I0760275

FACES OF ENVY

A PARANORMAL ROMANCE MYSTERY

J. K. GRUEBER

MYSTIC RIDGE PUBLISHING, LLC

COPYRIGHT

Mystic Ridge Publishing, LLC

Mysticridgepublsihing.com

ISBN: 978-1-965796-06-1 (Hardback)

ISBN: 979-8-9878673-3-4 (Paperback)

ISBN: 979-8-9878673-2-7 (Ebook)

Cover design by: Anne Graff, Andrew Grueber, and William Grueber.

Contributing cover photo editor: Sanderson-Decello Design, LLC

Also By J. K. Grueber

The Envy Series:
COLORS OF ENVY: A Paranormal Romance Mystery
FACES OF ENVY: A Paranormal Romance Mystery
ECHOES OF ENVY: A Paranormal Romance Mystery

The MacDade Brothers Mysteries:
EXPOSED IN THE SHADOWS: He Who Plays.
A Paranormal Mystery Rekindling Lost Love
The MacDade Brother's Mysteries (Book One)

EXPOSED IN THE CROSSHAIRS: He Who Rides
The MacDade Brothers Mysteries (Book Two)

EXPOSED BY THE RIVERSIDE: He Who Lives
The MacDade Brothers Mysteries (Book Three)

The Vampire Tales:
CURSED AT CONCEPTION:
The Vampire's Henchman

To my lifelong friend and soulmate, Steve. Life's an adventure and I'm glad to be sharing it with you.

PROLOGUE

"Painless," a low soothing voice chanted. "Nothing to fear . . . I don't want to hurt you, really."

Painless, his mind drifted with the word, no longer struggling, merely drifting. *Painless, nothing to fear* . . . but somewhere in the drifting tides of consciousness, he knew he should be afraid. Holding onto his fear, he watched a hazy image moving above him, heard scraping sounds, metal clinking like silverware shuffled in a plastic bin . . . a plastic bin in a restaurant. What restaurant? His thoughts snagged. Too rapidly, he slipped away again with a song lyric sliding through his listing thoughts. The Rolling Stones . . . something about the devil. He identified the melody, but the words muffled in his mind. He'd like to sing along or hum the tune, but his throat clogged, his mouth dried. With the effort to swallow, the sound skipped in his head. His attention floated within a myriad of flickering, dancing lights directly above, fascinated by the swirling yellow patterns on cracked plaster. He'd like to dance, too. Was that his own shadow hulking in that flickering light? Candlelight . . . a restaurant.

"Hmm, how we doing? Comfortable? Ah, yes. I see that you are."

The restaurant, his mind snagged, straining even as the shadowy image swam into his vision. The restaurant . . . he would be late. He should not be here—wherever 'here' was. Before genuine panic surfaced, he fascinated in the magnified appendages overhead, struggling to understand . . . to *feel*.

"You won't be needing these any longer."

These . . . *his clothes?* His mind stiffened, identifying a sense of touch, and tug down the center of his chest. 'No! No—don't!' The cry never reached his lips and drifted away too rapidly, lost within the beat and rhythm of another hit song.

Not a song . . . the whirl of helicopter blades intruded, rising from the edges of his drugged mind. Helicopter blades . . . transportation. Above him, through open dead eyes, he gleaned the glitter of diamonds, diamonds on black velvet . . . always blue diamonds on black velvet, and in his mind, he suffered the paradox to be delighted with the gift and know the ill-omen of the same. He'd found that necklace months—maybe years ago—and kept it safe for this moment . . . for what moment?

Drifting, he watched the images swirling through his drugged mind, felt the burn of the liquid jammed into his hip, taking his legs from beneath him . . . death. Surely an end with the last image of black diamonds.

A ball of flame blasting into the brilliant blue sky held him rapt, his focus following the wonder of vivid colors igniting like fireworks against blue sky and emerald forest. Death. Again, death. And his attention riveted yet again.

He'd seen these images, hazy images, gray on gray, marching in a bedraggled line . . . and the crackle of an old film accompanied the clatter of an ancient movie reel. Broken images flickered on the white screen. Every limp muscle attempted to cramp, collapsing as he found himself strapped into a stiff leather chair, the film scrolling through his mind's eye more clearly than on the wide screen directly in front of him. Puny, his body vibrated, jostling the thin wires attached to his skull, chest, his arms and legs. Caught as if in a spider's web, he rested helpless, watching the endless procession of hazy gaunt faces, male and female, young and old. They clung to one another in their bulky coats and sweaters, dull black and gray stripes running one into another, and he understood the significance. The beginning of his own end. These were the pictures and the knowledge behind them, and only in his mind, he shook his head, denying, rejecting . . . *elating?*

Nooo. How was that possible?

But in the next instant, he knew, he understood. Even as his young mind recoiled, repulsed, another young body rested in the leather chair, reveling in the images, anticipating more of the gruesome film. And the monster grew, becoming more enthralled each time the other viewed the wicked film.

'I will meet him in the city by the lake,' his own young voice transcended time, a mere whisper then.

'What city, child? When? Do you know?'

'Cleveland . . . he will begin in Cleveland,' he heaved softly, eager to please before the pain could strike again. No lights now, no film. Behind the thick black mask, he saw only the mind pictures as Dr. Carson prodded in gentle tones.

'When, child? Do you know the year?

'1989.'

Confusion and fear vied for attention in his frazzled mind. 1989. Still, the pictures continued to scroll across his mind's eye driving a moan off his lips, sweat from his brow. Tossing his head, growling, he sought a different view and again the propellers whirled overhead, drawing his focus to find the murky white face hovering over him.

Behind the mask to cover half the face, the man sniggered, and above the mask, the eyes remained hidden behind reflective lenses. Without a need for clear sight, he grasped the triumph and anticipation, oddly in conflict with the hostility swirling around him. He was alive . . . barely . . . but not meant to be alive. Someone wanted him dead . . . wanted them both dead?

Confusion spilled through his senses, his attention keening. *The past?*

The vision erupted, neon in his mind's eye, a black-winged angel spread within the points of a star. He'd seen this image—past or future. The black angel sprawled, arms flung wide to greet him, and his breath weighted his breast as he stared, as uncertain as ever another moment in his life. Past or future . . . would this moment come, or had it gone? Like the ghosts of Christmas in Dickens' novel, would it come, or had it passed?

The stillness suddenly floating in his mind created another quandary and abstracted the fear threatening to explode inside him.

On a slow tide, the images continued to glide, rippling in spirals outwards where every image created another, overlapping, replaying in new dimensions.

People were dying, had already died, would die . . . but some could be saved. Surely.

The birth of a madman . . . Cleveland.

'Mom'ma, nooo,' he moaned.

'Re'd for me, bab'be boy,' the voice of an angel, the grip of a demon with the fingers clasped like an iron cuff on his puny wrist, forcing his trembling hand down.

Paper—just paper. Silk—*just silk?* Words, just words . . . a *letter, a single capital letter embroidered on the silk*? But another hand had touched that stationary—*handkerchief*? And a conduit would open. Backward, forward, he knew enough to be terrified. No going back! He knew! He always knew! He always recognized the catalyst, and this one would spin him out of control!

Ah, and she stood in the center, his center. The vortex. A pillar of white light, a beacon in the night, illuminating the path as clearly as a lighthouse beam. He would find her. Had found her. Fore or aft? But oh, the madness to spiral around him and he saw her then, streams of black silk floating and sinking with the face as pale as a milk-glass bust, lips parted, eyes wide . . . and the terror gripped him as he watched the current drag her downward, fading into the murky depths . . .

"Forgivvve meee . . . I haaad nooo choooice . . ." a voice cried out in the night.

Devastation stole his breath as more pictures sped across his stricken mind, then rage . . . and he knew himself changing, evolving, darkening.

A lively tune erupted from his childhood, but a different melody intruded. A cradle song, rocking him, swaying him. Somewhere nearby, plastic crinkled in weird contrast to the scent of cow manure brushing against his senses. This wasn't a barn. A basement. Candlelight images danced within his distorted vision. A face appeared above him, a silhouette, no more intrusive than the faces of people he passed on a busy street, just another face in a crowd moving too fast for his slow ebbing senses to collect any details. An uncanny urgency to see, to remember, touched him briefly. The voice—too—came and went, no differently than fragmented conversations heard on any street corner or bus stop.

"This will be a little uncomfortable," the voice told him, and the hands momentarily blotted out the dancing patterns overhead. His nostrils flared and something slid into his skull sending a dull panic across his mind, but the discomfort passed, distracted by a weight stroking his breast. That too, confusing. Troubling. The restaurant . . . his thoughts floated. Late. He'd like to wake up now from this lazy dream, but again the melodies danced in his head. Images—faces—familiar and unfamiliar frolicked inside his mind. He should know them—did know them—but they were strangers, too. At a tug in his right shoulder, he flinched mentally, seeing a red halo arc through the flickering light, hearing uttered soft sounds. Disturbing, that red arc. His mind snagged as a series of dull tugs rippled through his collarbone. For an eternity, he thought he could feel a bulging pulse in his throat, a hollow drumroll in his chest.

"Painless. Just as I promised, and you should be grateful even though it's not your fault . . . I understand that better than you think . . . ah, there. Few more seconds . . . We can't help the faces we're born with . . . and yours is flawless. Yes, it is," the low voice chided, embittered.

A touch of fear scattered the devil music and images in his mind. He wanted up now . . . wanted to wake up. Late. Yes, he was late. *Mick would be worried.*

On the ceiling, the hulking shadow bisected the light. Tearing sounds accompanied a suctioning, breathing sound, but that wasn't a human breath. An artificial hiss.

"One down," the voice announced with a touch of satisfaction. "On to the next . . ."

Panic ebbing, he watched the flickering light, his mind floating to a lonely sound of a boat engine grinding through the river; car engines automated in a near constant hum as unobtrusive as his own breathing. If he wasn't asleep, he would like to be, but more melodies joined the noisy raucous in his mind.

The image had moved to his left, and the sounds seemed more distant. Another rippling tug, a red arc, a rapid jostling through his limp body. Panic came and went, a sensation of being trapped surfaced. Images of handcuffs fluttered in his mind, first on his wrists, then in his hands. He tried moving his hands, struggled to move some part of himself. Nothing moved. His senses swam to more sounds and songs, to a thickening fog. A sound escaped, scraped from some distant place deep inside.

"Hush now, nothing to fear," the low voice soothed, distracting.

He would like to see this face, tried to move his head. Nothing moved. Only the hulking shadow trailed into the flickering light, and for just a second, he understood the voice came from somewhere near his feet. His thought rippled a cord in his drifting mind. Something wrong. He needed to wake up.

"Lovely, yes you are," the voice spoke in a low, scathing tone.

Even in his distraction, he sensed the mockery in those words. Mockery. Hatred. Contempt . . . *envy?*

"Don't worry, now. I know what I'm doing. Yes, I do. You are lovely, but you'll be beautiful . . . a work of art," the deep voice chided.

Part of the fog lifted with the chant. Panic fleeted as a weight pressed down on his abdomen, and he might have been an under-inflated balloon—like the balloons wilting at the end of a party. Laughing voices reeled in his mind as his numb body fluttered to an external-internal tug and another part of his consciousness jostled. Something was happening to him. Something being done to him. Fear flashed neon. Sound gurgled in his throat.

"No distraction, now. I need to concentrate . . . I haven't much time. You don't want to distract me, now . . . one slip and the night is lost. Ah, there . . . finished. We'll just open this clamp . . . Beautiful. Not even a tiny leak. Painless as promised . . . Pulse, slow and steady. Breathing . . . fair. You should be waking soon . . ."

He was waking. Waking to a sense of fear and slow creeping panic. The voice belonged to a stranger; an animated specter as lifeless as the shadows flickering on the ceiling.

"Don't be afraid. I've taken care of everything now. You won't feel any pain, and we can chat while I work," the disembodied voice adopted a musing tone, more unsettling than soothing. "Of course, you won't be able to talk. Certainly, you can listen though. The bleeding is minimal, but I don't suppose that should concern you . . ."

No, his own internal voice chanted slowly. No . . . no . . . no. A dream . . . a dream. No candles. No voice. Wake up soon. A nightmare . . . just another nightmare. Even as his mind ejected denials as if chanting a holy mantra, he heard that low dead voice as clear as automobile engines passing on a nearby boulevard. He knew those sounds, familiar sounds. A jet engine rumbled lazily outside this small black space where he lay immobilized. His senses awoke to a tug at his hip, a sound like a champagne cork popping . . . his limp body jostled, plastic crackled, and he could feel it now, cold and sticky against his numb flesh.

"Ah, perfect. Just perfect . . . Would you like to see?"

He saw the shadow on the ceiling, twisting, turning. A long narrow shaft gyrated through the spiraling flicker of candlelight, magnified in the space directly above his face. A child's baton . . . a little girl's baton like the one he—she'd played with as a child? A little girl's toy dripping with glossy red paint . . . except the rubber end wasn't blunt. Knobbed. *Not a baton*, his cluttered mind struggled, *not a toy*. Above his face, swaying back and forth in his isolated vision, he focused on something more resembling a chicken bone—a magnified chicken bone with red gristle and clinging tatters of raw meat.

Like in the film, he grasped, *like in the film!*

"Perfect. Just perfect . . . Its technical name is the femur, but you probably know it as simply your thigh bone. It's one of the hardest bones in the human body. Very difficult to break. But then you probably didn't know that either, did you?"

The swaying mass retracted, and the single amplified snap was as much a physical as a mental sound lost within an endless silent scream.

CHAPTER I

Armed with the early edition of the Pittsburgh Press, Ronnie Bryson-Laquette strode through the dusky halls of what she'd begun to call Chateau Laquette, named exclusively after the object of her current frustration. The man had more places to hide in his collection of shadowy rooms than a mole in a maze. And he'd apparently decided to find every one of them in the past week.

Ronnie supposed he had good reason, but that offered little consolation under present circumstances. Women in her condition weren't supposed to go spelunking into the vast unchartered regions of a monstrosity that covered half a city block. Well, perhaps, not half, she connected while pushing open a small door. More like an eighth block and Bentwood wasn't a city by any stretch of her vivid imagination.

Like most other rooms in Jade's fortress, this one lacked a window, and what scant light filtered through the door barely offset the night shadows within. Unless he'd truly decided to play hide n' go seek—a thought to send a mild shiver down her spine—he'd not ventured into this nook. Pulling the door closed, she stood listening for the telltale rustling of packing paper or scraping boxes or the frustrated grumbling sounds to escape her husband when he believed no one stood within earshot. A proper gentleman, this wily husband of hers; a man born out of time for the customs dictating modern man that allowed public ranting and verbal tantrums.

Whatever he was up to, he was apparently satisfied with his undertaking, which only annoyed Ronnie more as she retraced her steps to the short connecting hall on the second floor. How dare he be happily engaged in something undoubtedly constructive when she felt like a ship about to break its moorings? He had a lot of blasted nerve leaving her to fend for herself... even if she had been a little snappy this morning. What the blazes did he expect when she knelt worshiping the porcelain god like a blasted derelict after a week bender? 'Lovely morning, sweetheart. Just give me a second here. I have a few more shreds of stomach to spew . . ..'

According to Dr. Blackwell, these *little bouts of nausea* would pass soon, and she'd feel *fit as fiddling*, but what the blazes did that old fart know about it? He was a man. Doubtful he'd ever overindulged. The closest Blackwell had probably ever come to spewing his guts daily, was a case of twenty-four-hour flu. A week, for God's sake! An entire week of rushing to the commode for a few seconds of relief was nearly more than her generally sturdy countenance could endure. That country squire of a doctor who dressed like a Dickens character probably hadn't even delivered a baby since 1909! Well, she knew that wasn't exactly true. The old goat had delivered both Deedee and Tee Spencer, the latter of whom would turn five in December. So, maybe Blackwell had delivered 95% of the healthy functioning adults in Bentwood . . . that still didn't make him an expert on morning sickness.

Knowing the friendship between Jade and Blackwell, Ronnie wouldn't be surprised to learn the old goat had advised her husband to steer clear of her in the mornings. Smiling wryly, Ronnie remembered the second box of crackers mysteriously perched on the headboard of their waterbed.

Morning sickness, hell—she was probably suffering seasickness from his tossing and turning over the past few nights, and that thought only strengthened her determination to find him. When a man like Jade Laquette starts mumbling and sweating through the night, doubtful, he suffered from indigestion.

Descending the steps to the first floor, Ronnie paused, listening to the symphony music emanating softly through the door to her right. Elaine Connelly had opened Olden Time as she did every weekday. By now, a half dozen collectors, dealers, and regular customers probably meandered through the shop seeking treasures or bargains. Jade wasn't on the showroom floor peddling his antiques, nor in his office behind that single locked door juggling numbers. If anything, the ability to sense her husband's presence had enhanced over the past few months. Whether she followed the soft musk scent of his imported aftershave or caught another, near primal scent, she dared not ponder.

The overwhelming agitation which had driven her from the privacy of their suite on the second floor, ebbed as she passed smoothly through the warehouse door on the first floor. Above head height, metal racks, and wood shelves, crammed full of cardboard boxes and paraphernalia, formed narrow tunnel-like aisles. Tract florescent light filtered over the highest peaks and passed through the towers of tables and chairs stacked at random between the shelves. Toward the deep end of the warehouse, Jade's collection of sports cars stood bumper-to-bumper, barely leaving space for the little black pickup that stood in a corner like a repentant child. Wading through the narrow aisles, she spotted the daylight glow from the open garage doors at the end of the warehouse. The sound of scraping, minus grumbling, reached her, along with the tangy scent of paint thinner. Without a doubt, he sensed or heard her arrival, but the sound of scraping continued uninterrupted.

Content to watch his gloved hand slathering paint thinner on another curved leg of the 19th-century farm table, Jade reveled in the natural sounds of dogs barking, children playing, and engines rumbling in the distance. Home. The sounds of home. The awe of being caught in the moment never ceased to thrill him. For a few moments or an hour at the least, he could remain fully rooted in the simplicity of October 1989. Neither moving forward nor back, aware of his lover, his friend, his *wife*—although that revelation still baffled him—somewhere just beyond his immediate sight.

Veronica was hunting for him. He sensed her need, but for a split second, he'd rather not be found. Barely that thought crossed his mind when he suffered the guilt of it. He loved her more than life itself, would walk through the fires of hell for her . . . but he'd prefer putting that off just a little longer.

As confused as he was irritated with the quandary in his mind, Jade studied the bubbling clear liquid on the walnut wood, and he felt it then. Like a living, breathing beast, his curse pulsed at his temple, and the images began to surf across his mind's eye.

A playground . . . Clearly, he saw the teeter-totter, the sliding board, and the fading brown grass spreading across the yard. In a flash, he recognized the red-black stone walls of St. Augustine's Academy and knew himself leaning against the slanted blue bars of a swing set in the attached playground. He need not even sit on the freshly painted seat or touch the rubber-coated chains to know who'd swung last—or first. If he tried, he might see the face of every child who'd enjoyed the swing . . . and in a flash, he saw Lincoln Bryson with his curly brown hair and round blue eyes as he tumbled off the seat, landing and battling tears as he picked himself up. Troubling, that flash . . . Jade had never met the child, Lincoln Bryson—

Veronica's brother.

Jade shook his head as if he might turn the dial and change the picture in his mind's eye . . . and saw her then. Veronique. His lady, his love, a mere child standing within a small circle of other little girls . . . and a smile played on his lips as he tipped his head of dark, unruly curls and studied her intently.

She was lovely, from her big blue eyes to her long, streaming locks. Askew, those black, silky curls slipped over her shoulder, threatening to escape the blue ribbon at her nape. Even in the shade of one of the immense oaks that circled the playground, her hair shimmered . . . she shimmered. Barely able to contain his awe, he watched the white light spiraling, spreading to encircle her as if she carried a beacon at her center. Like a miller to light, he was drawn to her, his entire ethereal essence reaching out to her, brushing against her . . . and she felt it, too. Her pale blue eyes turned toward him, riveted.

She felt him! But how was that possible?

Locking on her gaze, he knew the strangeness of himself held in stasis, unable to read a single thought or glimpse a single vision, but he felt her still. As if the light were saturating him, sucking on his soul, tugging, and bonding. Stunned, numb, and excited in the same instant, he grasped only a sense of knowing her, of being known by her. A white witch! He'd found his white witch!

And the recess bell clamored, startling him—

'Painless,' a soothing voice chanted. 'Nothing to fear . . . I don't want to hurt you, really.'

The ill-omen touched him, sending a shiver through his slight frame, and without a thought, he started a backward step. Faster, like a lightning strike, the slender fingers caught his wrist and froze him, rooting his tennis shoes to the floor, but his fingers fisted, recoiling in the iron grip.

'Mom`maaa, nooo,' he pleaded, again looking up at her, begging her to look at him. Sometimes, just sometimes if he looked into others' eyes, he could alter their intentions toward his own end. Nanna said it was a gift; Mamma said it was his curse.

She wouldn't look at him, ever. He was different. She knew it. Nanna knew it. No playing ball like other boys. No walking to the park with Nanna now. Different. He was different. Like his pappa 'A warlock like your pap`pa,' that's what his mother told him, but sometimes she seemed proud or pleased with that fact. He wasn't like other boys. Things he touched, talked to him. The dead talked to him. He had to read . . . learn to read. *A monster* . . . and they would come for him.

". . . He's getting restless . . . due for meds . . . How soon before we land . . . make sure the unit's on standby . . ."

"How the hell did this happen?. . . .That wasn't supposed to be a goddamn lethal dose!"

A monster . . . to be feared . . . to be afraid. And he was afraid . . . as afraid now of living . . . as of dying. What they could do to him . . . would do to him. Had *already* done to him?

'Do you want them to take you, bab'be boy? Is thot whot you want?, . If they knew whot you were . . ..'

'Blood pressure's climbing . . . pulse . . . He's waking up, Conners . . .'

'Calm down,' the husky voice demanded. 'We'll have you down in a few minutes. Just relax. . .'

'He doesn't look so tough. Surely not a threat to national security.'

Americans, the son of Jean-Pierre Jardonet trusted them no more than he trusted the French, but Jean-Pierre had spared his son this final odyssey.

In confusion and sudden fear, he strained to keep his fist from lowering, meant to keep his fingers locked, but his mother's hand was so much larger, stronger. 'Mom'ma, nooo, please . . . She's touched the hand of the devil,' he heaved softly, tears springing over his emerald eyes. 'Nooo,' he moaned as the images began to swirl in his young mind. He'd been here before, at this moment, knowing a catalyst lay before him, knowing too early what that word meant to him, for him.

Before his knuckles could be bruised on the ceramic tabletop, the long red fingernails clamped into his wrist, springing his fingers open, and his palm slammed down over the black J.

He saw the young face, the black and white light flickering over his pock-marked cheeks, accentuating the scars and pits . . . but the black eyes glowed, black from the drugs, black from dilation, black with his mad, maddening anticipation.

The eyes were blue.

Ronnie found Jade resting on an overturned milkcrate, close enough to the open doors, he might be sitting in the alley—undoubtedly, to keep the fumes away from her and their creation. Pausing, she stole the odd moment to admire the sight of him absorbed in his task. Even now, with a rare blue diamond and an intricate antique wedding band on her finger, she sometimes doubted this man was her husband. Whether he wore faded jeans and a flannel shirt—his present ensemble topped off with work boots which came straight out of an L.L. Bean catalog—or a tailored Armani with a silk shirt and oxfords straight from Italy, he remained the epitome of male elegance. Like silk, his walnut waves tumbled rakishly over his brow, glistening in the sunlight that streaked through the open doors. Long thick lashes shaded the unique green color of his eyes that flashed from emerald to pale jade depending on his mood. Framing full lips, his dark mustache twitched at one corner, evoking an instant image of cocky arrogance . . . and the devil wore a dimple to offset her unruly temper faster than she cared to consider.

As if the rake had timed his reaction, which he probably had, he paused from scraping and tipped his shaggy head, favoring her with a hesitant smile. "Feeling better, mon amour?"

"Don't you start," she snapped and noted the lift of his brow, the flash of his gaze heavenward, undoubtedly, seeking God's favor.

Damn it. He'd attempted to sound lighthearted despite the genuine concern behind his pale green gaze. Stifling another misplaced snippy remark, Ronnie continued forward.

Conversations between them hadn't greatly improved from the onset. He tended toward the mundane when something troubled him, and if she intended to engage in a serious conversation, she couldn't afford to be distracted by his laissez-faire attitude

The attitude was a ruse anyway.

"Something you uh . . . need, sweetheart?" he asked a little more warily. With his scraper poised, prepared to strip bubbled varnish from the spindly leg in front of him, he epitomized the busy man rudely interrupted and itching to return to work. That he chose to refinish the small table himself confirmed her earlier thought of his restless sleep; only two days past, he'd mentioned setting Cy Trascar to the task. Either Jade needed to keep his hands busy to offset his own nervous anxiety, or he truly had chosen to keep his distance from her without fully taking his leave.

"You're avoiding me this morning," she said simply, her cool blue gaze pinning him and reading his slight surprise.

"Sweetheart, you made it abundantly clear. I should become invisible posthaste or suffer your wrath," he said with a slight twitch of a smile. "I apologize if I chose the coward's route."

"Brat," she snapped, only more irritated with his ability to soften her mad . . . until she remembered exactly why she'd sought him. Glancing at the folded newspaper at her side, she lost her anger and noted the wariness leap into his jade-tinted eyes. The man already knew her too well. Her own slight smile notched his wariness by several degrees, and by no surprise, a tremor jostled his scraper. Doubtful, her intimidation techniques were the cause.

Sighing in mocked bewilderment, his timing and drama skills off, Jade shook his head and ran the scraper up the leg, leaning into the task in a posture of concentration. "Sush abuse," he muttered with more than a trace of a French accent slipping unnaturally into his words.

How many times in the past week had she detected that accent? An accent, more English than French when they'd met nearly four months earlier. Almost like a cold creeping up on him, traces of his heritage—those five years spent with his father in France—had begun to inflect his words. Curiously, she studied his profile, the feigned concentration on his kinked lips. The man was still an enigma.

Distracted, she tapped a drumroll against her thigh, drawing her own attention to the newspaper. Suddenly, the paper seemed more an ill-omen than the source of a solution to her recent anticipation. Too well, she knew his distaste and contempt for reporters. In his opinions, even the most respectable publications no more than tabloids to be viewed for entertainment rather than informational input. Books, first edition books, he'd professed, were the only genuine source of knowledge. Unfortunately, she didn't share his sensitivities to reap the ultimate benefits from inanimate objects. She needed to read the words to gain insight, where he need only to touch the damn things.

"Jade," Ronnie began carefully, not daring to draw his attention to the paper despite how much she suddenly wanted to throw it open in front of him. "We um . . . we need to talk for a minute."

"I am listening, mon amour."

By his low dry tone, she knew abruptly. "You already know what I'm going to say."

"I'm hoping you're wrong," he said cryptically.

Whether he meant about himself knowing or about her intentions, she wasn't certain. "You know how I've been irritable the past few days?"

"Days?" he asked with mocked shock, flashing a lifted brow and bemused glance. "Ma copine, you jest. You? Irritable . . . for days?" He paused and shook his head, fleeting his gaze to the spindle. "I haven't noticed any sush thing."

"I think I know what's bothering me," she continued, ignoring his attempted subterfuge.

"Ah, so you have realized, you are ahhh . . . pregnant, perhaps?"

"What I'm feeling has nothing to do with carrying our child," she said shortly, annoyed with his weak attempts to sidetrack her. Obviously, she had no choice but to plunge headlong into the subject—one he undoubtedly, anticipated. "I came upon something in the paper this morning, hon, and . . ." How to say it, now that she held his silent, if somewhat troubled, attention despite his hands working busily at the spindle? "I think it's something we need to do," she blurted. "If not both of us, then at least, me," she continued, and saw his hand jerk, miscalculating a careful swipe.

A gouge of ancient walnut wood curled and slipped to the cement floor. Another man might be cursing. He simply paused and studied the wound.

"Jade, a man died yesterday." And it occurred to her suddenly. "And you've seen it . . . or something of it, haven't you?"

He shook his head with a shallow denial and lifted his murky green gaze. His smirk strained. "Mon amour, men die every day. If I saw them all, I'd go mad within an hour. Whatever you've read—"

"Someone else will die unless we help," she said bluntly and watched the flash of concern in his studied gaze. "I've felt like this before, hon. It's what led me to you, to Bentwood, remember? I know . . . I feel a connection to this case. I can't explain it any more than you can explain what you feel, but it's something I know."

"I thought you decided you would not return to your profess`sion?" he said weakly, his brow lifted in mocked speculation.

"I'm not saying I'll write about this, hon," she said unwavering despite her curiosity over his thickening accent. Rather than 'tion', she heard a definite 'she-on' drawled at the end of his words. Concentrating, she continued, "But I do feel a connection."

"Veronique," he said with that rolling French rhythm that always touched her at the deepest level. "Leave this be."

Dumbfounded, she read the tension he tried to cloak behind his gaze. Not a hunch any longer. She was right. Somehow, they were already or would be soon, involved in the investigation of Jack Trumble's death. "If that was your idea of persuasion, hon? It worked admirably, but I ought to mention, not in your favor," she said with a faint smile that furrowed his brow. He had the damnedest ability to appear thoroughly bewildered while knowing precisely what she meant. "We're going to Elmview, aren't we, love?"

He parted his lips to speak a denial; the sound never reached his tongue. A flash of annoyance slipped across his eyes before he turned his attention to the spindle. Distracted, he picked at the gouge, blending, and mending the wood until the nick began to ebb.

Sensing the deeper emotions welling beneath his surface calm, Ronnie moved to him and stooped down. According to Donna Spencer, in another few months, Ronnie wouldn't be able to tie her own shoes, much less balance on the balls of her feet, but that thought slipped away as she touched his forearm, feeling a tingle at her fingertips.

Canting his head, he studied her with a warm gaze despite his troubled brow.

"We can't keep denying what we are, Jade," she said softly. "I know you're a fatalist by nature, love, but there has to be some reason we're together."

"You shouldn't be this close to these fumes," he said and dispatched his scraper to the floor, removing his rubber gloves before clasping her arm and lifting them both smoothly. Without a need for words, Jade ushered her into the alley where a warm breeze dispatched the fumes between hedges and fences. Between buildings, Maine St. traffic muffled, sounding miles away, along with distant sounds of dogs barking and children squealing in backyards.

Unconsciously, Ronnie spied through the wall of Rose of Sharon, hoping to glimpse Hazel Handler, their octogenarian neighbor. By routine, the woman generally spent a good bit of her mornings and afternoons rocking within her rose-shrouded cove. Three months earlier, even that slight view had been obstructed by the shaggy crop of Rose of Sharon overrunning her back lawn. Still, Hazel had never missed a glimpse of one of Jade's vehicles backing from the warehouse, or anything else for that matter. Octogenarian status bedamned. Hazel had more on the ball than most women half her age.

Considering Hazel's request for help to thin her backyard, Ronnie smiled faintly. The folks in Bentwood had adopted her as readily as they'd accepted Jade, and Hazel's invitation was just one more indication of acceptance. As far as Bentwood's citizenry was concerned, she and Jade would remain permanent residents. The apartment above Olden Time's showroom, however, was no place to raise a child, which probably explained the recent visit from Hal

Cartney, the only realtor in Bentwood. Equipped with a handful of available listings in and around Bentwood, including four chunks of forest land, Hal had nervously offered a sales pitch. Undoubtedly, he'd been persuaded, if not threatened, by at least one local lawman to approach them. Most folks had ignored the strange circumstances surrounding Jade's more recent past, but some, like Hal, remained leery.

Perhaps, for Jade, she should accept his advice and ignore the feeling which had stolen over her while breezing through the Press. People, far worse than Hal, existed. People who'd persecute her husband for the uncanny talents that he struggled to conceal.

Aware of him standing in front of her, his hand still resting idly on her arm, Ronnie looked up into his intent gaze. He'd allowed her those few seconds to reconsider and undoubtedly followed her every thought, hoping for her better judgment. Still, she gripped the newspaper at her hip and felt a connection. Why . . . why she felt this internal tug, she couldn't explain. "I need to do something, Jade. I can't just sit around getting fat and feeling useless."

"Sweetheart, as I recall, you've lost weight rather than gained, and I can safely say, you are anything but sedentary. Our apartment hasn't been so clean since its original occupants moved in a century ago, and Meg's still marveling that her stools stand on chrome bases."

A faintly amused smile slid into her lips, mirroring Jade's as she recalled the Sunday morning a few weeks past. Nesting, Meg had declared after Ronnie had acted upon an insatiable desire to use Jade's chrome cleaner and silver polish on Meg's diner stools. Ronnie shrugged. "I suppose I've managed to keep busy, but that's not what I mean, and you know it."

"Mon amour," he breathed in mocked exasperation. "*Bizzy* hardly describes your appetite for motion."

"I'm used to being in motion," she said and touched his side, applying just a little of her female charm while reaching one conclusion. "I need to do this, hon. For me," she said smoothly. "I don't know why this fellow's death caught my attention, but something's not right. I need to find out what." Before he could interrupt, she continued quickly, pressing her hand more fully against his side. "It's probably nothing. Maybe just botched female hormones sending me a few wrong signals under the circumstances. But I can't ignore this."

"Veronica—"

"I don't think it's a good idea that you come with me," she persevered. "In fact, it's probably better if you stay here and keep the peace—"

"Veronique—"

"Hear me out, honey," she said quietly. "I've already checked my map. Elmview's not too far from Johnstown, which means it's not much more than two hours away. I could leave tomorrow morning and be back tomorrow night. If anyone in town asks, as they surely will, you can tell them I went to visit friends in the city."

"You are a stubborn woman, madame," he said with a curt tone emphasized in the rolling French accent.

She smiled, seeing resignation creeping into his lofty voice and warm eyes. "You knew that before you asked me to marry you, hon. A little late to find that trait offensive, don't you think?"

"Show me this article that's captured your curiosity," he said and sent a mild, scathing glance toward the paper as he stepped back a pace, deliberately escaping her touch.

Only for an instant, she considered handing him the paper. Knowing how he reacted to certain things he touched, she unfolded the paper and pointed to the six-line obituary to catch her attention.

Jack Trumble, age 46 . . . survived by father, mother, wife, Jenny, brothers, a sister, two sons, and a daughter . . . viewing hours, today only. He would be buried in the morning.

The obituary contained nothing of curious content, and yet, even as she watched Jade's gaze dart over the few lines, she knew her accuracy. His brow furrowed, his eyes sparked an emerald hue, and his mustache twitched at one corner, offsetting a flash of pain. In a few fleeting seconds, his anxiety became apparent along with the headache drumming at his temple. By habit alone, he ran his fingers through the unruly locks at his brow, and a tremor slipped through his hand. By the time his murky gaze lifted, he was hooked. Uncomfortably, Ronnie wondered what she might be getting them into this time. "You do feel it, too," she said quietly.

"I'll go. You stay," he said carefully. "If it is nothing," he shrugged, letting the sentence dangle.

"It doesn't work that way, dear," she said bluntly.

"Veronique, you are carrying our shild. I'll not put either of you at risk. There's plenty to keep you bizzy—"

"Listen, bub," she cut him off shortly, seeing the dread livid in his halted expression. "We're in this together. Mamma, Pappa, remember? According to your pal, Dr. Doolittle, I'm as healthy as a horse. There's absolutely no good reason for me to sit at home like some fourteenth-century maiden awaiting her knight to return to hearth and home. If you insist on coming with me, I suppose I can't stop you, but you're certainly not making this trip alone. Get it?"

"Mon Dieu," he uttered and ran his fingers through his hair again as his gaze listed toward the hedges, down the ally, seeking solace anywhere other than her firm gaze. Shaking his head, his focus returned with a fair imitation of dismay. "Is there no argument I shall ever win with you, milady?"

"Probably not in this lifetime, sire," she mused and stepped closer, rubbing his side, and feeling her heat merging with his tingle. His eyes flashed wariness even as he reacted to her subtle seduction and leaned down, tasting her lips. A muttered sound, nearly a groan accompanied his defeat, and Ronnie almost heard him chastening himself for being won so easily. "If we're leaving in the morning, I better get the laundry done—"

With a low laugh, he leaned and scooped her off the gravel. "Like hell, mon amour," he mused while imitating a barbarian of old intent upon a single goal. Without pause, he carried her into the warehouse.

"Put me down, for heaven's sakes, you brute!"

Chuckling, he bounced her up and down in his powerful grip, forcing her to cling more naturally to his neck and shoulders. His eyes glittered with as much heat as mischief. "You interrupt a man in his constructive labors and test your female wiles?" he shrugged. "*C'est la vie, ma copine.*"

If any other man ever pulled this stunt with her, she'd put red racing stripes down his cheeks, but this arrogant devil had been getting away with it—regularly—from the start. In truth, she never minded, but to save face, she commented, "You left the doors open, hon . . . And you really should cap that paint thinner."

The unruly devil simply favored her with a deeper smile and notched his brow while continuing between his Jaguar and Maserati.

"Really, dear. It's not safe to leave flammable substances lying about unattended!" And she should have known better than to doubt him. They barely passed into the small bisecting hallway when young Wade Kreider opened the office door.

"Ah, Wade, just in time!" Jade stated, addressing the golden-haired twelve-year-old with an anxious note. "My lady's feeling a bit faint."

"Do you need the doc?" Wade asked anxiously.

"A natural event. We'll not need the doc just yet," Jade said as he started up the narrow steps, looking over his shoulder at Wade. "I left a can of stripper near the alley doors. If you'd cap the can and lock the bay doors, I'd be grateful, lad."

"No problem," the boy said quickly, already headed for the warehouse doors and probably questioning the *faint*. As Ronnie had noted months ago, the youngster was extremely bright, and not quite as naive as he should be at such a tender age. "Hope you're feeling better, Mrs. L."

Idling a chuckle once the door closed, Jade cleared the top step. "The lad's timing was excellent, don't you agree?"

Where exactly her husband's talents began and ended, doubtful even he knew for certain, but Ronnie knew better than to question Wade's arrival or consider it a coincidence. Whether Jade had known Wade would arrive or sent a silent signal to summon him, remained a mystery.

"Brat," she said bluntly, and before he could even think to make one of his lofty remarks, she nipped his ear.

"Mon Dieu, the woman's hungry!" Jade said in exasperation and hastened his pace.

Stifling a laugh, she kissed his neck, slipped her fingers into his hair, and turned her full attention to seducing him proper, enjoying every instant of his rare vulnerability. Before they ever reached the shadows of their bedroom, she loosened his flannel shirt, and her hand played in the soft mat of fur on his muscled chest. Her heartbeat matching the tempo beneath her palm, she began slipping the shirt off his muscled shoulders.

Upon a time, not that long ago, she'd only imagined the delight to revel in a male anatomy. She'd never risked taking liberties with a willing partner for fear of the inevitable consequences when starting something she wouldn't finish. To think now . . . she'd waited twenty-six years and stored up every female intuition to unleash on this single man.

Already, his eyes glittered nearer to emerald. His mustache quivered with anticipation and promise as he laid them both down gently. Barely, the water mattress rolled beneath them as Ronnie continued sliding the flannel off his shoulders.

She wanted him, every inch of him hot and heavy in her arms, his lean muscled limbs tingling against her palms. That hadn't changed. No matter how often they joined, she wanted more, needed more. Resting her palm over his heart, she drew in the prickling sensations as his heartbeat accelerated under her touch. As if caught in a wicked dance, their tongues twined and wrestled as they shed their clothes, tugging and pulling, rocking and tumbling over the velvet spread.

Lost in the turbulence, Ronnie whispered his name like a holy mantra as his low voice vibrated on accolades. By tone, she understood his need, his desire flaming with his love, but the words—spoken in French—were lost.

With his shaft rising, throbbing at her abdomen, she squirmed higher, capturing his ear, clasping his shoulders as she arched to take him in.

"Mon amour," he heaved against her neck where he burrowed as he began the slow glide, taking her to the higher planes where light and dark collided. "Mon amour . . ."

Like the rays of the sun, his hands kissed her skin, heating her from the inside out, driving all thought and reason from her mind as they found their rhythm, matching stroke for stroke. Only on the periphery of her vision, she beheld the tiny sparks of light, like dust particles floating in a stream of brilliant light, glittering sequins in the shadows.

Sweated and satisfied, their bodies twined like a modern art sculpt, twisted in a posture that might appear impossible, Ronnie began to rise from the post haze. Jack Trumble's death slithered to the surface of her mind, a lighthouse beacon in a thick fog tugging at her consciousness to steer her toward another story. Impressions. Forever, she'd relied merely on impressions and intuition to guide her toward her next assignment. For a half dozen years, she'd followed her senses to weed out criminals while honing her professional skills as an investigative journalist. Finding, falling in love with the man in her arms had been a result of those talents . . . and she'd nearly lost him.

For just for a moment, she considered ignoring the lighthouse signal, considered remaining in Bentwood, safe and secure with her husband and child to fill her every moment.

Something Jade had said to her before they'd married blazed neon in her mind. They'd been discussing the future, her career, a career she'd already decided to quit. 'It was never the story to attract you . . .' Never the story or the writing profession, never the Pulitzer Prize to send her flying into the dangerous situations she'd encountered in the past. Had she ignored her impressions of Bentwood, others might have died, and she might never have found the man in whose arms she rested.

"Jade," she uttered in the shadows, sensing his thoughts were not far from her own. "I do have to go, hon, but you don't."

“We’ll both go, m’ love,” he muttered softly and brushed a kiss on her forehead, apparently finalizing his decision.

“You . . . you’ve seen something of this, haven’t you?” she uttered while searching his face in the shadows. She could barely make out the contours of his sculpted features. Their room forever lingered in twilight even without the drapes drawn about the seventeenth-century style bed.

“Enough to know your accuracy,” he answered after a moment, his voice fading with the onset of sleep. “Something’s not asss it shooould be . . .”

With the heavy French accent lingering in his muffled voice, Ronnie recalled the moments of lovemaking, the French words whispered in her ear between kisses. An enigma . . . one she might consider questioning aloud if not for the soft contented breaths wisping against her forehead. After the past few restless nights, the weariness lingering behind his eyes, she didn’t have the heart to wake him. Content to rest in his arms, listening to his heartbeat and steady breath, she plotted their course until the need to act sent her slipping carefully from his grasp.

CHAPTER 2

The muffled sounds of retching, cursing, and coughing breached the bathroom door, awakening Jade to the new day, stunning and startling him into motion. By the stiffness in his leaden muscles, he knew his accuracy, not entirely certain whether he should be delighted or annoyed to have slept an entire afternoon, evening, and night away. Sleeping had always seemed like such a waste of precious time, and man had little enough to spend, let alone any to waste.

Good God, an entire day wasted. Igniting the lamp outside the curtain, he rested on his forearm, shaking his head in disgust.

As he listened to the muffled sounds, he found himself caught between amusement and empathy, a bit nauseated himself, although he dare not mention that detail to his beloved. Nor to anyone else in town unless he intended to suffer the banter a hundredfold. Jade could just imagine how much fun Tim Spencer would have with this wretched twist of fate. By God's grace, Jade hadn't yet buckled to the need to vomit, but unless this phase of pregnancy ended soon, he had no doubts that he'd join Veronica in her morning ritual. What a spectacle that would be, them kneeling and taking turns over the commode . . . and he saw himself then, himself and not himself . . .

Cracked linoleum under his blue-jean-covered knee. The vomit and bile mixed rancidly with the smell of urine rising from the stained bowl below his face . . . Himself and not himself, his body lurched, convulsing on the cramps and heaves. Modern conveniences surrounded him . . . them. He wasn't alone. On dual planes, Jade recognized the aged fixtures, from a porcelain sink on metal legs to a rust-stained tub against which he rested. A shabby motel . . . and above him, Veronica hovered, leaning on the sink, recovering, wiping her face in a wet, dull white towel as he spiraled toward misery. Her blue gaze drifted down to him, speculating in musing contempt . . .

Shuddering, he drew from the vision, willing the queasiness away. If he suffered this badly over morning sickness, how the hell would he fare when labor struck?

And how long did morning sickness last? How far away were the moments that he'd just witnessed? Not far—not far at all, he feared.

Uncomfortably, his thought shattered, and his attention turned to the dual garment bags standing at the wall near the bedroom door. A shiver slid down his spine. Jack Trumble . . . Elmview.

If he'd ever met the man, the memory was lost, but Jade pictured Trumble in vivid detail. A stout fellow with a shiny, balding pate and a strip of graying hair at his crown. Dark eyes, rounded flushed cheeks, cotton shirts pulled taut over his rounded girth . . . a car salesman's smile . . . though something felt slightly off with his thought. Sales . . . the man was . . . had been in sales of one sort or another. Dress slacks, a loose tie . . . *Trumble sat behind a cluttered desk in a beige-walled office . . . a windowed wall mixed daylight with florescent tract lighting, like a restaurant . . .*

He gripped the wheel of his late model LeBaron. Tires squealed; gravel flew. Shocked, shouted curses flew off his parted lips as he struggled to spin the wheel, jerked like an unstrung marionette as the car lurched, rammed—

Shaking himself from a momentary daze, losing the image, Jade shoved off the bed too quickly. Vertigo staggered him a few clumsy steps. Perhaps, today, he would resign to the nausea. He caught his balance against the corner bedpost, feeling an urgent desire to empty his stomach and calm the rocking and rolling in his gut. The thought of dry heaves—considering his already empty stomach—steeled his nerve.

Clinging to the bedpost, recovering his breath, he was grateful to hear the sounds ebbing in the bathroom. With genuine relief, he heard the water spigot ignite. If it was this bad on the outside, he could only wonder at Veronica's grit to endure those retching fits.

Forcing himself into motion, Jade collected clean clothes from the closet and dresser, timing his arrival at the bathroom door to coincide with Veronica's exodus. How she could appear beautiful, her black curls catching the bathroom florescent light in silhouette, her face radiant despite the soft light in their bedroom, remained a mystery. She even managed to smile slightly, if not just a trifle resignedly. "How is it you can be so beautiful when I know you feel wretched?"

"Are you sure you're not Irish?" she asked smoothly, this once not stinging him when he might deserve it.

"Not even slightly, that I'm aware."

"Yes? Well, I'd almost bet you have an Irish ancestor or two, dear, because you have more blarney than all three of my brothers combined."

"You're in rare form, milady," he said while bowing slightly and stepping aside, motioning his free hand in a courtly gesture to let her pass.

She hesitated. A more natural smile slipped into her lips as she sized him up from head to bare heel and back. "It's hard to be snippy with a man wearing his birthday suit," she mused and stepped close. Rising on her toes, she brushed a kiss on his cheek and sent sparks through his anatomy with a warm palm slipping down his abdomen. Blue diamond eyes sparkling mischief, she held him, waking his nether regions and aware of her effect. "Besides which, I was beginning to worry. When you decide to catch up on sleep, you don't fool around."

"You could have awoken me," he said while sliding his hand to the silky nightie at her spine, drawing her to rest against his rising shaft. Not another woman in his past had ever affected him more fully or aroused him more deeply. With a word, a smile, a touch, she could raise him from zero to sixty and leave him throbbing in anticipation. "You should have awoken me, mon amour," he corrected while considering how they might use this morning more productively.

"Awake with a vengeance, so you are," she taunted gently, appearing genuinely dismayed as she withdrew from his embrace. "Unfortunately, I feel as lousy as I probably look, and I suggest you take a cold shower. I need a cup of tea and a few more boxes of crackers."

With his nausea amplified after her touch, effectively withering him, he knew her accuracy on dual planes. "Why don't you lie down? I'll get your tea."

"Get your shower," she cut him off, already gliding toward the door. Pausing, she looked back at him, again captured beautifully in the bisecting light. "I'd like to be in Elmview before ten. Think we could take the pickup?"

Not only stubborn, but pragmatic as well, and he wouldn't dream of having her any other way. Considering her question, the logo 'Olden Time Antiques and Collectibles' etched on the pickup's doors in Old English script, he nodded. "The pickup's fine." And a fine choice, he might have added with a thought of where she was headed and why.

They!

Where *they* were headed! If nothing else, they might pose—honestly—as antique dealers in search of treasures. Certainly, better than admitting the true nature of their visit to Elmview . . . *Elmview* . . . something wrong. Their . . . her. *Her trip*?

Uncomfortable with his thoughts, preoccupied, Jade muddled through his morning ministrations. Showered, shaved, and dressed in jeans and a flannel shirt, he started through the bedroom but stopped halfway and stood looking at the suitcases, turning his gaze slowly toward the closet. He'd need his other bag . . . and the revelation sent a wave of vertigo through his mind. Shaking his head, he started toward the door but veered off course and reached the closet.

Months ago, the Federal Bureau had ransacked his domain with an official search warrant, but none had bothered searching too closely, thanks to an agent with an attitude. Stooped within the walk-in closet, Jade dragged the leather bag from the back wall, then slid his fingers along the wide baseboard to the corner, pressing lightly. A twelve-inch section of baseboard sprung free from the wall, and Jade slid the narrow drawer outward. At the edge of his mind, he heard Veronica moving about in the kitchen, heard the toaster pop and the refrigerator door snap shut. Heart hammering a leaden beat, fingertips prickling, he withdrew one of the thin leather pouches from the collection. Trembling, he pressed the drawer back into place. Even in the shadows, the elaborate gold embossed "D.P.J." glowed neon within the black leather. If the Bureau had been serious. . . .

Wrong . . . this was wrong. Another way . . . has to be another way . . . wrong. But even as the words sailed through his mind, his hands moved, sliding the small leather pouch into his back pocket as he rose. Swaying, Jade collected the garment bag off the floor, unclasped the leather straps, and hung the bag over the closet door, packing in automation. Shivering internally, he folded a leather backpack into the depths and zipped the case before he could change his mind. Adding the bag to the others at the door, Jade stood momentarily, collecting his balance with a hand clasped on the bedroom doorknob. Whatever this strangeness, whatever this sense of dread hovering inside of him . . . Elmview? *Wrong* . . . and yet right. Something he needed—something left there that he would need—

Drawing a breath, Jade forced himself calm and stepped from the bedroom in time to find Veronica finishing a piece of toast. Over the past few mornings, he'd crossed the street to Meg's Diner for breakfast rather than risk upsetting Veronica's precarious balance. Generally, he merely drank a few cups of coffee, not tempting his fate with anything more substantial. "Things are certainly looking up this morn if you're re—"

"You don't even realize you're doing that, do you?"

Halted, he searched her critical expression, bracing for her unpredictable temper. "*Excusez-moi, mon amour*?" he asked hesitantly.

"And there it is again," she said bluntly, studying him intently. "What's going on, hon?"

Apparently, she intended to lure him into another bewildering conversation, and he wasn't entirely disappointed. Whatever had affected him a moment ago was ebbing swiftly with a need to concentrate. "I'm at a loss, sweetheart," he answered carefully, honestly, and moved to the counter. Bringing a cup from the wooden rack, he glanced to find her still watching him. What had he done?

"You're going French on me," she said lightly, a tiny smile on her lips.

Bewildered and amused, Jade commented, "Unless that's an Americanism that I've not heard before, m' love, I should mention, I *am* French."

"Two weeks ago, if I hadn't known better, I'd have bet you were English," she said without a trace of amusement, only more curious if the cant of her fluffy curls were any indication. "Now, there's no mistaking it. You're sounding more French by the day, and I've noticed you're speaking more French than American English lately. Not that I mind, mind you, but I am curious."

Tim Spencer had mentioned the same thing a few days earlier, but Jade hadn't given it much thought since Spence was notorious for his bantering. In retrospect, Jade realized Veronica's accuracy.

"You don't even realize you're doing it, do you?"

"Suppose I can't deny that," he said carefully, articulating each word with American emphasis. Not since returning to the States, more than a half dozen years earlier, had he needed to concentrate to speak concise English. Adopting Americanism and losing his bastardized French accent had taken the better part of a year. To hear it creeping back was something of a problem, if not a serious curiosity. "But if you're looking for an *explication*, I—" He'd done it again, he realized, if only by the flash of amusement in Veronica's pale blue eyes. Shrugging his annoyance, he stated, "I do not have one."

Slipping from her chair, she came in front of him, sliding her arms about his waist and looking up at him. Her laughter rose fully to the surface beneath a fan of thick natural lashes. "I probably ought to warn you, dear," she said with a fleeting smile. "I find that accent extremely sexy . . . a little like Morticia on the Addams Family if you get my drift."

“Hmm, and sush may be an expli`nation in itself, eh?” he said as he ducked his head to taste her lips, drawing her against him more completely. “Perhaps, I am feeling . . . How’s it said . . .? Neglec`ted? Abuzed?” he considered while brushing another kiss against her cheek, hearing her stifled laugh, and feeling the warmth of her arms locking more firmly about his waist. “You have not been the most pleasant companion of late, ma copine. Perhaps, it’s mon unconscious wish to have your favored atten`tion.” *—she-on?*

“You are a brat, mon husband,” she laughed lightly and slipped away before heating him too fiercely. “I better get my shower and get dressed. I might be able to handle the smell if you want to dine in this morning.”

“I’ll not tempt fate,” he decided. Not hers or his own, he might have added, and an urgency niggled at the edges of his mind. “I might’s well carry our bags down and pull the truck to the side street. Did you . . .? You did speak to Elaine about opening the shop.” *Shope?*

She nodded. “Done. Wade’s going to stop after school and help until we get back. I told them we’re going to visit friends for a day or so.”

Why that thought bothered him, he couldn’t decide, not then, not as he loaded the bags into the bed of the pickup and backed from the warehouse. As he stepped from the cab, he heard the shouts . . . *voices.* His senses keened; his attention pivoted toward the alley entrance. Caught, trapped, he stood swaying as the morning light faded toward evening. At the edge of his mind, he heard the voices echoing from the side street. Closer, an engine purred softly, and he identified the pitch of his Maserati. *Night . . . no headlights. Reporters?*

Shaking the floating sense from his mind, blinking, and clearing the darkness from his vision, he recovered with a thought of Hazel Handler watching him. Too early for Hazel . . . dawn light spread through the alley. Uncomfortable, Jade strode around the end of the pickup to the garage door, and just for an instant, he saw Wade . . . young Wade Kreider standing in night shadows just inside the entrance, the garage door lowering over his wide stricken eyes.

Uttering a curse, Jade engaged the locks, hitting the electronic keypad to lower the door, then strode to the cab, half expecting to hear Hazel shout at him from her back porch. Even without the early hour, doubtful Hazel would harass him. Like most others in Bentwood, Hazel had fallen under Veronica's spell and by extension, forgiven him for his apparent sins. Over the past two months, the old woman had even begun to wave to him, and twice, he'd seen her ambling in his showroom. For over five years, she'd visited his shop only when he traveled abroad.

Respectability, stability . . . those were the side benefits of becoming a married man, starting a family. The true joy existed in waking every morning with the little minx in his arms, seeing the sparks in her eyes, feeling her love, whether raging or purring.

A smile slipped into his lips as he backed the pickup onto the one-way street parallel to his building. At the awning-covered side entrance, he parked and climbed from the cab.

Sunlight had not quite reached the canyon, but overhead, the sky had turned a platinum blue with a promise of another fine autumn day. Not a cloud in sight, Jade verified in a glance, daring to believe he would live through another uneventful day. By routine, he crossed the street and rounded the rear of the diner, entering Meg's through the open screen door without bothering to knock.

Officially the diner would not open for another ten minutes, but Meg was already in full swing. Freshly baked biscuits cooled on one long counter, along with four dozen immense cinnamon rolls, which had become something of a trademark. With her silver-flecked blond hair tucked under a white fishnet and a fan of locks across her brow, Meg could pass for a woman in her thirties, though he ventured she was closer to sixty. Fit and trim, wearing an apron already flour-dusted and streaked with dough, she acknowledged him with a smile and lifted brow as he helped himself to a cup of coffee.

"You need more than a cup of coffee on your stomach if you're planning on driving a while," Meg commented.

Apparently, she'd seen him coming. The crack of an egg drew his attention to watch the slimy contents start to sizzle on the hot griddle. His stomach backflipped. "I don't—"

"Nonsense," Meg commented, leaving him to wonder why he even bothered attempting to finish a sentence in the female company he kept. "I'd almost be willing to bet you haven't eaten since the night before last, and a few sympathy pains are no excuse to fast." She flashed him a twinkling glance that spoke volumes about her knowledge of his latest digressions into morning sickness. "It's not unheard of, dear. A lot of young couples, especially those in love, share the burdens of childbearing. It'll pass."

"Should I even wonder how long you've known?"

"Probably since last week when you turned a little green at the sight of my eggs," she said with a fleeting smile, splattering another egg on the griddle. "I don't generally see that shade until Cy decides to climb back on the wagon. It's a sure sign of a queasy stomach, and since I doubt you're spending your evenings clutching a bottle of Jim Beam," she shrugged. "Just simple logic."

"Hmm, then you won't be offended if I pass on those eggs, will you?"

"I most certainly will," she said bluntly. "Unless you can tell me you sat down to a three-course meal between yesterday morning, night, and now."

In spite of himself, Jade couldn't outright lie to this woman who'd become something of a mother—if not, a mother hen—to him over the past several years.

"Just as I thought," she said and waved him toward the entrance to the dining room. "Go sit, dear. I can't bear to watch you turning all those fancy colors over the sights and smells in here."

"No qualms about seeing me race to the men's room, obviously," he said dryly and decided to accept at least part of her invitation. If Veronica could hold down two slices of toast, he might fare well with a couple eggs.

In the dining room, he settled at his usual swivel stool near the register and breezed a glance to the folded Bender Falls' Trib in front of him. He hadn't perused the morning paper, not since the Trib had headlined the news of the second farmyard slaying. Current events were his wife's forte, and apparently, she fully intended to entrench him in the present. He preferred the past, preferred books . . . His thoughts turning in weird circles, he rested looking at the headline, not registering the words. *Sensationalism . . .*

In a booth at the front of the diner, a lone patron rested behind a heaping plate of home fries, bacon, and eggs, a newspaper folded to be read alongside his coffee. Gray streaked hair pulled tight in a rubber band at the nape of his neck, his shaggy brows furrowed above pale blue eyes that sprinted furtively to spy Meg as she chatted with another customer at the Formica counter. If he tried, Harry could make the meal last a good two hours, which would put him back at the municipal airport with time to spare.

Meg never minded him occupying her booth for the duration, and eventually, she'd meander in his direction to spare a few words. She was something, this handsome woman who could whip up a full-course meal faster than some folks could change their shoes.

One of these days, maybe he would get the nerve to invite her for dinner. Maybe in Pittsburgh to one of those fancy restaurants at the top of Mt. Washington. Maybe court her the way any beautiful woman deserved.

She'd lost her husband in Korea, she'd told him once, and they weren't too far off in ages. He'd mentioned Nam, and she'd appeared only sympathetic, not judging, or condemning him . . .

Preoccupied, Jade barely glanced at Laura, one of the morning shift waitresses who'd arrived in his mental absence. She passed him a smile while sliding a heaping plate of eggs and home fries in front of him.

Jack Trumble . . . Elmview . . . the images assailed his mind, none stabilizing long enough to grasp a clear vision nor even a sound impression. Discomfort, if not genuine distress, niggled at the nape of his neck, and a faint pulse at his temple enhanced his dread. He wouldn't gain the luxury of choosing an alternative course of action. As much as he might like to consider Veronica's stubborn will his nemesis, he couldn't fully win himself over to that belief. If he could thwart their course, he would have argued effectively and stood firm against her impulsive nature. His ineffectiveness told him more than he needed to know. *Fate dictated,* and when his wife was involved, the future was never carved in stone.

Not pleased with his revelation, Jade finished nearly half the mounded plate before his tension added to the nausea already gripping his stomach. No choice. As he'd learned a few lifetimes past, he had no choice but to ride out whatever blasted storm fate lay before him and hope for the best.

Hope . . . that word had been missing from his vocabulary, from his life, until Miss Veronica Bryson, ace investigative journalist, had stepped into his path. For her, he would walk through the fires of hell and dare to hope he could remain unscathed . . . but how much simpler life could be if they could remain satisfied with the suburban lifestyle of antique dealers in the small quasi-farming community.

Hah! And if wishes were horses, beggars would ride.

Unconsciously, Jade shoved the ravaged plate aside and in the same instant, suffered short hairs lifting under his collar. In the next instant, a familiar husky voice slipped through the service window, bidding Meg a pleasant amenity. Len Devinio wasn't alone.

Jade knew his accuracy when Meg's voice carried a slight edge to comment, "You and your pal can help yourselves to the coffee."

"Any chance Jade's around?" Len asked while accepting her offer.

Devinio's presence was neither unusual nor alarming. Between assignments, the federal agent had often spent time in Bentwood over the past few months. If local gossip, for which Ronnie was becoming a homing device, carried a grain of truth, the fellow's days as a bachelor were numbered. Mark Jarvins, however, had not set foot in Bentwood in several months.

Uncomfortably, Jade glanced toward the kitchen entrance as both men appeared. Both wore leisure dark suits, white shirts, and loose ties, but the likeness ended there. Where Len could pass for a mafia don, tall, broad-shouldered, and dark-haired, Jarvins was fair-haired, blue-eyed, and tailored in ivy school arrogance – a poster child for the Aryan race.

"I was hoping I'd find you here," Len said while rounding the end of the counter, apparently running block, and attempting to sound casual. This wasn't a social visit, despite the half-hitched smile on Devinio's mustached lips. "Mind if we join you?"

"Do I have a shoice?" Jade asked and withheld a curse over the slip of his accent to sharpen his sarcasm. For Veronica's sake, he'd forfeited his animosity toward Jarvins, but apparently, a few sore spots remained.

"G' morning to you, too," Len sniped as he settled onto the next stool, coffee cup in hand. "How's Ronnie?"

"Still a bit under the weather, but improving," Jade answered. Not bothering to apologize, he reached for the thermal pot Laura had left for him. Filling his cup, he set the pot aside and reached for the creamer as a tremor slipped through his hand.

"Any chance you know why we're here?" Len asked quietly.

In a lightning flash, Jade glimpsed a red-smudged baton and nearly missed his cup with the stream of creamer. Muttering a curse, he clattered the small pitcher to the counter and rested momentarily, looking at his coffee cup. Was it his imagination? Or was this the second time he'd heard that question recently? "No," he decided.

"You're full of it, paisano," Len said quietly, carefully.

Looking over into the dark Sicilian eyes, noting Devinio blocked Jarvins entirely from view, Jade shook his head. "The answer's no, Len. Whatever la reason for your vis`et? The answer is no."

Devinio's head canted more, his dark eyes critical. "I'm going to take into consideration that we're probably on the same wavelength here, paisano, and I'm going to be blunt. I'm here on official business." He paused only a half-second. His voice lowered an octave, apparently not happy with his position. "Like it or not, your reputation precedes you. Your name came down through channels, and we've been ordered to enlist your help. Knowing how you feel about this, I don't like asking, Jade, but uh . . . the fact that you already know something about this, leads me to believe we don't have a choice. Are you seeing this one?"

Jade shook his head, denying the words, willing himself to believe it. Turning his attention, he lifted his coffee and downed a few swallows.

"You knew we'd show up here," Len said quietly.

"What I know," he said as he lowered the cup and met Devinio's gaze. "Is that I do not want involved in whatever you're attempting to involve *moi*."

"Jade, this one's nasty," Len said.

"All unnatural death is nasty," Jade said smoothly, his gaze unwavering. "But in your profession, unnatural death is natural. You don't need my help."

"How many more have to die?" Len asked.

Jade parted his lips to curse the question, to curse Devinio, but his thoughts halted. Others would die . . . how many others . . .? His hand, still wrapped about his mug, shuddered with a force to plop hot coffee over the rim. Jolted by the hot sting, he withdrew his hand, breaking the start of a trance. Cursing, he yanked a few napkins from the metal holder and wiped his fingers. *Death. Unnatural death.* Shaking his head, he looked to Devinio far more desperate than he cared to consider. "Don't ask this of me, Len. Find another way. What Veronica and I have here . . . it's too impor`tant to risk."

"Mr. Laquette," Jarvins spoke in a voice striving to sound casual. Tipped back, he looked past Len, continuing carefully. "Knowing Ronnie as I do, I don't think she'd agree with you. If she believed there was even a slight chance that your assistance would stop a crime, she wouldn't let you walk away."

Neither the accuracy of Jarvins' words nor the attempted goading had an impact on the revelations tumbling through Jade's mind. He'd known. On some deeper level, he'd known these two agents would arrive, had known his past would catch up to him. Months ago, when he'd reclaimed the identity of his childhood, he'd known the risks. For Veronica, he'd recovered that name. No illusions. No deceptions between them. He was Jade Laquette, bastard son of Felicity Laquette who'd been murdered eighteen years ago . . . and he'd known it was merely a matter of time before his name circulated. More than one government had found him.

Drawing his gaze away, Jade lifted his coffee. He'd known, maybe days . . . weeks ago. Elmview . . . not Elmview. "Where is this madness happening?" he asked absently, his gaze fixed on the ravages of his breakfast plate, his stomach knotting.

"Ohio," Devinio answered. "A few hours' drive from here."

Jade looked over. "Cleveland."

Len nodded, not surprised. "I'm hoping you can convince Ronnie not to insist on coming along."

"Can't imagine why," Jade said dryly, and his gaze listed. "And I sup`pose it is lucky for you, we had other plans." He needed only a second to consider. "In the back of my pickup, you will find a garment bag. Black leather vs. brown. Take it with you. I'll meet you at the first rest stop on the Ohio Turnpike in about an hour."

"It'd be easier if we went in the same car," Devinio commented.

"On second thought, I will meet you at the first ex`et off I-80 into Cleveland in about three hours. That should give you plenty of time."

"Plenty of time for what?" Jarvins asked.

"To get there obeying safe speed limits," Jade answered and pushed off the stool, rising as Devinio likewise climbed afoot. Shrugging, Jade met the bemused brown eyes. "If fate intrudes, I trust you'll bail me and my car out of jail, eh?"

"I'd really rather not have any delays. Why don't we pick you up in about a half hour? The drive will give us some time to cover the details."

"Your associate will withhold, and I'll become annoyed. I'll meet you in Cleveland. Now, however, I need to adjust a few plans. If you'll *excusez-moi*?" Not awaiting a reply, Jade acknowledged Jarvins with a glance and nod then strode around the counter. Preoccupied, he tossed Meg a parting amenity as he passed through the kitchen.

CHAPTER 3

Months ago, Jade had known this moment would come. No matter how he'd attempted to deceive himself, he'd known the past would not remain as buried as his mother and too many gaps remained in his memory. Forward or back, the past or future. He'd known months ago—Veronica was his catalyst.

To go forward, he would need to return to the past... His past, his mother's past—and the past was nearly as dangerous as the future. Too many ghosts... And even as he considered that revelation, the details slipped away, the visions flashing as if sifting through a kaleidoscope. It would begin in Cleveland...

Crossing the side street to his warehouse, he fumbled with the keys, cocking his head to the sound of car engines, a steady drone of car engines idling slowly down Maine St. in a solemn parade. He heard the soft echo of sobs, a child's sobs. Deep voices vibrated in low, shaky tones, wispy breaths, and his heart hammered a leaden beat. A funeral procession . . . he knew those faces. Someone was going to die . . ..

Automated, he passed through the side door entrance, seeing, feeling himself launched against the beige wall within the shadows. He continued past the hazy outline of himself landing clumsily on the floor, Officer Tim Spencer hovering over him. Had it happened? Or would it come to pass? Had Tim already pushed him?

Out of control, the images assailed him in a whirlwind, not slowing, not stopping.

Even as Jade settled behind his desk, reaching in a top drawer for his stationary, his senses continued to spin. A phone call, he considered and slid the paper aside, drew the telephone receiver from the base. Without conscious thought, he placed the overseas call, reciting a series of numbers to connect with a living entity. In French, he issued the orders to put the travel arrangements in order, and for several odd moments, he rested in his comfortable leather chair, contemplating the familiarity of this undertaking. He'd spoken those numbers on other occasions and had listened to the familiar female voice reciting coded confirmation.

Had he called this number just now, or days ago . . . or somewhere in the future?

Rudemonje . . . Claude Rudemonje . . . Paul Lejeune . . .

An airport . . . Cleveland . . . municipal . . . short trip. Jade Laquette . . .

Whether he dialed the second or fourth number from memory, he consciously counted seven rings before the delightful young voice answered with a cheerful "hello." "Hi, ma cherie. Is your mom around?"

"Hiya, Uncle Sax!" Deedee nearly shouted. "Hold on a second, please! Mommy's in the kitchen!"

In his mind's eye, he saw the lovely auburn-haired child holding the phone away from her mouth. Her voice echoed on every plane, and in the pristine rustic-style kitchen, the beautiful blond rinsed a plastic mug and overturned it on the drying rack.

"Mommy! Uncle Sax is on the phone!"

From a distance away, Donna Spencer called, "Coming, hon."

Somewhere within shouting distance, Tee's young voice called, "M' gonna talk to him, too!"

God, how he loved these kids! Their love, their laughter . . . but in a heartbeat pause, he heard Deedee weeping, great heart-wrenching heaves. Troubled, Jade's smile wavered, his brow furrowed. How could such a small child suffer such wicked sorrow . . .?

"Hi, Jade!" Donna started then: "Tee, just hold on a second, sweetie."

"But I need a talk to Uncle Sax, too, Mommy. It's 'portant."

"I'm sure it is, sweetie, but mommy needs to talk to him first," Donna said diplomatically. "Sorry about that, hon. What's up? Everything's okay with Ronnie, right?"

"Everything's fine," he said smoothly despite a hitch in his voice. "Well, . . . almost fine."

"Aren't you supposed to be leaving in a little while?" she wondered. "Ronnie said you were going on a buying trip this morning and planning on an early start—maybe an overnight."

"Actually, that's why I'm calling. I wondered if you'd be interested in taking a road trip and maybe accompanying Veronica to Elmview. We were only planning on an overnight, but something's come up that I can't postpone . . . ."

To the sound of Jade's voice, Ronnie veered off the steps and reached the open office door in time to see him replace the receiver, his gaze already lifted toward her. By his expression, she knew something troubled him, and again she suffered a few second thoughts. Before he could speak a single word, she decided, "Hon, you really don't have to come along."

Leaning back rather than rising from his chair, he swiveled slightly toward her and attempted a smile that failed miserably. "As much as I know I may regret this, m'love, I've already reached that same conclusion," he said quietly. "Something's come up that I need to handle personally. Would you be terribly disappointed if I've already arranged for Donna to accompany you?"

"Jade—"

"Please, bear with me, Veronique," he said as he rose smoothly and came to her. His eyes conveyed his apology as well as his concern. "I know you are more than capable of traveling alone— that you work well solo—but under the circumstances, I'd feel better if you had someone with you." His hands slid to her shoulders, drawing her against him, and he smiled a little sadly. "Humor me?" he asked softly. "I feel bad enough that I'm backing out of this trip with you. To think of you traveling alone would drive me crazy."

Wrapping her arms more fully about his waist, she felt the tension coiling through him, sensing his turmoil on a deeper level. Far more curious than disappointed, Ronnie studied his shaded gaze, worrying. He wasn't one to renege on an agreement or change his plans without a damn good reason. In one respect, his decision reflected well on her trip, suggesting, nearly guaranteeing the uneventfulness of her venture. "Am I wasting my time looking into this?" she asked, and his tension hiked a notch. Concern and doubt fleeted across his brow. Already, she regretted asking. "Never mind, hon. I'm sorry—"

"We have a strange relationship, ma cherie," he said quietly, his smile softening. "Never apologize for asking what's in your heart and mind. When I can, you know I'll answer you. Unfortunately, I'm not sure how to answer you," he said with a slight smirk, a shrug. "I know you'll reach your destination, and I know I'll miss you tremendously, the instant you climb into the pickup. I have a feeling you and Donna will have a grand time despite your mission." He paused and seemed, belatedly, to realize the soft accent sliding off his lips. No mistaking the French rhythm; '—tion' had just become '—she-on,' rolling off his tongue with the end drawled. "You must promise me," he continued with a slight effort to pronounce each American syllable. "You will take time to peruse a few shops, and if something catches your eye, you'll buy it. Ahhh . . . and you must promise to miss me as mush as I'll miss you. That, I'm afraid, is as mush as I can tell you."

"More than I had a right to ask," she said lightly, struggling not to get lost in that lyrical, hypnotic pitch. On his troubled hazel eyes, she concentrated. "Don't suppose you'd want to tell me what came up so suddenly, would you?"

"Something from the past, mon amour, and I'd rather you are not involved," he answered quietly.

"That's not relieving," she noted and read his discomfort. "If it's something I should know about, something I could help with, I can—" She halted with her thought. Apparently, she couldn't postpone her trip. If ever he'd foreseen something that didn't come to pass, he'd never mentioned it aloud. This once, however, she'd prefer to doubt his talents. "Jade, I can postpone this trip."

"You have one mystery to solve, m' love, and apparently, I have another," he said soberly. "Was it not your words only yesterday, we cannot keep denying what we are? Who we are? I don't know why we're being torn in separate directions, but I sense that neither of us can avoid the inevitable."

The conviction in his voice and eyes held her rapt. He wasn't easily sidetracked despite his subversive tactics. Whatever had cropped up in the past hour carried a great deal of importance. Turning her thoughts to the more practical aspect of this change in plans, she wondered, "What did you tell Donna?"

"Nothing more than you told her. That we'd planned a short buying trip. Tim's parents are watching the kids, and I should mention, Donna was more than happy with the idea."

"Does Tim know?" Ronnie wondered and noted the mischief spark in her husband's eyes. The man was a devil, pure and simple. She smiled slightly, knowing how Jade enjoyed every opportunity to give Tim Spencer a taste of his own medicine. "What exactly did you tell him?"

"Not a thing," he said innocently, but she knew better than to fall for that expression.

"Darling, you're a horrible liar," she mused. "What did you do?"

"Well, I uh . . . I might have mentioned to Donna that there's a specialty shop in Elmview."

Ronnie caught on abruptly. Music boxes. Only a few weeks ago, Tim had threatened to strangle a certain antique dealer if he even mentioned another antique music box to Donna. "You really are a brat," Ronnie said with a laugh.

"*Moi*? A brat? What a horrible thing to say about your husband," he played indignantly, but his voice vibrated with a touch of laughter. "And after sush a statement, I probably shouldn't mention that it's a good thing you're taking the pickup."

"Tim's going to strangle both of us if we come home with a pickup full of music boxes," Ronnie mused.

"Naaa, he's been looking for a good excuse to add another room," Jade commented, and his sobriety returned too quickly. "When you reach Elmview, m' love, ring Elaine. If it's possible, I'll join you there this evening. In the meantime, I'd imagine we should get underway. I told Donna you'd pick her up directly."

"And I thought I was pushy once I made up my mind about something." Ronnie mocked a sigh. "I don't hold a candle to you, bub." She barely lifted her hands, intending to step away. He ducked his head and wiped out her thoughts with a quick kiss. A far too quick kiss, she decided, and slipped her hand to his neck, drawing him deeper. If anyone had told her even six months ago that she'd find her heart's desire in a sleepy little farm town, she might have roared with laughter. No mistaking it. Just the thought of parting for a lousy overnighter made her unnaturally anxious for his embrace, and by the strength of his hold, the heat of his lips, he was likewise afflicted.

Against her ear, he whispered. "Mon amour, I love you more with every day. How is sush possible that I should be so lucky?"

Even now, the timbre of his voice sent tingles down her spine. Holding him, hugging him, was nearly as rewarding as seducing him. Breathing in the exotic scent at his collar, she listened to the rapid pulse in his chest, echoing the beat in her own breast. Between them, quicker by two, another tiny heart hammered, cradled within the warmth of their molded bodies, and in a weird moment, Ronnie knew he felt it, too. His hand slipped down her side, touching the slight mound between them.

Parting slightly, his eyes softer, warmer, he looked down between them, and a smile played at the corner of his mustache. "Take care of your mother, little one, and spare her a morning's ill, if you will." Without missing a beat, he looked up again. "I hope you packed crackers just in case."

"I left a box in the pantry," she said lightly and stood on her toes to brush a kiss on his lips. "I'll call with the number as soon as we check into a hotel and if, as I'm beginning to suspect, you're not here when I call . . .? Do the same, will you?"

"I'll call you as soon as I can," he agreed and started them through the door. Keeping his arm about her waist, he opened the second door and escorted her to the pickup. Far more soberly, he peered into her. "If you even suspect foul play with Mr. Trumble, Veronica, please don't take any chances. Report what you find and come home. Promise me?"

"I'll be careful," she said and studied his critical gaze. "And you better do the same, honey. Whatever you're doing, be careful."

"Always, ma cherie," he said and ducked his head, brushing a kiss on her cheek.

Parting hurt. Only that thought held firm as Ronnie pulled away from the curb, watching Jade in the side view mirror and tossing a wave through the window. At the stop sign, she nearly rammed the gearshift in reverse, then cursed her weakness. They'd made a promise at the onset, promised themselves to maintain their independence and identities. Investigating and solving violent crime was as much a part of her nature as loving the big handsome devil poised as if to give chase at any moment. Perhaps, in his way, he'd understood her need, had bowed out gracefully, but even that thought failed to counter her sense of his honesty when mentioning his own mystery to solve. Whatever had 'come up' was neither pleasant nor a ruse. For a few seconds at the second block, Ronnie hesitated. She should turn around, should insist on helping him.

At times, his gifts truly were a nuisance.

Muttering a curse, she turned the corner, marveling briefly at the absence of traffic.

By this time in Arlington, the rat race for offices had begun, and a traffic jam clogged every main artery. In Bentwood, fewer than a dozen vehicles navigated Maine St., and those probably belonged to commuters who made the hour drive to and from Pittsburgh. Bentwood still surprised her. Deceptively serene, the town relied on more than oats and corn to survive and flourish. Many of these country folks, like Tim Spencer, had attended decent colleges from business to medical curriculums, returning with degrees tucked in their back pockets. Tongue-in-cheek, they meandered about town, pouring on the old country-boy charm.

Driving on autopilot, Ronnie turned off Maine and headed for the Spencer abode. Unconsciously, she scanned the forests and fields, considering a few of the real estate deals Hal Cartney had offered. Buying land, buying a house was a natural progression but not an instant necessity.

By Ronnie's calculation, they had at least eighteen months to reach a decision. The apartment above Olden Time would accommodate an infant. By mutual agreement, they'd find a more suitable atmosphere . . .

Hopefully, a house with a big backyard or a few wooded acres, where an inquisitive child—or two—could find adventure without the harsh realities of city life. She and Jade had both endured too many of the trials of urban living. Possibly, too early in life.

At some point, she may need to change her profession as well. She might need to find a slightly safer direction for her career, but there was time. First stop, the Spencers' abode.

CHAPTER 4

Irrationally, uncontrollably, Jade took a single step as the pickup turned at the far corner. At the speed of light, he contemplated grabbing his car keys and racing after her or calling Donna and demanding Veronica's return. Never just 'Ronnie.' From the first time she'd spoken her name, she'd been *Veronique* in his mind, no differently than he'd become 'Jade' to her from the moment she'd discovered his identity. But how much simpler life might be if he'd stuck to his 'Isaac Bently' identity . . . And it was too late to consider the ramifications. He was Jade Laquette, according to at least one official birth certificate, and Veronica was right. He couldn't keep denying what he was, who he was. . . .

Muttering a curse, Jade turned and passed through the side door, pausing to engage the lock, and moving to his office. Writing a brief message to Elaine, he passed into the shadows of his showroom and taped the note to the vintage 1800s cash register.

For a long, unaccountable moment, he stood scanning the shadows as if he needed to record every detail. At the front of the store, daylight filtered under the canvas awning, spreading a soft glow to add to the few fluorescent lights which remained lit throughout the night. In lightning-quick flashes, he remembered all the hours and days he'd spent rearranging the armoires and tables, repositioning chests and trunks, poster beds. In a style to compete with the finest shops in any metropolitan area, he'd designed his shop in showcase fashion, displaying his wares with a touch of class and elegance to defy the stereotypical secondhand store. Whether he offered a cut-glass piece of signed Fry on a sideboard or a first-edition book on an oak shelf, the items rested in a setting to enhance buyer appeal. Until Veronica had come into his life, this shop, this showroom, was as close as he'd come to inviting anyone into his living room. But he recalled the emptiness, the abandon to afflict his manse before Veronica had breezed into his life. The loneliness was gone. Even without her physical presence, enough of her warmth lingered like a soft perfume to offer comfort. The dark shroud to encase him forever had lifted. So, and it was, to hope.

Shaking off the melancholy, Jade drew from his thoughts and returned to his office, locking the door behind him. For a moment, he stood, feeling as though he'd forgotten something or left something undone. Uttering a curse, he continued through the second door, forcing himself to cross the hall to the warehouse door. He'd reached a decision, made a promise . . .

Cleveland. There it would begin . . . and end.

His thoughts carried him to the electronic locks at the garage doors, and he barely keyed in the last number before he sensed the change in his immediate plans. Annoyed, Jade stood waiting for the door to lift, not surprised to see the dark sedan blocking his entrance. Obviously, arguing would be futile. Len stood outside the dark sedan, casually leaning at the front fender. Arms crossed and a bemused smile on his lips, Devinio had apparently taken lessons from Spencer to appear nonchalant.

"We decided we couldn't afford to waste time bailing you out of jail, and you'd have been pissed when we left your wheels in the impound yard. How about a lift?"

Glimpsing Jarvins in the backseat, apparently attempting to appear relaxed and accommodating, Jade considered and decided, "We have exactly two ways of handling this, mon ami. You and your comrade can ride in that workhorse, or you can grab your bags and toss them in the trunk of my Maserati and park that beast in my garage. Either way, I'm driving."

"I like the third choice," Devinio commented and dropped his hand, lobbing the sedan keys to Jade. "At least it has government plates. I'd have a helluva time explaining to my boss how the three of us landed in jail."

"Have I ever mentioned what a pain in the ass you are?" Jade said as he slapped the security panel and stepped through the opening as the door started to descend.

"Not in at least a few weeks," Len commented and pushed off the fender, moving to the passenger door. "Look on the bright side, paisano. We have a blue bubble just in case your foot turns to lead."

"You do realize you've posed a challenge I couldn't possibly resist, oui?"

"As long as you realize, you're not driving a Maserati, and you remember we're not running the Indy Five Hundred. We shouldn't have a problem."

Tossing Devinio a smile—that undoubtedly sent a few second thoughts through the agent's mind—Jade strode around to the drivers' door. Without a doubt, driving remained one of his favorite sports. Spotting Hazel on her back porch, Jade tossed her a wave, mildly bewildered when she returned the greeting rather than a few choice words and a raised fist. Hard to believe this was the same old woman responsible for putting him and Chief of Police Sam Hayward on a first-name basis.

His thoughts idling, possibly deliberately evading the purpose of his unlikely traveling companions, Jade tested the sedan's get-up-and-go power at a few stop signs. He swung onto Maine and neglected the brake while passing beneath all three yellow lights. Amused, he noted Devinio watching him, and his smirk enhanced when he spotted the Bentwood Police cruiser in his rearview mirror.

"Lousy bit of luck, this," Jade commented as the blue bubbles ignited and the sharp, quick siren hailed him. Barely slowing to turn under the final yellow light, Jade pulled to the curb and lowered his window, watching the cruiser angle into the curb, nearly smacking the government issue's rear bumper. As both agents cursed, Jade leaned out and looked back, watching Tim emerge from behind the wheel.

In his crisp black uniform sporting silver ornaments, standing a solid 6'3", Officer Tim Spencer could intimidate even the unruliest miscreants without a need to draw his weapon. Tossing his hat back in the cruiser, Tim straightened, already shaking his head as he bounced a glance off the government plates. Alarm flashed in his blue eyes, countering the smirk as he strode forward. "Funny, I was just thinking about you," he said offhandedly, sparing a glance through the back window. His blue eyes darkened a few shades. "Want to tell me why you're in such prestigious company? And terrorizing my town at the crack of dawn?"

"I've been commandeered," Jade said smoothly, smirking. "And I can't say I'm disappointed to run into you like this. Did you get my message?"

"The one about our wives on a treasure hunt? Sure," Spencer said and ducked his head. He offered Len a friendly smile without betraying his curiosity or forfeiting his hostility toward the passenger in the backseat. "Hiya, Len. What's shakin'?"

"How do you justify letting this cracker keep his license?" Len asked with a good-natured growl.

"What I don't see, can't hurt him," Tim fired back and met Jade's gaze with silent critical speculation. "Was there another message I missed?"

"I didn't tell Veronica what company I'd be keeping, Spence," Jade answered. "With any luck, I'll join her this evening, but if I'm sidetracked, how about letting her know I'm in good hands and make sure she's all right."

"Will I be lying?" Spence asked.

"I'm not under indictment. I've been asked, and I've accepted their request for assistanz. You won't be lying, that I'm aware. I'd just rather not worry her, needlessly."

Doubtful, the words countered his concern. Nodding slightly, Tim considered what questions he should ask and apparently, reached a single conclusion. "If you need anything, give me a ring."

"*Merci.* Will do."

"And for future reference—yellow means slow down, not stomp the gas. You pull that shit again, I'm not even going to bother writing a ticket – I'm just calling Grant."

"You really should consider running for sheriff next term, Spence," Jade said dryly. "See you in a day or two."

Stifling a laugh, Spencer leaned and tossed Devinio an amenity, ignoring Jarvins altogether.

Sober, Jade rolled onto the highway and maintained a reasonable speed until he turned onto the interstate ramp. By the time he reached the dual lanes, the speedometer needle tipped passed the big eight, but neither Devinio nor Jarvins offered a comment. The sedan wasn't a Maserati. Muttering disgust, Jade nudged the gas pedal deeper and backed off when the chassis shimmied. For several moments, the hum of tires offered the only sound, and Jade remained content to watch the white lines and traffic, whizzing passed a few semi-tractors on the inclines and weaving between a few slower vehicles.

"What did you tell Ronnie?" Len asked.

"Very little," Jade answered while rolling up his window, slipping his cigarettes from his shirt pocket.

"She wasn't curious?" Len asked.

"You know her better than that. Fortunately, we have a relationship based on trust, and I don't intend to compromise that bond," Jade glanced over to find Devinio studying him. "Had she pressed the issue, my friend, I would have answered her honestly, and if the need arises, I won't deny her the details. Be aware of that before you make a final decision concerning how much you ask of me."

"How much do you already know about what we're asking?"

His attention cast forward; his thoughts turned inward. Only the tension lingered, now, a forewarning and ill-omen to suggest he'd crossed the line between the realm of possibility and probability. If ever he had a choice, the moment had passed.

"I know that at least one person has died violently. Without insight, I can surmise, by the presence of our silent companion, that your case involves more than one victim. Judging by your attitude toward eh . . . shall we say—my methods of investigation? You were not lying when mentioning an order from a higher source. Knowing my attitude toward what you're asking, I'd imagine the case is eh . . . serious enough to justify an alternate source of enlightenment?"

"What have you seen so far?"

"What I have seen is inconsequential," Jade answered, and a prickle lifted the hair at the nape of his neck. A mild pulse thumped at his temple. Flinching slightly, he caught a cigarette butt in his lips and canted his head to catch the flame. With an exhale of smoke, he continued, "What I will see, barring complications, is the only significant point of reference."

From the backseat, Jarvins spoke for the first time. "Would you mind being a little more specific, Mr. Laquette? What exactly do you know about the case thus far?"

"Your associate listens no better now than when we first met, mon ami," Jade commented and tossed Devinio a half smile. "He's a born skeptic. Or is it cynic? Or need I wonder if it is even more basic? He still doesn't trust me?"

"Give him a break, paisano," Len said in a low voice. "He's never worked with an uh . . . alternate source of enlightenment. How bad do you think this is going to get?"

"You could answer that better than I, Len," Jade said soberly. "You've either seen the crime scene or photographs. I have only impressions to suggest I will not enjoy the coming events . . . And as much as I would like to believe that I will join Veronique this evening, I have sense enough to doubt. My own skepticism? Or more basic? I've taken precautions to suggest she will need the support of friends in my absence. Does that mean I will be gone indefinitely? Or does that mean I'm still a fatalist, anticipating the worst that I should be delighted for anything less? Therein remains the travesty of my curse, my friend, Questions, never certainties. Answers, only in hindsight. A waste of brainpower." He barely paused and again glanced to find Devinio gazing almost listlessly through the passenger window. "You are worried now, eh? You would like nothing better than to order me off the next ramp, to return me to my hearth and home, but I should mention, it is already too late. The game, as the saying goes, is now afoot. To reverse the order could lead to disaster."

"It's not a game, buddy," Devinio said gravely, his gaze pensive. "I've seen what you do, and I know what it feels like to be on the outside. And you're right. I'm having a helluva lot of second thoughts." He turned partway to meet his partner's gaze. "We're changing plans, Mark. We're not taking him directly to the crime scene."

"You know where I stand, Len," Jarvins said lightly. "I won't argue that point."

"You should," Jade commented. "As uncomfortable as I find this situation, I am aware of my sensitivities." He glanced in the rearview mirror, catching Jarvins' pale blue eyes. "What I might tell you could be to your benefit." Returning his gaze to the highway, he continued, "How better to profile a maniac than to receive an eyewitness account of his actions? For you, sush an event could prove crucial. For me . . . painful."

"For the record, I should mention, I am a skeptic," Jarvins commented. "But I won't deny there's a certain intrigue in learning what Len seems to believe about you, Mr. Laquette."

"If we're to be associ`e ahh . . . partners? Perhaps, we should dispense with formalities. As much as I know my given name defies the mundane, I'm getting accustomed to wearing it again."

"Is it my imagination?" Len interrupted before Mark could react to the word 'partners.' "Or are you adopting a French accent to go with the name?"

"Your imagination," Jade decided and awoke fully to the accent slipping smoothly off his tongue. He lost the blasted 'T' and found a 'sh.' "Damn it, tis is ah . . .." He'd found the 't'. "Getting fucking ridicu`les." And he'd done it again. "Lus. Ridicul-laus—us, damn it," he snapped and caught Devinio's curious glance. "Don't even ask and . . . do not men`syohn—shion—t-ion. Shit! From bad to worse, obviously."

"Anybody ever tell you, you're a little strange, paisano?"

"*Moi*? Sh-stranje? Mon Dieu." Lifting his hands off the wheel, he offered a helpless gesture. "*Ne jamais* . . . uh nev`air."

"Then let me break it to you gently, you're out there," Devinio said gravely. "But since I've gotten used to that detail, don't sweat it. Just tell me this . . . are you practicing that accent for a stage performance, or are you really having a rough time with the basic English language?"

"If uh . . . if I slip fully over to français—French, damn it. Find an interpreter. I'm not having this conversa-asy-tion with you again."

"To hell with the interpreter," Devinio mused. "I'll find you a shrink."

"Hmmm, it could be I'm ah . . . suf`fairing a . . . interferenz of a sort," Jade shrugged despite his genuine discomfort, not happy to hear the 'zzz' dangling in the atmosphere. If he were entirely honest with his present companions, he might admit this turn of events—or tongue—was slightly more disturbing than he cared to consider.

To his recollection, he hadn't spoken French fluently since leaving his father's realm nearly ten years ago. On his eighteenth birthday, he'd changed his name for the second time, but the accent had lingered as he'd traipsed through a few of the more influential circles in France. In England nearly eight years ago, he'd adopted the King's English. Somewhere in that very long sojourn, he'd lost his American heritage along with the relaxed dialect. But he'd certainly mastered at least the proper pronunciations in the six years since. So, what the bloody hell was happening to him to bring that accent full-blown into his speech? His father—

"You know, you still haven't answered our earlier question," Jarvins commented. "How much do you actually know about the events transpiring in Cleveland?"

"Several months ago, you asked me similar questions," Jade answered, glancing into the rearview mirror, refusing to acknowledge the continued speech impediment. "I told you what I could then. What I believed relevant. I withheld nothing deliberately and cooperated as best I could." Considering momentarily, recalling the chain of events that had nearly led to disaster, he continued, "Had I a true gift, I'd have foreseen events and delivered a name into your hands. What I possess is a curse, Mark, if nothing else, believe that. What I know . . . is that I do not sleep well even on a good night, and some are worse than others. I would like nothing better than to give you a description of the maniac you are searshing." He shrugged, sincerely troubled. "Impressions and glimpses . . . bloody glimpses, I'm afraid. The victim, I am guessing is ah . . . *jeune femme*. Impressions or common sense . . . *terror*." With the car listing toward the median strip, Jade shook off the momentary daze and recovered his attention in time to avoid the grass. "We will save this discussion for a later time."

"Good idea," Devinio stated, apparently aware of the near miss with the gravel. "Unless you want to pull over and let me drive for a while?"

"I want to get there today, my friend. No offenz intended."

"We're not traveling across the country."

"Lucky for us," Jade drawled. "I don't think this heap would make it that distanz."

"You really are a smartass," Devinio commented.

"Thanks to Veronique, I'm becoming immune to abuse, Len. Your flattery is wasted."

"Want to tell me what's bothering you, Ronnie?" Donna asked, breaking the silence that had occupied the better part of a half hour.

"That obvious, huh?"

"I'm guessing here, but I'm betting it has something to do with Sax changing his plans," Donna said lightly. "Did he give you a reason?"

"He still has a tendency toward subterfuge," Ronnie commented while thinking of how little he'd said while saying a great deal. "I could've pushed for details, but . . . tell me something," she said and glanced to find Donna watching her.

Over the past few months, they'd become close, as if they'd known each other most of their lives. Despite her thirty years, Donna could pass for twenty with her flawless complexion, long blond hair pulled in a ponytail, and wispy curled bangs. In her fawn-colored eyes, however, the warmth and wisdom of her years countered the cheerleader style. Without much effort, Donna was a knockout, and regardless of the rumors boasting of Tim's affairs with any number of available females in town, Donna never needed to doubt his fidelity. The man knew what he had and was smart enough to appreciate it. If Tim ever needed to handle something privately, doubtful he'd resort to evasion. Comparing Tim Spencer and Jade Laquette could equate nicely with a dissection of Charlie Schultz and Rembrandt. And why bother? What she and Jade shared was different, but she trusted him. When or if the time came, he would talk to her.

"Uhhh, it would help if you told me what you want me to tell you," Donna commented.

Flashing a smile, Ronnie collected her thoughts, wondering, "What all did Jade tell you about this jaunt?"

"Only that you made plans to visit a few shops in a little town near Johnstown and uh . . . in your current condition, he'd rather you don't travel alone," Donna added with a touch of amusement. "But don't hold that against him. As I've come to know, men have no concept of the female anatomy, and childbearing is a mystery beyond their comprehension. When I was pregnant with Deedee, Tim wouldn't let me walk off a sidewalk without taking my hand."

"Just a little overprotective, huh?" Ronnie mused, thinking of Jade nearly sitting in the alley rather than in his warehouse workshop.

"Don't tell Sax I said this, but Tim and I can't wait to see how he handles it when you really start to show. I'm betting he'll install an elevator to keep you off the steps."

"Don't tell me, you have a wager on us?"

"Just a friendly wager," Donna said with a laugh in her voice, a glimmer of amusement in her eyes. "Tim's extremely sure that Jade will remain his unshakeable self, and I'm just as certain, he'll be a basket case before you hit your eighth month. In the calm, cool, collected department, you'll win hands down."

"Don't bet on it," Ronnie mused. "If the past week is any indication, I'll be a raging elephant by the eighth month and Godzilla by the due date."

Donna laughed. "My money's still on you, kid," she said in a macho voice and barely paused for a breath. "So, you want to tell me what he didn't tell me about this trip?"

"Pretty sure he left something out, huh?"

"Deductive reasoning," Donna said only slightly more seriously. "First, foremost, unless the sky was falling, I don't think Sax would change his plans to be at your side. Second, I don't think you'd take this trip without him unless you felt it necessary. No offense, hon, but antique buying is Sax's specialty. So, are we investigating someone?"

The only surprise was the surprise, itself. They'd talked about everything from kneading bread dough to a few of Ronnie's most hairy past cases. In a rare moment, Ronnie had even mentioned her intuitive senses, which preceded every investigation. Donna was far too smart not to guess the true nature of this trip, and there was no reason to withhold that information.

In rapid-fire, Ronnie recapped Trumble's obituary and the sense of something amiss. "The problem is," she admitted. "I'm not as convinced of a problem as I was yesterday. I almost feel as if I'm chasing a red herring, and honestly, Donna, the fact that Jade asked you to join me only strengthens that belief. If he sensed trouble, I don't think either of us would be in this pickup."

"He uh . . . he really is psychic, isn't he?" Donna asked quietly.

Glancing over, recognizing Donna's faintly troubled brow, Ronnie knew the hesitation reflected nothing of either skepticism or judgment. Generally, they avoided discussing Jade's talent, but not for lack of trust. Neither of the Spencers would ever breach that trust by carrying rumors. In fact, Tim had walked a fine line to disclaim the gossip concerning Jade's participation in discovering and stopping the killing four months prior.

"Ronnie," Donna continued quietly. "We never really talked about it, but the fact is, Tim and I both knew he had a little more on the ball than base intelligence. Every once in a while, something would happen in town, and uh . . . Tim generally traced it back to Sax."

"What sort of things?" Ronnie asked, genuinely curious.

"Just little coincidences. Like a few years ago when the Mason boy disappeared. The little guy wasn't gone more than a few hours when Tim ran into Sax in town. They got into a discussion about searching land deeds — something about Sax wanting to search for treasures in the old Forbes homestead and needing to get permission from the heirs. Tim might have blown it off, except that Sax said something to the effect that even an old bucket from an open well could be valuable. Tim never told anyone why he went in search of the well, but sure enough, he found little Rickie Mason clinging to an old bucket down the Forbes' well. It wasn't the first coincidence nor the last."

"Did Tim ever question him about it?" Ronnie wondered.

"I wouldn't consider Tim psychic, but he's pretty perceptive," Donna said reflectively. "I think he came close to asking outright about a few things, but he backed off before getting any direct answers. Tim sort of fell into the old saying, 'You don't look a gift horse in the mouth.' Besides which—despite the years Tim spent away from Bentwood—he lives by the dictum of a small town where some things don't need spoken aloud.

"For the record, we uh . . . we both knew Sax wasn't born Isaac Bently. I think Sam Hayward investigated him right after he came to town."

Remembering her introduction to Police Chief Sam Hayward, Ronnie believed that. In no uncertain terms, Hayward had warned her about stirring up trouble for an innocent man, alluding to the fact that every man had a right to his privacy, and that didn't make him a candidate for homicide. Doubtful Tim Spencer was the only Bentwood officer who'd received a few benefits from Jade's unruly insight. How her husband had believed that he'd silenced his gifts for eighteen years remained a mystery. But then, perhaps not. Deliberately, consciously, Jade hadn't tapped into his talents—not before four months ago.

Shivering despite the warmth within the cab, Ronnie remembered another incident with the physical manifestations akin to an epileptic seizure rather than a psychotic break. To this day, neither Jade, Tim, nor Len had discussed what happened later inside the Englers' barn. By whatever his methods, Jade had spooked two of the most unshakeable, confident men Ronnie knew. Only once, Ronnie had asked Jade about that event, and his reaction impressed her even in retrospect. Humbly, he'd attested to playing a minor role in solving the crime and suggested his participation wasn't worthy of further mention. She'd known it was a misdirection if not a blatant lie. Len Devinio, whom she'd known for several years, didn't use words like 'instrumental' without justification, any more than he'd grant a near stranger instant respect and friendship. Whatever had transpired in the Engler barn had resulted in both. She'd seen the interaction when Jade, Tim, and Len gathered in the same room, often enough to realize the integrity of their alliance.

As unlikely a trio as the Three Musketeers, antique dealer, local cop, and federal agent could bicker and banter while meeting minds on some mysterious level of intellect and friendship. A lot like the Three Stooges, except this threesome, generally left her to wonder what transpired between them behind the stage curtain.

"You're still bothered," Donna noted quietly. "And I think that's our exit coming."

"If I forget to tell you later, I'm glad you're copiloting," Ronnie commented and flipped on the turning signal. Freeing one hand, she barely reached toward her overstuffed purse when Donna handed over the ticket and toll. According to the map, they needed to exit the turnpike at the Irwin exit and travel via two-lane to reach Elmview. If not for Donna's interruption, they might have landed in Harrisburg.

"Good thing one of us is on the ball. I keep meaning to get a smaller purse, but I doubt it would help."

"You're worried about him, huh?" Donna asked lightly.

Ronnie rolled onto the exit ramp lane and glanced over. "He is psychic," she said quietly, not consciously gliding into the appropriate lane. By God's grace, she avoided a collision as other vehicles converged on the tollbooths from the westbound lanes. "For the most part, we don't discuss it. It's just a given that I admire, and he more often despises." Without losing her thought, she handed the ticket and toll to a stout, balding fellow, flashing a smile and greeting. Following the road signs, she veered toward the far left to hit Route 30 east. "I think he blames himself for his mother's death," she confided and glimpsed Donna's understanding.

Her thoughts divided, Ronnie glanced into oncoming traffic, picked a slot, and sped onto the busy thoroughfare, appreciating the pickup's acceleration. Like all his vehicles, the little Ford could zip through traffic with the ease of an eel. Good books, fast cars, and privacy—those were her husband's first and only loves before her arrival in his life. If nothing else about him, Ronnie knew she'd taken priority over all three, but if he even suggested buying a more practical car, like a station wagon, to keep her safe, she might slap him silly. God, she loved him, even if he made her half crazy.

"He's up to something, damn it," she muttered, more to herself than her copilot. "The problem is, I love him too much to interfere. My heart's telling me I should have insisted on staying with him. My head's telling me if he wanted me there, he'd have asked me to stay. The other problem is that I'm not used to letting someone else take the reins. There's my pickle. I've handled things solo and acted on my own intuition for so long, I'm having a hard time letting him get away with this."

"Excuse me?" Donna asked with a touch of amusement.

Glimpsing at the sparkle in Donna's eyes, slightly irritated, Ronnie confided, "I think he set me up. I think he's manipulated me into following this 'lead' to clear the way for whatever so 'unexpectedly' came up this morning. And don't ask for explanations. Let's just say, there's far more to my wily husband than meets the eye. So, where does that leave me? Taking a little jaunt to a little town to buy a few antiques like some fickle housewife who needs to be appeased . . . And on the flip side, he probably knows, that I know, that he's sent me on this excursion with his blessing. In the same respect, he knows I love him enough to let him get away with it, even though I'm now worried sick about him."

"You uh . . . do realize, you're not making any sense, right?" Donna asked if only to counter Ronnie's growing agitation.

"An undoubtedly anticipated event, compliments of my be-wedded," Ronnie said bluntly. "So, do we continue this jaunt and ride blissfully toward what is sure to be 'a grand time?' Quote—unquote? Or should I find somewhere to turn around, track him down, and demand a few answers despite how futile that exercise might prove to be?"

"If you're asking for a serious answer, hon . . .? From a purely selfish perspective, I wouldn't mind continuing," Donna said carefully. "But if you think Sax is in trouble, maybe we better turn around."

Therein lay the problem. If Jade foresaw trouble, he wouldn't risk her or their unborn child, and he did know her. Without half trying, she would land in the thick of things, and her interference would only distract him. "Damn it," she uttered resignedly. "I really don't have a choice. I'd trust him with my life, and knowing that he is my life, I have to trust that he'll take care of himself. God, the man still makes me crazy, but I can't afford to second-guess him. Forward, then," she said bluntly without a need to press the gas or change lanes. "When he needs me, if he needs me, he'll find me . . . And if he doesn't, I'll find him."

"I don't know about the *housewife* part," Donna mused. "But you have *fickle* covered."

"At least at the moment, I can claim botched female hormones," Ronnie said, feeling slightly more relieved with her decision. "If I still seem fickle a year from now, you can let me know, and we'll think up another good excuse."

CHAPTER 5

Traffic had increased considerably, leaving Jade no choice. Beneath the heady volume of a rock 'n roll tune, he muttered a curse and slowed his speed. Neither passenger apparently minded. Neither protested. Irritated, he sped between a few cautious drivers, taking the fast lane to bypass a few of the first Cleveland exits. Without forewarning or fanfare, he wheeled across the two lanes of traffic and shot onto an exit ramp.

Devinio leaned and spun the volume down, commenting, "This isn't our exit."

"A pity then. I'm getting off," Jade answered offhandedly.

"Need to use the john by any chance?"

Neglecting a response, Jade slowed, paused at the stop sign, and sped onto a four-lane. Barely traveling a few hundred yards, he pulled into a hotel parking lot. Beneath the carport entrance, he rolled to the curb and stopped, shutting off the engine before looking over at Len. "Tell me. What arrangements or provisions have you made to account for my presence? Providing, you intend to introduce me to your comrades?"

"Unofficially, you're here as a consultant. Forensic specialist," Devinio answered.

"Hmm," Jade uttered, a spark of enlightenment and amusement in his eyes. "I'll receive one of those dime-store laminated cards then, eh? The kind I could reproduce in any decent novelty shop?"

"We don't intend to put you in a position where you'll need to produce a badge," Jarvins answered.

"Now, I am offended," Jade mused, fleeting a glance at the rearview mirror. "Whoever has demanded my presence in this affair hasn't the clout to see that I'm properly equipped. But I'm expected to actively participate and offer insight? Poor planning," Jade commented and connected with Devinio's gaze. "Suppose I'm expected to check into a room under my given name, too. Is that so?"

"We'll put the rooms under my name. Officially, Jade, you're not here."

"Don't suppose you'll issue me a firearm, unofficially," he commented.

"We're not putting you close enough to the action for the need to arise," Jarvins stated.

"Meaning no offenz, Mark, if you believe you or I will be invisible beyond this point, you are not as worldly as I believed. Unless you have wound a magic spell to keep this event from the media, we need to anticipate the inevitable."

"So far, this case isn't in the public domain," Len stated. "If it was, I wouldn't have invited you on this trip."

"How many times has this killer struck?"

"Three over the past three months," Len answered directly, his dark eyes unwavering. "The fourth was found late last night."

"And you truly believe you can keep the public in the blind?"

"You'll understand this a little more when we go over the details."

"We're not playing this your way, mon ami," Jade said with equal gravity. "Forensic specialist," he considered and fumbled with his cigarette pack, breezing his gaze through the windshield. Halfheartedly, he scanned the gray sky beyond the covered portico. For a morning that had broken with such bright promise, the world had darkened. With an exhale of smoke, Jade looked over his shoulder to catch Jarvins' gaze. *A storm coming in off the lake . . .*

Blinking against the vision of black rolling clouds and frothing waves, Jade refocused and collected his thought. "As much as I know you are anxious to meet your associates and begin, I'd appreciate it if you'd book a room for me here."

"It's a little early to register," Mark commented. "And I'm fairly sure we could find suitable lodging a little closer to police headquarters."

"Precisely why I prefer this hotel," Jade stated. "And you really shouldn't have much trouble securing an early registration. Your credentials and all."

"We're not advertising our official status."

"You assume this city is large enough to swallow your identity, and thus, your participation in this investiga`tion. And I believe you're wrong," Jade said with a subtle edge. "Even if you slide through a backdoor, your profes`sion will become public knowledge. Humor me, Lenny. Secure a room here for me, then we'll continue this excur`sion."

Jarvins seemed to consider an argument, decided he would waste whatever time Jade's driving afforded them, and glanced at Devinio while opening his door. "I'll get the rooms."

When Jarvins had stepped out and started toward the entrance, Jade leaned and slipped the black pouch from his back pocket. For a long moment, he gazed at the scrolled gold-embossed monogram, then sighed and unzipped the pack. Already tense, he extracted the passport from the fold and looked over to find Devinio already studying the official seal. Handing it over, Jade commented, "If I am making a mistake, mon ami, it's too late to consid`air the consequenzes."

Devinio studied the passport momentarily, then lifted his steady black gaze. "Tell me this isn't exactly what it looks like, Jade."

"You would prefer for me to lie?"

"Do you have any idea how much trouble you could get into just for showing me this?"

"By your reaction, I don't think you'll like what I'm about to say."

"I don't even like *thinking* about what you're about to say, paisano. You're walking a fine line between what I'd consider a federal offense and what I can consider a hoax."

"*Mon pere* is an extremely wealthy man," Jade said quietly. "As much as I once despised him, I knew enough to learn from him, and he introduced me to a society where ah . . . multiple identities were easily accessible." He shrugged, dragging off his cigarette, and listing his gaze through the windshield, scanning his surroundings inconspicuously. No choice. Unless he wanted to risk the life he intended to live, he had no choice, and the wheels were already in motion. A phone call . . . a few lousy phone calls . . .

"Geesus," Devinio muttered, again looking at the passport. "Just to make me feel better, tell me this is not an active, legitimate passport."

"I'd be lying."

"Tell me you didn't travel around Europe on this name about five months ago."

"All right, I won't," Jade said and met Devinio's critical, doubting gaze.

"Oh Christ," Len said and shook his head, closing the thin book. "You have others."

"Hmm, a good time for me to stand behind the Fifth, eh?" Jade asked with a slight smirk.

"You do realize, Mark and I went about half nuts trying to figure out how a man disappears when he walks out of a busy airport."

"You're neither naive nor innocent," Jade said gravely. "You knew when you hit the blind, I wasn't all I seemed. Eventually, you would have discov`aired my uh . . . indiscre`tions, oui?"

Far more critically, Len studied him. "Just tell me this, paisano. Were you using Ronnie to cover your indiscretions four months ago? Was she part of a smoke screen to get me and Mark off your ass?"

"I resent your implication," he said honestly, his gaze and tone darkening. "But since I know your affection for Veronique is sincere, I will admit—what I share with mon amour is not based on a lie. Not then, not now. For her, I will walk in those shoes," he said and reached over, sliding the passport from Devinio's grasp. "Jade Laquette will not be implicated in this investiga`tion."

"Mark still doesn't trust you, and this won't improve his opinion, Jade," Len said gravely. "In fact, I think you better put that away, lose the accent, and forget whatever you're planning."

"I can't do that," he said simply. "You've asked for my assistance, and I'm here. Obviously, I cannot turn my back on this ah . . . venture? But in the same respect, I refuse to appear at a crime scene wearing my married name. So far, we've been lucky to avoid an onslaught of reporters beating on our door. In Bentwood, we have friends. We have a life. We have peace and quiet. If my name arises too often, and this soon again, in connection with a crime, solved or unsolved, we will lose that serenity. Eventually, I, my wife, and child would be hounded. Fan mail, hate mail, the curious and obsessed."

Genuinely angry, Jade's voice lowered on a chilling note, his gaze unwavering. "For the first ten years of my life, I lived under that pall, and my mother's life was forfeit. Do you understand, my friend? The risks are not merely the printed word. I am cursed. In my attempt to protect my love, I opened Pandora's Box, but I refuse to let the evil touch her or my son. Either I appear here as Dominique Paul Jardonet, son to *de renomm`e internationale entrepreneur*, or I rent a car within the next half hour and live with the nightmares until you catch your maniac."

"Jade, you could end up in Leavenworth," Devinio commented. "Or someplace just as unpleasant . . . like the French equivalent."

"*Tout ce qui sera sera,*" he said smoothly, shrugging indifference. "My life, as it would appear, is in your hands, but should you decide to have my assistance, perhaps, you would point out to your comrade—Veronique would not divorce me for landing in a federal prison. She would not be happy, howev`air, and her happiness means as much to me as her safety."

"Why do I hear the jingle of a warning bell?"

"You are an intelligent man, Len, and you have seen things in my presence that you still cannot explain."

"Are you truly planning on staying in this hotel?"

“Our companion is booking three rooms. The police headquarters is about a mile from here,” Jade said absently.

“How do we explain the presence of Dominique Jardonet? What . . .? Should we introduce you as a member of the French Foreign Legion, or do you have a doctorate in forensic medicine that we should be aware of?”

Amused, Jade stifled a smile and leaned, crushing the cigarette butt in the open ashtray. Leaning back, he met Devinio’s unpleasant gaze. “A foreign exchange student, perhaps? Or a liaison to the Gendarmerie—the French equivalent of the FBI. Perhaps, my ah . . . organization has experienced a similar case, and you are acting on diplomatic orders to cooperate with my government?”

For a long moment, Devinio studied him. “I have to admit, you sound more like a fucking French foreign correspondent than an American at the moment.”

“I’m a little old to pose as an ex`shange student,” Jade mused. “Unless I am in an advanced forensic school.”

“Christ,” Devinio hissed softly and glanced toward the hotel entrance. “I can’t believe I’m even considering this.”

“You need my help,” Jade said simply, and their gazes connected. “If what I’ve felt is any indica`tion, you have a madman on the loose in this little city. If he slips through the cracks here, he will reappear somewhere else.”

“You know more than you’ve admitted,” Devinio commented.

“I know what I feel, mon ami, and that’s enough to give me a few shills.”

Devinio quirked a smile on his thin black mustache. “Shills huh?”

“Shills. Shivers. Shit.”

“Chills, right?” Len mused.

“Oui, that is what I said. Shills—damn it.”

“Try this one—Chinchilla,” Len stated.

“Shinshilla,” Jade stated and nearly cursed as Len’s mustache twitched. “We are not having this conversa`tion,” he decided and glanced toward the entrance as Mark pushed through the glass doors. “And for the record,” he said and found Devinio more amused. "I am not practicing this bloody accent with the passport in mind. The opposite holds true, I'm almost dismayed to admit."

"One question. Is Dominique Jardonet married?"

Jade glanced down at the stout gold wedding ring on his left hand and suffered sudden dismay. As intricate and sturdy as the thick ring glittering and weighting his right hand, the wedding band seemed to squeeze his ring finger. Uncomfortably, Jade shook his head and looked at Len, unable to hide his discomfort. "When you've spoken with your comrade, I'll make the proper adjustments. Not before."

"Just don't do it in front of Mark. Even though he's accepted your marriage and he's attempted to be civil, I have a feeling, if he sees you discard that ring, he won't take it lightly. In fact, he's liable to be more pissed over that than he will over the passport. He still cares for her, Jade."

"That is ah . . . his only redeeming quality in my opinion," Jade said sincerely and held Devinio's gaze . . . *and if that ever changed* . . .? "Between us, know that regardless of what name I wear, in my heart, I'm married and 'to thine own heart be true.'"

Jarvins opened the backdoor and slid onto the seat. "Drive around the side. We're staying here, after all."

"Let me guess," Len said while looking over the seat. "Police headquarters is about a mile down the road?"

"Any chance you have some outstanding speeding tickets in this neck of the woods?" Mark asked, directing his question to Jade.

"*Aux contraire, mon ami*. Not even in-standing speeding tickets to my credit," Jade said lightly and ignited the engine. Driving sensibly to the far side of the building, he pulled into one of a dozen open parking spaces without verbal direction. Belatedly, he realized he'd parked directly in front of the center rented room. If anything, the coincidences that forever haunted his life and actions had increased tenfold over the past several months. And it wasn't a condition he found either comfortable or relieving. Too often, he moved to an unnatural sense, directed by internal impulses for which he had neither conscious grasp nor explanation.

Refusing to acknowledge the estranged glance Jarvins directed toward him, Jade stepped from the driver's door and moved to the trunk. Pandora's Box. What he'd feared for the past eighteen years had come to pass. No longer could he consciously deny whatever dark forces moved through him. No longer could he hold the lid in place and consciously suppress the premonitions to haunt him in the darkest hours. A coincidence or an irony? Or something far darker, that he should choose to use the name his father had given him nearly sixteen years earlier?

Preoccupied, Jade lifted his suitcase from the trunk, accepting the key from Jarvins without more than a fleeting glance to either his benefactor or the room number. If he was wrong, if he'd made a mistake in confiding in Devinio or choosing his present course, it was far too late to worry. The sooner he finished his business here and joined Veronica, the better he would feel. Consciously, he chose not to search too far ahead and concentrated on reaching his room—the center room. Jarvins truly didn't trust him, and in an odd moment, Jade blamed the agent, not at all. At times, Jade doubted he could trust himself.

Veronica was his only connection. She'd remained his only anchor to the material world from the moment her light had reached out to him across a playground. Through her, he'd found the integrity that he'd feared himself lacking. Before finding her, he'd never fully trusted, never fully loved. Even now, the bond seemed too new, too precious to fully comprehend. He missed her already. Wanted nothing more than to return to the car and set course for Elmview.

Instead, Jade flipped open his garment bag and began unpacking, hanging his suits in the mini closet. Contemporary, the room was as inviting as a doctor's office with a matching bed, nightstand, small table, and two chairs. A single long dresser doubled as a television stand. A plastic card boasting "Cable and HBO," stood atop the portable set. Upon a time, "Color" would have been the main attraction. Times changed. Progress. He should have brought a book, but then, he knew he wouldn't be here long enough to become bored.

Time had sped up. He could almost hear a clock ticking as if a countdown had already begun inside his head.

Without more than a fleeting thought to his actions, he stripped and changed, donning a French-cut black suit, charcoal silk shirt, and black tie. Forfeiting his tennis shoes and white socks for oxfords and black silk, he stood momentarily, slicking his hair into a more subdued style. Hesitating, he studied the effect and muttered a curse. Ten years wasn't that long ago . . . and it had been nearly ten full years since he'd last officially, consciously worn the name Dominique Jardonet. Without any serious effort, he enhanced the shade of his eyes. When he looked again, a more naturally hazel-eyed stranger stood in his place, and for a moment, he suffered the disorienting effect of his transition.

Shaking his head, he turned from the mirror and started collecting his discarded clothes, pulling the smaller backpack from his garment bag. The glitter of gold on his hand halted him. Already tense, he loosened his tie and fished the heavy gold chain from his neck, tugging it over his head. Trembling slightly, he slipped the wedding band off his left finger and switched the signet ring from his right to his left hand.

His birthright. An albatross. A talisman . . . and for seconds on end, he studied the intricate, ancient scrolls and script twining about his finger.

Uttering a curse, he fisted his hands, suffering the transition as if a living thing crawled into him, through him. The dangling gold chain quivered, glittering, drawing his attention to dance like fire in his emerald eyes.

"Damn it."

On his third attempt, Jade unfastened the gold clasp and slid the wedding band onto the chain to clink against the antique cross. He held both in his right palm. A matched set.

Eighteen-carat gold scrolled etchings from an era when true artisans used concentrated candlelight through water-filled glass bulbs, intensifying the wattage to create intricate designs under a magnifying glass—as old as the signet ring. Where his talisman glistened an oval of black onyx, both blessed ornaments wore marquise diamonds refracting the dull light in the room to sparkle magnificently.

Who was he attempting to deceive by wearing a cross? He could not even recall bringing the cross from his jewelry cache, could not consciously remember when he'd begun wearing the holy icon. His wedding day? Something old, something powerful. Something reflective of hope and decency. Hand in hand, his love for Veronica and his trust in something far more powerful than the bastardized forces created and manipulated by man . . . *and others.*

Veronique was the light . . . and him the darkness.

With the sudden memory of his father, a shiver skittered down his spine. For a split second, he stood within a tarry blackness, as oppressive as a physical cloak to wrap about him, torment him . . . And in those moments of physical blindness, Jade remembered his fear, terror, that his father had rendered him permanently blind. If nothing else about Jean-Pierre, Jade knew his father possessed an incredible power. Like oil and water, they'd clashed from the moment they'd met. A sense of what lay beneath the surface of his father's green eyes had countered whatever paternal bonds might have formed between them . . . but that had never altered Jean-Pierre's decision to consider his son his prodigy.

'You will grow into your own,' his father had promised while dropping the weighted gold chain over his head. 'There will come a day . . .'

On October 31st, at the stroke of midnight, unless Felicity Laquette had lied to him long ago, Jade would turn twenty-eight, and he wondered absently, would another year make a difference? Would he, as Jardonet had prognosticated years ago, become the man's prodigy?

'Green-eyed devil's son,' Veronica had said on their wedding day, and in fleeting thought, Jade recalled calling her, 'white witch.' Would she balance whatever darkness lingered in him still, offering light where the propensity for evil reigned far too supreme inside of him?

No answers, only questions, and concerns to disturb him too frequently. That he wasn't worthy to even stand in her presence had occurred to him more than once.

Muttering a curse, he donned the thick gold chain, tucking the ring and cross down his shirt collar, feeling the warmth like a comforting touch of Veronica's hand. Oddly, uncomfortably, he wondered at the sacrilege, or worse, the blasphemy. For Veronica's sake—at her father's request—they'd married in the Roman Catholic Church. The two months of religious education preceding that event, compliments of Fr. Paul Grogan, isolated the extent of Jade's religious experience. If Felicity Laquette had worshiped a god, it was 'currency' and the accumulation of wealth. By comparison, Jean-Pierre was a zealot, forever striving to perfect his abstracted arts, though toward what end or in whose name, Jade had never discovered. What little he'd learned about God in those early years contradicted his father's methods . . . and there had been another in his life.

Lighting a cigarette, killing time, Jade settled on the bed, relaxing against the headboard. How long had it been since he'd seen or spoken to Maggie Duncan? What had become of her? Fleetingly, he remembered the elder woman, realizing in retrospect, she wasn't that old. To a ten-year-old, she'd seemed ancient in her mid-thirties, more like a grandmother than a housekeeper and nanny. But then, compared to Felicity, anyone over twenty had seemed old. Stout, hardy, always welcome with a comforting hand and warm gesture, Nan Duncan had posed as the only stabilizing factor in those hectic first years, as much his mother's guardian as his own. In some things, however, Felicity could not be swayed, and Nan's attempt to steer him toward a heavenly host had remained a constant contention. That he could recall, Nan had managed to introduce him to her faith only once—barely managed to lead him into the comparably small church before his mother had stormed the doors and a battle had followed. In retrospect, Jade wondered at his mother's motives. Perhaps, in her estranged way, she'd attempted to honor the love she'd harbored for Jean-Pierre. At the time, Jade remembered being terrified, tempted to believe that if he set foot inside a church, the ceiling would collapse on his head. Such had been his mother's tempest that no other explanation had seemed plausible.

He was different . . . 'A warlock like your pap`pa,' that's what his mother told him . . .

Lurching at the memory, Jade sat forward and reached, turning the telephone toward him, and lifting the receiver. A sudden thought stopped him. The accent. This confounding accent, undoubtedly, compliments of Jean-Pierre! American . . . he was still officially an American citizen. English. The King's English or American English, either would be fine for the next few moments, and whether his tongue would cooperate remained to be seen. Engaging an outside line, Jade dialed the long-distance number, sitting through only two rings, checking the time. Robert Bryson should be home, undoubtedly in his office.

Familiar, the smooth deep voice announced, "Yes?"

Concentrating on articulation, Jade spoke carefully, "I hope I've not caught you at a bad time, m . . . sir?"

"Jade?"

"W-yes. I have a ques`tion and a fav`air to ask of you."

For a moment, Robert Bryson hesitated, questioning the authenticity of the caller, but apparently, not surprised. "Ask. If possible, I'll answer and oblige."

"Are you responsible for the re`quest I have re`ceived this fine morning?"

"What request would that be?"

"Con`cerning a pair of Federal a`gents and a mishap discov`aired last evening?"

Again, Bryson hesitated. "Your name arose in an early morning conversation. For purely selfish reasons, I attempted to thwart the possibility of your involvement. Apparently, if you're asking, then my persuasion wasn't enough. Whatever you've been asked to do, I suggest you decline."

Sound advice. "Who contacted you?"

"Since I'm not entirely certain I'm speaking to whom I believe, I wouldn't answer that question even if I felt at liberty to discuss it. Which I don't."

Damn it. Concentrate! "I assure you, I am the same man who betrothed my life and love to your only daughter. For her sake, howev`air, I cannot re`fuse the re`quest of your comrades. I would like only to know whom I need to thank for this enterprise."

In a flashing instant, the face appeared, there and gone, leaving an impression of familiar features rather than certainty. An older version—

"Jade, if it was a request, then you can refuse, and I would have phoned you shortly to suggest exactly that. If I understand even part of what you've been asked to do, this is not something I want my only daughter involved in. Bluntly, steer clear."

"I'm afraid, it is too late for that, but I will men`tion, Veronique is not involved, nor will I allow her to be touched by this evil."

"I doubt very much you can avoid that," Bryson stated with a subtle edge. "Or do I need to point out the difficulty we've encountered attempting to keep your name out of the papers? Frankly, if something like this leaks to the press, as it surely will, I doubt either of us could counter the publicity. As I recall, you were no happier with that possibility than I was. If you truly love my daughter, Jade, avoid this."

"It's because I love her, it is already too late," Jade said while crushing out his cigarette. "Whish leads then to my re`quest," he said decisively. "Jade Laquette is not answering this call to ah . . . service. Problems will arise, m-sir. If you have the influ`enz I believe, I may need your assis`tanz to counter the legal issues. To be blunt, mon ami, when the name Dominique Paul Jardonet surfaces in certain circles, have it understood that the son of Jean-Pierre should not be ah . . . deported? In fact, if you would tele`phone a friend in the French consulate and have that name re`quested, such would be greatly appre`ciated. He is in this country."

"What the devil are you up to?"

"You must act quickly, sir, and the fewer questions, the better. For my own protec`tion, my father nev`air acknowledged Jade Laquette, nor did he flaunt himself at my wedding. You, Veronique, and a few others whom I trust explicitly know from whom I've inherited cer`tain attributes."

"That's not necessarily true, there were a lot of people in attendance."

"People saw what he allowed them to see," Jade admitted aloud for the first time. "Inform only those you must that Dominique Jardonet is as capable as Jade Laquette at off`airing insight. Have it understood, if it is a psychic your comrades wish to employ, they will accept the man I hov given them."

"If this is supposed to be clear, Jade, perhaps, you should start over," Bryson spoke carefully.

"You and I have a similar goal, sir, to protect my wife and shild. And I have anoth`air fav`air. I'll give you a number now. Call it immediately after you speak with the consulate. Mention only that Dominique Jardonet is currently a liaison to the Federal Bureau, and sir . . . acti`vate your secure line before dialing. It is not a call your government would appreciate intercepting."

CHAPTER 6

No longer prejudiced against the simplicity of small towns, Ronnie enjoyed the even blend of farmhouses and more modern brick ranch homes which had grown steadily closer to the highway. For nearly fifteen miles, farms and fields had erupted between forests. Even in the predominant farmland, however, industrialization had reared its head. They'd passed at least one working mine and a functioning power plant with smokestacks that reminded her of futuristic sci-fi flicks and a wide paved entrance, complete with diamond-shaped restrictions and security placards. Yet the town appeared removed from those supporting anomalies.

Like Bentwood, Elmview sported tree-lined two lanes, a few red lights, and townhouses stacked like bookends to either side of a short business district. All the modern amenities existed, from gas stations to fast-food minimarkets, and to her immediate surprise, at least one major hotel chain had staked a claim on the edge of town. The reason became apparent when Donna spotted the signs for a state college. Elmview was no more an isolated farming town than Bentwood, and it was probably twice the size, with houses clustered several rows deep on either side of the main thoroughfare. Traffic was heavier, too, though not on a scale to equate with a city.

As Ronnie practiced her old habit of driving through the heart of town, she noticed the pedestrian traffic, deciding she might have judged Elmview a college town without the need for a sign. The walkers ranged between late teens and early twenties, with a few old-timers lounging on door stoops or weathered park benches smacked against brick storefronts. She could just imagine a few of the elders' observations and nearly laughed aloud when she spotted a boy with a streak of purple hair escorting a young woman with a butch.

God, be merciful, had she ever been that young? That rebellious? Had she ever suffered such an identity crisis? God knows she'd never followed a fad, choosing to define her personality by the mundane. If she'd ever entered the Bryson mansion with her head shaved, her mother might have suffered a coronary, and her father . . . he would have waged war on the governing bodies of the nation's capital to ban hairlessness.

Snapping her thoughts to the present, she glanced to find Donna likewise smiling at the passing sights. "Wonder if Jade would like me with a butch?"

"Somehow, I don't even want to think about what Tim would say," Donna commented on a similar wavelength. "And I thought I was the cat's meow when I came home with the Charlie's Angels' look in my senior year."

"Maybe I really should change my hairstyle," Ronnie considered. "I've probably had this same stylish lack of style since grade school."

"Don't even breathe that thought around Amy Sue," Donna warned with a laugh in her voice. "You'll end up looking like Madonna."

Stifling a laugh, considering the local hairdresser's enthusiasm over any challenge, Ronnie idled, "Maybe that wouldn't be so bad. I might look good as a blond."

"If you're going blond, I'm going brunette," Donna played. "Could you see the reactions we'd get?"

"Might be worth the effort just to see which one of our hubbies faints first," Ronnie said and glanced off a passing storefront where a few brass antiques glimmered in the sunlight. Braking at the yellow light in her path, she started, "Think we'll get a room first . . ."

The sight of the gray hearse halted her words, and a glance at her watch verified her sudden thought. Stopped, wondering at the coincidence, Ronnie watched as the hearse pulled onto the main drag with a silver limo in its wake. Purple flags and glowing headlights designated the procession pouring onto the highway in front of her. An even blend of late-model sedans, economy cars, and several shiny pickup trucks countered any indication of social status. Apparently, Jack Trumble garnered a wide range of acquaintances. The light changed from red to green, and still, the procession continued.

Watching the faces in passing windows, Ronnie judged the ages ranged from young adult to elderly, with a few smaller heads bobbing in backseats. Who exactly was this Mr. Trumble that he would warrant a second red light to accommodate his parting procession?

"Gees, whoever they were, they had a lot of family or friends."

An understatement, considering the size of the town, Ronnie nearly spoke aloud. Estimating, not counting, Ronnie guessed at least three dozen cars had passed before the final funeral car, equipped with a yellow strobe light on the fender, sped past her front bumper. Overhead, the light remained red. Behind her, the traffic had backed up to the preceding stoplight. Pouring from the opposite side street, several vehicles joined the line minus headlights and taillights. With a funeral procession of this size, gossip would likely run rampant. Deciding, she awaited the light and followed the parade at a respectable distance. Whether Jack Trumble was a red herring, or a genuine victim of unnatural death no longer mattered. He was a curiosity. Perhaps, her botched hormones were not quite as botched as she'd believed.

Intent on keeping the cavalcade in view, Ronnie barely glanced at the storefronts to either side, maintaining a casual interest if only for Donna's benefit. When the houses began to grow farther apart and hedges cropped up to border long front lawns, she couldn't pretend her indifference. To Donna's credit, she remained mute even when the traffic slowed nearly to a stop as the procession turned onto a private, pillared entrance ahead. The need to uncover details enhanced by the time the last car crept through the pillars.

Considerably large with an abundance of trees and shrubs to conceal the nearest headstones, the cemetery spread out onto a rising hillside offering a splendid view of a mausoleum where the lead cars had already stopped. At least two separate paved lanes bisected the hillside. Ronnie followed the rear car through the stone pillars.

'Oak Orchard Cemetery,' a stylish sign indicated.

Taking the first turn to avoid the traffic jam, Ronnie drove on a parallel path, following the lower road. Dividing her attention between staying on the pavement and watching the mourners climb from stopped cars, she maintained a steady crawl. Snubbing modern trends, very few of these folks had betrayed the norm and worn a color other than black despite the range of followers. Her attention snagged, she glimpsed two men wearing military regalia and a few others in what appeared to be full police uniforms. A sixth sense, a niggling at the nape of her neck drew her attention to a pair of gentlemen dressed in casual black suits who kept pace from a distance. Surreptitiously, they trailed behind the main body of mourners who hiked up the paved lane. When Ronnie lost her view, she turned her attention to the lane. Plainclothes policemen . . . or federal agents?

"Why do I get the impression we just found Jack Trumble?" Donna asked as Ronnie navigated another intersection to avoid the mausoleum.

"That feeling I get . . . it's back," Ronnie said offhandedly, glancing absently off names and dates, noting a few old and weathered headstones. With the oaks spread overhead and more than a few hints of red in the branches, the lane might resemble a park avenue if not for the gray and black masonry jutting from the earth in uneven rows. A few elaborate crypts dug into the hillside, appearing undecided whether to remain above or below ground for all eternity. One truly magnificent black-stone construct boasted marble pillars and mahogany doors with the name 'Savrel' etched in Old English script at the ornate stone crown.

They had reached the older section of the cemetery. That much Ronnie gathered before taking quick note of a more recent fissure in the earth. Unconsciously, she slowed to creep past the recent grave and read the name on the new, pink-tinted marble. Duncan . . . Emmet Duncan. Reading the dates, she calculated the deceased's age. Sixty-nine.

"Should I start to worry?" Donna wondered, sounding slightly uncomfortable.

"Think we'll go check into a hotel," Ronnie decided and touched the gas, maintaining a respectable speed to pass the circumference of the cemetery. She pulled onto the highway without a backward glance.

"I noticed, you didn't exactly answer me," Donna said quietly.

"Sorry. Preoccupied," Ronnie commented and flashed Donna a quick smile. "I don't think we have anything to worry about. I made a promise to a certain fellow that I wouldn't become actively involved in an investigation. If I even think this could get hairy, we'll call in the proper authorities."

"Somehow, that's not a relief," Donna said, but she wore a slight smile. "But for what it's worth, this trip already beats my morning routine, and to tell you the truth, I wasn't looking forward to spending my afternoon studying art deco. At times, I truly despise working with the nouveau riche, and my latest client is determined to reach new heights of haute couture."

"Don't tell me—white on white?"

"Don't I wish," Donna huffed in a musing, dry tone. "This lady sincerely believes that plaids and stripes are great partners."

"Oh God," Ronnie laughed. "That sounds lethal."

"Try fitting a Picasso in a kilt-patterned frame, and you'll have a clear picture."

"Heck, with that kind of challenge, this trip really is a vacation for you," Ronnie laughed.

"My girl Friday, right?" Donna mused.

"We really need to work on that. You look more like a Wednesday kind of girl."

"Code names . . . Uh huh, let's work on this. I always wanted an exotic name."

"Orchid?" Ronnie mused.

"Too mundane. Snapdragon?"

"Petunia?"

"Good grief, that's awful," Donna laughed. "Natasha?"

"Right. And I'll be Boris."

"From bad to extremely worse. I have it! We'll go for the cloak and dagger image. I'll be Serpent, and you can be Tine."

"You really are lousy at this," Ronnie laughed. "Let's try something novel. I'll be Ron. You be Don."

"We'll sound like a comedy routine, and I didn't think to bring one of Tim's cigars."

"Code names, huh . . .? Ozzie and Harriet?"

"Don't tell me. You're a closet old-movie buff?"

"My secret's out. You pick something. You're the artist."

"Monet and Rembrandt," Donna decided.

"Ooo, I like that. As long as I get to be Rembrandt."

"Fine with me. Mona and Rem or Rem and Mona. Now, that has flair," Donna decided. "Settled. From this moment until we hang up our inspector caps, I'm Mona, and you're Rem."

In the wake of his discussion with Robert Bryson, Jade paced within the room, not entirely disappointed when the knock interrupted. By the time he reached the door, he knew the hostility awaiting him on the other side. Jarvins would not appreciate the transition or the proposition. Prepared for the anger, as well as the surprise, Jade granted entry, stepping aside. Jarvins would not be a problem. In a half second, Jade glanced off the blue glare and connected fully with the dark brown eyes.

Mamma would beat him again if she caught him mind-bending—

Done. In a half second or less, it was done, and Jade watched as Devinio's step faltered partway through the door.

The agent's attention darted over his shoulder, distracted and tense. A crease sped across his brow, and for an instant, Len hesitated, looking as if he might give chase. Clearly, he'd glimpse a man striding past the crowded gas pumps in the adjacent gas station. Blue jeans, a flannel shirt, dark hair . . .? For an instant, Devinio had seen Jade Laquette, but he rejected his belief for the obvious reason. Jade Laquette had just opened the door and stood inside the room . . . *or did he?*

Giving the door a shove to snap shut at the agent's heels, Jade returned his gaze to Jarvins whose twitching cheek betrayed his tension.

"Let me see your passport," Jarvins stated in a voice straining to remain civil.

Extracting the thin pouch from his jacket, Jade leafed through a wad of French and American currency and slipped out the passport along with a current driver's license issued to Dominique Jardonet. Handing them over, he watched as the agent dropped his attention to the genuine articles. Four months wasn't that long ago, and the events of those few harried days were clear in both their minds. Would Jarvins reconsider the profile he'd attempted to create in that brief sojourn? Or would he simply realize that he'd come close to the truth? Too well, Jade knew he reflected the character traits of an amoral personality. Before meeting Veronica, he'd maintained quasi-friendships, but no close personal relationships. He'd lived alone and engaged in token physical affairs with indiscriminate regularity, accountable to no one. He'd never even owned a cat. Antisocial. No intimacies. On the surface, even his relationship with Tim Spencer and his family could be a contrived convenience.

Heated, Mark shuffled the passport and driver's license, scrutinizing the words and dates for discrepancies, searching for an indication of forgery and fraud. In the authenticity, the documents were evidence enough. Lifting his critical, steel-gray eyes, Mark commented, "You realize, we could have you deported if not imprisoned, Mr. Jardonet? The Federal Bureau frowns on impersonating an American citizen, especially when engaging in legal, binding contracts. With the documents in my hands, you could face a few serious charges."

Jarvins had no idea who or what he was dealing with, and Jade had no intention of enlightening him just yet. "I'm counting on the fact that you will re`cognize the mutual benefit of these ar`rangements, Mr. Jarvins, and perhaps, that you will consid`air our mutual friend."

"Believe you me, Mr. Jardonet," Jarvins said in a low, lethal tone, poised now as if he would like nothing better than to strike. "I am considering our mutual friend, and I don't appreciate the vibrations I'm getting. Does she know about these . . . documents?"

"She knows I have not always been the man she married," Jade answered. "She knew that before we were married, as did you."

"You didn't answer the question. Does she know about these documents?"

"You are asking, does she know I have in my posses`sion, a means to become someone else whenever the need demands . . .? And my answer will persecute me regardless of the integrity of my motives. Is that ans`air enough?"

"You son of a bitch," Jarvins hissed softly, his gaze heating. "Did you marry her for the pure hell of it?"

"Consider this, before you cast a stone, Mr. Jarvins. If my motives were any but pure, would I have handed you the evi`denze to incriminate me? A man in your eh . . . posi`tion? For Veronique, I have resurrec`ted a name I once swore an oath nev`air to consciously wear. Now, you de`cide, mon ami. Do we continue with this sharade, or will you singlehandedly attempt to destroy what matters most to me in this wre`shed world?"

"Have you even considered—remotely—the ramifications if you're linked to Jade Laquette and my partner and I are implicated as coconspirators?"

"Your ass is cov`aired," Jade said simply, his gaze unwavering. "Jade Laquette and Dominique Jardonet can be connected only through a select few. Those I would trust with that information would not dare to interfere as it is in their best interest to accept me as I am."

"If that's supposed to reassure me, Mr. Jardonet, the opposite holds true," Mark stated crisply. "Just what—or who—the hell are you? And don't give me a song and dance. Are you in some way genuinely connected to the French consulate? A fucking spy?"

"Monsieur, if I were thus, do you truly believe I would answer you?"

"Under the circumstances, I don't think you have a choice."

"Do you want my help to stop a killer, Mr. Jarvins, or do we have time to waste on argu`ments that will prove counterproductive?"

"Regardless of the authenticity of those documents, Mr. Jardonet, we can't very well justify bringing a French civilian into this case—"

The telephone emitted a quick, piercing ring, and Jade hesitated only a second, glancing at Mark with a polite, "*Excusez-moi.*" Even half expecting the phone call, Jade was slightly startled when the faintly familiar French words spilled into his ear. In rapid fire, he heard the words he'd anticipated. If ever he'd doubted Jean-Pierre's influence, those doubts had vanished.

Transformation, complete.

"Oui. Merci," he responded politely and lowered the receiver to its cradle while suffering more than a few second thoughts. Officially, he'd just become a French foreign dignitary, the son of a man he'd loathed for more years than he cared to consider. For anyone interested, his presence could be traced to a branch of the French intelligence community where the trail would end. As of this moment, he could refuse to offer even a single detail and if the agents attempted to imprison him, he could simply stand behind diplomatic immunity. Deported. "*Merde.*"

"What was that all about?"

Slightly uncomfortable, Jade looked over to Jarvins, then Devinio, who studied him with an intensity to betray his slight smile. "The moment for doubts has passed, messieurs. Officially, I have become a participant in your investiga`tion to assist however I can. For the record, that thought pleases me no more than you," he said as he connected with Jarvins' perturbed gaze. "*Quoi qu'il en soit.* Shall we go?"

"I don't think we've covered—"

"Mr. Jarvins, pardon *moi*, but it is no longer in either of our hands. You asked for my help. Demanded it, in fact. You now have it. If an introduc`tion becomes imperative, introduce me as Jardonet, and we will both pray for your unflagging faith in security that my presence avoids notice by the press. If sush comes to pass, I've become profi`cient at two choice words. No comment."

"This doesn't fly, pal."

"We're wasting time," Jade stated and started toward the door. Coming face to face with Mark Jarvins, Jade stood close enough to feel the heat of the agent's tension and anger, if only in the ether. "Ring your superiors from headquarters, monsieur. The sooner we learn the details and thus, profile this mon`stair, the closer we may come to put an end to our affilia`tion. Frankly, I trust you no better than you trust me, but I will put my differences aside for the common good. Bear in mind, howev`air, if you do anything to jeopardize Veronique Laquette's safety, I will succeed where a psychopath failed a few months ago."

"If you're threatening me—"

"Consid`air it a promise, mon ami," Jade said quietly, his sincerity not betrayed by the indifference in his tone.

"Jade," Devinio started.

"Jardonet, my friend," he interrupted smoothly and looked at Devinio. "A mistake like that could be disast`air from this moment forward. Dom—Dominique—Monsieur Jardonet. Do not slip again, *si`l vous plais*. We are treading dangerous waters."

"Somehow, I don't doubt that in the least," Len stated. "Monsieur Jardonet."

Appreciating Devinio's acceptance, Jade eyed Mark, knowing the man strained against every ounce of his better judgment and contempt. Nothing Jade could say, however, would relieve the man's suspicions or distrust, and they were wasting time. With a sense of urgency nipping his neck, Jade tempered his silent challenge and glanced toward the door. A slight troubled smile haunted his lips. "I don't think we can afford to be enemies at this moment,

Mark . . . Is it possible—this situa`tion is volatile in a public sense beyond the mere atrocities of a murderer?"

"Excuse me?"

"Is there . . . I don't know," Jade said honestly, becoming slightly more distressed with the sensations increasing to thud at his temple. "A public outcry . . . Something's ah . . . We should go now, messieurs. Whatever's transpiring could ah . . . affect . . ." Unconsciously, Jade lifted his fingers, rubbing his temple, his gaze listing. A sense of something . . . no images, no flashing visions. His talents were never truly stable or predictable. Shaking his head, he sidestepped clumsily and leaned at the wall, not at all certain why he suddenly felt as if he stood within a roaring crowd, a tunnel of sound.

"Ja-ardonet?" Devinio stuttered and stepped closer, clasping Jade's elbow. "What's—"

"A . . . ah riot?" Jade said absently, eying Devinio as if the agent might explain that possibility. "If not now . . . soon, Len. We should not waste time. Whatev`air you are not telling me . . . it is volatile, and I am not an optimist. The press . . .? Someone's done something . . . Will do something . . . A mistake."

"Goddamn it," Len uttered, suddenly appearing more angry than worried. "The last time you looked like this and said something like this, all hell broke loose. Can we avoid it?"

"I . . . fear we may be too late, but we . . . we can try, oui?"

Devinio looked toward his skeptical partner. "My vote's in, Mark. Let's roll. Whatever questions remain can wait."

"I can't believe you're buying into this, Len—"

"We both received that directive," Len stated. "The way I see it, we don't have a choice other than to play this out. And he's right—we're wasting time." Len sidestepped, using his considerable brawn as a shield, and motioned Jade toward the door. "Let's go, and don't even think about driving this trip."

CHAPTER 7

Even if he might have preferred sliding behind the wheel, Jade knew better than to attempt it. Accepting Len's invitation, he passed through the motel door and continued to the rear door of the dark sedan. Temples thudding, Jade settled into the corner of the backseat, leaning his head against the back post. Whatever had affected him continued pulsing, demanding the massage, and more than ever, he wished Veronica stood within his reach. She had a knack. With a touch of her fingers sliding through his hair, she could warm the chill and calm his trembles, pressing her slender body against him to saturate him with her comfort. His chilled fingers and the car's vibration only fused and enhanced the tension tingling through him.

In the front seat, Jarvins continued his low, angry oaths and argument, citing Director Lakeland issuing the request for Laquette, not Jardonet. If Devinio even humored him with a response, the sounds were lost.

"Hurry, damn it," Jade said, his tension rising, his voice lowering. "A mistake, damn it . . . one of the detectives . . ." Ducking, he tried pressing his head against the vinyl to offset the pulse thumping at his temple. Darkness . . . a weird, chilly darkness . . . but there were faces . . . and sounds.

"Voices . . . whispers," he uttered under his breath as the images began to appear. Pale faces, frightened faces, eyes glazed with confusion . . . he should understand. Something seemed familiar to him suddenly. Something . . .

"Fear," he said softly. "Confusion . . ."

In clusters, the bodies moved through the gray mist, converging, uttering. Children clutched the dull tattered skirts and jackets of elders. Men and women . . . gaunt faces and ashen complexions.

"Uncertainty," he said as he watched a young woman turning her face upward, besieging her mate, a man of slight build and waxy complexion, glazed eyes. "Uncertainty," he confirmed. Knowing, sensing the confusion, he waded through the thickening mass. As if he moved against a tide, the faces drifted past him. Some seemed to look at him, others through him. "Who are you?" he asked as one of the faces, an elderly man, slighter than him, hovered in front of him. "Who are you? What are you doing here . . .?" Words . . . he heard the words, saw the lips move, but no understanding came. "Please . . . anglais . . . francais? Please . . .?" *More words slipped off the parched lips; the ashen forehead lined, and gray brows dipped, but the eyes . . . dark brown eyes dulled with resignation, sorrow . . . no fear.* "Where are you going. . .? Why—"

"What the hell . . .?"

Words, foreign words Jade understood and jolted to an external shout, a mental force to drive a spike of pain through his temple. "Mon Dieu!" he heaved and slammed his palm full against his pierced skull, anticipating blood, expecting a cut. Slowly, surely, the shouts filtered through the closed windows. Anger rose in the voices. Shaking his head, grateful for the pain receding, Jade lifted his head enough to glimpse the crowd of bodies filling the street a half block ahead.

"Take that side street. There has to be a rear entrance," Jarvins stated.

As they sped onto a narrower side street, Jade glanced over the crowd, spotting several uniformed police at the fringe of the gathering. Alike, but different from what he'd viewed a moment ago. Time . . . by the colors and styles, he knew at once, this was the present, the reality of the moment. The mist . . . all had appeared gray within the mist.

Shaking his head, he focused again, glimpsing the shiny bald heads, recognizing the deliberately tattered shirts, chains, leather boots . . . A biker gang? Wrong. The revelation slammed him. "White supremacists."

“Looks like you were right, Ja-ardonet,” Devinio said as he wheeled past a car double-parked, nearly blocking the side street. “Someone made one helluva mistake.”

A rear entrance existed. Unfortunately, whatever had demanded the crowd at the front entrance had carried to the rear. An angry mob filled the gravel parking lot; several reporters, cameramen, and at least one news van added to the frenzy.

“Goddamn it,” Jarvins stated.

“Forget this headquarters,” Jade said calmly and caught Jarvins’ angry gaze over the backseat. Shrugging, Jade continued, “The latest victim will be found at the morgue, oui? Perhaps, we should leave this situation to the local authorities. You ah . . . have a collection of informa`tion which is relative to this case. A quiet place, the morgue.”

“He’s right, Mark. If that mob is an indication, our arrival here will only fuel the fire.”

“Find the damned morgue.”

“I’m guessing it will be found near the courthouse,” Jade offered.

“Find a goddamn phone booth with a local directory,” Jarvins snapped.

“Was just a sugges`tion,” Jade said, mocking a wounded tone while rifling in his suit pocket for his cigarettes. And a lie, he might have admitted, furthering his intentional mistake by adding, “And the courthouse is toward the center of town.”

“How many times have you been there?”

“Nev`air,” Jade commented, deciding not to mention from where his knowledge stemmed. Fleeting, he recalled spending a blissful weekend with one of the clerks from that fine establishment after a chance meeting at an auction. Like all his encounters before Veronica, that affair hadn’t held his attention. Mutual physical satisfaction. If he recalled accurately, the young woman planned to flock south with the geese and relocate permanently in Miami. Just as well, winters with the winds off the lake could be brutal.

Lighting a cigarette, Jade cracked the rear window a few inches, not truly considering the passing scenery nor the slight chill. Once again, Len had sped onto a four-lane, and offhanded, Mark voiced his annoyance, mentioning the phone booth. Devinio never said a word, just continued driving, and in an odd moment, Jade grasped the reason, stifling a humph. Devinio was no stranger to Cleveland. The wily Sicilian knew exactly where to find the morgue . . .

Ten minutes later, Devinio exited the interstate, circled the courthouse deliberately, and drove the few city blocks into Cleveland's east side before pulling into a parking space near the entrance. "What do ya know?" he said as if astounded. "The city morgue."

"Cute," Mark stated, not amused.

Smiling despite the circumstances, Jade joined Devinio on the sidewalk, masking his voice to mention. "You, mon ami, are pas`sive-aggres`sive."

Dark eyes glittering, Devinio maintained a straight face while commenting, "Don't mention that too loud. I'll be up for a psych evaluation."

"You would not fare well. Take my word for it," Jade countered with mocked sorrow and glimpsed Len's smirk.

Agitated, apparently unwilling to concede, Jarvins joined them and attached himself to Jade's hip as if flanking a criminal, prepared to intercede if said miscreant decided to bolt.

No longer even slightly amused, Jade's stride slowed as they approached the glass doors. With the moment closing fast upon him, he wondered at his ability to carry through with this enterprise.

At Jarvins' hip, the agent carried a briefcase, undoubtedly, packed full of details and documentation that they might have openly discussed throughout the drive if the fellow had an ounce of trust or a flutter of decency.

To walk headlong into what was sure to be a gruesome experience carried no appeal whatsoever, and without a conscious thought, Jade veered before reaching the entrance. Breath tight in his chest, he leaned at the redbrick wall, turning his gaze toward the dark sedan. Doubtful either would let him wait in the car, but by God, neither would drag him through those doors before he was ready. Fumbling in his jacket again, he drew out his cigarettes, unconsciously cupping a flame to the butt, his attention listing between passing cars and pedestrians. Across the highway, some sort of park . . . a college campus. His senses keening, acclimating, he gathered details from the aether. A taste of lake water touched his tongue and filled his nostrils. The chill breached the black jacket and snapped the cuffs at his heels.

Tunnel vision. All too rapidly, the cars were expanding and contracting like cartoon caricatures, the colors intensifying, the sound echoing between the brick walls and windows as if filtered through a hollow drum. In a staggered breath, Jade exhaled wisps of smoke, shivering internally and lifting his free hand in a nervous gesture to slick the hair off his brow. What the hell was he doing in Cleveland, standing outside a morgue? Shaking his head, he found Devinio in a spooked shine, suddenly lost.

Genuinely concerned, Devinio broke from his slightly startled, frozen pose and came toward him. His dark eyes intense, he deliberately ran block on Jarvins' far more aggressive advance. "What's the trouble, paisano? You uh . . .? You already feeling something?"

"Shaky," Jade answered honestly, a little desperately. Only once—only once in the past eighteen years had he deliberately, consciously, set out to use his talents to alter circumstances. For Veronica, he'd entered a crime scene, and even now, most of those moments remained a mystery. Through Spencer, through Devinio, Jade knew the effect of that experience, and he needed only a glimpse of Devinio's eyes to grasp the man's genuine concern.

"Not chaky, huh?" Devinio said in a futile attempted jest.

"What's going on now?" Mark asked with an edge.

Hot, Len riveted his attention on his associate. "Go on ahead and make the introductions. We'll join you in a few minutes."

"That's not how it works—"

Turning slightly, Devinio stood nearly two inches taller and wider than his sophisticated associate. Despite the stereotypical brawn vs. brains, Len was as quick-witted and well-educated as his senior partner. "Let's get something straight, Mark. Mr. Jardonet is here of his own free will. If he wanted to walk away, I wouldn't blame him, and I wouldn't stop him. And neither would you. Capisce? So, this is how it works," he continued in a low volatile tone. "We're giving him as much time as he needs to make his decision before he commits fully, and if he changes his mind, you can go inside and talk to Roberta while I find a rental agency to get him a car. If he decides to assist—and bear in mind, we were ordered to invite, not coerce Dominic Jardonet—then we'll continue. Now, either stand aside and give the man some space to breathe. Or go inside and secure a room where we can all get comfortable. Either way, if you try cramming both of your number ten loafers down his throat again, we're pulling the plug on this arrangement right here and now. I'll be goddamn if I'll fuck up a case of this magnitude because you have a bug up your ass. It's your call. Do we work together or put in for immediate transfer?"

"I'm not walking away from this," Mark stated, his cheek muscle pulsing with his restrained temper.

"Then quit acting like a jackass," Devinio stated crisply. "Go find us a room and see if Roberta finished that autopsy. And one more thing," he said as Mark's jaw stiffened with the tension and anger. "If Mr. Jardonet agrees to continue, we're not walking him into that room blind. He's going to have some idea of what he'll encounter."

"Anything else?" Jarvins asked snidely.

"Cold," Jade said absently. His gaze had dropped to the pavement between them. Within his quivering vision, his black shoes and pant legs appeared fuzzy. "Aah a-I hate the cold," he stammered and sank a fisted hand into his jacket pocket. Shivering internally, his hand trembled as he lifted his cigarette and took a long drag.

"Damn it," Devinio stated. "I was hoping this Goddamn chill was coming off the lake."

Jade shook his head slightly, lifting his gaze to Devinio, attempting to stabilize his focus. "Y-you have to . . . to clear the room," he managed in a quivering voice. "Re`move the forensic doct`airs and staff. The deci`sion is made, mon ami . . . It is coming. Whatev`air the reason, I can no longer shange my mind. I am too close . . . Already, it is happening. This . . . this victim? I have s-seen . . . felt. I think I knew this morning I could not avoid this event. Conceivably, long`air, soon`air. I felt this coming. We will go inside, mon ami . . . Et will not be plea`zaunt, but et will be."

"That latter observation didn't exactly relieve my mind, paisano," Devinio said gravely. "So, this is how we'll play this. We'll go inside and find a quiet room where we can brief you on what we have so far. I meant what I said. You're not walking into this blind. After you've seen some of the documentation, you can decide how best to assist."

"I appre`ciate your concern, but I fear et is wasted," Jade said in a breath and dropped his cigarette, crushing it under his heel as he gestured his free hand for them to continue.

Passing through the glass doors behind Mark, in front of Len, Jade shivered within his jacket, shoving his fists deeper in his pockets. Whether the cold was inside or out no longer mattered. The tunnel vision lingered, distorting the sterile lobby and the long, lean-faced secretary who appeared more annoyed than impressed by Mark's credentials. Within seconds, they were secreted through a varnished door where several other bodies animated, advancing through a tunnel of dull yellow tile and shiny terrazzo floor.

Lean and lovely, the mid-aged woman led the small procession with a quick, confident stride. From her frosted fluffy bob of brown hair to her sensible brown flats, she was color-coordinated in a fashion to suggest affluence. With her stark-white lab coat in sharp contrast to the fitted chestnut-brown jacket and skirt, she looked like she'd just come from a medical convention rather than an autopsy. Only the tension around her brown eyes betrayed her profession and tainted the pleasant smile as she reached them, "Lenny, Mark, it's good to see you."

All business, perhaps for the benefit of their audience, Mark established his seniority, thrusting his hand, speaking first. "Roberta, likewise."

"Roberta," Devinio replied with an easy familiarity.

Curiosity quick in her eyes, she sized up Jade in a glance, offering her palm and a smile. "And you must be our consultant—"

"Roberta," Devinio interjected with the introduction. "Dominique Jardonet. Monsieur Jardonet, Dr. Roberta Lincroft. Forensic pathologist."

Jade barely started to lift his hand from his pocket when his attention dropped to her slender palm, and abruptly, he sank his fist deeper. Looking into her light brown eyes, noting her clinical observation, he stifled an apologetic smile. "Doct`air," he said, canting his head in greeting. Hopefully, he hadn't offended her too badly by rejecting her handshake, but he wasn't about to make amends. Another time, another place, he could accept her greeting. Not here, not after what she'd so recently touched.

"Mr. Jardonet," she said while eyeing Len, then Mark with a quirked brow. Apparently, she'd anticipated another name, or she found the circumstances irregular enough to be curious.

"Roberta, we could use a private room," Jarvins spoke before she could voice her curiosity. "Hopefully, a room with a telephone. I'd imagine Tagger and Springer are looking for us by now."

"I spoke with Springer about a half hour ago," she confirmed while turning and nearly running into the brawny, white-smocked man hovering at her shoulder. Apparently remembering protocol, she offered the introduction without missing a beat, "My colleague, Dr. Albert Rhoades, and his assistant, Amy Addison. Dr. Rhoades, Amy, my associates. Agents Jarvins and Devinio and Mr. Jardonet."

The fellow appeared less than pleased to make their acquaintance. "Gentlemen," he managed collectively, not bothering with a handshake. Like Lincroft, he wore a lab coat, but it hung open over a plain white cotton shirt and black trousers, both in need of ironing as though he'd spent the night in his clothes. A white mask dangled at his collar, framing his day-beard like a second chin. He was probably one of those fellows who could grow a full beard overnight. Not even mid-morning, and the dark brown haze shaded a hint of acne scars on his cheeks and jaw.

His young assistant wasn't nearly as reserved. A smile lit her brown eyes and swelled onto her perky, pink lips as she thrust her hand toward Mark first, if only by his proximity. Jarvins paid her the equivalent of lip service, barely touching her fingers, and looking like he might draw a handkerchief from his suit jacket and wipe cooties from his hand.

If not a developed sixth sense, Devinio had an innate perception, recognizing Jade's reluctance for physical contact. Congenially, Lenny accepted the young woman's greeting and started the procession in motion, sparing Addison from an insult.

On dual planes, Jade grasped her disappointment on par with his relief. Over her shoulder, she sent him a bright, come-on smile in perfect conflict with their surroundings.

Shivering internally, his sense of alarm keening, Jade trailed after the blur of bodies, his fascination rising with his distress. Like a kaleidoscope, the browns, blues, and blacks swirled and swelled, changing patterns. The funhouse effect. Familiar and disorienting. The dull yellow tile walls expanded and contracted; the utilitarian terracotta floor shifted under his shined shoes. They were traveling through an administrative wing, passing an open door where office staff fused with the desks and blind-covered windows, a collage of moving, speaking images. Important. He grasped the abstracted importance of the moment despite overlapping tangible visions of beige walls, doorways, and voices. Images wavered and rippled in Jade's sight. Slate-gray one moment, black and pitted the next, the walls throbbed to either side, disorienting with a fun house effect. Faces swirled through the unsteady tapestry, and, in a paradox of dread and anticipation, he knew the transition of time and space. A white projected light flashed, strobe-like in his eyes . . .

'*Nooo, Pleeease nooo, doctooor . . . nooo more,*' the words echoed from the past, fading into the clutter of his whirling senses. Like an overwound clock, the images gained momentum, spinning.

Rather than the casual exchange between doctors and agents, Jade heard a clamor of iron links, slamming iron doors, a low drone of voices like a human generator. The sounds vibrated at the edges of his mind. Internally, he flinched against a hiss of iron scissor-slicing iron. A hollow thud preceded a roar of approval erupting in a tremendous crowd. A guillotine. He knew it, felt it, glimpsed its red-glistening razor edge for a split second, and drew a soft breath in the next instant. The *Place de la Revolution* . . . Marie Antoinette, Queen of France . . . her stunning white face glowed from the depths of the basket. He stood in that place where her head had rolled. The same and yet different . . . there and here.

Shaking his head, Jade saw the thick gray mist, then heard a more innocuous hiss of steam releasing and the echo of a train whistle in a distant place. His heartbeat quickened; breath thinned—

In a droning pitch, Roberta Lincroft mentioned the size of the city staff vs. the local census.

Keeping pace, Jade struggled to grasp her words, and cling to the present. Only at the edge of his awareness, he heard her speaking. Grasping the significance. The Chief ME had recently suffered a heart attack, public knowledge, leaving Dr. Rhoades in charge for the moment and him not that well versed in running the morgue. Overworked and understaffed, she professed kindly. The coroner's office lingered on the brink of chaos which Lincroft added carefully without faulting the lumbering young doctor in their company, perhaps, to explain his harried appearance.

Clearly in temporary control, which likely accounted for the contempt flowing off Rhoades, Lincroft ushered them into a large room that resembled a classroom—one geared toward advanced medical students. A conference room, she announced, motioning toward a small table where coffeemaker, cups, and condiments disturbed the atmosphere. On the walls, posters and charts, graphs and graphic depictions of human frailty reigned supreme. Just inside the room, a dangling life-sized plastic skeleton stood in a pose to offer a greeting, with ankle bones crossed and jointed fingers lifted and flayed. Either in honor of the coming holiday or a need for levity, someone had loaned the plastic corpse a top hat and wedged a thick cigar between his yellowed teeth.

The paper pumpkins and smiling black cats littered throughout the graphic art countered nothing of the grim atmosphere.

Halloween . . . Halloween was coming . . . the chocolates were ordered—

Far more clumsily than intended, Jade accepted a suggestion and settled into one of the nearest chairs at the end of a long, pock-marked, ink-blotted table. Whatever his curse, he couldn't contain it much longer. Internally, his muscles gripped, and his breath lodged, burning in his chest, the images pulsed behind his distorted vision. Detached, his attention floated, aware but indifferent to the verbal exchange between partners and doctors. He barely understood the dismissal, recognized only the silence as the door snapped shut behind Lincroft, Rhoades, and Addison.

"How are you holding up, paisano? You all right?"

With the internal vibrations, Devinio's ruggedly handsome face rippled in Jade's vision, but he nodded. "H-ave to be, right?"

"Answer me this, honestly. Have you ever visited a morgue before now?"

"Ah-a dungeon once," Jade managed. "Noisy . . . like this. It g-gave me night`mares," he said, attempting a smile, shrugging.

"All bullshit aside," Len spoke while tugging out the end chair, and settling into it. "The pictures you're about to see are extremely graphic and uh . . . grizzly. Are you sure you can handle it?"

"Show me these pictures and . . . we will see," Jade decided, aware, but not acknowledging Jarvins rifling through his briefcase across the table. Now that the moment had come, neither man appeared anxious to begin. Devinio wanted to pull the plug with the fleeting memory image of a dairy barn. Jarvins' reasons were far more complex. He dreaded divulging confidential information to a man he neither liked nor trusted. Jade Laquette a.k.a. Dominique Jardonet fell into that category . . . *but there was another agenda to consider.*

Looking into Jarvins, Jade grasped an echo of thought, not surprised when Mark buckled to a personal indulgence and slid the stack of black and white photos across the table.

Rather than the graphic art atop the pile, an image of Jarvins holding a telephone slid like a phantom across the face of the photograph, and on another plane, Jade witnessed the pulse in Jarvins' cheek as his blue gaze riveted, his anger ascending on equal planes with his surprise. 'That's impossible, goddamn it . . . Laquette's been here the entire time! . . . I know what you were told, director, but it's a ruse. Laquette's posing as Jardonet . . . I'm telling you, sir, no way was he on a plane . . . I'll take him at the hotel . . .'

Backpack slung over his shoulder, Jade strode from the white block building, following the directions toward the hangers. If he'd ever met Harry Windell before today, the memory was lost, but surely, he'd met the aging pilot whose image remained on the surface of his mind. Short, ripcord lean, Harry could pass for Cy Bender's brother, if not his twin. Overhead, the rolling gray clouds added to the melancholy as he grasped the gray shroud surrounding the slim image. Harry wasn't long for this world . . . *Oh, but he loved his jets . . . Lears, Cessnas . . .*

Checking his logbook, Harry stood at the bottom of the short staircase, his gaze lifting, shifting as if searching. Tufts of thick gray brows shaded his eyes as his forehead creased with confusion or doubt. On the lone suited gentleman striding through the bay doors, his attention riveted. Black hair trimmed in a classic business style, his substantial image overlaid another wavering image of a more casually dressed fellow . . . and like an audio recording dubbed over, several voices converged, turning to word salad in Harry's confusion.

'. . . Hello . . . Ready when you are . . . He'll be along shortly . . . I'll just put his bag inside . . . You'll need to change planes . . . Cincinnati . . .'

Overlapping, one image ascended the steps, another descended, passing through one another as if stepping through a looking glass. Disoriented, Harry Windell stood at the steps, his head pivoting as if watching a pinball. His lined lips creased in a curious kink, then clearly relaxed as another familiar man strode into the hanger.

Blinking, clearing his sight, Jade focused on the photograph deliberately placed first for its shock appeal. If Jarvins anticipated a reaction, he was disappointed. Indifferently, Jade studied the photo, seeing, not feeling the images. The photo might be a stop-action scene from a movie script for as little effect as it created. Even in monochrome, Jade recognized the blackened texture of puddled blood, which silhouetted the human form lying on a smooth, bright surface. Human, and not human, he considered with the pulse thumping at his temple, his brow furrowing from his physical discomfort. As if the carcass had deflated, the depth and thickness of this apparition appeared wrong . . . lacking substance. He might be looking at a gelatin sculpt molded on a plastic mat.

Curious, uncomfortable, Jade slid a hand from his pocket for the first time since entering and reached, touching the edge of the top photograph, and feeling a tingle in his fingertip as he nudged the picture aside. All too swiftly, his stomach rolled; he retracted his touch, fisting and dropping his hand to his thigh. Muffled voices accompanied an inanimate snap; a shutter lens clicked. In front of him, another angle of the sculpt came into focus, and his senses floated with the tangy petrified odor of dried blood, death . . . more muffled voices. Shaken voices. Hushed, as if they feared waking a monster inside the room.

Seeing, not truly seeing, Jade heard another click of a camera, tasted bile threatening to rise in his throat, and stifled a cough, a breath. Swallowing with an effort, he continued studying the gruesome stop-action set. The sculpt had flaws—major flaws distorting the edges of the silhouette. Desecrated, fissures appeared at every joint. The gelatin had been sliced and folded back on itself, depicting rolls . . . And abruptly, Jade knew what he was seeing, knew this wasn't a grizzly movie set despite the shutters snapping and cracking in his amplified senses.

Uttering a breath, he pushed smoothly backward and rose, darting his gaze between Devinio and Jarvins. His eyes stung suddenly. Shaking his head, his lips parted to deny his vision as he landed his unsteady focus on Devinio.

"Jade," Len stated, pushing off his chair, rising. "What—"

"Mon Dieu," he heaved softly, shaking his head. "What have you gotten m-me into? What mad`ness?"

"What are you seeing?" Devinio asked, not moving forward, though he strained against revulsion and the need to react. "What can you tell us?"

"Your photograph`air was sick by the time he finished," Jade stammered softly, fleeting a wary glance to the black and white picture, shaking his head. Uncontrollably, tears lifted, further distorting his vision, and suddenly, he felt like he'd stepped back in time, suffering a child's fear, a child's nausea. "Mon dieu . . . a sick`ness. What kind of mon`stair have you discov`aired here?"

Drooly, Jarvins commented, "Obviously, we're hoping you can tell us something about that."

Hot, angry abruptly, Jade leveled his distorted gaze on Jarvins. "If I judged you as you judge me, monsieur, I would walk away from this. Not anoth`air word would I off`air, but you are nothing. A pompous ass to believe yourself so pure of heart and mo`tive. Wonze, perhaps, you believed in what you are doing . . . But was et conven`ienze to drive you toward this end? Or arro`ganze?" he asked, his accent thickening to roll his Cs to Zs and Ss.

"We're getting a little off track here, aren't we, Mr. Jardonet?" Jarvins said in a mocking tone.

"What do you feel when you look at those photographs? Is et sorrow or pain? Or is et a shallenge to prove yourself superior to this mon`stair? What demons do you face, monsieur? Or do you believe yourself so re`moved from humanity? You are a coldhearted bastard who could not have given Veronique as much love as I feel for her in a day if you had an entire live`time. And for that, you still envy me, judge me."

Jaw twitching, Jarvins glared at him, restraining his desire to rise by a thread. "If you're finished, Mr. Jardonet, maybe it's time Len finds you that rental car. Obviously, you have nothing constructive to add to this investigation, and we've wasted enough time—"

"Do you fear what I can tell you about yourself? Or about this case?" Jade interrupted; his gaze heated. "Do you fear to find the similarities you share with a mad`man"

"I don't fear a goddamn thing, let alone anything you would propose to offer to this investigation. I wasn't in favor of bringing you into this case—"

"Ah, but you had your reasons, eh?" Jade said in a low tone, his gaze unwavering. "What was that you said in the diner, eh? For Veronique? What would she think of me? How would she re`spond to learn that I'd turned my back on this investiga`tion? What is your long-range plan? To discred`et me? To put me on a collision course with a maniac and have me re`moved once and for all? And then whot, Agent Jarvins? Will you rescue mon widow from her misery? What evil lurks behind your eyes, monsieur, so and et is re`flected by this maniac. Profile yourself, monsieur, and you'll have the mechanics of a psychopath."

His pale blue eyes chilled, Jarvins looked up at Devinio. "We've fulfilled our directive, and this hoax has gone far enough. I suggest you take your new friend back to the hotel—"

"He's right, isn't he?" Len said quietly, poised to meet Mark's gaze head-on. "You saw this case as a means to an end?"

"I won't even humor you with a comment, Len. We've known each other too—"

"You know, you're one of the best profilers in the Bureau, and for the most part, we've always worked well together. But I'll tell you, paisano, you're losing your perspective."

"You'd accuse me of losing perspective when you've bought into this hocus-pocus, and you're willing to put stock in what this lunatic says? Maybe you better consider taking a vacation, old friend. You've been hanging around that shit-stinking town too long, listening to little old ladies winding tall tales—"

"You really are a pompous ass," Devinio commented. "And I'll take that into consideration while mentioning, I'm getting engaged to a woman who hails from that shit-stinking little town." His dark eyes flashed to Jade. "And if you tell her that, paisano, I'll kick the shit out of you, French passport or not." Without losing his thought, he pivoted his gaze to Jarvins, who appeared slightly sidetracked by Devinio's announcement. "Now, we're back to playing this one of two ways. You can accept that Mr. Jardonet is officially on this case, or I can make a phone call to have you transferred out of here."

"You'll have me—"

"Cut the shit, Mark," Devinio stated darkly. "Whoever requested we enlist outside assistance is a little higher on the food chain than you and me. If it comes down to you or him, who do you think's getting a plane ticket?"

"If one of you would care to men`tion who I need to thank for this hon`air, I would appre`ciate et," Jade said sincerely, but neither man betrayed his knowledge if either, in fact, knew. The command to secure Jade Laquette's assistance had passed through one of the directors, Assistant Director James Lakeland, but the order had originated elsewhere. Uncomfortable, Jade glanced between them, judging the hostility belying Jarvins' resignation. Apparently, Devinio's words held merit, which only enhanced Jade's discomfort. Who in Washington had decided to enlist Laquette . . . and what was the ramification when said benefactor discovered Jardonet's enlistment instead?

As an afterthought, Jade recalled suggesting his father-in-law spread the word that Laquette would not become involved in either politics or criminal investigations . . . And about now, someone in the upper branch of the FBI would be well-versed on the coincidental arrival of Dominique Jardonet. A mistake, perhaps, to use an authentic alias that could connect pieces of a puzzle, one which might have ensured his safety for the past dozen or more years. Connections. Jean-Pierre had them. Bryson had them. And whoever ordered the execution of Felicity Laquette eighteen years ago had them.

Distracted, Jade dragged from his cigarette, his gaze listing toward the black and white photographs. A connection. Was it even possible that this monster was somehow connected to the total picture, or was it—as he believed—merely another cataclysmic, if not catastrophic, event to determine a given course for the future? Whatever the reason, Jade knew the futility of attempting to subvert circumstances. Sighing heavily with another exhale of smoke, his fingers tingling and temple pulsing, Jade caught Len's gaze. Only a few silent seconds had passed, and Jarvins had not reined his temper enough to attempt speaking. Just as well. The time for chatting had ended.

"Do you want to know about the mon`stair behind those photographs, Lenny, or should I continue to tell you things about the people who have handled those photos since they were taken and developed?" he drawled.

"Excuse me?"

"You have toushed those photos. Jarvins. The photograph`air. A technician in your lab. A few others have handled those photos." Jade shrugged. "I have ah . . . been to the crime scene. I've tasted the aether there through the breath of another. If you want me to read your madman, I need toush his victim. I have told you once, I am sensi`tive—re`ceptive to toush. Your madman nev`air toushed the photos, and he will not speak to me through the informa`sion in your files. You've seen how this works . . . and we have no shoice."

"We have a choice," Devinio stated. "I'm not putting you through hell unless we run out of options. How bad would it be if you touch something the killer touched . . .? Other than the victim? Like say—a melted candle? Could you get something off that?"

"I appre`ciate your concern, Len, truly, but if those pictures are re`flective of this mon`stair's handiwork, nothing I toush after him will fare me well. The body, mon ami," Jade said quietly, not entirely comfortable with his decision but sensing his accuracy. "Anything else would be a waste of time and energy when we have the source of his greatest emo`tions at our fingertips."

"You uh . . . you know this is going to happen, huh?" Devinio asked.

"I'm afraid so," Jade conceded.

"And it's going to be bad, huh?"

"Again, I have a feeling it will be ex`stremely unplea`zaunt."

"You nearly died a few months ago," Len stated gravely, his dark eyes intense and worried. "Did you know you'd get that close?"

"Nothing is without a prise," Jade stated.

"Price or prize?" Len asked, not amused.

"Eith`air or," Jade answered, likewise sober. "There is no dif`ferenze. In all things, there is a cost and a reward." He shrugged. "Philosophical, oui?"

Len twitched a slight smile without forfeiting his gravity. "How do you want to work this? You said clear the lab. That we can do, but uh . . . I'd like to get your reactions on tape. Any chance you'd agree?"

"That is not your desire," Jade said quietly. "How mush of this has already been ar`ranged in advance?"

"Probably more than I'd like to admit," Devinio answered honestly. "If the orders were followed, Roberta has a camera ready, and a crew's standing by in the event you agreed to visit the crime scene. Bluntly, paisano, we're supposed to document whatever happens here to have it analyzed by our technicians."

"You re`alize I won't agree to that, right?" Jade said. "For my safety and security, I will not have my face and act`tions re`corded on film."

"Then you really are finished here," Jarvins said in a tempered voice. "Those arrangements aren't optional."

Glancing indifferently off Mark, Jade connected with Len's uncomfortable gaze. "Perhaps, we have all wasted our time, eh, mon ami? No film, no option. I will allow your part`nair and your doc`tair to join us . . . and I will agree to have my words re`corded. You will not film this debacle, and I will know if you attempt to de`ceive me."

"Maybe you didn't understand me," Mark stated. "The arrangements—"

Jade leveled his gaze on Jarvins. "You have lost considerable ground, monsieur. Do not tempt fate by inter`rupting again, or you will receive no ans`airs to your ques`tions."

"If you're serious about the audio tape, we'll deep-six the cameras," Len said without acknowledging his partner. "No matter how this may seem and sound, paisano, I want this case closed neat, clean, and fast. I don't even like to think about some lunatic with that kind of potential walking the streets."

"If I didn't agree with you, Len, I would nev`air have climbed into that wre`shed car with you this morning. Let's get this ov`air with."

"You really didn't have to put it that way, Monsieur Jardonet."

CHAPTER 8

At the elevator, Jade bulked internally, but there was no turning back. Sidling toward the back of the steel box, he leaned, braced against the rail, and his attention dropped to the corrugated floor.

The new arrangements were made and approved. Whatever conversations had transpired between Jarvins, Devinio, and some faceless entity on the opposite end of a telephone line had left the unlikely partners tense and disgruntled. In the interim, Jade had waited in the hall, host to at least one secretary and Roberta Lincroft, who rose to her natural curiosity to ask a few questions, not excluding the mention of Veronica Bryson-Laquette. Feigning indifference and ignorance had ranked as one of the worst moments of the day, second only to slipping his wedding ring off his finger. What he would give to have Veronica beside him was a sacrilege. Fortunately, he feared drawing her into this realm more than he feared forfeiting his immortal soul.

If ever he'd suffered second thoughts, none more than now.

Under his collar, a prickle lifted, and apprehension gripped him, paralyzing him as the elevator landed with a leaden thud and ping. If he could move at this instant, he might try jamming his index finger in the control panel to lift the elevator. Overwhelming, this sense of terror . . . and he needed only a mental flash of those photographs to understand his internal mechanisms. He knew . . . God, be merciful, he did know how his curse worked. He would step into that gelatin mold of human discard . . . would face the horrors which that no longer male or female carcass had encountered before a final breath. Madness. To walk willingly, voluntarily into that horror was surely madness.

Not even the memory of his mother forcing him to touch personal articles—to *read* inanimate objects for her personal gain—could compare with this event. A masochist, perhaps. Or a neurological defect that he'd need to torture himself to feel human. Or was he even more arrogant than Jarvins? Diving headlong into this madness to prove himself in some way superior to the human race?

For years, he'd lived without the ability to touch others through his abstract sense. He'd striven for normalcy and succeeded to an extent. Coincidences had haunted him, but none more alarming than a flutter of déjà vu. Madness, to tap into the source of all that he'd despised—and feared—for so blasted long. Madness, to agree to make intimate contact with a monster through the intimate contact with a corpse.

"God help me," he uttered, sounding more American than French, but too lost in abstracts to appreciate the return of his heritage. Around him, beneath him, the walls and floor rippled, as unsubstantial as smoke. A mistake . . . surely a mistake. But even now, an urgency, a need to continue this chosen course, pressed at his temples. To turn back now was no more possible than hours earlier.

"You don't have to do this," Devinio said quietly.

They were alone in the elevator; the doors stood open. In retrospect, Jade recalled Len suggesting the others continue ahead and get things ready. Things . . . The corpse. The room. The recorder that Dr. Rhoades and others utilized daily.

Shivering internally, Jade lifted his gaze to Len. "Promise me, my friend," he said quietly. "If . . . If anything goes wrong, you will speak to Veronica for me."

Devinio's tension ascended several degrees. "You promise me, paisano, nothing's going that wrong, and bear in mind, I can pull the plug on this thing here and now."

Jade shook his head. “You cannot. I cannot. We’re on a shosen course. Maybe et is . . . my fear talking? I’m not that brave . . . a born shicken, honestly. What’s inside of me has scared me forev`air. This is no dif`ferent. Just promise me, mon ami. If . . . if I cannot speak with her, you will tell her I love her with all that is real inside of me. That I have loved her from the instant we met years ago. Will you promise?”

“Stand in my shoes, damn it, paisano,” Len said quietly, his intensity a force within the frozen iron cube. “I do know you’re legit. God knows, I never believed this kind of shit before I met you, but I’m damned sure a believer now. In my place, faced with a man of your uh . . . power? What the hell would you do if he suggested something is about to go extremely wrong?”

“I would uh . . . consid`air the source.”

“That’s exactly what I *am* doing and exactly why I think I’m pulling the plug—”

“Lenny . . . I cannot accurately predict the fu`ture,” Jade said honestly, uncomfortably aware of his accent thickening by the moment. “What I feel more often de`rives from the tangible past. Impres`sions, oui. But none based on concrete evi`denze, and I am a fatalist. What can go wrong, will. I have felt that way all my life. Et is a crippling fear that any forward step shall result in a backward mo`tion . . . or annihila`tion.” He shrugged, wanting to be understood, still needing the promise if only to cover his bases. “Perhaps, *ma mere* understood the need for force. She nev`air gave me a shoice, knowing I would shoose stasis over possible disaster. I have nev`air been the bravest idiot or most courageous fool. Don’t let me shange your mind. Demand my service, mon ami. Make et easier on both of us. Right after you promise to carry the message for me.”

“Damn you,” Devinio stated, frustrated. “And if something does go wrong? If what you’re feeling, is based on a premonition? What do I do then? Tell Ronnie you loved her right after I admit I’m responsible for whatever happened to you?”

Smiling faintly, Jade shook his head. "Blame me, Lenny. Tell her I forced you. She'll believe you. She thinks I'm intelligent and forceful. So et is, love is blind, oui?"

"The lady has her intuitions, paisano," Devinio said gravely. "And I'd wager she's not blind or easily deceived. We'll do this your way. You have my word. I'll speak to her if for any reason you can't. If, however, that comes to pass, I'm never speaking to you again."

With a handshake, they sealed the pact. Not entirely relieved, still more tense than he cared to analyze, Jade accepted the hand signal to step from the elevator. No turning back. This was it. As if a conduit had already opened, tunnel vision warped the walls, rippling the floor beneath his soles. A chill started at the nape of his neck and spilled outward, effecting Lenny if his soft curse was any indication.

Out of control, the power within him fed upon itself as if somewhere between a conscious decision and subconscious will, a silent communication had signaled all systems go. Before he passed through the door that Devinio held for him, Jade felt the external world fading, the walls closing in on him. Spiraling, his attention sped off the chestnut-haired doctor and Jarvins as they were apparently making last-minute adjustments. Far away, he glimpsed the only occupied table in the room. A sheet draped from one end to the other, no recognizable human shape beneath the cover.

"Mr. Jardonet," a faraway female voice reached him as he sidestepped from the touch of a slender hand. "I hope these two warned you about what you're about to see . . . And you better have a pretty strong stomach . . . ."

No more than a flutter, like the butterflies reflective of her one and only speaking engagement, the movement started just below Ronnie's waist. Startled, she halted mid-stride, at once delighted but oddly tense. Even her breath silenced, held, as though she heard a sound from the depths of her stomach. Something more than a gurgle of indigestion for a change. Had she heard something a moment ago? God knows, she'd felt that flutter on other occasions and simply accepted it, enjoyed it. Did a fetus dream? That spontaneous flutter was akin to a body jolting awake on the cusp of a sound sleep.

Uncomfortable, suddenly, Ronnie glanced about the contemporary room as if she might recognize the source of her distress. On the outside chance that Jade would join her, she and Donna—Mona—had booked separate rooms. Her attention caught on the king-sized bed, and a smile flickered on her lips, remembering. They'd made love for the first time on a rented bed, but the King-Edward-style bed they shared was far more comfortable. If—when—Jade came, they would inevitably try out the flower-covered mattress, and she could already hear him making some off-the-wall comment about the quality of the accommodations. Doubtful, he'd find fault in their coupling even if they landed on the floor.

But even that thought countered nothing of the sudden nausea threatening to erupt. Hurrying, realizing the unnatural timing, she fled into the bathroom, snapped up the toilet seat and stooped, prepared for the inevitable. Noon—nearly noon. By now, the fits of illness generally passed. A blessing, according to Ronnie's mother, who professed that most women didn't contain their morning sickness to the morning. Vicky, her sister-in-law, and Donna had verified Fiona's words, claiming they'd suffered ills morning, noon, and night for at least a few weeks. Morning sickness, Ronnie had vowed, would be confined to the morning come hell or high water . . . and apparently, her infant had agreed until now.

Cursing, gagging, she forfeited the battle to restrain the inevitable and emptied a few remaining gulps of coffee and toast into the commode. Below her stomach, like a fish out of water, the tadpole wiggled and squirmed, adding insult to injury.

"Shhh," she uttered, tucking a hand to her waist in a moment of genuine fright. On some weird plane, she sensed the little dickens' distress, wondering if her sudden tension could affect her unborn child. As much as she loved the thought of having this child, Jade's child, the mysteries of this event remained a little nerve-wracking. Nine months of weird epiphanies might drive her as mad as a hatter. In the meantime, . . . she swallowed the last of the dry heaves, settled unceremoniously on the tile floor, and leaned against the side of the tub. Inside and outside against her palm, the motion fluttered.

"Shhh," she uttered again, looking down at her hand as if she might calm the fetus. "Settle now, you're warm and safe, and if you're hungry, I have it on good authority, that part's covered around the clock. Just relax and sleep, li'l darling. Whatever's troubling us . . ." And it was an *us*, she realized abruptly. Whatever had started the fluttering might not have originated in her construction, but it was definitely a shared alarm.

Floating suddenly, his senses drifting, he swayed physically, staggered, and bumped into a solid body. "Owe . . . wha-what . . ." A stranger held him, halting him. The sting of pain, an insect bite? Suddenly the confusion set in. "Whaaat . . ." Around him, the world had changed, darkening, fading. He knew this street or should know this street . . . *work*. "Ha-ave to get t-to wooork," he moaned softly, ducking his head, shaking his head to clear the fuzz. At his hip, a hand clasped him; his knees had turned to rubber.

"What're you seeing?" a deep voice drifted. "What's going on around you?"

"Funnny . . . feeel funnny," Jade strained, his voice sounding different, softer even to his own ears. On dual planes, he understood a need to talk. "Sooo haaard," he moaned softly. "Haaard tooo talllk . . . tonnngue's nnnumb . . . ssswolllen. . .. Drrrugged."

"Where are you? Do you know?"

His head jerked with a nod, rolling against the solid chest. Devinio . . . a stranger. "Ohhh GGGod," he heaved as his soles scraped, dragging under him.

At his hip, a hand gripped, tugging him into motion. "Awwwake," he moaned, seeing the distorted images of a vehicle in shadows, understanding panic at the edges of his mind. "Nooo," he moaned and attempted to struggle. Nothing moved. Swollen, his hands dangled loosely over the massive arm about his waist . . . female. "Hhhelllp mmmeee," he heaved and felt himself sinking, even as he understood the woman's head lulling, dangling now like her arms. *Only the pavement, distorted within her line of vision. Somewhere nearby, a streetlight provided a dull glow, not enough light to see more than shadows and impressions of a man's shoes clomping on the sidewalk.*

"What do you see, paisano?" the deep voice nudged from far away.

"Shoooes . . . mmman's shoes," Jade answered, losing himself slowly, more fully within the haze of whatever synthetic had stung her. And abruptly, the world firmed. Images cleared. His muscles constricted with an incredible strength rising through his limbs. "Sleep . . . Just sleep now . . . Nothing to worry over. . ."

"Paisano?"

"Painless," he sniggered. "I promise you . . . you won't feel any pain." *Carefully, he lifted the limp woman and laid her gently on the van's floor, snapping the door shut.* "Van," Jade said as he moved within the weird hazy light, circling the vehicle, climbing behind the wheel. "Chevy. Late model. '82 – '83." *The engine ignited, vibrating through his palms, through his body. Hands . . . A glitter of light surfaced in his mind, darting up off the hands he held against the steering wheel.* His attention riveted forward. He understood a determined course and recognized only the essence of traveling a planned route. Hazy on either side, he knew buildings passing, lights flashing, traffic signals, street signs, traffic . . . *engine sounds fused with music from car windows and open bars* . . . "Painless . . . perfect. Planned. Such beautiful skin . . . flawless," he said in a far huskier voice. "Flawless . . . beautiful. A work of art . . . the stupid bitch. I'll make her a work of art . . . fools. Flawed . . . I'll make her flawless. Beautiful . . . you should thank me, whore . . . I am an artist!"

Waterfront . . . Jade glimpsed the dark reflections of lights on the waves. "Water," he snapped with a gunshot rhythm. A sense of anger, hatred flowed through his mind, through his veins. And images . . . strange images as if glimpsed on a movie reel. Black and white . . . the faces again.

"Faces," he said with a peculiar note, a question in his mind, in his voice. He'd seen these faces, or something similar. "Ah-ah . . . movie?" *Was this a movie reel? Crackling, as if from an ancient projector, and flicker of lights in the gray-on-gray images. People moving through the mist, tattered gray coats . . . scarves pulled tight on women's scalps. Skin taunt and pale, gray-on-gray.* "Movie . . ."

The images flickered with the broken animation of an old movie, the frames clicking and clattering, distorting the apparitions to appear clumsy as they trailed in line. The camera had moved back. He saw the bodies moving in a line, broken steps, trudging steps. Confusion haunted his mind as he saw some of the faces looking at him and heard the click and clatter of the film. *A silent film.* "Movie." *Even in black and white, he recognized the fear and intimidation as heads ducked away and hands clasped children's shoulders, drawing the smaller ones into a comforting hold.*

"What do you see?"

"Fear . . . Confusion . . ." he uttered, but that wasn't what he felt. Power. His limbs suffused with strength; he grasped the power of this combined fear. "Invincible," he snapped as the images changed again, and he found himself climbing from the driver's seat. *A building . . . a house?* Uncertainty haunted his mind as the van door sped open in front of him, and he saw the woman lying limp in the shadows. "Still resting . . . Lazy bitch . . . You're all useless . . . but I've found a use for you . . ." *Collecting the flaccid body as if it were already weightless, he shoved the door closed, turning within the shadows.* "I have everything ready for you, Jew-loving bitch . . . all ready for you . . ." But the words were muffled, drifting, becoming more difficult to hear. Understanding with the first hints of heaviness in his limbs, Jade uttered a breath, a sound. Dread and fear touched him on dual planes. "Nooo . . . ma-ake ittt ssstop," he pleaded in a far weaker voice, feeling his physical essence sinking, withering. "Mom`ma, helllp meee . . . mmmake ittt ssstop . . . baaad."

"What do you—"

His body jostled, landed in an uncollected heap, limbs akimbo. He heard them thud and thump, heard a crinkle of plastic, and moaned on another plane. He'd seen this before, felt this before. *Flickering, the lights began to ignite, a snap and scent of sulfur.* Disoriented, he shook his head, catching only glimmers of metal tables, faces he should know, waking to a scent of chemicals as strong as the scent of plastic. Sinking on rubbery knees, he settled on the shiny floor, heaving breaths as if he'd run a marathon. Not running, not moving. Weighted, his mind snagged between overlapping images of a shadow moving in flickering light and the dark-clad bodies on every side of him . . . and still another image swayed in his swirling vision.

Intense, the light glittered on a metal tray, sparking reflections off shiny metal instruments, plastic tubes, vials of clear liquid, and syringes . . . at least a half dozen syringes. To one side of the glistening table, several large plastic containers—food storage containers—stood in a neat row. His head shook, rejecting the images, refusing to acknowledge what his mind gleaned. "Nooo."

"Too long, damn it," a low voice uttered.

"He's not telling us—"

"Painless," the low voice issued off his lips, hissed in his ears. "We have time now . . . Plenty of time . . . And things are different now. Masters . . . they were masters. Artists . . . Ah, and they were brilliant. To create something beautiful from nothing . . . That was their goal. Long, I've listened and learned, and this is only the beginning . . . I will make you immortal . . . You'll like that, won't you? . . . To be flawless. An object of awe and adoration . . . useful," the voice dripped sarcasm, and in his line of vision, Jade watched as a long-bladed knife slid smoothly beneath the pale blue blouse, slicing cloth like butter. "You won't be needing these any longer . . . beautiful. That was their only mistake . . . They wasted so much. Hadn't the foresight to see the potential in each of you . . . Ah, but I have seen and understood. For these moments, I have lived, and you should feel honored that I've chosen you as one of the first . . . Together, we will break new ground and create something beautiful from nothing . . . Do not be afraid."

Terrified, stricken, he watched as the hands, an extension of himself, slid a scalpel through the flesh beneath the limp, pale arm. *Blood spouted and spilled over the edges of the cut, but the fingers worked swiftly, smoothly, collecting an instrument off the tray, sliding the blunt tips through the incision.* Rejecting, denying, Jade moaned a sound while at the same instant suffering triumph and contrasting flutters of confusion. Too many impulses, too many conflicting images. His senses swirled, struggling to make out the images in front of him, to find his own reality. Dark hair . . . dark hair spilled out around the pale face in front of him, but not even that could he see clearly as another incision sliced through muscle, squirting, flooding.

"Ouuut . . . gettt mmme ouuut," he moaned softly, struggling internally, externally to extract himself from these confusing, conflicting images. *Blood . . . so much blood*, and the visions were accelerating inside his mind, the woman waking, her senses keening to know fear, to struggle for understanding. In the same instant, the knife slipped through the top layers of flesh, descending the underside of the exposed arm to the elbow joint. *Blood . . . turning red. All red now, spider-webbing over the bare flesh. And he felt it, suddenly. The pain of that incision piercing his own arm, slicing over the nob of his shoulder.* "Ohhh GGGod . . . no. No . . . hurrrts! Helllp! Helllp mmmeee!"

She felt nothing. Triumphantly, the surgeon worked steadily, his words a calm mantra, a balm on the rising awareness of his patient. "Nnnooo," he moaned as he tried twisting, but something—someone—held him! And he felt panic inside, outside, and heard anxious voices far away, just beyond his reach. Blood . . . he tasted it. Smelled it. Felt it! He felt it! Her blood, his blood. Mixing and dripping, saturating the cloth on his arm as the acidic pains swept through his arm with the precision of the scalpel lifting, detaching the outer layers of his flesh. In an instant of stark, crystalized terror, he understood — saw a large swatch of red tissue-thin cloth dangling before his eye and knew that was his skin. The scream never reached his lips, endless the sound carried through the vacuum of his collective consciousness, but even in blackness, no relief came . . . she was awake . . . he was awake . . . and they were both bleeding.

"Jade," Ronnie uttered absently and looked through the open connecting door into the compact bedroom, half-expecting to see him standing in her presence. Suddenly, she needed to see him, and she cursed whatever madness had carried her a few hours from their home. Pushing smoothly off the floor, keeping her hand over her wiggling anatomy, she strode into the main room, settling on the edge of the bed and swaying slightly, more surprised by the floating sensation. Was she about to pass out? Alarmed, uncertain whether she feared something wrong with her body and the baby or with Jade, she reached clumsily, dragging the phone receiver off the hook, and jabbing the buttons for Olden Time. If Jade answered . . . he wouldn't answer. If nothing else, she knew, abruptly, he wouldn't answer. And the thought firmed her resolve.

"Olden Time Antiques and Collectibles," Elaine said brightly.

"Hi, Elaine. Is Jade there?" Ronnie asked in a clipped, no-nonsense tone.

Only an instant of hesitation passed before Elaine recovered from her surprise. "Well, that sure explains why he left this note. I thought he was going with you, honey? Is everything all right?"

"What note?" Ronnie asked.

"I found it taped to the register when I came in," she said lightly. "It's to me, but it says here, when you call, I'm supposed to tell you not to worry. Says here though, he might have to be away for a few days. He says . . . well, let me read it."

"Good idea," Ronnie said in a more tempered tone, not quite relaxed.

"He says here, 'Elaine, read this verb-a-tim if you please.' I'm not sure exactly what that means, but I'll read you the rest," Elaine said. "Says, 'When two hearts beat as one, so and they are three forever. Trust that union, my love, and find time to enjoy your shopping spree. I'll be home as soon as I'm able. Love forever and always, Jade.'"

With her final words, Elaine sounded slightly choked up, and Ronnie smiled faintly.

"That's it, then," Elaine managed, clearing her throat discreetly.

"Thanks, Elaine," Ronnie said while picturing Elaine's rounded cheeks flushing just a little. All too well, Ronnie knew her husband's effect on women, and for all Elaine's brusque, all-business manner, she wasn't the exception.

"There ain't many men who'd write those kinds of words to his wife," Elaine said in a rare moment of confidence. "Sometimes, I think maybe he was just waiting for you to come along all this time, Ronnie, and I sure am happy for both of you."

"Thanks, again, Elaine—"

"Honey, how you feeling? You're not overdoing it, now, are you? You oughta be putting your feet up and resting some in between your shopping. There's nothing this old store needs that bad that you need to run yourself ragged."

"Why do I get the feeling you were talking to Meg?" she asked, amused again. Compliments of her husband, she'd inherited a plethora of adopted mothers, aunts, and grandmothers. It was a wonder she'd managed to survive all twenty-six years on her own.

"Meg's a good one for worrying. Now, after I got this note, I got to thinking. If Jade's not with you, who is there with you?"

Good grief. Would Elaine offer to close the shop and race to her side? "No need to worry, Elaine. Donna decided to take the day off. We should be back sometime tomorrow. Is everything else all right?"

Hesitation, then. "Right as rain, honey. Don't you worry about a thing. I've been minding this old place for a while now."

Something was bothering Elaine Connelly. "Elaine, what's going on?"

"Nothing at all, honey," she lied poorly, hurrying just a little. "I'm going to have to run here. This ole place is filling up. Was there anything else?"

Obviously, Elaine wasn't about to air her concerns over the telephone. "Let me give you the number here to reach me. If or when Jade calls, tell him to call me immediately." She recited the number, then added, "If anything urgent comes up or any of my family needs to reach me, you can either call or give them this number. If I'm not here, just leave a message at the front desk."

"Will do. You take care, now, you hear?"

One would think she was the only pregnant female on the blasted planet for as often as people told her to 'take care.' Either that or they seemed to believe she lacked the mental capacity to ensure the safety of herself and an infant. "Will do, Elaine. See you tomorrow." Being pregnant was the most natural thing in the world and certainly not cause for ceasing and desisting from life. She was no blasted incubator to sit around getting fat and lazy, nor to act as if she carried a gut full of crystal. God knows, the cargo was precious, but on at least one score, Ronnie agreed with Dr. Blackwell—she knew her own body, its strengths, and weaknesses. A few months from now, she might need to prop her feet on a pillow for a while. At the moment, she suffered an insatiable appetite for motion, and her little passenger seemed more than happy to oblige. In fact, the little worm had settled down considerably, as though Jade's words had filtered through the phone and reached the watery depths to calm the tide. "Ready to rock 'n roll, tadpole?" she asked, glancing downward, half expecting a few flutters. Apparently, the little dickens agreed. Silence. Stillness.

Smiling slightly, Ronnie pushed off the edge of the bed, catching sight of herself in the mirror across the room. Turning sideways, she sought visible signs of occupancy, not sure whether to be relieved or concerned by the absence of a bulge. She still wore the same size jeans she'd worn three months ago, but according to Mr. Laquette, at least a few subtle signs were occurring. Considering his powers of observation, he was probably a fair judge. Her bras were a little tighter.

Smoothing a hand over her nearly flat stomach, she slid her gaze upward. On a scale of one to ten, she could still not consider herself more than an eight on a good day. Lips too full, a nose too long, eyes too big. In long loose black curls, her hair remained her only redeeming quality, and she probably should forget attempting to go blond. She would end up with orange hair, and she could just imagine looking like a pumpkin in another six months or less.

How had it happened? How had she, Veronica Bryson a.k.a. Ronnie Bryson, landed a man like Jade Laquette? Canting her head more naturally, she studied her image in the mirror for a telltale sign. She certainly wasn't any raving beauty, though she was conceited enough to consider herself fair. Jade, on the other hand, was the most attractive man she'd ever met, barring none. Physically, he was so blasted sexy, with the kind of long, dangerous looks to drive any sensible girl crazy. He could've picked any woman he wanted, and he'd wanted her . . . as much as she'd wanted him—

Abruptly, her reflection began to ripple; her attention riveted. Lips parting, she watched the colors swirl. Her black curls spiraled in a tremendous arc as if caught in a funnel cloud, fusing, blending with the colored quilt behind her. Her jeans, her yellow blouse, all became a blur of rainbow color, darkening first, then turning white for an instant.

Frozen, mesmerized, Ronnie watched the images emerging from the light, the whiteness clearing, fading, taking on other shapes. A room . . . and bodies. Black-clad bodies . . . a white smock. Florescent light spilled over the shiny metal carts, but it was another color, and a single image drew her undivided focus.

In a scattered collection of long limbs, her husband lay as still as death, jostled only by the others who tugged anxiously, drawing his legs from an awkward twist. Clearly, smudges of red spread over his face as the picture began to turn slowly on the glass. His mustached lips parted, blood glistening on the black bristles, spilling over his sturdy chin. Red spirals rolled off his temples, flowed from his ears, stained the silver-gray cloth on his chest as a pair of female hands yanked the tie and ripped at the silk. His thick lashes lay in a red mat, framing the almond shape of his eyes, motionless . . . And even as she stood swaying, staring, blood lifted thin slices beneath the roots of his thick wavy hair. Paralyzed, she watched, uncomprehending, as the others, mere shadows worked anxiously over him, shouting orders she couldn't quite hear, frantic in their efforts to begin CPR.

Swaying, sensing, feeling the integrity of this mirror image, Ronnie barely parted her lips to scream when the scenes again began to change, swirling, spiraling, turning to gray smoke on the glass . . . And he stepped fully from the mist. As vivid as her own reflection a moment ago, Jade stood within the glass gazing at her with a familiar cant of his head, a smirk on his lips. His eyes, as pale as oriental jade, studied her with an intensity to wipe the hysteria from her mind. No blood on his face, none on his clothes. He simply stood, wearing a familiar black suit, shirt, and tie, the epitome of male sensuality. Posed as if for nonchalance, his hands rested casually, hooked at the thumbs in his hip pockets, holding the jacket aside. "White witch," he said with a soft, wispy tone to send a tingle down her spine.

"Jade," she uttered, reaching toward him as if to draw him from the glass.

He shook his head almost sorrowfully. His eyes filled with such sadness she felt tears lifting in her own eyes. Slowly, he lowered his gaze, closed his eyes, and vanished.

Off balance, she watched her reflection staggering a backward step and thrust her hands to the side as she plopped clumsily on the bed. Shaking her head, shaken, she continued to stare at the glass, at her own wide-eyed reflection. A hallucination! A hormonal imbalance! A premonition . . . or a reality she could not bear to accept? Nothing could have happened to him! He was alive and well! Nothing else could she, would she even dare to consider! But a horrible fear swam in her mind. If she lost him . . . no! He was alive!

'Two hearts beat as one . . . three forever . . . love forever and always . . .'

Tears streamed down her cheeks. Ronnie rested, swaying, her body vibrating. *Dead*.

"Nooo!" she heaved on the brink of a cry.

"No," she breathed and drew herself up. "No."

Whatever had just happened here, whatever she believed she'd seen, or thought, or heard . . . no. *Not possible. Unthinkable.* Jade Laquette would not have walked into something from which he could not have walked away. If nothing else, she needed to believe that. Whatever the madness to affect her, his health and welfare were no part of it. Wherever he was now, he had the situation well in hand.

CHAPTER 9

Endless, the scream echoed, piercing the nebulous into which Jade had fallen. Endless, the agony and horror, the denial which offered no relief. *Dying. She was dying . . . nothing moved. No word escaped her parted, parched lips. Only the jostling and tugging, the tearing and ripping prickled her ebbing awareness. Inside her, her heart thumped a leaden beat . . . a slowing drumroll that she wanted only to end. No conscious thought remained. Only the madness reigned as the scream continued in an endless crescendo . . . and it was endless. Eternal . . . Forever she screamed as the madman hovered, a fading, phantom shadow on the wall, his words no longer reaching through her madness. A breath, a scream, a sound . . .* darkness.

Nothing moved. No light of heaven. No dark of hell. Floating within the nebulous, he knew only the sense of weightlessness. A beginning and an end. Nothing and everything. Peaceful oblivion . . . But too soon he felt the change coming. A ripple, a tug, a rage blasted his weightlessness . . . rage. Delight. Euphoria . . . dismay. She was gone.

"Bitch," he uttered. "Ungrateful bitch . . . I've given you immortality, and this is how you repay me . . .? You expire? You're like all the others . . . Unworthy of the honor I'm giving you. No appreciation for what I'm doing for you . . . How dare you deny me the audience I deserve . . ."

In front of him, he saw clearly, the red bulging muscles and corpuscles, strands of sinewy tendons, and fragmented veins. Something had gone wrong this time; he knew if only by the amount of blood leaking from those frayed pores. Possibly he'd administered slightly more coagulants than necessary. If the blood had thickened, it might explain the loss. He'd prepared for a great deal more than he saw. The others had bled profusely . . . filling the plastic mat as if lying on a sacred alter.

"An altar—" Of sorts, *he considered with a smile concealed behind the* "Mask" *at his lips. The others had honored him with their offering, but this bitch . . . Well, he couldn't blame her entirely.* "Magnificent. Flawless," *this human flesh. A few imperfections to be expected. He held up the flesh, holding it against the backdrop of candlelight. His eyes and mind lighted with delight. A pity, he considered as he detected the faint dark patch of flesh, like a brush stroke. When he'd found it on her thigh, he'd known how it would look under the light, in this light. That, he would keep for himself . . . He kept a tiny bit of them, all of them, for himself. His reward. In time, he'd possess enough to create the ultimate work of art. For now, he had everything he would take from her. He wasn't greedy. There were others. Plenty of others were willing and prepared to help him perfect his art, his talent.*

One day, they would appreciate his contributions. These ones would be forgotten, but they' live on . . . "Exalted," *he thought bitterly, while tucking the swatch of flesh into the open container where a saline solution would keep it supple for a time. How dare they exalt these worthless bastards. One power. One race. One way of life. Hah. That was the only truth, the only beneficial contribution made by the others. Art. Art would live on . . . and he had the talent. He'd known forever that he'd make use of his talent. The greater good . . . fools. Old fools. They'd the power at their fingertips, but they'd squandered it. Using their gifts toward the wrong end. He would show them. Give them true purpose. Lend them a concrete reason to carry out their mission . . .* "Profit." *To take a life merely to take that life was madness, a betrayal of the Hippocratic oath. To make something beautiful from nothing, to create art . . .*

"Justified" *He understood that, now. Understood far better how the others had salvaged their conscience. He, too, was* an artist." *He understood.*

If only she'd stayed longer, he considered as he collected his tools, tucking the instruments into the cases and cleanser. Disgusted, he fleeted a glance to her dead, staring orbs, her red glistening face, bulging eyes waxed eternal.

He no longer had a desire to touch her, or even look at her. Dead, she was useless, and she'd not lasted even as long as the others. He'd need to keep the next one more heavily sedated. Letting her rise to appreciate his accomplishment, his talent, had been a mistake. He should have realized that much, should have remembered that others had tried that technique long before him. He should have learned from watching those films. Perhaps, he would need to reconsider his methods. There was something to be discovered here and worth the effort. The others had lasted longer, adding hours to his quest. Living tissue was so much more supple. Live and learn. He would try something different on the next one. When he perfected the process . . . "Mass market. Riches and fame." *Nothing was more beautiful than human flesh . . . A work of art to be molded and remade . . . like clay. Modeled into works of wondrous art.*

He'd be famous. More so than the others who'd pioneered his field. His name would rise to the pinnacle of success, a household word. A name to be revered and feared, secretly envied, openly adored. He'd found the key, to greatness, to world order, to world dominion. His would be the only way! A leader among men! This was only the beginning . . .

As he cleaned up his workspace, his thoughts sailed in ever greater circles of grandeur, no longer as annoyed with his benefactor as he had been earlier. Without conscious thought, he tugged the tubes and syringes from her orifices, placing everything in the last container. There would come a day when he'd have more equipment at his disposal, when he wouldn't be forced to work in such humble surroundings. In due time, he'd have a theater, a studio . . . and it wasn't that far off. Already, others sought to know his trade, to see his work. In a short time, he would find the permanence he sought. For now, he didn't mind. All artists struggled in the beginning. He, too, would rise above the loathsome conditions. In the meantime, . . .

Dipping his gloved finger in the bloody offering, he moved to the wall between the candles. Smiling behind his mask, he delicately traced the straight lines, vertical and horizontal. Backing away, he snapped his heels together sharply and raised his hand. "Heil Hitler!"

Sniffing, uttering a curse, and drawing a calming breath, Ronnie barely started on the road to recovery when the rap of knuckles intruded. In a flash, she rose, flying across the floor, tempted to believe, daring to hope Jade stood on the other side. Even before she yanked the door open, she knew better.

Far too perceptive, Donna read the signs, and her smile flashed to serious concern and alarm. "Ronnie? What's—"

"A nightmare," Ronnie heaved, swinging away from the hand reaching for her. A little clumsily, she moved into the small bathroom, spinning the faucet nobs to full blast, and leaning, cupping, and splashing cold water onto her flushed face. Ice water was the swiftest cure for a nightmare according to her husband. And he should know. Far too frequently, he climbed into bed after an icy shower and jolted her awake with a touch of his chilled fingers. Nightmares were Jade's forte, and these most recent episodes were terrifying, for her, if not him.

"Do you want to talk about it, hon?" Donna asked while touching, rubbing Ronnie's shoulder.

Shaking her head, Ronnie collected a breath, reaching blind, gathering the towel Donna delivered into her hand. "Hormones," she huffed in the towel. "Must have do-ozed off."

"You're still shaking," Donna said worriedly. "And I don't buy it, hon . . . You don't doze off. Are you feeling all right? Physically, I mean? You're not having any pains, are you?"

Abruptly, fear leaped a few degrees with the thought of something happening to the baby, with the mere suggestion that something could be wrong. Sobering rapidly, she reviewed the progression of events from the odd timing for morning sickness to the rolling and kicking . . . The bloody images in the mirror followed by Jade's appearance, and the sorrow in his eyes. '. . . hearts joined . . . three forever united . . .' Their child? Was there something wrong inside of her? Something happening with Tadpole? Had Jade just tried to warn her . . . or was he reassuring her?

"Ronnie? Are you having any pains?"

Her eyes clearing, conviction firming, Ronnie dried her face and met her own bloodshot eyes in the mirror, shifting her focus to find Donna studying her. "I'm not doing this," she decided abruptly. "I'm not about to turn into some crying, whining sissy. I'm fine. The baby's fine. Jade's fine. That's all there is to it."

"Maybe you better tell me what happened," Donna said soberly, searching and worrying a glance over Ronnie's face.

"No," she stated simply.

"Ronnie?" Donna urged carefully.

Turning to meet Donna's alarmed gaze directly, Ronnie decided, "Yes, something weird happened a few minutes ago. Yes, I lost it for a few minutes. No, we're not discussing it. I'm just not buying it, and if you're the friend I believe you are, you won't ask me to cough up the details. What we are going to do, is . . . go shopping and pretend nothing happened."

"I wouldn't mind that if you weren't still so blasted pale, hon. Maybe we better just hang out here for a little while, and you can rest for a few—"

"The last thing I need is rest," she said bluntly. "I promised Tadpole a jaunt."

"Don't tell me you're going jogging," Donna said in an attempt to relieve the tension.

"Worse," Ronnie decided. "We're going to park in town and window shop. I noticed a little diner on Main. It sort of reminded me of Meg's. With any luck, by the time we get there, I'll be able to hold down a few cups of coffee . . . maybe a slice of peach pie."

"Peach pie in October?"

"If it upsets you, Mona, I'll be sure and tell them to hold the pickles," Ronnie said and waved Donna through the door. "Let me just grab my purse."

"Be easier carrying your overnight bag," Donna played, sounding relieved but not entirely satisfied. Her sobriety returned in spades when Ronnie joined her at the door. "Are you sure you're up to this?"

"I'm fine, okay?" Ronnie said with a slight smile. "I just had a couple bad seconds. Usually, when I get like that, I track down my wily husband and spar a few rounds. He gets the cutest smile . . ." The same kind of smile he'd worn in the mirror, she considered, feeling somehow better with the thought. "Of course, I get more irritated," Ronnie continued as she tugged open the door, forcing Donna through it. "Which lasts for about thirty seconds or less. He suckers me into forgiving him a world of sins without half trying."

"You're good for each other," Donna said with a more natural smile.

Which was one more reason she could not afford to humor that nightmare. If anything happened to him . . . she wasn't altogether sure how she would handle it. Without betraying her internal thoughts, Ronnie commented. "I know he's good for me. About now, he probably has a few doubts about how good I am for him. You think I was bad when you came in? You should see me after a few hours of morning sickness. I think he's considering moving into the warehouse permanently."

"Right," Donna laughed as they stepped into the elevator. "I can really believe that. I mean, I've seen how he tends to steer clear of you at any given moment."

If they were within shouting distance, they were generally within touching distance. Ronnie smiled faintly and shrugged. "As I said, you've never seen me at the crack of dawn.

"I guess I'll find out in the morning, huh?"

"I guess," Ronnie said distractedly, thinking how much she would rather be heading home even at this very moment. Only the revelation that she would return to an empty apartment countered any thought of returning home early.

CHAPTER 10

"Can you hear me, paisano?"

Not clearly, he might have answered if not for the exhaustion tugging at the edges of his frayed mind. The words came to him, muffled, far away, as if the speaker shouted through a faulty bullhorn over a great distance. Only the urgency of the voice prodded him to attempt a response and struggle to understand. Tired. Exhausted. He pried his eyelids open with an effort, but his vision remained as muddied as all else in his mind. The light hurt, blinding his sleep-sighted eyes. Squinting, he found a silhouette above him, not nearly focused enough to judge the face, to recognize features.

"That's it, pal. You're coming around now. Just relax. You're going to be all right."

Another voice from the same faraway place carried a different tone, a female timbre. "I don't know what the devil just happened here, Len, but I don't think we can afford to make that assessment without a full battery of tests."

"I know how this looks, Roberta. I've been where you are. Just don't panic when he comes out of this looking no worse for the wear."

"Lenny," the woman stated in a softer tone. "I'm not sure I believe what I saw, but I do know *what* I saw. We should have him on route to the nearest hospital."

"What do you think happened downstairs? Honestly, Roberta, what's your take?"

"I can buy into a psychic connection," the woman said quietly, her voice closer, more distinctive, less shouted. "I'm old enough to admit I don't have all the answers to the mysteries of the universe. Whatever our friend saw created a physical breakdown, and he went into cardiac arrest."

"Have you ever seen blood evaporate?" Devinio asked quietly. The silence lingered a few seconds before he asked, "How you doing, Dominique? You coming around yet?"

The English words were directed to him, and he understood them. In fact, he could make out the rugged face above him a little more clearly. Head canted, the black hair shimmered in the bright light; the nearly black eyes wore a genuine concern and scrutiny. Somewhere, recently, he'd seen this face, but the circumstances eluded him. English . . . déjà vu. He rested on US soil . . . but he'd never worn the name Dominique in the US. Or had he? Damned the weariness to tug at his every fiber!

Realizing the time lapsing, the man's concern, he nodded, managing a weary, "Oui, monsieur."

The black mustache kinked at one corner; the eyes flashed a spark of humor. "You're looking a little better. Any chance you feel like getting up?"

Considering the heaviness in his limbs and lingering confusion, he shook his head slightly, dragging a hand to wipe the fuzz from his eyes or block the light. Shading the glare, he moved his head enough to view the strange room, aware of a hard surface beneath him. His attention held momentarily on the female speaker. She studied him as critically as her comrade. Her walnut-shrouded head tipped, her soft lips curved in a pensive smile, and her brow furrowed beneath a few loose locks. Managing a faint smile, his brow troubled, he continued his slow scan, not relieved by the graphics on the walls.

Familiar . . . he'd seen this room before. More seconds dragged as he again sought the dark-haired fellow, 'Len . . . Lenny.' They'd met . . . the circumstances . . . revolved around a murder . . . more than one murder. A morgue. He knew abruptly, he rested within a conference room in a city morgue . . .

Cleveland, Ohio, USA. A murderer . . . he'd come here to find a murderer, to stop a madman . . . to remove the threat.

He needed to get up, get moving. Urgency crawled at the nape of his neck, but when he started an attempt to rise, the hand landed on his shoulder, halting him without much effort. The weariness still held him, threatening to take him under. "Have to get up . . . get out of here."

"English, paisano," Lenny said with a twitching smile. "My French still isn't that good."

Stopped, slightly more confused, he studied the agent for a joke. "English."

The agent nodded. "I happen to know your English is almost better than mine, paisano. So, tell me, are you really feeling good enough to try getting up?"

He was lying on a table . . . a solid metal table, and something in that thought only troubled him more. Nodding, he decided, "The sooner the better. We must leave."

Canting his head slightly, the smile no longer as apparent, the agent studied him. "English, Monsieur Jardonet. Try that again, this time in English."

Devinio, he remembered abruptly, Len Devinio. But the revelation offered no quick relief, not when this federal agent had just called him Jardonet . . . and he hadn't worn that name in quite some time.

Worse, even worse, he grasped the fellow studying him, waiting as if he had no grasp of the words. "What the hell's wrong with you? Have you gone deaf?" Far more slowly, carefully, he articulated the words, "Remove your hand and help me up. There's something . . . some thing. . . coming." And with his words, he started moving again, knowing only a sense of urgency, a need to rise and escape this room. "Running out of time, Leonardo. We must move . . . I must—"

"Damn it, just rest a minute," Devinio stated.

With his wrist caught and the agent pressing his shoulder, he had no choice. The woman had stepped closer, drawing his swaying gaze.

Her hand clasped his other wrist, lifting it, moving his shirt cuff, and pressing her fingertips to his forearm. "Just rest a minute, honey. I just need to get your pulse. Do you understand?"

Annoyed, agitated, he commented, "I'm not a moron. Of course, I understand."

"Somehow, I don't think he appreciated that question," Len stated.

Intent on her apparent activity, the doctor refrained from answering.

Devinio's comment, however, drew his attention upward to realize the conflict of amusement and concern. Unless this agent was a moron, he shouldn't need to guess to grasp the simple words. "Leonardo?" he said carefully. "Do you understand anything I'm saying to you?"

The troubled lines across the brow suggested his effort to respond or understand. "Cut the shit, all right? English, paisano," he stated carefully, his gaze far more intent, troubled. "I know you tend to revert entirely to French when you're excited, but I'm lucky if I understand enough of my ancestors' native tongue to talk to my grandfather. English, all right?"

"I'm speaking English, for God's sake. What's wrong with your hearing? Your ears? Your mental acuity? Listen carefully. I need to get out of here." And he would need this agent's physical help. Clearly, he realized the drag of his words, the weariness weighting his limbs as if lead ran through his veins. "Now, Leonardo . . . we have to move, now."

"Goddamn it," Devinio uttered, looking at him far more critically. "You said it earlier . . . Goddamn it, you knew this would happen. I'm going to need a fucking interpreter."

"You need your fucking head examined," Jade stated. "Help me up!"

"Lenny?" the woman barely started to speak when the muffled sounds erupted, growing louder swiftly, drawing her attention and Devinio's gaze away.

Rolling his head to follow their gazes, he found the door to the room, and only one thought started him moving, attempting to roll and turn. He needed to get up! Get out! Whatever that noise advancing, he wanted no blasted part of it. Something, somewhere he needed to go! Someone he dearly needed to find, to see. The reason he was here. The reason he'd returned to the USA. He needed to find someone. A woman! His wife! His love! How the devil he had been caught up in this madness . . . caught. Caught was the operative word, and as he tried shoving the hand off his shoulder, his attention riveted on the door swinging open. Caught. Whatever had been chasing him forever, had just caught up to him. Nothing else held more firmly in his mind as he watched the life-like bodies flooding into the room. Only for an instant, his attention darted, then riveted on the blond-haired man coming toward him. The fellow seemed to burst through the oncoming rush . . . and that rush of oncoming bodies had been averted. The phantom images dissipated like apparitions turning to dust. This was Jarvins . . .

"What's going on, Mark?"

"We're circumventing an international incident and getting Mr. Jardonet out of here," the man stated with a touch of sarcasm. "And this isn't a good time to argue with me, Len. We're taking him to the hotel for the moment. If we help, do you think you can walk, Mr. Jardonet?"

A lie . . . the man was lying, but this wasn't a good time to argue, not with the echoey vibration of a chopper engine at the edges of his mind. A helicopter . . . not yet. Nodding, Jade pushed onto his elbow, resigning to wear the name Jardonet. Dominique Jardonet, a name, an identity, a curse from the past, and he had no choice now. As he'd known several hours earlier, he'd need to become Dominique Jardonet once again, though the reason eluded him.

Sliding his feet off the table, he pushed partway up as Devinio clasped his arm either to halt him from falling or to force him back down. Bracing a hand on the table at his hip, Dominique rested momentarily, collecting his balance, firming the world around him. Still, he heard it, a scramble of activity, firm anxious voices relaying medical terms, snapping orders. Significance . . . he knew the importance of those sounds. A medical emergency . . . *and he was destined to become that emergency.*

His gaze lifted, passing between the agents who stood to either side of him. Murky, he sought substance and recognition in the room. A classroom . . . a conference room. The images overlapped, only more confusing by the similarities as if green boards and blackboards separated and floated, immaterial, one over the other.

"Mon Dieu," he uttered. A funhouse. Forward and back . . . *a fireball exploded on an emerald blanket, spewing flaming airplane parts into the afternoon sky . . . a helicopter rose above the city lights . . . medical jargon spilled off the lips of the bodies hovering over the stretcher where another body lay, appearing more dead than alive . . . a face he knew—*

"Can you walk, Mr. Jardonet?" Jarvins asked again.

"Death," Dominique muttered, pushing off the table and gaining his balance on his own feet as both men clasped his arms. Looking into the tense dark eyes, he asked, "Where? Where were the other victims brought?"

"Damn it, try that again in English," Devinio stated.

Annoyed, Jade found the pale blue eyes, noting the cant of the head emitting a question mark while the tight smile conveyed arrogance. French, damn it. As he blasted well feared, he'd lost his English as completely as he'd lost his birthname, Jade David Laquette, as if he'd just misplaced the damn thing. Disgusted, he asked, "Do you speak French?"

"Obviously, not as fluently as you, monsieur, but passable," the man answered in English, somewhat chiding. "Why are you asking about the other victims?"

"Too many impressions, perhaps," he said with an offhanded shrug and another scan of the room. A morgue, he reminded himself. If nothing else, he knew the possibility of an endless chain of grizzly images assaulting him. Lingering too long within the apex of death would not fare well on his psyche, and currently, he was having enough trouble with that blasted anomaly. Connecting with the blue eyes, he decided, "You were right. An international incident, notwithstanding. We should leave, now. It would take weeks to sort through the things I could tell you within these walls, and I doubt we have the time."

"About that, I concur," the man said in a lofty tone and removed his hand, gesturing. "After you, Mr. Jardonet."

Hesitating, Jade looked more deeply into the pale blue eyes, sensing, feeling something hidden behind the gaze. A trap? A mockery? Distrust. Unconsciously, his internal mechanisms rose, conveying indifference as he nodded his acceptance as though it should be no other way—this fellow playing second fiddle. Glancing off Devinio, suffering the estrangement to accompany his name change, he stepped out of the loose grasp and found the forensic doctor watching him with a critical concern. Smirking, he shrugged and held out his hand to her. "I apologize if uh . . . this experience disturbed you, madame. I assure you, I am well, and I only wish we had met under different circumstances."

By her expression, she had no idea what he'd just said. Her gaze flashed toward Jarvins before she accepted Dominique's proffered hand. "If you won't go to the hospital, Mr. Jardonet, at least promise me that you'll see a physician soon. I can't begin to know what—"

Snapping his hand back, flinching uncontrollably against the electric jolt in his palm, he studied her startled eyes even as he flexed tingles from his fingers. By expression alone, he conveyed the apology for his unorthodox behavior becoming far more aware of his sensitivity enhancing. "Your profession and my nature do not fare well together, madame. *Pardon moi*," he said smoothly and glimpsed Devinio's flash of relief as they started toward the door.

Barely a few steps into the hall, Devinio commented, "I was beginning to think you truly had forgotten how to speak English, paisano."

"*Excusez-moi*?" Dominique asked with a lifted brow and glance, a serious curiosity haunting his mind.

"We'll talk about it in the car," Devinio decided as they passed an open door.

A few assistants and the acting chief medical examiner lingered in the hallway, the latter of whom attempted to mask his interest in the departing visitors. Whether he was intrigued or resentful of the interlopers remained a mystery; he merely nodded to acknowledge their departure.

Looking toward Jarvins, Devinio asked, "You collected the tapes, right?"

"We have an interpreter flying up from Quantico," Jarvins answered. "On the outside chance that Mr. Jardonet offered something of value, we should have the translation within a few hours. Now, however, we may have a more immediate problem."

"Such as?"

"Reporters," Dominique answered and halted a few steps from the final door. His gaze spun to land on Jarvins, annoyed and angry. "You knew they were outside?"

"I know if we don't hurry, we could have a problem," Jarvins stated and looked at his partner. "I just got off the phone with Springer. About twenty minutes ago, the local in charge of last night's murder, Captain Schleger, made another statement to the press, announcing that the FBI's handling the autopsy. Sooner or later, this building will be jammed—"

"Sooner than later," Dominique interrupted shortly, his gaze still heated, and enhanced by the certainty of his identity changing . . . or *changed.* "They are here, Agent Jarvins. I would suggest we leave by an alternate route. Preferably, a backdoor . . .."

Out of sorts, Ronnie listened to the chatter in the diner, her attention keening at the gossip she'd expected to hear. Jack Trumble . . . a real estate broker. Halfheartedly, Ronnie nodded to something Donna said. Sitting in a window booth, they were privy to more than a few dozen patrons at tables and booths in either direction. Outside, the sun had shifted behind clouds, offering a bright, unoffensive glow on chrome and paint. Her attention caught briefly on the shiny black surface of their pickup parked directly across the street. In old

English script, the "Olden Time" logo scrolled across the door, neat and tidy, classy.

Despite her protests, Jade had mentioned, after the fact, that he'd enlisted an attorney even before their wedding, rewriting every thread of legal documents to put her name on the business. According to her husband, since he'd needed to change his legal name on the records, it only made good sense to add her name at the same time. Money, she knew, meant absolutely nothing to her spouse . . . and she supposed, she shared his opinion. If she never wrote another article or engaged in another moment of manual, money-earning labor, she could live comfortably even without their joint finances. Trust funds, set up years ago by her father and grandfather, had assured her of a lifestyle consistent with her upbringing . . . and even that, she and Jade shared. Despite his chaotic childhood and tragedies, he'd never lacked material comforts. They'd attended the same private school in those first years, and later, he'd admitted having private tutors under his father's roof. On his eighteenth birthday, he'd struck out alone with a few dollars in his pocket, and within six months, he'd accumulated a small fortune. He had the Midas touch, which he considered a curse.

Smiling faintly, she remembered his slight disgust and arrogance when he'd admitted, Olden Time was more of his hobby than a source of income, and she believed him. The man thought absolutely nothing about spending a few hundred dollars on a ceramic doll and giving it away as a gift. Even the items he bought, allegedly to sell at a profit, generally departed his shop under market value. Despite that, however, he'd built "Olden Time" into a lucrative, thriving enterprise.

Considering the past few months, she understood his base attraction to the business. Not only were they surrounded by beauty and wealth, but they also enjoyed the rare pleasure of brightening other lives with nonessential items. More than a few housewives in Bentwood purchased a crystal bowl or lovely piece of jewelry, which they might not have otherwise afforded, and her wily husband had a talent for concealing his goodwill as if he had no idea how to read a price guide.

"Mind telling me what's so interesting out there?" Donna interrupted.

Still smiling slightly, Ronnie drew from her distraction. "Sorry, just thinking."

"I'd have never guessed," Donna smiled. "Bet I even know what—or who—you're thinking about."

"You'd probably be absolutely right," Ronnie said, deciding she could not, would not return with an empty truck. At some point, she would engage in some serious antiquing, and try her hand at seeking items that the local citizens in Bentwood might enjoy. The trick, Jade had confided, was to think about a specific person, then judge the potential purchase accordingly. In other words, if this was Hazel's week to browse, Ronnie dang sure better have a few rose-colored or painted bowls on hand. Like Donna and music boxes, Hazel loved roses. Maybe a rose-colored basket, something with a touch of gold and brilliant red.

Ronnie barely reached her decision when her attention riveted on the male voice in the booth behind her. Consciously, she hadn't seen the two men arrive and had no idea what either looked like, but the words caught her ear.

". . . I'm telling you it wasn't an accident. Jack's been driving that stretch of highway for thirty years."

"I'm not saying I buy Logan's story about a deer, Ray. The thing is, Jack was hitting the bottle pretty hard lately. Could be Logan's covering a few details for the sake of Jenny and the kids."

"According to Les, Jack hasn't been in the Wayside since last week, and he damn sure wasn't drunk when he left his office three days ago. Cindy was pretty damn sure he had an appointment to keep."

"If you're even suggesting what I think, Ray, you better keep that to yourself."

"All I'm saying is, I don't think it was an accident," the man at Ronnie's back growled, his voice tempered. "Jack's been acting funny for the past couple months . . . Ever since he took on that Ryder estate deal."

"You better be damn careful who you mention that to." The other spoke in a voice barely above a whisper. "Far as I'm concerned, that's none of my business either. Jack's dead. Stirring up a lot of trouble won't make him living and breathing again. If Rick Logan says a deer's to blame, that's good enough for me."

"Yea, good ole' Logan. Wouldn't surprise me to find out he's on somebody's payroll. If Whitman was still the chief around here, we wouldn't have near the shit we've had to contend with—"

"Can I get you ladies anything else?" the mid-aged waitress interrupted, reaching across the table to top off coffee cups. A little on the heavy side, she wore her hair in a tight perm and fishnet, not quite complimenting her round face, but her smile and friendly manner compensated.

"I'd love a slice of peach pie if you have some," Ronnie said and flashed Donna a quick smile.

"We happen to have the best peach pie this side of Georgia," Lena stated.

"Great!" Ronnie commented and slid her empty sandwich plate aside. She had to admit, eating something slightly more substantial than pie at the onset had revitalized her.

Stifling a laugh, Donna decided on a slice of pumpkin pie. "With plenty of whipped cream."

"You sure you're not expecting?" Ronnie mused, and the fleeting sparkle in Donna's eyes halted her started jest. Studying the slightly sheepish grin on Donna's lovely face, Ronnie felt her excitement igniting. "I'll be damned . . . Does Tim know?"

"Not yet," Donna said and stifled a laugh. "And it's not definite yet, so how about keeping it under your hat for a little while? I'm barely a couple weeks late."

"This, from the lady who told me she's been as regular and dependable as an eight-day clock since day one," Ronnie huffed, smiling, and happy for the first time since leaving Jade standing on the sidewalk several hours ago. "God, this is so neat. If you are, how far along would you be?"

"About six weeks behind you," Donna said.

"And you're happy, right?"

"Let's say, I'm not looking forward to dirty diapers again, but uh . . ." Her eyes brightened. "I don't think I'd mind too much."

"Tim's going to be thrilled," Ronnie knew.

"Which is why I was going to wait for a special occasion – like the next time Tee's wrestling with Scotts and takes out another lamp."

Remembering Tim's disgruntled rendition of the event in question, recalling how he enjoyed blaming their Irish Setter puppy for the woes of his life, Ronnie laughed. "Sounds like a great plan, but I noticed . . . was?"

"Depending on that little shop with all the music boxes, I may need to break it to him much sooner and much less subtly," Donna said with a wry smile.

Catching on, Ronnie laughed again. "You're rotten."

"A girl's gotta use whatever she's got," Donna said, sounding like a good ole girl, undoubtedly, in reflection of her husband. "Besides, it'll be easier convincing him to add a few rooms if we have another very good reason."

"Funny," Ronnie laughed. "Jade mentioned something to that effect."

"He's a shit, and he probably already figured this out."

The conversation had fallen silent at Ronnie's back, and a glance over her shoulder toward the oncoming waitress told her what she already suspected. The bolder fellow had taken his leave, and the other appeared intent on the scenery outside his window. What exactly had those words meant . . . and should she bother checking the local library? Should she stick to her main goal? Or simply let the locals deal with their own dirty laundry? A coverup. From those few words, she sensed the accuracy of her thought. Apparently, the real estate agent's demise wasn't nearly as accidental as the hotel clerk had mentioned.

Offhandedly, Ronnie had mentioned running across the lengthy funeral procession, and the young woman behind the counter at the Inn had gladly filled in a few details. Real estate agent, fatal car crash, wife and kids devastated. '. . . A doggone shame, too. Mr. Trumble was one of those guys everybody knows and likes, ya know? I'm glad if a lot of people showed up. If I wasn't working this morning, I would've gone. Me and Jimmy went to high school together . . .'

In the hallway upstairs, before parting to acclimate in their rooms, Donna had shaken her head. 'You're good, Rem. No wonder you get the big bucks.'

Jimmy, twenty-two, attending Penn State, the main campus in State College, PA. Damn it, she was working on this story, Ronnie realized while logging a few more names. Rick Logan . . . Chief of Police Logan, no doubt. Whitman, former police chief. The Ryder estate. Ray and Tim somebody. Old pals apparently. Something fishy in the wind.

With the sizeable slices of pie delivered, Ronnie dug in gladly, noting Donna equally thrilled with her mountain of whipped cream. "I think I should have asked for whipped cream," Ronnie commented, eying the fluffy glob.

"Here, slide your plate over. I'll share," Donna offered.

"Far be it for me to get between a starving woman and her whipped cream."

"This conversation could go downhill very quickly," Donna mused and dug a hardy spoonful off the side of her plate, affording Ronnie no choice but to hurry her plate toward the listing glob. "There," Donna said and offered one of her sly smiles. "That's what . . .? About one-half calorie, I won't wear?"

"More like a few hundred," Ronnie guessed. "This tastes too good to be healthy."

"I really should insist you take another few hundred off my hands," Donna said while scooping pie and cream onto a spoon. "According to Sax, you've lost about ten pounds."

"I have a feeling as soon as the tadpole quits rushing me to the bathroom in the morning, that will change. Keep your calories, hon. You'll need them if your mornings get anything like mine."

"Your mom still trying to get you to see her doctor in DC?"

"I'm sure she is, but she gave up on me. Think she's working on Jade to convince me, but he and I both agreed, Dr. Doolittle knows what he's doing."

"God, I'd love to see Dr. Blackwell's face if he heard you call him that," Donna mused.

"He did appear a little piqued until I pointed out that as long as he keeps telling me I'm as healthy as a horse, the nickname stays. Tit for tat, that's my motto."

"You know, I have a feeling between us, he's going to wish he retired years ago," Donna said with a conspiratorial smile. "Dr. Doolittle, huh? I like it, Rem. We're going to make a helluva team."

"What do you say we hit the Music Box, first? If I saw right, there's a brass dealer right next door. With any luck, we can have a full load before we call it quits for the day."

"Depending on the wares, Rem, if we hit the music box store first, we could have a full load long before then."

"I'm still game, as long as I get to be there when we ask Tim to unload them."

"And you call *me* rotten?"

"Tit for tat, honey," Ronnie played. "Hurry up with that mountain. We have things to do, places to go."

"No people to see?"

"Maybe just a few," Ronnie said, and by her smirk, Donna knew the agenda would not remain limited to antique hunting.

CHAPTER II

Alone in the backseat of the government-issue sedan, the man posing as Dominique Jardonet rested uncomfortably, drawing his focus from the passing scenery long enough to catch a flame to his cigarette. Not a great deal of the past several moments – if not hours – made sense in his mind. He'd begun the morning as Jade D. Laquette, husband and father, that much he recalled. Waking in the morgue, suffering the floating sensations of enlisting his curse, ducking from the American Press through an alley . . . Cleveland, Ohio. USA.

Upon a time, those words had seemed foreign to him, as foreign as the language slipping smoothly off his lips, despite the first ten years of his life. He had, however, reclaimed his American heritage, had even found a pastime within the borders of his adopted homeland to keep himself occupied for eleven months of every year. An antique dealer . . . Isaac Bently. Was it no more than four months passed when he'd realized he would need to leave that name, that identity behind? Whatever serenity he'd found within that guise was gone now. Jade David Laquette had reemerged like a ghost refusing to pass fully over to the ethereal plane. Resurrected, Dominique knew, by the white witch who'd haunted his dreams for eternity. For her, he'd opened the lid on Pandora's box, and the evil that he'd sensed throughout his lifetime had leaked out. The name he'd sworn never to wear again—both of them—were now strung about his neck like an albatross, and to his dismay, he wasn't two people even if he could claim a few biological half-brothers who bore a striking resemblance to him.

Vaguely, Dominique recalled speaking with the agents within that conference room. '. . . the price . . . the prize.' Everything has its cost and its reward. If he'd enlisted his curse months ago? If he'd concentrated and resigned to use the talents his father had attempted to unleash, Dominique wondered now what choice he would have made . . . and knew, by the ache in his chest. He would've chosen the same course. To save Veronique, to stop the maniac who would have taken her life, he would and had walked into the fires of hell. What he might have mentioned only a few hours ago, if Devinio had asked, was the irreversible course that decision had laid before him. He'd known the cost of finding his love . . . and the price he would undoubtedly continue to pay. No turning back. With a phone call, a few words . . .? He'd forfeited his life to spare her once again, to spare the child she carried within her. Such was the cost of his birthright. His reward and his comeuppance for seeking her light. If he'd rejected that glimmer of hope she'd cast out to him nearly two decades earlier, would he be here now, striving to do the right thing when the wrong thing would be so much more appealing?

He would like nothing better than to descend on the nation's capital and wreak havoc on those who had destroyed his life.

He could. With little to no effort, he could track them down, every last one of them, and destroy them.

Anger relieved nothing of the pain spiraling through his system. Whether he felt more suffocated by hatred or love, he couldn't decide. He knew only the lethal combination swirling in maddening circles within his mind. Irreversible. Only this morning, when his heart had chased Veronique to the corner, he'd known the irreversible course of their separate ventures. Hope, he remembered and cursed that word in his mind now. With the flicker of hope she'd kindled, he'd deceived himself to believe all would be well, blissfully unaware of what his wretched curse held in store for him.

Evil, he should have known even then, played upon such volition, twisting and turning those tiny flames to bend the fool to his ruin. Well, and it was done. He'd believed, *hope reigning eternal* and all that nonsense, that he would survive unscathed and salvage the life he'd meant to live. A temporary step into his past, as if he could shed the darkness like a cloak. A grand irony. After everything he knew about evil from a master of the craft—to believe he could waltz with the devil and escape unscathed.

And here he was, so thoroughly submersed in that blasted identity as the youngest son of a warlock that he could not even speak the goddamn English language. Damned Jean-Pierre's talent. Just damn him.

Shaking his head, uttering a curse, Jade caught the dark eyes watching him in the rearview mirror, and that annoyed him even more. Damned Devinio and his normalcy, his decency, his firm grasp of the natural realm. Just damn him.

Restraining his resentment, Dominique commented, "If, as I suspect, you are traveling toward the hotel where this odyssey began, I suggest you reverse your course."

"English, paisano. On the outside chance that you'd like me to know what you're saying."

Annoyed, Dominique addressed the passenger, who tipped his head and looked back at him. "Did you understand?"

"We don't have an audience, Mr. Jardonet," Jarvins commented with stark sarcasm. "I suggest you drop the act and make this easier on all of us. In fact, if you're up to the challenge, possibly when we return to headquarters, you'd agree to translate the tape we made."

"On this tape . . . I assume I spoke only French. Is that right?"

"I said let's drop the act," Jarvins stated. "Bluntly, I don't know how you pulled off that hoax, and I really don't want to know, but you should know, I'm not buying it. Not your melodramatics in the morgue or this uh . . . Frenchman crap. We've already wasted more time with you than I care to consider—"

"You are a fool, Mr. Jarvins," Dominique said evenly and held the cool blue gaze, his own indifferent. "But you are right. You have wasted your time. Ask your comrade to find the nearest car rental agency or a telephone booth."

"Doesn't work that way, Jardonet. Someone seems to think you can add something constructive to this case, and until we hear otherwise, you're staying in our company. I do have a few questions you might clear up though," Jarvins said, his lips tipped in an angry smirk. "Just little curiosities, mind you, but it might explain a few things," he said snidely.

"How long have you worked for the DGSE? What—maybe about ten or twelve years?"

Darkly amused, Dominique let the smile slip into a corner of his mustache. "How long have you worked for the FBI?"

"What's going on here, Mark?" Devinio asked, glancing over.

Rather than answer, Jarvins continued studying Dominique over the back of the seat. "Why don't we just skip that one, and you can tell me how much you already know about this maniac's MO? And while you're at it, tell me where he struck before hitting US soil?"

"I am at a serious loss," Dominique said with a half-hitched smile. Undoubtedly, Jarvins' believed that Jade Laquette/Dominique Jardonet had received a full brief from his French superiors.

"I don't like to break this to you, but you have two choices. Either cooperate and start talking—in English—or I'll make damn sure you're on the next trans-Atlantic flight."

"That would be a mistake," Dominique commented indifferently.

"Don't test me or tempt me, Jardonet," Jarvins said in a lower tone. "The only reason we're not on our way to the airport right now is because someone pulled a few strings. And honestly, that doesn't improve my opinion of you. Frankly, I'd like to know who the fuck you really are, because I'm about 99.9% sure that you're not Jade Laquette, which means that you've not only taken the identity of an American citizen, you've married under an assumed name. I shouldn't need to tell you exactly how that affects that contract. To be clear, monsieur, the gig is up. Now, what the fuck do you know about this maniac? And why is the French government interested in this case?"

"To my knowledge, the French government has no interest in this case," Dominique said in an amiable tone despite his chilled gaze. "You came to me, Agent Jarvins. Recall that if you will."

"What I recall is finding you as much as waiting for us in Meg's Diner, and you conveniently mentioning a trip you were planning. I also seem to recall you didn't need a great deal of convincing to join us, and you didn't need too many details. Add in the fact that you weren't shocked by those photographs, and you did speak a few keywords which I was able to understand . . . and what I want to know is, who contacted you before we arrived? And answer me in English."

"Even if I could answer you as you request, how would those answers further our joint mission, Mr. Jarvins? I would think the end results, or our liaison would justify whatever curiosities you have, and offer a degree of . . . how do you say it, relief?"

"Don't fuck with me, Jardonet—"

"Would not dream of it," Dominique said with a slight smirk. "But I should admit, comrade, I have no control over the uh . . . difficulties with my current dialect. Training, perhaps," he said with an indifferent shrug. "Dominique Paul Jardonet wasn't born on American soil, and uh . . . his English is not what it should be. Do you understand?"

"Neither me nor my partner are wired, Jardonet, and even if we were, it'd be a little late to worry about our sharing your confidence. We did pick you up in a little town called Bentwood, remember? And we're obviously not the only ones on American soil to know you're wearing an alias."

"I see your predicament," Dominique commented, affecting a reflective tone. "Unfortunately, I really do not give a bloody damn what you propose to understand, nor am I even slightly concerned with whatever you feel is uh . . . your right to know?"

"Listen asshole—"

"No, you listen," Dominique stated, his gaze heated and intent, locked on the angry blue eyes. In a low silky voice, as different from the man they'd picked up in Bentwood as the color of his eyes, he continued, "I am not, and have never been a man easily intimidated by authority. That much you should have realized months ago when you attempted to destroy me through your jealousy. I will warn you, now, sir, do not attempt to test your government clout or affluence with me. I will assist with this case because I choose to assist, but the rules have changed, comrade. If nothing else about Dominique Jardonet, you should know, he is the youngest son of Jean-Pierre Jardonet, French entrepreneur and diplomat. Fuck with me beyond this point, mon ami, and you will be swabbing the loo in Quantico when next you visit there. Are we understood?"

In the rearview mirror, Devinio's dark eyes flashed, shooting over to Jarvins as he asked, "What the hell am I missing?"

Jarvins hesitated only a second before commenting, "You're no more the son of a French diplomat than I'm the prince of—"

"Careful, asshole," Dominique interrupted quietly, a smile twitching in his mustache. "You have no idea who or what you are dealing with, and such a disadvantage could be detrimental to your future."

The mobile phone emitted a signal, interrupting and drawing Jarvins' angry attention. Cryptically, he answered with a few words, only more annoyed when he leaned and returned the instrument to its holder. Looking over to Devinio, he snapped, "Find somewhere to turn around and head back into town. We have a meeting with the state and county investigators."

Harry Windell might have experienced a stranger afternoon, but none since swearing off hard liquor a decade passed when he'd totaled his Harley after a few too many shots. He'd walked away without more than a few bumps and bruises, rather like his return from Vietnam, except those bruises were on the inside and came in the form of flashbacks. The same and yet different, these vivid

hallucinations . . . and slightly unsettling when he was solely responsible for the two occupants strapped into the seats behind him.

With the turbulence of the winds off Lake Erie, he'd suggested seatbelts, and just for a second, he'd spied over his shoulder to see that his passengers obliged. Only one man rested in the seat within his view. The fellow had been traveling to and from DC for the better part of a year; the other, a stranger, was apparently in the john. Harry dared not contemplate that detail too closely. He'd heard them speaking—or thought he might have heard more than one voice . . . but audio hallucinations were not unheard of either.

Clearly, he recalled the sound of bullets striking the propellers, the engine hissing and sputtering as the wind rushed through the open doors. Going down! The chopper spiraled; the control panel screamed warnings as surely as the men scrambled into the compartment behind him. No time for parachutes or prayers . . . the tail sliced through jungle vines and saplings, snapping, sizzling, exploding . . .

He'd crawled from the wreckage, dragging an unconscious man at his hip, blood spilling into his eye, flashing a red haze to enhance the crimson shine on Brewer's forehead. A gash, nothing more, Brewer was alive – surely – and they needed to get as far from the dead bird as possible. The gooks who'd fired those shells couldn't be too far away . . . and Harry had heard enough horror stories of American prisoners tortured to aid in the propaganda . . .

Waking to the voices calling through the earphones, Harry drew from the memories though he still smelled the chopper fuel, still heard the explosion, and felt the woosh of heated air. Through the windshield, he saw only a gray sky, and panic raced into his stricken mind. Had he descended into clouds? Fleeting, he spied the gauges, judging the instrument readings at normal ranges. For a few crazy seconds, he'd believed the small jet plummeting, and he wanted nothing more than to land his boots on solid ground and to hell with his passengers' intended destination.

Spooked suddenly, he realized himself descending and managed to recite his call letters, requesting permission from the small municipal control tower . . . Cincinnati.

By the time they found a parking space near the courthouse, even Devinio's attitude had changed, far more subdued and preoccupied. In Devinio, however, Dominique sensed genuine concern within fleeting glances of the dark eyes watching him, judging him, searching for an explanation where none existed. Whatever changes had begun days or weeks ago, were complete. Even concentrating, Dominique couldn't form the English words that Jade Laquette and Isaac Bently had spoken so smoothly not long ago. The changes were inside of him, and he needed little thought to realize the mechanics behind the changes. His father's words, his father's tutelage, his father's goddamn curses . . .

In the back of his mind, Dominique heard the low angry voice hissing at him, demanding, *'French, my son . . . you will speak French or not at all . . .'*

'American! his angry cry echoed over the distance. *'I'm an American! English!'*

'English . . . to hell with your English, obstinate child. French or not at all . . . that is your only choice . . .' And when a man like Jean-Pierre offered an ultimatum, there was no arguing.

Still, Jade had screamed, *'Go to hell!'*

'Hah, and you think that a curse upon me? Silly boy. Make it easy on yourself, my own little bastard . . . Learn to speak the words or resign to babble . . .'

Standing at the single window within a comfortably modern waiting room, Jade nearly cursed aloud while remembering that sojourn. He'd learned to speak French, had spoken only French for at least a few years. English had sounded to him like gibberish. Not until he'd begun forming even his thoughts in French had he mastered the basics to begin speaking English again, and by then, he'd begun answering to the name Dominique Jardonet. By what trick he found himself once again confined to his father's dialect, he couldn't quite decide.

Dominique Jardonet.

As he might have mentioned inside the car, Dominique Jardonet wasn't born on American soil and were he entirely honest, he might have admitted, nor was Jade Laquette. Semantics, Dominique considered as he drew from his cigarette, a twitch of a smile on his lips. If he claimed the country of his birth as his origin, he would consider himself English; after all, he'd been born in the back room of a boarding house somewhere near London. Perhaps, his father's arrogance had created the need for his bastard to speak French rather than English, and Jean-Pierre wasn't a patient man.

Sensing the advance of someone at his back, Dominique looked over as one of the younger agents came alongside him. Small-boned, petite, the blond . . . Chelsey Davis smiled somewhat boldly as she asked, "Can I get you a cup of coffee, sir?"

Nodding slightly, he managed, "Cream." Distractedly, he glanced toward the door through which the agents had passed. Without a need for his talents, he knew what the discussion entailed behind the inter-sanctum of the locked doors. The lid was about to blow off the best-kept secret in Cleveland, thanks to a municipal police chief with an understandable grudge. If the madman behind these crimes had meant to create havoc, he'd chosen the right method along with the right location. Capt. Daniel Schleger had wasted no time pulling in the neo-Nazi leaders in connection with this murder, and it was only a matter of time before someone from one of the three other precincts began speaking to the Press to admit a similar case. The riot outside of Schleger's precinct was only the beginning.

Accepting the coffee cup, Dominique barely acknowledged the young woman with an uttered amenity. His attention pivoted toward the door as Devinio came partway through and motioned to him. "We're setting up a room with a tape recorder," Devinio said as Dominique joined him in the hallway. "Our interpreter should be here pretty soon, and uh," he hesitated, his dark eyes searching, tense. "Apparently, you have a few countrymen flying in from New York at the request of Ambassador Leonet . . . any chance you're on a first-name basis with him?"

Dominique shrugged. "We might have met once or twice."

Troubled, dismayed, Devinio halted Dominique and turned on him, glancing in either direction before meeting his gaze directly. "What the fuck's going on here, paisano?" he asked in a low, careful tone. "And try this one in English."

"Pandora's box, my friend," Dominique answered and read Devinio's more troubling intensity. The fellow had understood at least the pertinent words.

"I'd appreciate it if you'd at least try to cooperate and translate some of that tape before our interpreter arrives. Despite Mark's opinion, I'm still inclined to believe that what you said and saw in that room could add a great deal to this case. Anything you could tell us at this point would be appreciated. Those pictures you saw," he hesitated. "Multiply them by three, and you'll realize what we're up against here."

"A madman," Dominique stated, halfheartedly considering a means to enlighten Devinio of his own serious predicament. To translate the tapes, he would need to speak English . . . or would he? Possibly, he would have more luck writing the English script than speaking it. With a hand gesture, he motioned Devinio to continue and show him the room, managing the words, "Paper and pen." Possibly Devinio understood at least that much French. They no sooner entered the compact conference room, probably one designed for interrogating or holding prisoners for processing, when Devinio produced a pen from his breast pocket and asked the technician fussing with the recorder to bring another tablet.

No pictures on the walls, no windows to the outside world, the room contained a single square of screened glass in the door, and a two-way mirror suggesting an audience on the other side. Centering the room, a table no larger than a small dining room table and a half dozen cushioned office chairs attempted to offset the institutional image. Uncomfortably, Dominique settled into one of the chairs near the recorder, glancing at Devinio as he motioned with his cigarette, the need for an ashtray. The room far too closely resembled another room where Jade Laquette had spent several hours at the mercy of a federal interrogation team. Presently, however, his wrists were neither ringed in iron nor connected with chains; a shallow relief considering that Agent Jarvins stood, even now, behind the darkened mirror. That, too, familiar.

In an odd moment, Dominique gazed into his reflection on the glass, finding Jarvins as if the mirror were a natural window, but it was his face looking back at him, his hostility trapped in the mirror. Jarvins . . . Mark Jarvins might have given Veronique the life she deserved, a lifetime of quiet happiness and serenity. If nothing else, Dominique knew the respect and pride Mark Jarvins carried for himself, his ancestors, his birthright. In fleeting instants, Dominique knew Jarvins had been born and raised in the upper-class suburbs of the capital. Jarvins had attended Ivy League schools alongside Veronique's brothers. He'd lived a normal life similar to Veronique's though more clandestine and protected. Their ancestors had probably fought side-by-side in the Civil War along with both World Wars.

Dominique's ancestors had probably tutored under Merlin, but the longevity of his lines offered no comfort. Myths and fables, folklore and tales . . . should he take pride in his father's often ranted diatribes concerning their ancestors descending from the Druids? Or worse, to believe his mother's mention of gypsies and the fantasies rooted in the hills of Transylvania?

And Felicity Laquette had the bloody nerve to consider him a monster?

Annoyed, angry, Dominique barely glanced off the ashtray as he crushed his cigarette, then reached for the tablet. A fool. He'd been a fool to believe he could fall in love – even with a witch – and live a normal life. His father had left him alone for nearly the past six years, which was no longer a great mystery. The bastard had known where to find his youngest son; might have manipulated a few circumstances to keep his youngest son busy. Jean-Pierre had known enough about the future to remain in the shadows for these last six years and had probably merely rested and waited, anticipating the meeting and union with Veronique to propagate their lines.

God be merciful, he still loved her, still loved the thought of their joint creation. He need only recall that moment in the wee hours when he'd stood holding Veronique in his arms and slipped his hand to her waist. As awed as he'd been startled, he'd felt the lifeforce brush against his palm, stood in fascination at white light so bright that it pierced the darkest corners of his mind. This tiny creation, a mere whisper of life, already possessed a soul so pure it had held him enthralled in those few seconds. No, he would not change a single moment in time even if he could have spared himself the pain of this moment with the thought of leaving his wife and child behind forever.

Three together . . . forever.

She'd said it only yesterday . . . 'We can't keep denying who we are, what we are.'

But he'd tried. With every ounce of his being, he'd tried to deny what lay within him, tried to hide from it . . . And to what avail? Whether he was Jade Laquette . . . or Dominique Jardonet . . . or Isaac Bently . . . or any one of a half dozen other names he'd taken in the past twenty-eight years, he continued to carry the seeds of evil, the curse of the devil. If not the American government, then the French, and if not the French, then the English . . . sooner or later, he would be dragged into the most macabre depths of the human condition, and if he remained with his wife and child, there would be no peace for them either.

The only decent thing he could do for them was to step away, sever all ties, and refrain from becoming his father's son. Veronique was strong in ways he could not begin to fathom, her white light as fierce as any dark force . . . but would he taint them as he'd been tainted? Would his need to perpetuate the dark forces inside of him be too strong?

With his anger on high, Dominique reached and shoved the appropriate button to start the tape player. What startled him more, the gibberish emitted from the machine or the near annoying static of voices just outside the room, he couldn't decide. Riveted, his attention fell and held firm on the recorder as if something in his immediate vision would explain the nonsense. He recognized the woman's voice – Roberta Lincroft – the forensic pathologist had spoken to him when he entered, he remembered, but her words on the machine sounded garbled. The tape was useless. Some interference. He heard only gibberish. Shaking his head, lifting his gaze to find Devinio, he barely started to curse the incompetency of the machine when his own words erupted. His gaze shot to the machine.

"... Wh-what ... wh-whaat ... ha-ave to get to wooork ...."

His senses floating momentarily, Dominique reached and slammed the off button.

Across the table, settling into a chair, Devinio said something.

Something indiscernible, Dominique realized and studied the dark eyes, seeing, sensing the man's concern . . . and at a loss to understand the words spilling off the agent's lips.

"My God," Dominique uttered, his senses sharpening. He knew, abruptly, the voices he'd heard sounding like static . . . English spoken words. For the second time in his life, those words . . . gibberish. English . . . as foreign to him now as French a few lifetimes past. As if Devinio spoke in fast-forward, the sounds fused, the syllables merged. Dumbfounded, Dominique studied the face across from him, searching for some word or syllable he understood.

"... Mr. Jardonet ..." Only those two words registered as if a spark ignited and doused.

Tense suddenly, Dominique shook his head, halting the cluttered sounds. Before the panic could set in completely, his attention pivoted toward the door, and relief ignited before the knock interrupted and the door opened.

CHAPTER 12

Dressed in a dark-blue form-fitting jacket and slacks, the young woman passed her escort, who offered a few words of gibberish. Across the table, Devinio rose, extending his hand to the female, likewise offering a few words. In a soft sing-songy rhythm, she responded, apparently, in English. Blond hair cut in a carefree style to sweep smoothly off her brow and shoulders, makeup applied with an eye for detail, she might have stepped off the cover of a business journal for the young female executive. As Dominique rose, she sidestepped Devinio and offered smoothly, "Pleasure to meet you, Mr. Jardonet."

"If you please, Dominique," he answered, relieved until he realized she'd spoken in French. "Miss . . .?"

"Duran," she offered, still holding his hand. "Anita Duran."

"You are not from the French Embassy. You are the interpreter from the Federal Bureau of Investigation?"

"Yes," she answered, her brown eyes holding his gaze even as Devinio interrupted.

By impression and expression alone, Dominique knew Devinio had interrupted deliberately, apparently anxious to get started. Flashing a glance toward the agent, Dominique slipped his hand away, agreeing wholeheartedly, looking again at the woman. "I am almost ashamed to admit, I have a great deal of trouble with the English language and even more so with American English. A communication breakdown," he said with a slight smile and shrug, motioning toward the chair he'd occupied. "Hopefully, you can translate the words on this tape. If they wait for me to make sense of them, they may wait a while."

She smiled understandingly and flashed her glance toward Devinio as the man started speaking again, apparently addressing Dominique.

Uncomfortably, Dominique met the intense dark eyes, not entirely oblivious of the agent's agitation nor certain how to admit his declining condition without inviting trouble. Looking toward the interpreter, Dominique commented, "Please, miss, explain to him, I am not intentionally being difficult. I just don't understand enough of his words to know what he expects of me." As she began relaying the words, Dominique looked into the dark eyes, conveying the integrity of his meaning, seeing and sensing the fellow's growing anxiety. Shrugging, Dominique offered a slight smile which by no means countered the message. Glancing at Duran, he commented, "Translate for me, please?"

"Of course," she answered.

Toward Devinio, he commented, "I mentioned the need for an interpreter, and now it has come to pass. An inconvenience, comrade, but one I cannot change any more than you can learn to speak French in the next ten minutes. For now, we need to rely on the services of your associate."

When Duran finished, Devinio started to speak. Dominique tipped his head, searching, trying earnestly to grasp something of the words, gaining only impressions from the agitation flowing off Devinio in a nearly visible wave. Annoyed by his shortcomings, Dominique looked to the woman for the interpretation. "Please, what was that?"

"He uhm . . . he said you could understand English a little while ago," she said hesitantly.

Dominique shrugged and looked to Devinio, gesturing his loss with an open palm. "C'est la vie, mon ami."

Devinio's eyes flashed doubt, and Dominique grasped the reason . . . the words had parted his lips in English! With an effort of concentration, Dominique formed his thoughts in French, speaking carefully and realizing the broken English off his tongue. "Clearly . . . et is . . . eh . . . not clear? What I say . . . you do not . . . Bloody hell. Forget it." Looking over to Duran, anger flashing in his eyes, he continued smoothly. "Tell him I don't care to sound like a moron. If he intends to carry on a conversation, he'll need to speak through you."

The woman flashed a worried frown as she eyed Devinio and apparently translated the words. When Devinio responded, Dominique continued to watch Duran, awaiting her interpretation. Her eyes flashed worry, then fleeted a glance to Devinio, who apparently urged her to speak. Drawing a breath to muster her courage, she spoke simply, "He asks that I translate verbatim. He said—you're still an arrogant son of a bitch."

Smirking, Dominique canted his head to Devinio. "We understand each other, my friend." As Duran spoke, Dominique motioned Devinio toward the tape, continuing. "I'll listen to this tape, Agent Devinio. Perhaps, I'll have more impressions or insights to add, and Miss Duran can interpret those as well. The uh . . ." He considered absently, his gaze listing toward the woman and back toward Devinio, concentrating and speaking only. "Clearance?"

Annoyed, Dominique awaited Duran's interpretation. "What do you mean? Hers or yours?"

"La mademoiselle?"

Duran started to answer, "I'm cleared—"

Dominique flashed her an annoyed glance. "I'll hear his words, his verification, miss. Meaning no offense to you, but he'll understand the significance of my question."

Devinio awaited the woman's translation, then tilted his gaze to Dominique and conveyed the integrity of Duran's words. "Miss Duran carries the credentials to hear whatever's said. Nothing will leave this room unless it's cleared by the Bureau. You have my word."

Doubtful, Dominique might have answered, but in a fleeting instant, he realized the futility of his concern. He'd already offered the Bureau whatever evidence they'd sought when enlisting him for this investigation. If he worried about security, he would have walked away from this endeavor when leaving

Meg's Diner a few brief hours earlier. Had he consciously realized how deeply he might become submersed . . . *for Veronique, for Tad.*

Something of his wariness and second thoughts appeared in his eyes and expression, apparently, misinterpreted. Devinio reached over, speaking carefully, demanding Duran's translations. "Sincerely, Mr. Jardonet, whatever happens in this room is extremely classified information."

"For whose classification?" Dominique asked and studied Devinio's eyes, seeing the brow furrow with his doubt. Continuing, he commented, "You have enlisted my eh . . . services, Mr. Devinio, and I still wonder who believed in my . . . qualifications? What I have already given you is enough to create problems in my personal life . . . and I am on . . . foreign soil? Will you guarantee my personal safety? Can you guarantee that nothing I have done or can do will reach the ears and eyes of those I would consider an enemy?"

"I'm not sure I am following you," Devinio answered through Duran, still studying him. "And this would be a helluva lot easier if we were both speaking the same language."

"We are worlds apart and growing further with every minute," Dominique answered, his gaze unwavering. "I asked something of you earlier, Mr. Devinio . . . I will ask you to keep your promise to me, nothing more." In English, he managed, "Understand?"

For a long moment, Devinio studied him, his dark eyes spiraling with thought before he looked to Duran and spoke a few words of English. When she answered, "I understand," Devinio looked over and repeated the French words, "*Je comprends.*"

Nodding, Dominique barely glanced at Duran, intending to suggest they start on the tape. A second thought intruded, drawing his attention toward the door. By what sense he anticipated the interruption, he needn't wonder. On an even par, his senses enhanced as his American heritage deteriorated.

The knock intruded, announcing the same young detective, Shawn McAllory, who'd met the Federal delegates in the reception area. Overqualified for the position of goffer and escort, McAllory made eye contact with Devinio, spared a glance to the female agent and Dominique, then began speaking. Not visibly irritated, the detective conveyed more by his tone than his words. The fellow hadn't made detective status by accident or affluence; he was a top-notch investigator, and he wasn't pleased with the recent developments in his case. In fact, he was damned annoyed with the FBI's belated attention and interest; after all, as much as a month ago, the Bureau had been invited into the case. Thus far, neither local agent had offered anything of significance . . . and now, when McAllory should be visiting crime scenes and neighbors, he was playing host to a growing number of out-of-town and foreign dignitaries. He wasn't a happy man.

Reading McAllory in the space of a few seconds which was far easier than reading Devinio, Dominique turned his attention to the mid-aged, well-dressed man who excused himself past McAllory. Medium built, tailored, sporting a thin mustache, the fellow approached Dominique, sizing up the two others in the room in darting glances while lifting a billfold from his jacket. Meeting Dominique's gaze with an intensity to betray his slight smile, he spoke smoothly, "Insp. Jardonet, a pleasure to make your acquaintance. I am Claude Rudemonje, and this is my associate, Paul Lejeune. We are from the Embassy."

Dominique accepted the billfold for inspection and drew far more than words from the official credentials. They were, in fact, native sons of France, recently employed in sensitive positions within the UN building in New York . . . and both were acquainted with Jean-Pierre Jardonet. Rudemonje . . . Dominique was certain he'd met the fellow somewhere in the past, grasped the significance although the details eluded him. Returning the billfold, Dominique fleeted a glance and nodded toward the second fellow. Before he could comment one way or another, Mark Jarvins and the county deputy sheriff in charge of the investigation arrived outside the door, crowding the entrance, and filing into the shrinking interrogation room.

Obviously, no one knew exactly what protocol to follow, least of all Deputy Vince Dartworth, who wasn't in the habit of entertaining the FBI, much less foreign visitors. Belatedly, Dartworth regretted sending McAllory to collect the agents. In his book—apparently influenced by the romantic endeavors of such greats as Sherlock Holmes and James Bond—gaining the interest of a foreign diplomat in his case outweighed the overdue participation of the Federal Bureau. Jardonet had, after all, visited the morgue, and unlike either agent, offered something of value that the Bureau considered important enough to enlist a translator from Washington. Stout of build with the mid-aged spread of a man accustomed to riding a desk and barking commands, Dartworth insinuated himself past his junior detective, took a few seconds to size up his guests, and extended his hand to Rudemonje, judging his seniority by age. "Mr. Jardnay," he said in a voice striving to sound authoritative despite the contrast of his flushed, rounded cheeks.

At a loss to grasp the words, Dominique collected only the impressions to know Dep. Vince Dartworth apologized for his negligence, overemphasizing his self-importance in the case.

Glancing off the proffered hand, Rudemonje looked to Dominique, his pale blue eyes conveying his disgust. "Please, tell me this isn't an example of the hospitality and reception you've received in this company, Insp. Jardonet."

With a dismissive gesture toward Rudemonje to accept the handshake, Dominique commented, "Explain his mistake kindly. He has a difficult task for which he is sorely ill-equipped, and our arrival has only complicated his life."

Rudemonje wasn't inclined toward forgiveness. He considered the oversight and neglect a direct affront toward his countryman. Whatever words he began speaking started the deputy blinking and flashing his stunned gaze toward Dominique, which transformed into weird awe.

Dartworth's wasn't the only expression to change, and Dominique tipped his head, judging the various reactions, sensing anger behind Jarvins' gaze, confusion in Devinio, slight amusement behind Lejeune's otherwise calm blue gaze, and doubt in the young woman. Only McAllory seemed to consider the words with an odd combination of relief and respect and in a flashing glance, Dominique noted the man's genuine apology for dismissing him earlier out of hand. Curious, Dominique captured Rudemonje's gaze and wondered, "What exactly have you told them?"

"Only what is appropriate," the fellow said with a slight shrug. "That Dominique Jardonet is considered one of the most accomplished and respected investigators in all of France, and you are here as a favor to an American diplomat. I suggested he telephone the Director of the Federal Bureau of Investigation to verify your credentials, and if he has further doubts, he should telephone Ambassador Leonet directly."

Only on the surface, Dominique maintained a slight smirk to suggest amusement. In Rudemonje's eyes, the details spiraled beyond the scope of his words, and Dominique received the verification of his earlier thought. Jean-Pierre's influence had transcended the ocean, and Jade Laquette was dead. With a phone call, a few words, he'd become Dominique Jardonet . . . and there was no turning back. Jean-Pierre had paved this road for a dozen years, if not longer. No turning back. He was Dominique Paul Jardonet, and the darkness which had threatened him for a lifetime crept through his mind, over his soul.

The need to protect his wife and son had just increased a hundredfold.

In the space of a few fleeting seconds, Dominique felt the transformation, feeling the changes within himself as his nature merged with the identity he'd attempted to deny. An accomplished and respected investigator . . . of *unnatural* methods of investigation. Changes complete, he knew who . . . what he was, and he wasn't the same man who'd held his love and touched the child he'd created.

"Mr. Jardnay," the deputy nearly stammered while extending his hand toward Dominique, continuing in a slightly more reverent tone.

Glancing off the beefy hand with an air of indifference, Dominique addressed Rudemonje. "Translation?"

"He extends his apology and offers his name once again."

Dominique nodded curtly toward the deputy then spoke to the agent-interpreter. "A change in plans, miss. My associate, Mr. Lejeune will assist in the translation. When the transcript is finished, I will read over it and add what

I can." Without pause, he glanced off Rudemonje, then toward the younger detective, and asked, "Will you show me what you have collected to date on this case, Det. McAllory? The sooner I learn where you've been, the sooner I will determine where I will go."

As Rudemonje translated, the detective flashed his gaze between them, then looked to his apparent commander and spoke a few words to which the deputy responded.

Jarvins interrupted momentarily and drew Dartworth's attention, as well as Dominique's gaze. Flashing angry glances, Jarvins snapped a few words to Rudemonje, who appeared unruffled despite the heat in his eyes as he looked at Dominique. "He asks to speak with you privately for a few moments," Rudemonje commented, and Jarvins apparently took offense to the delay, managing a few bungled words in French to demand the audience.

"As much as I would like to accommodate you, Mr. Jarvins," Dominique started and shrugged. "Your French is as faulty as my English. If you don't mind the presence of a translator, by all means, we can talk."

Jarvins appeared only more annoyed and angry when Rudemonje finished. He met Dominique's gaze with an equal glare, speaking in English and conveying his demand through the tension spiraling in his eyes.

As Rudemonje began to translate, Dominique commented, "You believe I am playing games, and I resent the implication." Without pause, his gaze unwavering, he continued, "The game has ended. Your superiors apparently knew who they sought when they asked for my assistance. Ergo, I will assist, but unless you put aside your personal animosity, you and I will not work together beyond this point. I can and will have you removed from this investigation regardless of your respected skills . . . And a shame it would be since I am in a position to know you are very good at your profession . . . Consider what you know of me and what you believe you know and ask for no further explanations of either my skills or credentials. Between us, if we reach a detente, we can solve this case. If I believed otherwise or doubted the integrity of this killer's intentions, I wouldn't be here. I will not, however, continue to defend or justify myself to you. Are we understood?"

"What I know," Rudemonje translated the words off the mustached lips as the pale blue eyes continued to drill Dominique. "Is that I intend to make the phone call your associate suggested before I allow you further access to this case. Do you understand?"

Considering, Dominique shrugged and looked to Devinio, sensing the man's troubled expression and confusion. "Assist your comrade in verifying whatever he feels the need to verify, Agent Devinio. Waste whatever advantage of time remains on our side. When or if you are satisfied, you'll find me and my associates at the restaurant ah . . . Dioganni's? Believe it was down the block . . ." And as Rudemonje finished the translation, Dominique smiled slowly and spoke in Italian. "If you would care to join us, feel free."

"*Dannazione*," Devinio uttered, and Dominique understood the curse, shrugging, smirking as he motioned toward his comrades.

Dominique barely started toward the door when Jarvins stepped and reached for his arm, intending to stop him. In a split second, Dominque deflected the grasp and landed his palm on Jarvins' chest. Under the impact, the agent staggered a few backward steps, and in a single smooth motion, Rudemonje and Lejeune stepped between them before Jarvins could fully recover his balance. By actions or words, Rudemonje forced Jarvins back another step, and Devinio clasped his partner's arm, adding a few words to stifle his aggression. Still, his blue eyes flashed fire toward Dominique as he hissed a warning of sorts.

Annoyed, as much by his inability to understand the spoken words as by his hostility toward Jarvins, Dominique refrained from a verbal response. Flashed a dismissive gesture, he sidestepped past his countrymen toward the door. Barely fleeting a glance at the stunned deputy and his younger counterpart, Dominique passed through the door and continued toward the exit. That he'd lost all traces of his American heritage, even his natural grasp of the damned language, fared not well in his mind. A handicap, this communication barrier, and one he should be able to remove.

Like in Bentwood, locals in Elmview enjoyed browsing in the quiet atmosphere of the half dozen local antique shops, and Jack Trumble had become a topic of conversation in more than a few. Between buying antiques and dickering prices with one old shyster of merit, Ronnie had learned a great deal about the late realtor, not to be mistaken for 'agent.' Trumble had begun his career as an agent nearly twenty years ago, a young 'Upstart . . . fresh from the eight-month course offered by the local college.'

"He used to work with Parker . . . That would be Lyle Parker, not to be confused with Sam Parker, who owned the tool and die shop out on Slinger's Rd. Now, there was one shrewd old timer," the equally shrewd old timer had commented.

Relaxed, amused, Ronnie leaned at the front counter, ever the good listener. Around them, the smell of old wood, rust, and dust, offered an attic atmosphere that embraced Finn Briggers—nicknamed thus, colorfully, for always having a fin in his back pocket. The old timer, as reed thin and weathered as the flute hanging on the wall over his shoulder, had been something of a lady-killer in his heyday. To keep the wolves at bay – and a noose from his neck—he'd allegedly kept a five-dollar bill handy, ever ready to pay for his indulgence in the finer pleasures.

"In other words," his equally weathered, lovely older counterpart, Lucy, had whispered. "He was always one for visiting a certain house at the edge of town, if you know what I mean."

At that instant, stifling a laugh, Ronnie had fallen in love with the old pair, content to listen and pay whatever price they saw fit to put on the brass spittoon lying haphazardly alongside a collection of old buckets. How exactly the conversation had veered to Jack Trumble—not to be confused with his brother, George, who ran the only beer distributor in town up until a few years back when 'Kennedy took office'—Ronnie hadn't decided. One minute, they were discussing Finn's love life and the price of "good scrap iron." The next, they were discussing the length of the ". . . biggest damn funeral precession Elmview had seen since Ethel Savrel had passed on to the big cathouse in the sky." Forever, Ronnie had been a good listener, especially when faced with a good storyteller. Delighted, amused, and enthralled, she'd listened to a few of the wilder tales concerning Ethel's endeavors, which according to Finn had begun around the time of Prohibition. ". . . A few of the good ladies of Elmview damn near shut her down with their temperance movement, but I'll tell you, Ethel was no kind of lady to get on the wrong side of . . . She had a set of—"

"Finn," Lucy warned, pursing her lips, and eyeing him with a withering look.

Sheepishly, Finn lowered his weathered hands from the suggestive position about a foot from his baggy coverall bib. "Well, hell, Luce," he grumbled and eyed Ronnie and Donna with a spark of mischief. "You lovely young ladies know what I'm getting at . . . And I'll tell you, you didn't want to be standing too close when she got to whirling around in a catfight."

"I don't think I'd want to be in a catfight with her," Donna commented, innately instigating the old timer to continue, which he obliged willingly.

"No, sirree," he said smoothly. "She'd a made a good two or three of either one of you girls. Ethel was the type of woman when you needed a good ass whoppin—"

"Finn, I swear, you ole goat. Where's your manners?"

"Sweetie, if you ain't figured that out by now, then it's too damn late for me to tell you," he said with mocked reverence. Between his shag of long gray hair and a day-beard looking a week old, he was about the cutest old man Ronnie had ever had the pleasure to meet. Not only was he a grand storyteller, he was as sly as a politician knowing damn full well his old-timer routine covered a world of sins – not excluding the fact that he knew the difference between brass and scrap metal. If he suspected she might harbor an ulterior motive for listening, he never let on, but as the story veered again from Ethel to Jack Trumble, Ronnie's suspicions grew.

"Fact is, ole Jack's been making a mint ever since he split off from Parker and went into business for himself. Jack always had a way about him. Falling in shit and coming out smelling like a rose."

"That's no way to talk about the dead," Lucy, pixy-faced and equally skilled as an impersonator of old age, sent her old friend and obvious mate, a chastening scowl. With her round face and full lips, she looked like a child pretending to pout.

"Dead or not, Luce, a fact's a fact. Remember the time him and his brother Nate went out fishing on Shocklan Lake? Was Nate who damn near drown."

"Sure heck wasn't because of Jack," Lucy defended as if doubting Finn could even suggest such an absurdity. "The good Lord knows, nobody knew that flood was coming."

"Anybody with a lick a good sense wouldn't go boating on Shocklan Lake after the friggen spring thaws."

"They couldn't have been more than ten years old, Finn. I swear."

"Was Jack who went and snatched his daddy's boat," Finn said bluntly. "Old Mase used to tug his whiskers something fierce whenever he lost sight of Jack for a few hours. Always falling into a world a shit . . . and this here, don't strike me much different," Finn continued without any help or persuasion. "I figure there's more than a grain of truth to what we been hearing about that Council meeting a while back."

"Finn, don't you start spreading rumors."

"Hell, Luce, not much of a rumor," Finn said and looked to Ronnie, silently supporting her thought of his ulterior motives. "See, girl, here about eight or nine months ago, old Hank Ryder passed on . . . Now, there's a fella who had a lot on the ball. Must a been close to ninety. Outlived three wives and a passel of kids. Has maybe four or five of them left, but they're damned near as old as Methuselah, the whole lot of them. When old Hank passed on, his whole place went up for sale . . . We're talking maybe close to five hundred or so acres, a whole lot of it's prime farmland. The way I hear it, old Hank got wind of some big company wanting to buy up a big parcel of land . . . A lot like when the power company came in a few years back. Hank . . . he was a farmer like his daddy and probably his granddaddy before that. From what anybody who knew Hank can tell you, he wrote it in his Will that the whole place had to be sold to a private citizen. With a stipulation. No corporation could purchase the land for no less than fifty years. Guess he figured, he'd need fifty years in heaven or hell before he'd give up full title to his hills. Tell you, wouldn't be a bit surprised if old Hank didn't appear in front of Jack out on that stretch just out of pure meanness."

"A corporation bought the land?"

"Damn near worse, sweetie," Finn said with an edge in his voice, a twitch in his bristled, sunken cheek. "I don't know if Jack finagled it or if he was pressured into helping, but the town of Elmview, about a dozen councilmen altogether, ended up with title to the land. Hear tell, they brought in a couple big lawyers from Pittsburgh or Philadelphia to get around Hank's Will. Last I heard, they've had surveyors out there for about three or four months now. And I'll tell you something else that you'll not likely hear spoke too loud . . . There's been a whole lot of whispering about the EPA snooping around out Ryder Rd. What I'm thinking and hearing, is that they're planning on turning the whole damn place into one of those cancer-causing dumps. That's real nice for some of the folks who can profit from the transaction right now, but I'll tell you, in the long run, I'd rather have teenagers cutting up on the sidewalks outside and egging my windows on Halloween. Chances are, that college will be the first to pull out of Elmview when word gets out. Not to mention, I sure's hell wouldn't want to start a family next door to a few thousand pounds of toxic waste. It'll be akin to that Centralia just north a here all over again . . . and those fires are still burning."

Somehow, the Jack Trumble affair had just become a whole new ball of wax. Maintaining her empathy, genuine, despite the need to cover her rapidly turning thoughts, Ronnie commented, "Is there anyone trying to fight against it? I mean, you could probably put together a group and lobby in Washington against something like that. If your reasons were strong enough and you had enough support, you could probably block it . . . Especially, if, as you're suggesting, Mr. Trumble's accident is connected."

"Now, did I say that, girl? No sirree. You didn't hear such a thing in Finn's Corner," he said tongue-in-cheek, his steel gray eyes as direct and sharp as a razor's edge. With his point made, he listed his gaze toward the tarnished spittoon, which rested albeit forgotten, on the wooden counter between them. "We got a ways off the track here," he said smoothly and canted his shaggy head, lifting his leathery hand to scratch his beard. "Let's see . . . Think your last offer was somewhere in the vicinity of twenty bucks."

"I think we settled on twenty-five," she said honestly.

He raised a gray brow and eyed her critically. "You accusing me a going senile, girl?"

"Not on a bet," she said smoothly. "Now that you mention it . . . I think it was twenty."

"You by any chance driving that little black pickup? The one from that dandy shop over in Bentwood?"

Sly as the devil, she considered. "As a matter of fact, I am," she said lightly.

"You wouldn't, by any chance, be the little lady who made an honest man of that young fella who owns the place, would you?"

Amused, Ronnie nodded. "I think he was probably pretty honest in most respects before I married him, but we're working on rounding out his reputation, which probably compared nicely to your own before Lucy snagged you."

"Snagged, being the right word, you can bet your boots," the old timer mused and feigned to duck as Lucy made to slap him. Chuckling, he flashed his wife a toothy grin and looked at Ronnie. "Me and that youngster traded off a ways back. He had a nice Sam Holt shotgun that looked real good over my mantel. I never felt quite right about taking him the way I done. Of course, I figure he was just learning and could use a few hard knocks. Why don't you tuck that bucket under your arm, there? And if you like those old candlesticks there," he said, motioning to a shiny brass set of sticks on the end of his counter. "You pick those up, too, and tell that young buck, Finn sends along a 'hey.'"

"He'd have a fit if I didn't pay for these," she said honestly. "The man loves when I spend his money."

Finn chuckled, and Lucy joined him. "You tell him we give them to you as a wedding present, Veronica. Me and Luce heard tell he hitched up over the summer. Don't figure I can blame him for not coming to the festival this year."

CHAPTER 13

Preoccupied, Dominique strode from the inter-sanctum of the Sheriff's Department and continued into the main hall, backtracking the path he'd traveled with the Federal agents to enter the building a short time ago. Taking a side entrance stairwell, he avoided the main flow of the justice-seeking or serving population within the courthouse and led his escorts into a small parking area.

"We have a car on the main avenue," Rudemonje commented. "If you will wait inside, Paul could retrieve it."

"We'll walk," Dominique answered and continued toward the alleyway that led to the main thoroughfare. Pausing to catch a flame to his cigarette, Dominique glanced over the buildings to either side, sparing a glance at the gray sky overhead. In an odd moment, he remembered his father's villa . . .

The gardens crowded on either side of a cobblestone path. Tremendous fountains and endless vines stretched beneath towering trees, offering a haven where an industrious child could hide and rest. But he wasn't a child in his father's realm. Not when he'd traversed those paths. By the time he'd gained his father's favor to haunt the gardens, Jade Laquette had lost half of his teenage years—the most important years of every young man's life. Like all other years past, nothing in that stage of his development had been considered normal.

Walking again, thinking, remembering, Dominique nearly cursed aloud at his nostalgia.

He'd learned to drive, to drink, to socialize with the influential men and women who forever frequented his father's abode. At fifteen, his father had brought him a whore . . . And what a wonder to learn the finer pleasures of that confounding species. Affairs of the heart were what others of his age learned in those delicate years, and Jean-Pierre omitted nothing from the education he bestowed on his young prodigy. Love them, leave them. Only after Dominique had believed himself in love with the whore, he'd learned firsthand what that word meant. The pain of betrayal had destroyed whatever hope he had of accepting a woman into his heart. The first of many, that sleek, over-endowed woman who'd held him enthralled for a few months.

Cloistered, those six years in his father's domain, but by no means ignorant. Jean-Pierre had found methods to bring the world to him, to show him the darkness behind every spark of light. That lesson, to see his lover in the arms of a dozen other men, had backfired like most others of that era, but in a stopped instant, Dominique wondered. He'd hated Jean-Pierre . . . and it seemed suddenly, every trial had led toward that ultimate end, to kindle his hatred ever darker. A plot, a manipulation, a finely constructed platform on which the future would be built. His father had fine-tuned the monster that Felicity Laquette had created, and Dominique was that monster.

The lid that an ignorant child had so thoroughly constructed to deny his teacher the ultimate victory, the only safety device that child had known—to deny the anomalies inside of him—had blown off. Pandor's Box. And Dominique understood even that part of the plan. Forever, the one thing he'd sought, the only thing he'd clung to, was a belief that he'd find the black-haired witch who'd haunted his darkness, who brought him light . . . And Veronica Bryson had come into his life, a tempest and a wonder like no other, offering him so much more than a physical embrace.

Love, it was the only weapon his father could use against him to break through the denials of a lifetime. The only weapon against the hatred and dark arts, which Dominique would've recognized if his father had wielded either against him. To save the only person who meant more to him than his own life, he'd allowed the lid to burst . . . and dived headlong into the darkness.

A bitter irony, he considered as he strode in silence, aware but disinterested in the passing pedestrians, as well as the predominately orange and black decorations to boast the coming of the devil's night.

Once, long ago, he'd determined never to use his dark talents. Out of fear and guilt that he was responsible for his mother's early demise, he'd rejected the inheritance of his nature, had vowed never to use the odd abilities that were as natural to him as breathing. Never would he read another item placed in his hands. Or search another past to determine the future. Never would he play inside the psyches of others.

His mother had been a grand one for welting him when he enlisted his mind-bending talents, but she'd never bulked at using his other skills. Weekly, sometimes daily, she'd forced otherwise innocent items into his hands, forcing him to see the past and utilizing his spoken words to bulge their bank account. Never again, the child had vowed and fought against his father's persuasion with everything inside of him.

A bitter irony . . . love should be his undoing and his ruin.

Damned fool that he was, he loved her still.

Walking from the light of day into the subdued candlelight of the Dioganni's Italian Ristorante, Dominique's eyes adjusted far more swiftly than he cared to consider. Nothing had ever been natural or normal in his life. Why should his instant acceptance of candlelight bear any surprise?

Standing aside, he listened as Rudemonje requested a table for three from a hostess dressed to look like a peasant maiden. Frilly flowered apron, more Dutch than Italian, pulled taut at a tiny waist and amply filled at the bib. She wore her hair braided and twisted into a drape around her perfectly rounded head, and her cow-brown eyes widened a notch, flashing over each of them with keening interest. An illusion. She was a part-time hostess, a full-time student at Ohio State University, supplementing her grants toward a business career. In another few years, she'd land a secretarial job and begin climbing the corporate ladder through a means she could implement now without the cost of an education. No surprises or mysteries. In freeze-frame, she rested atop a leather-topped desk, mini-skirt hiked to her hips, bare legs spread and wrapped about an older man's waist as he pummeled her.

Bleakly, Dominique motioned his countrymen to follow her before he veered toward the signs designating restrooms. Rather than enter the men's room, however, he continued to the cubbyhole notched into the wall where an ancient telephone booth would afford him privacy.

From memory, Dominique dialed the long series of numbers and waited as the long-distance line engaged.

Before the first ring ended, the low silky voice intruded, "So, you have answered your calling, at last, my own. I am happy for you."

"Bastard," Dominique answered, leaning heavily against the dark oak wall.

"Such a thing for a son to say to his father."

"My father's son, then. Yes?"

Sighing, the low voice mused, "Suppose I cannot deny that."

"No, I suppose not," Dominique said with an equally dry tone. His thoughts turning in slow, ever-darkening circles, he pictured the man—an older version of himself—resting comfortably behind a wide, mahogany desk. "Any more than you need deny that you anticipated this current event. My question is this, father . . . why? Was this another of your fucking tests? A lesson, perhaps? Allow me the freedom to love and keep me in the dark while finding a means to destroy it?"

"You either offer me too much credit or not enough, my own. Such has always been the way with you. Hence, I should mention, the darkness you chose to wallow in was of your own design, son. As for love . . .? We have in ourselves, even at our worst, a propensity to find even briefly, that which eludes us most often."

"Maudlin, father? I find that damned hard to believe," Dominique stated. "And don't consider me the fool you have always judged me. I've always given you the credit you deserve, which is why I know you're behind the steps I've followed. And don't bother to deny it, as you positioned your righthand man rather nicely. Just tell me this . . . Where do you expect me to go from here?"

"You could answer that question better than I, Dominique."

Damn him! Damn him for speaking that name again as if the past ten years never existed. "Into my own . . . Aren't those the words you spoke a lifetime ago, Jean-Pierre? Upon a time, I would come into 'your' own, and what a prophet you are, sir. I am obviously, once again your own, and with all my faculties intact despite my pact to the contrary. And to think, you put on such a grand act at my wedding reception. You son of a bitch, you knew when you made that off-the-wall remark about letting me change my name years ago, that I'd take it back—"

"I have always enjoyed your temper," Jean-Pierre interrupted, sounding slightly amused. "But again, you give me too much credit. I might have anticipated a need, but I held no gun to your head to lead you toward this end. Rage on, my son. When you finish, we'll talk rationally."

"Rationally," Dominique repeated in a descended tone. "By all means. Rationally. Or productively. How the hell do you propose I pull off this grand illusion you've created? As much as I have ah . . . a few qualifications for this post, I cannot very well claim any past fame in the investigative field."

"Hmm, I see your predicament," Jean-Pierre said thoughtfully. "You believe you have no documentation to account for your skills, and therein lies your doubt, along with your own blasted curse. Luckily, your father has supplemented your natural talents," he said with a wry note. "Dominique Jardonet's name has appeared rather often in connection with ahh . . . certain solved crimes. Have no doubts, either over the shoes you wear or your ability to fill them. I have every faith the answers will come when the questions arise. You are your father's son."

"A bloody curse if ever I've heard one," Dominique muttered, annoyed. "Now then," he continued. "About that debt I owe you? I'd imagine, with this turn, we are paid in full?"

"You honestly believe I have manipulated you into this event," Jean-Pierre commented, sounding slightly surprised and somewhat dismayed. "Has it occurred to you—my hand is not stamped upon this covenant?"

"I should believe you're merely the innocent benefactor in this course of events? Hardly," Dominique said dryly. "Even at my worst, I could sense your manipulations, Father. I have ah . . . undergone a few changes. Granted, I walked into this endeavor with something of a clear head, and I've resigned to the consequences, but I know this isn't an innocent act of fate. That debt. You will promise me now, you will place neither my wife nor child in jeopardy toward your own end. I will wear your name, and act on your behalf, but from this moment forward, you'll stay away from them. You won't interfere in their lives one way or another."

"Dominique, months ago, I acted on your behalf, sensing you lacked the attributes to protect them in your present state. Now, you accuse me of interference?"

"How long in advance did you know where I would be, Father? How many years in advance did you darken the skies over Bentwood and form that coven that certain events would play out to your advantage?"

"Credit where credit's due, my own. You wear the gift of the prophet."

"I wear the fucking stamp of the devil, and you know it, sire. You put it there," Dominique stated in a chilly voice. "Agree to my terms, father, or Dominique Jardonet will not survive through a single day," he barely hesitated before commenting quietly. "Credit where credit's due, you know my capabilities, and presently, I have nothing to lose."

"Ahh, my own, now you think me the fool," Jean-Pierre commented in an equally low tone. "You may never live the life you choose, son, but will you leave the life of another to chance . . .? I think not. You are your father's son. Near or far, you'll watch over those you hold within your heart, nothing else will keep that most vital organ ticking. A pity, my own, that we are both cursed with the ability to love in such great proportions that we must endure the darkness to ensure the light. Philosophical, no? Ah, but what is the light without the darkness, mon ami?" Jean-Pierre asked gently and hesitated only a moment. "Now, enough talk of debts and ultimatums. I am more interested to know what you have stumbled into."

"As if you have no idea," Dominique said, genuinely dismayed to realize the accuracy of his father's words. A shallow threat. Even if he'd contemplated physical suicide, which he hadn't, he wouldn't have risked such an undertaking, leaving his wife and child unprotected. Damned if he did, damned if he didn't. Damned. And his epiphanies offered no quick solution or resolution. On the opposite side of the Atlantic, his father waited patiently, apparently aware of the conclusions spiraling in Dominique's mind.

"When one such as yourself broods, you give me cause for concern," Jean-Pierre commented. "Knowing the battles to rage inside you, I wonder, have you sensed a threat to your ah . . . wife and child?"

The man had nearly called her a witch, Dominique knew, but the question itself disturbed him more. To spare Veronique and his child . . . a threat. If he were to believe the innocence of his father's question, Dominique needed to wonder what had lured him into this madness. "I know I'm here because I sought to protect them," he admitted, suddenly far more troubled than he cared to consider. Gratefully, his father needed no verbal announcement.

"Then perhaps, you need to concentrate on the moments at hand and spend less time blaming another for your confusion."

"Love to," Dominique stated, his thoughts transcending. "Unfortunately, I'm suffering a present handicap which carries a striking resemblance to a bit of your early handiwork. Bearing that in mind, I'd appreciate it if you'd lift this bloody curse off me."

Sounding slightly surprised, Jean-Pierre asked, "What spell am I accused of casting now?"

"I was, at one point, fluent in four of the six languages of the United Nations. Unfortunately, I am down by one, presently, and that one is vitally important, considering my present location. Why the bloody hell have you erased the English language from my mind?"

For a long moment, Jean-Pierre was silent, then slowly, almost carefully, he commented, "Believe me as you will or will not, but I fear the curse is not so much of my design as your own . . . You wear an albatross about your neck, and I fear, somewhere in your nature, you realize the handicap of that pendant. Learn from history, mon ami. Battles have been waged throughout history over that which you are now at odds. You are your own battleground, Dominique, as you were years ago. Remember, mon ami . . . you had both languages inside of you. Your mother spoke to you only in French for years, and it was your choice, your decision then, not to understand anything I said to you when you first arrived. Through your unruly obstinance, you defied and denied me. No curse have I used against you that you hadn't the ability to wield against yourself. Why, my own, do you believe I knew what was inside of you when nothing of yourself have you ever offered me as proof?"

Nothing else Jean-Pierre could have said would have been more believable. For several moments after hanging up the phone, Dominique leaned against the back wall of the phone booth, thinking, remembering.

Not once in Jean-Pierre's realm had Dominique ever consciously enlisted his talents to perform the side-show tricks his mother had drummed into him. Not once had he wittingly offered insight or suggested a sense of something not laid before him. Nothing of his psychic abilities had he consciously displayed, and yet, Jean-Pierre had never doubted. Until this moment, Dominique had believed his father had used his dark arts to look inside of him . . . but the revelation slammed him. In every moment within his father's dark realm, Dominique had displayed his talents, and his father had merely called on those internal mechanisms . . . perfecting them.

Damn Jean-Pierre for being so blasted smart and cynical. And double-damn him for not just pointing out the obvious.

An albatross around his neck.

Uttering a curse, Dominique reached with both hands, sliding his fingers under his collar, and catching the gold chain. His fingertips tingled, his heart banged a leaden beat, but he drew the chain up and over his head, lifting the ornaments from under his shirt collar. For a long moment, he held the glittering ring and cross in his palm, remembering those moments only a few hours ago when he'd last held the two binding trinkets. The battle . . . a religious quandary. A paradox, that he should attempt to waltz with the devil wearing a symbol of the Divinity. Shaking his head, he closed his fist over the gold and diamonds and dropped his hand smoothly, sliding his fist into his jacket pocket. The weight on his ring finger pulsed and throbbed, clamping like an iron jaw. The signet ring . . . the intricate weave of gold and black onyx, binding.

With only a fleeting thought of what he'd do with the ornaments in his right fist, his heart hammered a more leaden beat. A sense of abandon flashed through his system.

To protect them, his wife, his son . . .

Bereft, he pushed off the wall and shoved the glass doors apart. Several paces away, Paul Lejeune pushed off the wall, but Dominique barely spared him a glance and gestured to start him ahead toward the dining room. If anything, the discussion with his father had darkened his mood and cast more shadows than illumination. Jean-Pierre wasn't a man to be trusted. Admired and feared, but never trusted. Dominique harbored no illusions about his father's digression from the details of the debt. That, too, represented an albatross of sorts, but one not as easily slipped from his neck as the symbols of the life he would leave behind.

Depressed, Dominique slipped into the corner of the wide booth, not entirely surprised when Lejeune joined him on the bench seat. Lifting and opening the menu, Dominique needed only a glance to realize the curse had not abandoned him. Aside from a few words of Italian to suggest the cuisine, the menu might as well be written in hieroglyphics. Tossing it aside, he turned his attention to lighting a cigarette, barely acknowledging the waitress who bubbled outside the booth. The Italian words slid off his tongue without a hitch. Coffee with cream needed a few words from Lejeune to be understood.

Across the booth, Rudemonje studied Dominique for a few seconds, awaiting the waitress to depart before asking, "Is everything all right?"

"Fine," he said offhandedly and looked over, judging the man's age near fifty, close to Jean-Pierre's age. "What are your instructions?"

"To assist you however possible and see to your comfort and safety."

"Rather broad, those instructions."

"We were not versed on the nature of your business here, sir."

Whether the difference in their ages or something else about that formal address bothered him, Dominique couldn't decide. For a few seconds, he studied the older man with a natural curiosity. Abruptly, seeing himself as a child through this fellow's eyes, Dominique remembered. He'd met this Rudemonje years ago. "You never called me *sir* before, Claude. Do you think we could dispense with the formalities?"

A smile tilted the thin mustache; the blue eyes conveyed appreciation. "I wasn't sure you remembered me, Dominique. It has been more years than I can remember."

"I'd believe that more if you were not here at the moment," Dominique answered and looked at the younger man. They'd never met, but something in the dark eyes emitted recognition, and perhaps, a little . . . awe? "I am at a disadvantage, Mr. Lejeune. You appear to know me or about me. I would wonder what rumors you've heard?"

"No more than what Claude mentioned to the Americans," Lejeune said and studied him. "You are not what I expected, sir, but it is an honor to meet you."

"Ah, then rumors have exaggerated my credentials immensely," Dominique said with a wry smile as he extended his hand. "Forgive my earlier negligence, Mr. Lejeune, and call me Dom or Dominique. The pleasure is mine."

By the strength of his grip, Lejeune verified his genuine pleasure to receive the introduction, but Dominique drew far more than conviction from the touch.

In a millisecond, he understood the words his father had spoken concerning his airtight credentials and certainly explained Jarvins' mention of the DGSE, the equivalent of the CIA. Through Lejeune, Dominique learned that he was reportedly a member of a select group of secret service agents who acted under the orders of the Prime Minister of France. His list of accomplishments ranged from subverting an attempted assassination of a visiting dignitary from Russia to the apprehension of several terrorists to numerous other curiously solved cases in England, Spain, and Italy. Either Jean-Pierre had hired a band of exceptional investigators, or he'd taken up a second hobby, fabricating and staging an international crime spree to compare nicely with the antics of the original PLO.

The problem, Dominique realized as he retracted his hand, was the familiar essence of those events. He'd been in Spain . . . and Italy . . . and England . . . and at least a dozen other countries when deadly events had spiraled curiously around him. Until five years ago, when he'd taken the name of Isaac Bently and settled into the life of an antique dealer, he'd often found himself wrapped up in weird circumstances. And in a more unsettling moment, he realized the fabrications were based on fact. Only the name had changed, and how hard had Jean-Pierre needed to work to attach a single name to each of those isolated events? Damn him! The credentials which had apparently gained Dominique Jardonet a claim to fame were none but his own. If he weren't so blasted annoyed, Dominique might find that detail amusing. Not amusing. Jean-Pierre had apparently followed his endeavors from day one, and it wouldn't surprise Dominique to learn that his accomplishments, as well as his aliases, were listed on some penultimate list of secret agents in the *Direction Generale de la Securte Exterieure*.

How had his father justified the last six . . .? *Damn it*, Dominique nearly uttered aloud.

His father hadn't needed to justify a six-year absence. As little as five months earlier, Isaac Bently had traveled abroad, and it was no secret that he traveled every few months. Inevitably, he shipped a truckload of antiques to furnish his shop, but the nature of his trips entailed far more than treasure hunting. For nearly ten years, Dominique had, in fact, changed his name and occupation as smoothly and efficiently . . . and as blasted often, as most people changed shoes and like a comfortable pair of shoes, he'd held onto a few of those names to wear at whim and whimsy.

Who was he, then? What name did he truly wear? Not Dominique Jardonet. His father had given him that name at the age of twelve. Before that, his mother had dubbed him Jade Laquette, but even that name was an alias, scrolled on an American birth certificate to enable him to attend schools and collect social security, providing he lived long enough and worked hard enough. Isaac Bently . . . like a comfortable pair of shoes, he'd claimed that name when re-entering the states for the past five years, falling into the daily routine of a womanizer, bachelor, and antique dealer. He'd loved the serenity of Olden Time . . . and the people of Bentwood with their quirks and eccentricities. He'd loved being 'Uncle Sax' to the Spencer children and enjoyed the friendship of Tim Spencer, whether they argued over a deck of cards or wallowed in shared misery over a few too many beers. Not often, those wallowing sojourns, but he'd enjoyed them as much as sitting down to a homemade meal at the Spencer table or bantering with Meg over a stack of eggs and home fries.

Suburbia USA . . . he'd craved it as much as he'd craved the love of a black-haired witch. But he was no more Isaac Bently than he was Jardonet or Laquette.

The name . . . the only name which could apply, came to him as he accepted the cup of coffee in front of him, reaching absently for the pitcher of cream. Chameleon. He wasn't a man with a name to define his nature or volition. He was a chameleon, capable of changing his colors and blending into the world as if he need hide his trespass in the natural realm. His mother had been right to fear him, to fear her creation, to treat him like a blasted monster. He was to the world what a chameleon was to a blade of grass. An anomaly.

Lost in his idling thoughts, he sensed the arrival, not entirely taking notice when Devinio slipped into the booth alongside Claude, and a few words exchanged. Only when he sensed the man studying him, searching, and speculating, he collided with the dark, tense eyes. "Your associate has verified his curiosity and my credentials? Or does he still intend to complicate the issues?"

In Italian, Devinio managed, "You are cleared to assist in this investigation." His eyes betrayed the simplicity of his words. They'd received orders from the head of their revered organization to roll out the red carpet, and Mark Jarvins was still fuming. He'd wanted Jade Laquette, here. *Needed him here?*

Devinio, however, was merely more curious. What began as an odd directive to enlist the aid of an alleged American civilian with a questionable past, had become a matter of international intrigue. Devinio was no fool. He'd tallied the facts and reached a singular conclusion—the man he'd been calling Jade Laquette for the past several months, the man he'd met while investigating a serial murder case in a backwoods town, wasn't who or what he appeared. In a paradox, Devinio found that revelation far less unbelievable than unsettling. For Veronica Bryson-Laquette's sake, he harbored more than a few concerns.

"At some point very soon, you and I will need to chat, Mr. Jardonet," Devinio continued quietly. "But that can wait. I'm more interested to know what else you can tell me about this case. Miss Duran's working on the translation, but what I've already heard poses a few questions."

"You lied about your fluency with your native tongue," Dominique noted.

"My native tongue is American. My grandparents were from the old country. I'm second-generation American. And I don't think we can afford to bring up uh . . . lies?" Devinio commented.

"Touché," Dominique conceded. "I wasn't criticizing or casting a stone. Your lie benefits both of us, present circumstances withstanding. I should mention though, I am not a first or second-generation American. Honestly, I wasn't born here." He shrugged, holding Devinio's gaze as he canted his head to draw a flame to his cigarette. Continuing with an exhale of smoke, he commented, "Your questions . . .? I have the impression you aren't questioning who as much as what I am and wondering, perchance, if what you saw was the act your associate believed it to be."

"I heard part of the translation," Devinio said hesitantly. "I've also seen enough in your presence to be curious. Where does the act end and genuine uh . . . abilities begin?"

"Believe what your eyes and ears perceive, my friend. Whatever else I am, I am capable of what you have seen. This killer . . ." Considering, remembering, Dominique turned his gaze to the ashtray, thinking, speaking. "His victims are not random. He plans and stalks." Momentarily, his thoughts floated; his features tensed with the memory of his insight.

Shaking his head, Dominque firmed his gaze on Devinio, fleeting a glance at the waitress who flounced toward them.

Like the hostess, this young woman was destined for promotion. Her awe and excitement with yet another handsome, well-appointed customer in her section spoke volumes about her future. She'd like nothing better than to offer more than another menu to any one of these apparent businessmen.

Distracted and apparently annoyed, Devinio tempered his tone while addressing the waitress, breezing a glance over the menu, and speaking a few offhanded words. When she strode away, Devinio commented, "Nice restaurant. You're picking up the tab, right?"

"Naturally," Dominique said dryly, more grateful for that attempt at jest than he cared to consider. In the next instant, however, he knew the hollow beat of the words. They were not friends, not any longer. Whatever rapport they'd shared had ended, and it was futile to continue the charade.

Devinio spoke again in English, apparently addressing the others at the table, extending introductions on his own behalf, and offering a handshake toward both. Neither man accepted the amenity for anything more than a formality. In Italian, Devinio commented, "Your companions aren't the friendly type, eh?"

Shrugging, Dominique noted Rudemonje's skepticism as well as his concealed contempt for the agent. In French, Dominique asked, "What troubles you, Claude?"

"I doubt we can trust him any more than his partner, Dominique. I believe they resent your presence and assistance in this investigation. I don't believe you are a man to make an idle threat, and I would wonder if it wouldn't be prudent to have them replaced? Surely, there are others qualified who'd be less likely to sabotage your efforts or jeopardize your position."

"My position, or my health, my old friend?"

"Either or," Claude answered, his gaze steady. "The other one, Jarvins, seems to carry a personal grudge against you. Or is it his resentment toward the French in general?"

Twitching a smirk, Dominique shrugged. "I didn't win his friendship, I'll admit, but he is qualified to make a difference in this investigation depending on which way the wind blows."

Devinio interrupted, "Any chance you'll tell me what's eating him?"

"He's attempting to convince me to have you and your partner dismissed from this investigation," Dominique said with a slight smile. "And I'm considering it."

"A few hours ago, I might have found that slightly amusing," Devinio stated, his dark eyes more intent. "At the moment, I don't find it funny, and I don't think you should consider it. Mark's not the easiest man to work with, but he's a damn good profiler."

"You are better, Leonardo," Dominique commented. "But you missed the keyword. I wasn't just referring to Mark Jarvins exclusively. You and I—we have a different problem, but a problem just the same. I am not ah . . . a foreign exchange student," Dominique said quietly and noticed both of his comrades finding that comment amusing, at the same time verifying what he suspected. Both knew Italian as fluently as English. "The problem is this, my friend, I am not an amateur in this area, nor am I uh . . . fragile? Naive? As much as I would enjoy working with you, I wonder if you would trust my expertise or consider me as qualified as your superiors have suggested. We haven't known each other long, but the past few hours have left questions in your mind which could jeopardize this case if you second-guess the events to come. You tell me, Agent Devinio, can we put our uh . . . differences aside and work side-by-side with the doubts lingering between us?"

For a long moment, Devinio studied him, apparently searching still and reaching yet another conclusion before answering sincerely. “If you can, Mr. Jardonet, then I can. If that changes, I’ll let you know, and we can decide what to do then. And take into consideration, I intended to bring you up to speed before that fiasco in the morgue.”

“Point taken and accepted,” Dominique conceded and looked to Claude. “Does that satisfy you? Or do you have further doubts we need to address before continuing?”

“If I offended you by expressing my doubts, I apologize, Dominique.”

“I’m not in the habit of explaining or second-guessing myself,” he said bluntly, his gaze locked on Rudemonje. “Your concern is appreciated, but I suggest you let me worry about my safety and well-being regarding my temporary comrades. Regardless of whatever you may or may not remember, I am neither a naive child nor as vulnerable as you seem to believe. Understood?”

“Yes, sir,” he answered, sufficiently humbled.

CHAPTER 14

Striding up the street with a brass spittoon cradled under her arm and Donna holding the candlesticks, Ronnie decided, "I think I'm going to have to hurt him sometime soon."

"Since I doubt you mean Finn," Donna mused. "Mind telling me why?"

"The shit probably knows more about this town than I could learn in a year, and the only hint he offered, was his mention of music boxes before bidding me bon voyage."

"I see your point," Donna said lightly. "So, where to, now? The Hall of Records or the House of Wicker?"

"No slip of the tongue or attempt at poetry, that," Ronnie noticed.

"If even I can smell a rat, the stink has to be pretty bad. Tim's often told me, I don't follow the rules where a female's sense of smell is concerned. Of course, it has nothing to do with the fact that I've become accustomed to stuffing Odor Eaters in his work shoes. Sooo, are we shopping for antiques or facts this next round?"

Stopping at the passenger door, digging in her jeans pocket for her keys, a habitual parking place for those essentials if only to avoid losing them in her purse, Ronnie scanned the somewhat busy street. No farming town, this. The traffic maintained a steady stream in the afternoon hour. At least a few dozen teenagers loitered or meandered between pizza shops and bookstores which existed in abundance sporting a warehouse of specialty names. New cars, old cars, pickups and vans, and delivery trucks clogged the street, and at least one semi-tractor parked at the far end of the block from where they stood. Out of sorts, Ronnie scanned the storefronts on the immediate block, and her neck prickled with a sense of someone watching them. In the next instant, she muttered a curse under her breath. Maybe she wasn't personally a ten, but with Donna, sleek and lovely despite wearing a scotch-patterned flannel shirt and jeans, they probably topped off around a nineteen, losing a point for wedding rings on both of their fingers. They probably looked like bookends to a few libidinous college students – Donna's brilliant blond hair, her own as black as the pickup. If a few people, of the male variety, didn't take a quick interest, Ronnie would wonder if she was already beginning to show.

Distracted, she fumbled the key into the passenger door lock, her attention divided to notice a few boxes already pressed against the cab. If they bought too much more, chances were too damned good they'd get robbed. Elmview wasn't Bentwood. Doubtful anyone would keep an eye on the truck for them. Halfheartedly, she wondered if one of those storage garage facilities might have found a home in Elmview, then struck upon a better idea. "Didn't Finn say something about living on the outskirts of town?"

"A little shack," Donna agreed, emptying her wares onto the front seat. "Why?"

"If we get filled up, I'd rather not leave the truck hanging out in the hotel parking lot, and there's a rental agency down the block. What do you think the chances are that he'd let us park at his house? Maybe in his garage until morning?"

"Considering that he acted like he was Sax's Dutch Uncle, probably pretty good, but could I ask you something?"

"Sure. Shoot," Ronnie stated, leaning against the pickup's flank, noting the gravity in Donna's lovely amber eyes.

"Is it my imagination, or are you consciously attempting to avoid finding out whatever you came here to find out?"

"Excuse me?"

"Come on, Rem, this is Mona speaking," Donna said with a mocked Cagney accent and sincere speculation. She forfeited the act for more natural curiosity. "We've been here what . . .? About four or five hours, right? We followed a funeral and toured a graveyard. We had lunch and eavesdropped on an interesting conversation."

"You heard it too, huh?" Ronnie mused.

"Your eyes have a way of turning blind when you're listening. I don't know what was said, but I know you were listening and interested. To continue, I've heard you coyly pump a hotel clerk, a gas attendant, and several antique dealers, hitting pay dirt on nearly every occasion. And you still seem as if you'd rather not have heard a single word. So, is this how you always handle an investigation? Or are you attempting to botch this one for any particular reason?"

A damn good question. By now, under normal circumstances, Ronnie would have visited the public library and poured through old and current papers or microfiche. She would have collected the names of most public officials of merit, might have paid a visit to the hospital, or at least learned who handled the autopsy on Jack Trumble. She would have touched base with someone in the know and learned whatever the police knew about the alleged accident.

Instead, she'd dragged Donna through a half dozen antique shops, buying whatever caught her eye like some spoiled rich brat with her old man's credit card. Damn it. That she was spending cash—her own cash—offered no immediate relief or consolation. A day, she'd told Jade only yesterday morning. Originally, she'd planned to hit this town, spend only a day tracking down leads, and promised to enlighten the locals if she found anything amiss. Now, by God, she wouldn't mind if this case dragged out for six months, wouldn't give a damn if Trumble's apparent murder remained a mystery forever. Botched female hormones? O*r something far more alarming?*

What if she simply wanted to live the life Jade had created for them? Antique dealers, momma and pappa bear with baby bear safe in his own bed at night, every night? What if, somewhere in her nature, she would rather not endanger the family she'd found, the family she intended to raise, by putting her neck in the line of fire? She could write children's books . . . or a novel . . . or biographies on the rich and famous who would undoubtedly afford her the time of day when she mentioned her name. Damn it, she did not—absolutely—positively—did *not* want Jade hounded by the press, and as long as she continued to investigate violent crime, solved or unsolved, she was risking his peace and harmony.

Too damned many reporters would pounce on her rather than the story she might uncover in this town. She could almost hear the questions . . . *Did your husband assist in solving the murder? Did he use his psychic ability? Did he study the stars? Did he murder Trumble to create the story . . . ?*

Then the other questions would start again . . . *Does he know who murdered his mother? Why she was murdered? Who might have had a reason? Did he actually see her murdered? We heard he raced home from school to find her . . . Could he have raced home to murder her . . . ?*

Unconsciously, Ronnie lowered her gaze, staring at the pavement, oblivious to Donna stepping closer until the hand landed on her arm.

"Hon, if you don't want to investigate this, it's okay with me."

"I uh . . . I don't know what I want to do," Ronnie admitted, feeling the confusion of that simple confession. She'd never been wishy-washy. Had never not-known exactly what she wanted. Forever, she'd been accused of being spoiled, bold, aggressive, and determined, toward none of which she'd ever taken offense. Decisiveness had become her trademark long ago. She'd always at least claimed to know what she wanted and how to get it. Jade was possibly the only exception. Despite her instant attraction, she'd tried keeping her distance, tried masking her initial encounter behind an excuse. Even when attempting to accept the FBI profile to consider him a serial killer, her base instincts had defended him and prohibited her from making that ghastly claim. One moment, she'd wanted to hug and kiss the life out of him; the next, she'd wanted to pound him to a pulp for his arrogance if nothing else. In the end, just the thought of losing him had nearly killed her.

Where did that leave her now? Investigate Trumble's murder and this apparent conspiracy wrapped in a few thousand barrels of toxic waste? Or continue a shopping spree and pretend not to hear and feel the discrepancies around her?

'You never became a journalist to get the story . . .' Jade's words spoken months ago rang in her inner ear. In his own weird way, he'd known her decision to abandon her career, just as he'd known she'd entered the business to solve crimes, to prevent further crimes.

A toxic waste site on the edge of this booming college town would be a crime, and someone's pockets would need to be lined to change the legislature in Pennsylvania to allow the blasted dump.

Damn it, let these sons a bitches find an island . . . or some strip of desert land where not even birds bothered to land. Let them find a few hundred acres legally and legitimately where an old man's Last Will and Testament wouldn't be breached, or a realtor murdered as part of the package!

"All right," Ronnie said and met Donna's gaze head-on. "Change in plans. If we stop buying as of now, we can put all this stuff in the cab tonight. So, as of this moment, if we see something we want, we leave a deposit and pick it up tomorrow. In the meantime, we'll need to see it in passing. We're going to split up for a while." Pausing a heartbeat, she continued, "The local library's probably only open for a few more hours. Ditto on the municipal building, where I can probably find the tax maps. Depending on what we find, we'll hit the courthouse tomorrow—I think it's in Johnstown."

"I take it, I'm visiting the library, right?"

"Finn said about a year ago," Ronnie continued. "Unless you have a helluva memory, you'll need a notebook. Get into the archives from the local paper. Everything should be on microfilm. The less you say to the librarian, the better, but if you need a cover story, we're both here looking into the possibility of opening another antique shop. You'll want to know what kind of auctions were advertised, that sort of thing. With any luck, Mr. Ryder's estate consisted of something other than land. Regardless, estate sales would justify our market potential. What we need is Mr. Ryder's obit and anything in the headlines around his time of death. Skip through the local news for about a month fore and aft the date of his passing. If you have time, skim through the papers between then and now and jot any names that come up concerning waste management or public elections . . . And see if you can find out when Rick Logan became Chief of Police. Ditto on the councilmen. You have a good eye and ear for discrepancies. If something doesn't look right or sound right, no matter how silly it seems, make a note of it."

"Something tells me we just got serious."

"See, point of fact, you have a good eye and ear. I'll drop you off at the library and pick you up at closing," Ronnie decided. "Depending on how lucky I get at the municipal building, I might need the wheels."

"You certainly don't waste time when you make up your mind," Donna said as Ronnie started around the truck.

"We've already lost about five hours," Ronnie stated and reached the driver's door as Donna stretched across the seat. Without missing a beat, Ronnie climbed inside and added, "And I don't want to be here much passed tomorrow morning."

Within a back room, as far from the mainstream of the sheriff's department as possible, the team of state and county investigators had set up a base camp that equated nicely with a war zone command center. Maps, diagrams, charts, and graphs cluttered the walls; telephones, computers, and fax machines spread out over a half dozen desks crammed within the room. One entire wall defied and yet personified, the dictum of war, and at that wall, Dominique stood, scanning the faces and grizzly remains of all four victims. In an angry script, on a strip of blackboard not currently in use, a frustrated detective had dubbed the maniac "The Taxidermist."

Fitting though it seemed, the title was wrong.

Detached, Dominique continued to study the black and white photos, the faces, and names. One hand hooked at his hip pocket by a thumb, the other occupied with a cigarette, he read the name of the latest victim whose picture had been added only hours earlier.

Frances Cummings. Age 25 . . . In life, she'd been attractive. Dark hair, livid brown eyes, and aquiline features from high cheekbones to a long, lovely neckline. 5'5". 132 lbs. The numbers, the names, came to him easily, but the words . . .? If not for Devinio reading the title, Dominique might still be studying those letters and searching for meaning. Obviously, his handicap hadn't abandoned him, and it was an annoyance he could do without.

Behind him, the others in the room spoke in noticeably hushed voices as if he might overhear some nonsense between them. Impressions. Only impressions of their attitudes touched him, and those ranged from resentment and doubts about this French interloper to awe and hope that he might miraculously solve the case in the next ten minutes. Deputy Dartworth seemed to think Dominique might spin at any moment and announce the name of their maniac, then engage in a lengthy diatribe to explain how he'd solved the mystery. Unfortunately, no such development hovered on the near horizon. Of a half dozen names relative to suspects, none jumped spontaneously to the foreground of Dominique's mind. Like the victims, two young men, now two young women, the mug shots of a few suspects tacked to the opposite side of the wall offered little insight. Whether the distraction of his subdued audience or the mere detachment in himself stifled his insights, he couldn't decide.

He knew death. He sensed the absence of life when he looked at each of the young faces. The first victim – Abraham Lowenstein, had been only 22 years old. At 5'11" and 175 lbs., he wasn't the size or age one might expect to meet this end. Like his comrades on the wall, he'd been handsome . . . dark eyes, a sweep of brown hair, a high intelligent brow, and a friendly smile . . .

Moving along the wall, Dominique found Lowenstein's picture, aware of Devinio meandering a few steps behind him. The words, damn it . . . the words would help, but in a moment of crystal clarity, Dominique realized his temple thumping. Unconsciously, he reached his cigarette-holding hand and touched the note pages tacked under Lowenstein's picture. A tremor slid through his system, jostling his fingertips and breaking the connection . . . but it was enough.

In lightning strike flashes, he collected the details that one investigator or another had compiled since Lowenstein's murder nearly three months earlier. A student . . . a first-year medical student. Abraham – Abe, to his friends of which he had many – had been missing only a few hours before his roommate had begun making phone calls . . . nearly twelve hours before Carl Shumaker had called the police to report him missing. Punctual, conscientious, courteous, and an overachiever, Lowenstein had worked part-time at the Cleveland Clinic between taking summer courses, a routine he'd begun as much as five years earlier. His father was a prominent neurosurgeon, his mother a radiologist. The medical profession was his life and his goal. '. . . *But he always had time for his friends,*' his roommate had stated, a detail which led to Shumaker's concern. He and Lowenstein had planned a double date. '. . . *Sort of a celebration between summer semesters. It's sort of a ritual before we have to crack the books again.*' They'd made reservations at a decent restaurant and planned on visiting a few nightclubs. Lowenstein never phoned his date . . . Rita Marsell, a second-year med-student whom he'd dated on-again, off-again, for nearly a year.

From what the detectives had determined, Lowenstein had disappeared between leaving the hospital and reaching his apartment twelve blocks away. A dozen witnesses recalled seeing him before he left the hospital. Seventeen hours later, his car, a 1980 Chevy was found parked in an ally alongside a rundown apartment building ten miles from the hospital. What remained of Lowenstein was found in the basement. From dental records, he was identified nearly twenty-four hours later.

Daylight . . . in broad daylight, the twenty-two-year-old, athletically built medical student might have been forced to drive himself to his own destiny. The forensic technicians had lifted neither unusual fibers nor strange fingerprints from the vehicle or the crime scene. The Taxidermist had placed Lowenstein, believed to be alive, on a layer of plastic that remained at the scene draped over a handmade wooden workbench. Aside from the plastic, the killer left a half dozen melted candles on various makeshift shelves and tables, along with the symbolic Swastika painted in Lowenstein's blood on one of the walls. A great deal of blood remained at the scene, but neither footprints nor handprints were found. At least one detective hypothesized that the killer had stood on plastic and might have worn a plastic suit throughout the ordeal but no physical evidence had been found.

Standing square and firm, Dominique swayed only in his mind as the compiled details continued to spiral through his consciousness. In mere seconds, he knew as much about the Lowenstein investigation as the dozen detectives who'd spent weeks tracking details. Casting his murky gaze down the wall, he knew abruptly what he needed to do, how he needed to proceed, but a heaviness dragged at his chest and weighted his mind. With every detail, with every tidbit of information he digested from the papers that hung randomly on the wall, he would be drawn deeper into this madness, deeper into the realm of this madman . . . and it was too damned late to back away. He'd touched the mind of this monstrosity and formed an open conduit to a madman the instant he'd walked into the morgue hours ago, if not a helluva lot sooner. No longer could he consider his premonition a nightmare from which he would awaken, rattled but unscathed. This maniac existed in the material world, and, through physical contact, Dominique had sealed his fate.

Muttering a curse, he dragged from his cigarette, turning absently and nearly running into Devinio. Barely glancing at the agent, Dominique found an ashtray on the nearest desk and crushed out the butt. Resigned, he returned to the wall, hearing the soft static of foreign words as he touched the next victim's collection of clipped reports and copied notes. One-handed, he let the pages slip through his fingers, fanning them and introverting the details far more swiftly than he'd ingested the Lowenstein's report.

Another female, Erin Demarco . . . age 19. Light brown hair, brown eyes, 5'3", 134 lbs. Enrolled in Community College . . . Two months earlier, she'd walked across a parking lot outside the supermarket where she worked as a cashier, and no one saw her alive again. Her car, like Lowenstein's, was found parked in a driveway of a condemned house a few hours after her parents reported her missing. She was found in the basement. A different precinct, a different jurisdiction. The chief of police had clamped a lid on it and called the State Police, who then contacted the small task force already working on the Lowenstein murder. Same MO, no visible change, no evidence left at the scene. Like the first, the killer had used a surgical scalpel to remove large portions of skin but left the genitalia intact. Not a sex offender, one detective had determined despite flayed breasts and chest area in both cases. No evidence of sexual intercourse or sexual deviance to this killer's credit . . . but the maniac scored the faces off both victims.

Noel Labinski . . . age 27. Dark brown hair, blue eyes, 6'1", 195 lbs., graduated from a technical institute, a certified electrician who worked for the utility company and subcontracted for a construction company in his spare time. Single. He'd begun seeing a divorcee with two children six months earlier. Marriage in the wind. No one knew where he'd spent his last evening alive. No odd jobs were scheduled according to his personal calendar. He was last heard from when he radioed the utility company dispatcher to say he'd finished for the day and was headed home. Two days later, his girlfriend, Dolores Ruple, phoned the utility company. The company van was found parked in Labinski's driveway along with his personal 1974 Dodge pickup, a vehicle he'd kept in mint condition. No sign of Labinski. A week later, two officers in another precinct answered a tenant's complaint about a noxious odor coming through the heating vents; apparently, the landlord had ignored the tenant's complaints. Labinski was found in a storage room that hadn't been used in twenty years. The killer had gained access through a sub-level exit in an alley.

The abduction method had changed, but nothing else. No one had seen or heard a thing the night of Labinski's disappearance, and no evidence remained at the scene.

Frances "Franny" Cummings . . . age 25. Long, walnut-hued hair, brown eyes, 5'5", 132 lbs. . . . His senses floated momentarily, and his muscles threatened to cave. With an effort, Dominique firmed his stance. Officially, Cummings's boyfriend, Mick Jordan, had reported her missing two days past. Not a great deal had been discovered thus far. A copy of a brief report filed by a dispatcher who'd taken the call from the boyfriend hung on the clipboard with the preliminary notes and Dr. Rhoades's initial findings. Franny had worked as a waitress and covered the evening shift at a small all-night restaurant a few blocks from her apartment. Mick Jordan had spoken to her from his workplace—the post office—shortly before five o'clock. She was scheduled to work at six, and he planned to join her for dinner. He drove straight to the restaurant where her boss had already begun to worry. According to the almost incidental investigation by the officer assigned to the missing person report, Irma Bingle had considered phoning the police even before Jordan's arrival. Franny was never late, almost obsessively on time or early for her shift. The anonymous call that had directed police to the scene had been placed privately to an officer in the Hyde Heights precinct . . . an officer who'd recently made the local news. As a sidebar, the investigating officer had noted Officer Glen Benning's citation for an act of bravery, above and beyond the call of duty . . .

He'd rescued a woman from a burning car while off duty.

CHAPTER 15

"Justice," Dominique said absently as he slipped his hand away from the clipboard. That it was the first word he'd spoken since entering the command center occurred to him only as he sensed Devinio's start. Looking over, Dominique read the critical gaze and curiosity, repeating the word in Italian, and continuing, "He chose Benning to ah . . . punish him perhaps? Or worse, to mock the officer's humanity. Justice . . . or a sick sense of humor."

Every voice in the room had fallen silent abruptly, and in a glance, Dominique realized nearly every pair of eyes turned toward him. Most, he suspected, had been watching him, waiting for something as miraculous as Deputy Dartworth anticipated. Jarvins wasn't in the room. He'd apparently taken up personal residence in the sheriff's office, where he was currently searching through copies of the same information displayed on the walls. Profiling.

"I'm not sure I would consider anything about this maniac humorous," Devinio commented. "Sick or otherwise. That he chose Benning to make a statement—seek justice—I agree. Are you getting anything else?"

Sliding his gaze down the wall, Dominique glimpsed each of the suspects, then sidestepped again. Silently, he fanned through the collected information on the suspects. For the most part, they were convicted felons, who were in the vicinity at the time of the abductions or had known access or association with the victims. One man had been pulled in and questioned extensively because he'd stopped at the grocery store where Erin Demarco worked. Another had a friend who lived a few blocks from Labinski. Another delivered soft drinks to the vending machine on Lowenstein's campus. The suspects had a single common denominator and offered an advantage over the victims—they were all prior offenders. Dominique could have merely glanced over the mug shots tacked to the wall to reach that conclusion. The victims had nothing in common. The suspects . . . Dominique found a few exceptions, not entirely surprised to find a few old boyfriends and school chums in each of the younger victim's case. None were considered serious suspects, any more than Cumming's boyfriend or Labinski's dispatcher, both of whom had been questioned at length.

No common denominator, Dominique verified as he stood, gazing across the grizzly wall. Ages . . . the first two had been close. Male – female. Lowenstein first, three years older than the second victim, Demarco. Again male—Labinski, 27, two years older than Cummings. If this were a numbers game, Dominique might list the next victim as 32 and the one after that as 31, but doubtful this maniac planned to follow any chronological order. Far too quickly, he'd run out of ages, and this maniac planned to be around for a while.

"He stalks them, you realize," Dominique said absently and eyed Devinio.

"We've surmised that much."

"He is ah . . . doubtful on this board of suspects," Dominique considered with a fleeting glance down the faces. Locking on Devinio, he shrugged, "I don't believe he's ever been prosecuted for a crime. He is ah . . . too confidant and not . . . concerned with natural laws. Arrogant, this maniac. If nothing else, the Swastika is a sign of his own supremacy. And he is educated, Devinio. Meticulous," he added with fleeting thoughts of the information from each crime scene and his own deeper coalition. Clearing his focus, he found Devinio studying him still. "I notice the Federal Bureau's findings are available, but nothing of the profile thus far. Is it possible you are only now becoming involved in this case?"

"We've had men on it from the beginning."

"Men . . ." Dominique considered the evasive comment. The answer came to him and darkened the shade of his eyes. "You have left this investigation to the hands of agents who specialize in fraud? How is that possible?"

"Everything's gone through the Bureau, Mr. Jardonet," Devinio stated with a carefully controlled edge that hid nothing of his shared anger. The Bureau—his agency—hadn't afforded this case the attention or response it deserved, and another person had died because of that oversight. "The MO was cross-referenced at the onset—"

"Then ignored," Dominique interrupted. "Any blasted idiot could have viewed that first scene and evidence and known where this bastard was headed. What the fuck kind of fools do you work with—"

"Do you have something constructive to add to—"

"Constructive? Ah, yes. I am here with a purpose, yes? And not to criticize the incompetence of your associates. Profile, Mr. Devinio. You are searching for a professional entity. One with surgical skills, a working knowledge of medical science, and a romance with history. A fucking genius in case you've failed to realize it. Taken separately, any one of these cases could have told you that much. Ah, and he is morphing, growing, searching for his method. These – they are trial runs," he said with an offhanded, dismissive gesture toward the victims. "Look at them, Devinio. What do you see common in all of them?"

"Aside from the fact that they're all Caucasian and under thirty, they attended or were attending higher education facilities. In Cumming's case, she dropped out after two years. They were all from different areas. One lived alone. One with a college roommate. One with her parents. One with a boyfriend. Physically, they share hair color, but the shade in Demarco's case rules out a definitive connection. She didn't dye her hair; it was closer to blond than brown. The ages are too broad a spectrum—19 to 27. The height—too far apart, 5'3" to 6'1". Weight, we're in the stratosphere—132 to 195. Males, he apparently likes taller and well-built. Females tend toward average height-to-weight ratios. Skin color . . . that's this bastard's bag, Mr. Jardonet. I'm not sure he's selective beyond that point."

"Look again, Agent Devinio. It isn't the color, and there is a pattern relative," Dominique said absently, scanning the young, attractive faces. "Not just color . . . If he is allowed to continue, I think his next victim will be a Black man. If he hasn't already found him, he will. The complexion, the texture . . ." Toward Devinio, he continued, "Look at Frances Cumming's photograph, my friend. A driver's license photo, and yet, her complexion is perfect. Not a flaw or blemish to be seen. Driver's photos are not touched up. And if you check, I will bet the school photo of Lowenstein wasn't altered. Demarco's senior picture—flawless. Labinski's photo ID—flawless." As Devinio turned his gaze to the board, Dominique continued, "Now, consider the Swastika—a noted sign of supremacy. Perfection. Do not tell me this monster has no sense of sick humor, my friend. Look at the names. Lowenstein—Jewish. Demarco—Italian. Labinski—Hungarian or Polish."

"Cummings?" Devinio pointed out.

"Jordan. Jewish by chance?"

"Where's . . . damn it. Her boyfriend."

"A postal worker . . . Fairmont. He works in the office. Sense of humor. Justice," Dominique shrugged. "I will guess our madman visited that office once, if not a hundred times. Either he took exception to Jordan's heritage, or he spotted Cummings when she visited her boyfriend. In each case, we have the supremacy factor. Our madman's a bigot."

"Great," Devinio commented, taking slight exception to Dominique's indifferent tone. "That narrows it down to about a few million."

Taking a few steps, ignoring the tense, subdued audience, Dominique slid onto the side of a desk and lifted his cigarettes from his jacket. Shaking one out, he looked to Devinio. "Let's try this a different way, Agent Devinio. Find a pen and paper, and we'll attempt to profile your maniac in English for the benefit of our colleagues."

Devinio let the reference slide and strode to another desk, speaking a few words to McAllory, who rested silently watching, listening. The young detective had no idea what words had passed between them, but he recognized at least the heat of the exchange. He wasted no time delivering a pen and notebook into the agent's hands.

"Ready when you are," Devinio commented.

"Thirty to forty years old," Dominique said smoothly. "No smaller than six feet. I would put his weight around 185—give or take ten pounds. I will say medical profession – doctor. More specifically, I believe he's a surgeon, good with a knife. Possibly with a background in experimental procedures or some area of research. Caucasian. Light brown or blond hair meticulously groomed. Blue eyed. He is of Aryan persuasion. I would believe he is single—"

"Slow down," Devinio stated, though he finished writing a half second later and looked over. "Why single?"

"Perfection," Dominique answered and shrugged. "If he was married, he married young, and the illusion cracked swiftly. No woman would measure up to his standards, not of the human race or himself. Arrogance, my friend. Anyone less than Aphrodite would have outraged him."

"Maybe he found someone who fits that bill."

"Then he could be a widower," Dominique said indifferently and shrugged. "He is not married now. A wife wouldn't jive with his visions of grandeur."

"Even Hitler had his moment."

"Hitler is not his hero," Dominique said, never more certain of a thing. Shaking his head, his thoughts floating, he drew from the moments in the morgue, continuing absently, "He sees himself as an artist. Perhaps, a . . . a sculptor? He seeks beauty in the human form. Appreciates beauty in the human form even as he . . . determines to improve it?" His gaze slid to Devinio, finding the dark eyes studying him. "Does that make sense to you?"

"I'm listening," Devinio said evenly.

Dominique nodded, "I see that. But you should be writing, yes?"

"All right, I have sculptor," Devinio said with a slight twitch of a smile.

"He might have attended art classes, but I think it was long ago. His creations would never have satisfied him. Impressionist art . . . something off color. Movies," he said offhandedly, his thoughts floating momentarily. "Well, it will come to me," he said in a dismissive tone. "Profile. We know he drives a van. Undoubtedly recently purchased. Possibly directly before Labinski's murder. You might search for stolen vehicles though I doubt it would help. He believes himself immune to natural laws. He'll own the van if only to prove he's invincible."

"You think he took the van idea from Labinski?"

Dominique nodded. "The idea might have come to him as he stalked him."

"They're still running down Labinski's clients and utility routes . . . What's your take?"

"Our maniac could have spotted him hanging from a utility pole," Dominique commented and shrugged, unconsciously looking toward the handsome face of Noel Labinski. Several thoughts connected as his gaze skimmed toward Frances Cummings. "I'll be damned," he uttered.

"What?"

"Routes," Dominique said absently. In his mind's eye, he saw the map that one of the investigators had charted of Labinski's utility route in the last three days of his life. Slipping off the desk, Dominique strode to the wall, removing the clipboard and flipping through the pages. Greek. Goddamned Greek! Irritated, he studied the map for a few seconds before turning and returning to the desk. Handing the clipboard to Devinio, he flashed an annoyed glance. "Does it, or does it not say Fairmont somewhere on that page?"

Devinio accepted the clipboard and dropped his attention, breezing his gaze over the words before enlightenment crept into his eyes. He muttered something in English that needed no interpretation.

McAllory pushed from his chair, coming alongside them. He glanced off Dominique before speaking toward Devinio. The question and curiosity loomed large in his eyes.

Devinio might as well have been speaking Greek when he answered McAllory and handed him the map. His dark eyes returned to Dominique, "Nice catch. It looks as if Labinski crossed paths with the Fairmont post office two days before he died. That just might narrow the field if we can put together a composite with the sketch you're drawing. How sure are you about the height and weight theory?"

Fleeting, he remembered the large arm within his sight, the man's shoes scuffing the pavement. Before he could sway, he sidestepped to the desk and settled onto it, realizing, "Positive. He is ah . . . large to a woman of 5'5". With Labinski's size, it's a fair assumption . . . and we can add athletic to the list. A health spa . . . physical fitness club. Something with an exclusive roster. He wouldn't let himself be seen half-naked and sweating by anyone of an inferior race. He might have his own private equipment. He's not a man who socializes more than necessary, and he would ah . . . not be a nice person to work with, demanding of his coworkers. Anything slight of perfection would infuriate him, and he would seek command."

"Private practice, do you think?" Devinio asked.

His thoughts turning, Dominique scanned the picture board, his focus listing over the faces before settling on Lowenstein. "Damn," he uttered.

"Now, what?"

Rather than answer, Dominique pushed off the desk and strode toward the board, hesitating before lifting the clipboard. The words meant nothing, but the contents, the impressions, the details which others had collected . . . in a heartbeat pause, he knew he was onto the monster in the physical plane. Turning, he returned to Devinio, handing him the clipboard, and meeting his gaze. "Dr. Lowenstein . . . neurology, yes? Either our maniac met the son or the father through the hospital . . . a beautiful young Jewish boy. We need to know who works with the elder Lowensteins, and we need to search the hospital records where Abraham worked."

Devinio studied him momentarily, speaking carefully, "For a man who claims not to read English, you don't seem to be having much trouble here, and I'll be honest, friend . . . I know you didn't have time to read these pages."

"Then why wonder if I can read English?" Dominique asked.

"Son of a bitch," Devinio uttered as the enlightenment crept over him. "You really aren't reading words, are you? But you just inhaled every shred of information on those pages."

"I would prefer you tell our colleagues that you offered me prior access through a federal arc . . ." He'd almost said 'archives' and his internal alarms resounded even as he changed the word. "Channels. I wouldn't dispute you, my friend."

For a few seconds, Devinio continued to study him, then skimmed his gaze over the board and looked to the young detective who stood aside, the only member of the task force who'd braved close contact with the interlopers. McAllory wanted this case solved, and he couldn't care less about jurisdictional lines or who contributed to the case. Intently, he listened to Devinio, sparing a glance toward Dominique, nodding and moving, speaking at the same time. Undoubtedly, issuing orders, the young detective reached his desk as several others took his cue.

When at least a few voices rose in an excited tempo, Devinio smirked at Dominique. "Again, nice catch. I'm beginning to feel like an amateur here."

Depressed and distracted suddenly, Dominique cast his gaze toward the cluttered wall. The photographs ranked among some of the grizzliest images he'd ever had the displeasure to witness with his own eyes.

Not the absolute worst, he grasped as the gray film began the wicked march through his mind's eye. He'd seen worse . . .

He'd rested, strapped to a leather chair, force-fed a collection of images that had nearly driven his child-self over that precarious ledge of sanity. Human experimentation in the name of science or merely to aid the war effort, and by no coincidence, he was seeing those images now. This monster had seen those same films—

"Any chance you've done this a few million times before?" Devinio interrupted. Without a doubt, the agent was remembering an incident when newly resurrected Jade Laquette had handed him an innocuous, anonymous message, claiming that a killer would be found when the handwriting could be matched.

Grateful for the interruption, shrugging, Dominique drew from the started trance. To deny the agent's supposition, to admit this was only the second time in his life that he'd ever consciously, deliberately enlisted his curse . . . futile and counterproductive. The representatives of the French Embassy, one of whom waited for him in the reception area, the other who'd traveled to the Inn to collect his belongings, were more than enough to verify his surmise. The second, not the last time, he would enlist his curse. Dominique Jardonet wouldn't be allowed to slip through the fingers of his adopted homeland's government. Jean-Pierre had built this trap and the mouse had taken the bait even as another trap loomed on the horizon.

"Anything else you can add to this profile, Inspector?" Devinio asked, only half jesting with the use of the title. His disposition had already changed; their relationship transformed. In his dark eyes, the understanding and belief had firmed.

The revelation that Devinio would consider him an equal rather than an arrogant, half-crazy psychic should be a relief. Instead, Dominique knew only sorrow as he locked his gaze on the angrily scrolled words.

The Taxidermist.

"He is skinning them alive," Dominique said drearily. "Not stuffing them. He is using the parts for . . . something. And . . . he is building a trophy for himself," he continued, his gaze misty. "Birthmarks . . . those are his trophies . . . And his hero is not Hitler. The Swastika is a mockery on the wall . . . a deeper sense of humor. . . sarcasm. Movies . . . damn it. Old movies . . .."

Again, the faces marched across the screen of his mind as if he held an ancient projector in his head, and for the briefest moment, he suffered the fear . . . a child's fear gripping every fiber of his being. His own . . .? O*r the fear of a madman?*

Shuddering, he yanked himself from the image and firmed in time to halt Devinio from reaching for him. Not quite masking the shine in his eyes, he blinked the fright away and found the agent studying him far more critically. He attempted a smile, but no genuine humor touched his eyes or mind. "A momentary lapse."

"What were you seeing?"

"Better left in the dark," Dominique considered and reached unconsciously into his pocket as if to draw the warmth to him. Instead, he found the ornaments and chain. His fingers tingled and his palm prickled with heated sparks as he gathered the symbols in his grip. Looking down, he drew his fist from his pocket and studied his closed fingers. Slowly, he shifted his focus to Devinio, who appeared neither relieved nor appeased. Offering his hand, he commented, "Hold onto these for me, Lenny?"

Hesitating only a fraction of a second, Devinio lifted his hand, accepting the offering. Without a need for sight, he knew what Dominique had placed in his possession. "You'll let me know when you want them back, right?"

With every ounce of his willpower, Dominique refrained from wearing his answer in his eyes and nodded, but in his mind, only one thought held firm.

To protect his white witch, his warlock son, that day should never come.

CHAPTER 16

The tadpole was up to his tricks again, flip-flopping like a fish out of water, and creating a sensation of vertigo. Alarmed, Ronnie managed a few clumsy steps and settled onto the closest chair. This wasn't the way she'd intended to begin an interview, to stumble into the tax office like a drunken sailor. But it was a little late to save face. God forbid she'd need to vomit. Drawing breath, clasping the arm of the chair and her gut, she ignored the purse strap sliding off her shoulder. As hollow and loud as a bass drum, her purse hit the tile floor alongside her tennis shoes. Across the small room, the woman, Mabel Ross, the local tax collector, scrambled from behind her desk, apparently no more accustomed to people fainting in her office than Ronnie was accustomed to fainting in an office.

"Honey, are you alright? Did you trip?"

Right. Now, this dear little woman would believe her visitor a klutz. *Settle, Tadpole! Mommy's got work to do here*, she tried, silently, while attempting to still the little dickens under her palm. Unfortunately, the world had turned a little gray at the edges and her hair spilling about her face wasn't a good sign. Head between the knees . . . was that the cure for a faint? Deciding, she dropped her head a little lower, hoping, praying, this bout did not end with the usual round of retching.

Mabel clasped her shoulder, attempting to subvert Ronnie's intention and halting her from falling on her head. "Honey, what's wrong? Do you need a doctor? Should I call for an ambulance?" the anxious voice offered.

"Minute," Ronnie heaved. "Just give me a minute. It'll pass."

Apparently, Mabel accepted the words. Several seconds passed before she spoke in a slightly calmer, almost matronly voice. "Can I get you anything, dear? A glass of water?"

No dunce, this lady. Pregnant women were permitted to be clumsy and barring that, they were expected to faint on occasion. The logistics offered no relief. Fortunately, Tadpole decided to cooperate and settle down. If the dickens were this bad at the size of her thumb, she shuddered to think what he would do when he was ready for his final swim. A boy . . . If she harbored any doubts, none remained. Only a male of the species could be this much trouble. First a pain in the gut, then a pain in the butt, then a pain in the heart . . . and she had a feeling, this little dickens would be his father's son.

"How far along are you, dear?" Mabel asked while producing a glass of water.

"Not as far as I wish I were," Ronnie admitted, recovering enough to accept the glass, leaning back in the vinyl chair. Sipping the water, blinking spots from her eyes, she caught her first clear glimpse of Mabel Ross. The woman was nowhere near retirement age, as Ronnie had first guessed. Mabel wore soft, short, permed hair framing her face in a natural hazelnut shade. Big brown eyes magnified behind thick panes of glass, and pink-tinted lips offered a pleasant, engaging smile. No more than mid-fifties, if that, which defied the attitude of the man who'd directed Ronnie from the closed municipal building to Mabel's home office. A few streets from the main thoroughfare, the houses and yards were reflective of Bentwood's side streets. Plenty of trees, private driveways, flower boxes . . . Mabel's entry sported plenty of flower boxes, all gushing with petunias and impatiens appearing hardy enough to last the winter. 'Just look for the house that looks Dutch . . . Ole Mabel sure does like her flowers.'

Without a doubt, Ole Mabel liked her flowers. Even inside, the greenery bulged from ceramic pots, clay pots, and painted buckets. Spiked leaves sprang nearly three feet tall, slicing toward the ceiling behind the desk. Along with holding the tax collector position, Mabel probably boasted a sizeable, profitable greenhouse in her backyard. Crowded with so much green, the office reflected an exotic tropic atmosphere.

Maybe Tad suffered from allergies. That bout of wiggling had erupted with the spontaneity and ferocity of a sneeze. Then too, maybe he sensed her failed attempts at horticulture and decided to spare her the pain of seeing how plants should look. "These can't all be real," Ronnie decided and found Mabel looking around, somewhat worriedly.

"Oh dear, you don't have an allergy I hope?"

"Not that I'm aware," Ronnie admitted and softened her disbelief—and rudeness—with a slight smile. "I can't imagine growing even one of these plants, much less all of them. They're beautiful."

"Why thank you," she said sweetly, too polite to inquire directly about her unexpected visitor's business. "You have seen a doctor, haven't you, dear?"

"I've been told, in no uncertain terms, that I should expect to toss my oats a few times every morning through the first trimester. I do apologize for bungling in like this. If I've caught you at a bad time, I could probably come back at your convenience."

"I have time, dear. Is there something I could do for you?"

"Hopefully," Ronnie said, relaxing more with her stomach calm. "I set out intending to just buy a few antiques today. My husband and I own a shop a few hours from here. The more I've looked around though . . .? Well, I guess you'd say I'm sort of following a whim. We've talked about opening another shop, but where we are right now, it would be like competing with ourselves. Maybe you've heard of us . . . Olden Time Antiques and Collectibles? My husband generally comes here at least once a year."

"My goodness, yes," she said lightly, appearing to relax and smile more, taking in Ronnie now as if sizing her up for a photograph. "I've met your husband, Zak, isn't it?"

Close enough. "That's him."

"He generally comes around at our Fall Festival," she said, reflecting, probably realizing she hadn't seen him this year. With a glimmer of uncanny delight, she confided, "I can think of at least a half dozen young women who will not be too happy to meet you, dear, but I, for one, am delighted for both of you."

"Thank you," Ronnie said with a smile despite her sudden discomfort and mild irritation. Was there anywhere her husband had traveled and not become the object of female attention? *And wasn't that just a stupid question?* The man attracted women as if he had a magnet in his butt. One flash of those chilly green eyes and any sensible, red-blooded female over the age of ten—considering Deedee's protectiveness of her Dutch Uncle, Ronnie corrected, over one—fell at his feet. He should register himself as a lethal weapon, and she really might need to hurt him before she kissed the stuffing out of him. Blast him for being too far away to catch the brunt of her rising ire. A half dozen women falling at his feet . . . *What was he up to, now? About a thousand and six?*

"Now, what is it I can do for you, dear?"

These fits of fancy and fantasy had to cease! "Well, I was hoping I could collect some information," Ronnie continued as if she hadn't paused. "Like I started to say, we're thinking about opening another shop." *Maybe in Australia, if he'd never been there before.* "We didn't really talk about Elmview as a possible location, but I thought I might surprise him and look into it before I broach the subject. We haven't been married too long. Actually, about eight weeks," she added and knew Mabel had caught the connection. "In any event, I'd like to find out about the taxes. Maybe find out what properties are available in or around town. I thought about stopping in at the Realtor's office, but well . . . if what I heard in town's an indication, my timing leaves something to be desired."

Mabel's face shaded; her eyes dimmed. "I see," she said solemnly, not volunteering anything more.

"Anyway, I thought you might be able to help. The thing is . . . see, we're not originally from Bentwood, and we really haven't decided where we'll settle down. We've talked about buying land and living outside of town. I'm more of a city girl, but I really don't want to raise a child in the city. Elmview . . .

it seems a little like the best of both worlds. I really like the idea of a college close at hand. I'd imagine the elementary and high school curricula reflect that influence. We wouldn't need a lot of land. I'd be happy with maybe just a few acres, but we sorta agreed to somewhere between ten and twenty acres. If you didn't mind . . . about how much would the taxes be on something that size?" She caught herself and laughed just a little. "I probably should ask, is it even possible to find something that size?"

Mabel wasn't quick to bite. She hesitated, "I'm sure there is . . ."

The next half hour, Ronnie decided, amounted to the biggest waste of time she'd ever spent, and as she climbed into the pickup, the irony struck her. Was it some practical joke that the moment she decided to actively investigate the case, the well ran dry?

The flight plan had not changed, and that was perhaps, the only relief in Harry's mind as he rested at the corner table in the small pilot's lounge. Generally, his passenger spent a few hours in the city before traveling to his home turf in Tennessee. Once a month, as regular as clockwork, Mr. Smith, as he liked to be called, traveled the same circuitous route, making rounds between Pittsburgh, Cleveland, Cincinnati, and Knoxville where he remained until the next trip. What exactly Smith did for a living, Harry had never discovered. and he could think of a whole plethora of clichés to confirm his decision never to ask, only starting with 'curiosity killed the cat.' Very little conversation had ever passed between them, and in Harry's memory, Smith had never traveled in company before today.

So why today? And who was this illusive fellow who'd seemed to disappear into the small terminal the instant they arrived? If asked, Harry couldn't even readily describe the extra passenger, and that worried him at a base level. He'd always considered himself observant, with a keen eye for detail, and yet, he couldn't decide if the fellow was short or tall, rail-thin or as wide as a barn door.

The other fellow, the one who'd delivered the single piece of luggage, had been rather thin, and young—possibly no more than a teenager, though he'd walked with an easy confidence to suggest he was older. Early to mid-twenties then, and dressed like a gas attendant, though Harry couldn't recall the logo on the coveralls . . . Maybe an airline attendant, he corrected, thinking about the dark blue coveralls. Yea, probably one of the airport employees who Mr. Jones had enlisted to carry his luggage aboard. The young fellow had said something, something like '. . . he'll be here shortly . . .' After that, things got a little hazy. Mr. Smith had come aboard . . . and Mr. Jones had already boarded.

Shaking his head, Harry firmed his focus through the glass and found his Cessna on the tarmac, waiting. Waiting for what though?

Unconsciously, Harry rubbed at his temple, only vaguely aware of the headache thumping that had begun some time ago. He probably should have eaten slightly more than a bagel at breakfast. Time hadn't allowed. He'd barely had time to pick up the morning paper before his pager had sounded and he answered the summons to land himself and his plane at Cleveland Municipal. Grabbing a bagel rather than the full breakfast he'd intended at Meg's Diner, he'd hustled over to the private airfield and logged his flight plan.

Thinking about Meg's—and Meg herself—brought a smile to Harry's bearded lips. She sure was something. About the best dang cook Harry had ever had the pleasure to meet, and about the classiest older woman he'd ever encountered, barring none, despite how many fine women he'd associated with over the years. Blond wavy hair only sprinkled with white-gray strands, smooth, sculpted cheeks to accent her big blue eyes, and a sleek, trim build not nearly hidden by the checkered smock or apron she wore over blue jeans. At first glance, the lady barely appeared old enough to drink, but the mirth and wisdom in her eyes countered that thought quickly enough. She was something—

Something or someone who'd made those trips to Bender Falls worthwhile. Finding Meg's was, perhaps, the only highlight of those stops in Pennsylvania.

A good meal, a lively conversation with some of the locals, and time to daydream about what might have been if he'd met a woman like Megan Price twenty years earlier. All in all, it was a good reason to hang out in that weird little town while his passenger jaunted off to Pittsburgh to conduct his affairs.

Much as Harry preferred not to know Mr. Smith's business, he'd worked out enough about the fellow's trips to surmise Smith worked for the government in one capacity or another, and by his demeanor, he was probably a spook rather than an attaché. As regular as clockwork, Smith traveled between . . .

Pulling out of the flower-enshrouded driveway, Ronnie countered her earlier thought. Verbally, openly, Mabel hadn't added a single detail to the growing mystery, but what she failed to say spoke volumes. The few glimpses of the local tax map had helped, too. Just a little too cautious, this mid-aged woman who loved flowers. Taxes, they had discussed, with Mabel educating Ronnie on the assessment taxes, land taxes, municipal, county and state taxes as if Ronnie had never forked over a dime in her life. With firm resolve, the woman had hedged any indirect mention of Trumble, and Ronnie suspected she'd known him and associated with him regularly. The Ryder name was never mentioned. In fact, no names were mentioned directly. Feigning ignorance, Ronnie had brought up zoning laws as if she'd heard of the foreign word and needed an explanation. R-1, R-2, Commercial, Industrial . . . to open an antique shop on the premises they chose to buy, they'd need a special exemption which would be granted by the council. The process, Mabel assured her, wasn't that difficult. A matter of filling out forms, forking over a few bucks, and eventually attending a council meeting. All in all, it was more of a slight inconvenience, and Mabel doubted it would be a problem. Elmview was always open to new businesses.

Maybe not such a waste of time, after all. Unwittingly, Mabel had verified more than a few tidbits of gossip, incriminating the Elmview Council. Without realizing it, she'd even name-dropped a few of the council members. First names only, Ronnie considered while driving the length of the lane, but how hard would it be to fill in the blanks?

Stopped at a T-intersection, Ronnie hesitated, startled when she found the street sign. Finn had mentioned Shocklan Lake . . . and here was Shocklan Rd. Impulsively, she turned left, away from town. The old timer hadn't stressed any importance when telling that story, like a sidebar in a magazine, about the lake and Nate Trumble nearly drowning. A very long time ago, however, she'd learned to accept peculiar coincidences and follow the mundane, a condition which had increased tenfold since meeting her husband. No coincidences in life. If nothing else, she could enhance her feel for the town.

To either side of the asphalt lane, the houses crammed one against another, suggesting she'd found the slightly poorer side of town. With the scant yards, walking spaces between walls, narrow windows, Insulbrick siding, and missing rungs on aging porches, she could imagine these houses standing before the time of Prohibition. The larger houses, like Mabel's, would have belonged to the upstanding citizens. The folks who lived down here—and it was a downward slope—had probably walked to those fine houses, employed as maids, cooks, seamstresses, and liverymen or later, chauffeurs . . . and she was slightly miffed to notice the predominantly black population surrounding her.

Racism was alive and well in Elmview, a detail she'd not noticed when walking the main thoroughfare where an even blend of whites and blacks had meandered, intermixed. College students, she considered absently, young people had the right idea, but how many of the old timers in this backwater town still called this stretch of Shocklan Rd. by some indignant racial slur? And what did that tell her about Jack Trumble's past, his history? Had he hailed from a poor white family? At ten years old, carrying or dragging a boat, he couldn't have lived too far from Shocklan Lake.

Almost too quickly, the houses stopped, and the forest slammed into the last tattered remains of cottages and garages. Barely visible within a tangle of vines and ivy, a weathered gray shack leaned almost casually against the stout trunks of a couple wild cherry trees, a picture-perfect rendition of old town America. With the sun sprinkling through fall leaves, spackling the gray wood with a rainbow effect, the shed would make a great photograph in a historical piece . . . maybe something a little controversial.

Ronnie could imagine standing one of the locals alongside that shack, then putting a counter shot of one of the fine houses with a likewise inhabitant. Doubtful the good people of Elmview would appreciate the slant of that article if she chose to write it.

Onward, upward, Shocklan Rd. twined through tree trunks which seemed close enough to scrape the fenders if she needed to avoid an oncoming car. Not since turning onto Shocklan had she seen another car, not in front or behind. To either side, the weeds and briars crowded the lane threatening to overrun the pavement at more than a few junctions. Rounding one steep, sharp bend, she contemplated the possibility of reaching out her window and touching the back bumper. God help her if she'd driven anything larger than a pickup. A few of these bends would never accommodate a moving van. She barely considered that thought when she rounded another bend and jammed her foot on the brake. Stopped at the bright red stop sign, she rested momentarily, glancing in either direction on the wide, pleasantly paved road that sported dual-yellow lines and white guidelines to indicate gravel. If Shocklan Lake resided on Shocklan Rd., she'd missed it. And considering the flood Finn had mentioned, she judged her elevation as a confirmation. In fact, considering that she'd driven an incline since leaving the listing garage in her wake, she'd probably missed the lake by at least four miles.

Considering the need to turn around, Ronnie watched the dark blue sedan sail past her front bumper, and with her gift for recall, she knew she'd seen both the car and male passengers several hours earlier. The suited gentlemen had ambled toward the mausoleum, a part of and apart from the procession attending Jack Trumble's interment service. The car had passed her on Main, several cars behind the hearse. Executives . . . or government employees under one auspicious agency or another? With what she knew now, she might consider them advocates of the EPA.

Letting the car gain a fair lead, Ronnie awaited another car to pass, then pulled out, following. Hopefully, they were neither headed toward a golf tournament nor home. It would be awfully nice if they led her directly to Ryder Rd., and she wasn't above daring to hope.

Less than three minutes later, traveling a safe distance behind with a few cars passing, heading toward Elmview, Ronnie confirmed her belief in coincidence. With the brake lights on the small Dodge directly ahead, she likewise tapped her brake, and she wasn't surprised when the sedan turned right, ducking through a tunnel of trees onto a narrow gravel lane that could pass for a private driveway. She'd found Ryder Rd. and she was close enough to read the license plate as the sedan bounced over a few serious ruts at the mouth of the dirt lane.

Pulling a pen off the visor, she jotted the numbers on her palm while keeping the pickup between the lines. With a little luck and a bit of charm, she could learn those gentlemen's names and possibly, a great deal about their intentions with a few quick phone calls . . . and maybe it was just about time to turn her suspicions over to a higher power.

CHAPTER 17

Oblivious of the words, Dominique read enough in the voices around him and the repeated handshakes to know what Devinio had said after calling attention to the gathering. The profile and various insights opened several avenues of investigation. Attempting very few words of English, Dominique accepted the apparent gratitude and praise with an air of indifference. Any man among them could have found the same connections and made the same educated guesses if they'd looked at the entire case from a fresh perspective. Well, possibly not. He held an advantage that he was neither inclined to boast nor appreciate.

With several men on telephones and several others plotting their course of action with a partial description and a fresh outlook, the room had electrified. The search for a killer was afoot, and the direction of assault was well underway. One detective, Jon Mechlen, who'd considered the hospital angle, approached Dominique directly and, through Devinio, asked if the Inspector believed the man wore plastic or surgical scrubs.

Remembering the green fibers found in Lowenstein's backseat, a fact deemed to be a moot point by others considering Lowenstein's part-time occupation, Dominique had answered simply, "Hospital scrubs. I think he may be wearing a hospital uniform, and it's more possible—harder to prove—he's discarding his clothes in a hospital's laundry service receptacle. A guess, bear in mind, but it stands to reason he would use the industrial facilities at his disposal. If records are kept to account for such items, you might determine the number of surgeons vs. the number of soiled uniforms on the day following Lowenstein's murder."

"I'll be damned," the detective stated, and those were the first American words Dominique had understood in hours.

Curious and startled, Dominique watched the fellow turn away and the words were lost as he sped toward an empty desk. Still confounded by his sudden clarity, Dominique found Devinio, who wore a slight smirk.

"I'm beginning to think I should just toss my badge and accept the job of an interpreter," he said lightly. "You certainly don't lack surprises."

"Deductive reasoning," Dominique commented, annoyed by Devinio's voice of appreciation. "Your lab report stated that green fibers were found in Lowenstein's backseat. Someone apparently considered that detail odd despite Lowenstein working as an orderly. A first-year med student wouldn't wear surgical apparel."

"You're deducing that our killer either waited for him in the parking lot or in his car and possibly held him at gunpoint?"

"There were chemicals in Labinski's and Cummings's blood. Our mad doctor changed his MO. Maybe Demarco posed a problem," Dominique shrugged. "The only similar substance in the toxicology reports are the coagulants used to thicken the blood in every case. Cummings's lab report will be different," he said absently and pulled himself from the start of a sway, irritated as he found Devinio's critical gaze. "I am guessing."

"Like hell," Devinio growled. "You haven't guessed about anything yet. What changed with Cummings?"

"He uh . . . he let her wake up," Dominique admitted in a leaden tone and scanned the nearest faces, his attention returning. "He allowed her to come awake. The others, I believe, were kept heavily sedated . . . Anesthetized throughout the procedure."

"Another bit of guesswork, huh? Procedure. He sees this as an operation."

"He . . . attempts to keep it clinical, yes, as if he's merely experimenting with a corpse," Dominique verified. "He tested the effects of lower sedation on Cummings. She was awake, and the terror killed her. Your forensic doctor will verify that detail. She had a massive coronary on his operating table."

"I think this is a good time to tell you, Mr. Jardonet," Devinio hesitated. "I'm glad you're on our side."

He was on neither side, he might have admitted, but his attention riveted as Mark Jarvins, another man, and the interpreter, Anita Duran, entered the combat zone. In a fleeting instant, Dominique knew this confrontation with Jarvins would fair no better than any past. Carrying himself with the lofty arrogance of an Aryan leader, Jarvins glanced over the bustling activity, and his attention riveted on one of the detectives near the door, apparently listening, alerted by something the detective had said. Noting the stranger following, likewise appearing arrogant and intrigued by the activity, Dominique's senses keened. In his early forties, with dark hair, sharp angles and planes on his cultured features, this newcomer dressed in a conservative style in a classic, tailored dark suit. With his quick, intense eyes and politician smile, he was either the mayor, sheriff, police commissioner . . . or district attorney.

As if zeroing in on a target, Jarvins flashed his gaze toward Dominique and zipped his attention toward Deputy Dartworth, veering his course. A thick folder rested on his hip, held aloft in one gripped hand. Duran likewise carried a manilla folder clasped at her chest and her sculpted brow kinked as she veered toward Dominique.

The transcript from the morgue, Dominique knew and glanced at Devinio. "If it's not too late, Lenny, you could confiscate those papers she's holding and keep them for your eyes only. I wouldn't mind."

"I think we have bigger problems," Devinio commented, his attention on his partner for a half second before looking at Dominique. "I have a feeling Mark won't be as happy as the rest of these folks with our progress."

"Hmm, should I take that to mean, I should invest in a bulletproof vest?"

"I really wish you wouldn't say shit like that," Devinio growled under his breath and forced the twitch of a smile for the benefit of Miss Duran as he offered a greeting in English.

She responded in kind, then lifted her gaze to Dominique, offering a similar amenity before reverting to English and verifying Dominique's suspicions. Her brow still troubled, she spoke for several seconds before handing the papers to Devinio, who appeared likewise affected. To Dominique, Duran offered, "I finished transcribing the tape in English, Mr. Jardonet. I . . . I really don't know what to make of it, sir. Other than to realize, you had a few very bad moments." And those moments worried her even now. Genuinely concerned, she searched him, apparently, fearing he might pass out and die before her eyes. The words and sounds on those tapes had scared her despite her Quantico training. "Are you truly all right, sir?"

"Fine, miss, but I appreciate your concern," he answered indifferently, his attention shifting to Devinio who'd already begun reading.

Without lifting his eyes, the agent eased onto the corner of the desk, his attention riveted on the pages in his hand.

Before Dominique could decide on appropriate action, tempted to slide the pages from Devinio's grasp, he sensed the hostility and connected with Jarvins' glare as the agent advanced. A few paces further back, the stranger stood listening to Dartworth, who bubbled as he enlightened their guest to the developments. Devinio's prognosis of his partner's rage fell slightly shy of the mark, and as Dominique held the blue fire, his natural defenses rose.

Rather than address him personally, Jarvins leveled his gaze on his partner. "I'd like to talk to you in private, Len. Now."

Clear. Crystal clear those American words rang in Dominique's ears, but they were anything but music.

Toward the interpreter, Jarvins spoke in a controlled, quiet rage. "Tell our guest we'll be right back and stay with him. And do not translate anything he says, or anything said to him until I get back."

"Excuse me?" Duran asked, apparently bewildered.

"Just keep him occupied," Jarvins said and flashed a glance off Dominique to his partner.

Devinio had lowered the pages, at least enough to look at Mark. Too professional to betray his internal thoughts of Jarvins' mental state, he asked, "Don't you think that's a bit unfair?"

"You and I need to talk. Outside," Jarvins stated.

Agreeing, Devinio glanced at Dominique. "I'll be back in a moment." He handed the papers to Duran as he commented, "Keep those to yourself for the moment, Miss Duran, and if our friend gets antsy, maybe you can get him a cup of coffee. He takes cream."

Interesting, this new development, Dominique watched both agents striding toward the doors. Several others in the room had taken notice. McAllory, sitting behind his desk, had heard Jarvins' order toward the agent, and by his pensive expression and glance toward Dominique, McAllory wasn't happy with his knowledge. In fact, the second glance toward the federal agents suggested contempt which might have slid off his tongue if not for the telephone at his ear. An ally, Dominique judged him before looking to the female agent, who adopted a cool clinical expression. "Your comrades departed in a hurry," he said in French. "Is there something I should know?"

"I'm sure it's nothing," she answered smoothly. "Can I get you a cup of coffee?"

He made her nervous even without Jarvins' order. He shook his head, smiling slightly. "Have you worked for the government long, miss?"

"A few years," she answered, uncomfortable under his gaze.

"Often in the field, are you?"

"Not too often," she answered evasively, omitting the fact that this was her first field trip. She was a clerical technician, a linguist.

"Will you read what you've translated for me," he asked and noted her anxiety double a few degrees with the indecision. The request wasn't exactly against her orders. Still, she hesitated as if the papers in her hand were exclusively the property of the Bureau. "Miss, I should remind you, my voice is on that tape you transcribed. Read it to me in French, my dear. I would just like to be sure you have missed nothing. That is to your superior's benefit, yes?"

Relieved and deciding not to take offense at his suggestion that she might have made a mistake, she nodded and looked around for a place they might sit down.

With natural ease and arrogance, Dominique touched her arm and gestured for her to come closer and share the edge of the desk beside him. Her tension hiked another degree, and in a fleeting instant, he knew his proximity, the scent of his cologne, and his touch sent a tiny little shiver down her spine.

Unfortunately, he suffered no such affliction. Instead, his heart hammered a leaden beat, and a flash of a dark-haired enchantress fleeted in his mind. Anger and pain slid through his system like oil and water as he spied over Duran's shoulder. No relief came with his ability to read the typed English text; any more than he felt anything as she began speaking the French words that he'd spoken hours earlier. Nothing. He felt nothing as she recited the words off the victim's lips and felt little as she nearly uttered the words of a madman, sounding like the female version of a maniac to his ears.

The exercise served a purpose, however. He heard now, the anxious words snapping between Devinio and Lincroft as he'd suffered what appeared to be a heart attack. He heard the shock in Jarvins' voice as the man had seen the physical manifestation of blood that Lincroft had attempted to stanch in futility. For a few insane seconds, he knew what they'd seen, what they'd feared. . . and it was no wonder the forensic pathologist had suggested he see a doctor. She was convinced he hemorrhaged on the morgue floor, and he wouldn't be surprised if she soon scheduled an appointment with the Bureau shrink. If he wasn't in such a foul mood, he might find that thought amusing.

Not amused, he listened as the young agent innocently recanted Mark Jarvins' words which suggested the fellow believed this ordeal a staged performance. Jarvins had stomped out of the room, stating that he'd have this 'bullshit' stopped.

Jarvins hadn't returned, but another male had joined them, and Lincroft had addressed him as 'Doctor.' Dr. Albert Rhoades, the acting coroner. In Duran's soft voice, the doctor's words became as clinical and clipped as Lincroft's despite the lofty tone. With Rhoades's help, Devinio had carried Dominique from that room, but nothing of that ordeal registered in his mind even now. Blackness. As Duran had noted, at least a half hour lapsed on the tape before Jarvins returned and collected the cassette. A half-hour of dead time. The dead time between suffering an episode and regaining the function of his life and limbs. Dominique owed Devinio a few words of gratitude. Doubtful Lincroft or Rhoades had willingly allowed an unconscious man to rest without medical attention for that length of time. Dominique could only imagine the battle waged between the agent and the doctors.

Duran barely finished when McAllory sidled from behind the desk, drawing Dominique's gaze from the typed page to his tense blue eyes. Flashing a glance to Duran, McAllory stated, "How about telling him something for me?"

"I'm afraid I can't do that," she said simply.

"You're an interpreter, right?" he asked in a cold voice, his gaze fixed on hers.

"Sir, I'm afraid I can't help you," she said with a note of apology despite her conviction.

McAllory looked past her toward his superior and raised his voice enough to be heard across the room. "Hey ya, Cap?"

Duran rose off her rested rump, her tension leaping as the young detective flashed her a wry smile, then started to continue within the paused silence. "I think when you get a minute—"

"Sir," Duran started.

McAllory continued toward his superior. "You better hire an interpreter or get one of Mr. Jardonet's pals in here."

"Listen, mister," Duran stated, taking a step toward the tall detective, glaring up at him, and lowering her voice. "You could be interfering with Federal jurisdiction—"

"Who the fuck you think you're kidding, lady?" McAllory said in an equally volatile tone, his Irish temper rising in his stark blue eyes. "The only one I'm interfering with here is that dickweed boss of yours, and from what I can see, he's been gunning for our visitor since they arrived. Now, you want to relay a few words, or do I escort our guest out to the reception room where I know at least one of his buddies is hanging out?"

"What is it you want to say?" she asked in a cool tone.

"Tell him, I think we narrowed the time down when Labinski was around the post office. We have a confirmation of him answering a call about four blocks away on the 18th. Tell him I have a few of our guys checking the post office to verify Jordan's schedule. Got all that?"

She nodded and eyed Dominique, who feigned curiosity. "The detective just wanted to express his gratitude for your assistance, sir. He says they're making progress."

Nothing of the lie appeared in her eyes, and that thought darkened the anger behind his own as Dominique nodded and found the detective studying him for a reaction. "As I said earlier, my friend, your gratitude is appreciated. If you're making progress, stop wasting time talking to me. You should be on the phone with the utility company checking Labinski's schedule." Glancing toward Duran, Dominique commented, "Verbatim, please."

Instead, she translated, "Mr. Jardonet appreciates your efforts, and you can keep him informed on your progress with Labinski's schedule."

Not entirely satisfied, McAllory nodded, but Duran wasn't out of the danger zone yet, and Dominique sensed her alarm as the deputy and his austere guest started across the room. She looked at Dominique, deciding, "If you'll excuse me, I have a few calls to make."

Dominique touched her arm, flashing a dismayed expression. "If you would postpone those, my dear, I would appreciate your help. I believe I'm about to receive another introduction."

Maintaining her calm impressively, she resigned to the inevitable, appearing no worse for the wear as Dartworth arrived, cheeks flushed and his eyes brimming with gratitude. "Miss Duran, if you'd do the honors. This is District Attorney, Adam Macanders. Adam, this is Insp. Dominique Jardonet," he said with careful emphasis on the last name. As if Duran was no more than a mouthpiece, not worthy of introduction, Dartworth nearly stepped on her to present Dominique in the best possible light. "Like I said, he doesn't speak English, Adam, but I'll tell you what—wish I had fifty more just like him on our payroll." He looked to Duran commenting, "You don't have to tell him that, miss, but you could introduce them."

Apparently, she chose to comply at least that far, seeing no escape. "Mr. Jardonet, this is Mr. Macanders, the District Attorney."

Macanders wasn't a man easily deceived nor impressed, and he apparently knew Dartworth well enough to doubt such an enthusiastic accolade. "Mr. Jardonet," he said with precise pronunciation. In formal French, he managed, "A pleasure to meet you. My French is not . . . very good. But . . . I understand, I owe you thanks."

This was a turn neither Duran nor, obviously, Jarvins, had anticipated. Smiling his appreciation, Dominique accepted the proffered hand and commented in rapid-fire, "Your thanks I humbly accept, but I should mention, the killer is not apprehended yet. An investigation of this nature could take more hours than I have spent, and whatever praise is due, should go to the exemplary investigators you have working in this office." He'd lost Macanders somewhere in the first half of his speech. Smiling apologetically, he offered, "Pardon me." Slowing down considerably, he commented, "I have the same difficulty with your language . . . People speak in fast forward, and I am left speechless." He shrugged, and Macanders' smiled his understanding. "Your investigators in this office deserve the praise. When this madman is captured, it will be due to their efforts."

Macanders was confident enough to admit his limitations. Without reservations, he looked to Duran. "Have I understood him in saying that I should thank this department for the possible apprehension of this psychopath?"

"Yes, sir," she said uncomfortably. "He feels their efforts should be praised."

Looking to Dominique, then Duran, Macanders commented, "Tell him I agree, but I think he's being modest if what I've heard and seen is any indication."

Obviously, those words were innocent enough to receive a literal translation. Dominique gestured his hand in a universal sign of dismissal, wearing his resignation in a slight smirk. "I am glad I could offer assistance. I only hope what I've given is enough to stop this madness."

Macanders awaited Duran's translation which she offered literally. Toward Dominique, the DA continued, "Are you familiar with the American justice system, sir?"

Duran repeated, and Dominique nodded with his simple, "Yes."

"From what you know about this case, do you believe we could compile enough physical evidence to gain a conviction if this were to go to trial?"

Duran was stuck. Macanders quite possibly knew enough French to catch her in a lie. Rather than literal, she looked to Dominique, "Mr. Macanders asks if you feel any evidence could result in a conviction in a trial?"

Toward Macanders, Dominique spoke honestly, "It's too soon to discuss a trial, my friend. We have narrowed the field of this maniac, but we must identify him before we can catch him or convict him. If you have an accurate account of the profile, you know he's smart."

Macanders looked to Duran, and she started a liberal translation. "Please, Miss. Quote him if you will. This isn't an easy request, and I know I'm asking a great deal, but I would like to hear his take on this situation."

Stuck, she looked at Dominique. "Would you repeat your words, sir?"

With slight deviation, Dominique repeated the words, offering an understanding smile and looking to Macanders as she again translated at least the first part literally.

She added a few words, however. A few very important words.

". . . I would rather not discuss my thoughts yet."

Macanders looked at him, speculating and intent. "I assure you, I've been involved in this nearly from the start. Can you tell me this? Is it possible this killer came from France?"

Duran repeated the words loosely, obviously to suit her own purpose since she looked at Dominique with genuine curiosity in her eyes.

Likewise speculating, Dominique answered, “If so, my friend, I’m not aware of it. I was recruited by your FBI more by coincidence than by personal experience. France has its share of madmen, but this isn’t one of them.”

Duran translated, “I don’t believe that is possible, but the Federal Bureau who recruited me could tell you more. France has its own lunatics, but this isn’t one of them.”

At least she hadn’t jeopardized international relations, Dominique mused behind his sympathetic gaze toward Macanders. The fellow was no dunce; he appeared to doubt either the words or the translation. He apparently knew enough French to wonder if he’d heard an accurate account.

In a few seconds, he sized up the woman and her loyalties, judged the Federal Bureau’s track record in this case thus far, and realized her possible motives to cover the Bureau’s backside. He wasn’t a man easily fooled, and whether Duran realized it or not, she’d just singlehandedly destroyed whatever chance the Federal Bureau had of recovering the trust of this task force. Macanders wasn’t a symbolic figurehead paying a courteous visit to this backroom; he had, in fact, assisted in creating the team of top-notch detectives, working with the sheriff’s department and state investigators. This fellow wasn’t an outsider. He wanted this maniac in a courtroom with enough evidence to justify a few life sentences, if not the electric chair, and that was one case he intended to handle personally. Behind his quick brown eyes, the doubts spiraled and vanished as he nodded toward Dominique, the knowledge and understanding conveyed by his expression. In French, he managed, “Possibly we can talk again, Mr. Jardonet. If you need anything . . .” He brought his billfold from an inside pocket and removed a business card. Likewise producing a pen from his breast pocket, he added more numbers before handing Dominique the card. His gaze intent, he spoke simply, “Call me if you will.”

“I will. Thank you.”

Less than a half mile from Ryder Rd., Ronnie spotted the hand-painted signs tacked to trees, each spaced about a hundred feet apart, counting down to a pumpkin stand. Sure enough, in a wide dirt and gravel clearing tucked alongside a barn, an immense collection of pumpkins stood on fine display, crowded on the ground, on a hay wagon, on bales of hay. She nearly mistook the bib-coverall-clad man lounging in a modern lawn chair as a stuffed scarecrow; his straw hat befitted a stage prop in a movie set. As much as she feared betraying a few of her friends in Bentwood, she found herself stopped, climbing from the cab. A few small pumpkins, too cute to be ignored, littered the ground around the farmer's weathered boots.

"Howdy, miss," he said good-naturedly, animating to sit up from what might have been a doze.

"Hi!" she answered while striding directly toward him, her gaze darting over the fruits from softball to soccer ball size. Self-indulgent, she mused, deciding on the instant, the tadpole needed a pumpkin. Hollowed out, any of these gems might make a fitting fishbowl. Smiling at her introspections, she doubted the little imp would appreciate her thought of buying him a new home—something less apt to rock like a ship at sea when he needed to swim. Stooped, she scanned the cluster as if she might pin an award on the most pumpkin-perfect shape. "God, are these cute," she said honestly.

The farmer leaned on his forearms, now, governed by male etiquette not to rise and tower over her.

That she stooped less than a few feet from him, she lent no first or second thought while judging a few of the closest pumpkins.

"Me, I like those big uns over there," the man said idly. "A half dozen pies in any one of them."

Spotting exactly what she wanted, Ronnie leaned and plucked the bite-sized pumpkin from a slot between a few bully-sized brothers. With a stout little stem and perfect orange complexion, the pumpkin looked as if it'd been crafted by man and poured from a mold. She refrained from smelling it to make sure it was real.

"Any chance you have a little one you're looking to please?" the man asked.

"A very little one," Ronnie said with a smile. "And this is exactly the right size." *Too small to be considered a fishbowl. Perfect*. And with a thought of Donna, Ronnie continued a careful scan picking out another tiny-tot pumpkin and two others, slightly larger, for Deedee and Tee. Stepping gingerly through the makeshift pumpkin patch, she collected the others, returning to the farmer with her hands full. "Several little ones," she said lightly. "And I think this should do it." Until she spotted another, larger pumpkin standing out among the horde. Wade might like that one, and despite his uncanny wisdom beyond his years, he was still a kid. "I think I'd like that big one there, too," she decided and caught the elder man's peculiar gaze. For a few minutes, she'd entirely forsaken her more serious mission in Elmview, but something in the way the man studied her created a sobering alarm. "Something wrong, sir?"

Pushing off his padded lawn chair, his lined brow and speculating eyes remained pensive even as he glanced toward the pickup. "Seems to me it was a young fella driving that pickup the last time I saw it around here."

Big surprise. Relaxing, Ronnie smiled, "That would be my husband."

"Nice young fella . . . Zack, ain't it?"

Close enough—*again*, she noted. "That's him."

"He's not come by in a while. Everything's all right with him, isn't it?"

With an uncanny prickle at the nape of her neck, Ronnie maintained her smile. "Everything's fine. He was planning on coming with me, but something came up at the last minute. Do you know him well?"

"He stopped out this way a few times," the man commented. "Matter of fact, the last time he was here, he mentioned looking for a couple things. Told him if I come across what he was needing, I'd hang onto them for him, and so happens, I got around to cleaning out my shed. I set some things aside. If you're not in a hurry, maybe you'll want to take a look, see if he's still in the market for them."

Coincidence? Doubtful. "Let me just put these in the truck," she said lightly, noting the man ambling toward the large pumpkin she'd indicated.

All too quickly, she found herself standing just inside the open doors of the upper level of an incredibly huge barn. Below deck, the sounds of rutting, grunting pigs filtered through the wide planks and an open stairwell. To either side of a hay-dusted runway, mounds of neatly stacked hay bales towered to the sturdy 'beamed rafters overhead. Two tractors stood side-by-side directly in front of her, one new enough to appear straight off the assembly line floor. Hay wagons and farm equipment crowded the deeper regions of the runway. Without a doubt, this was a working farm . . . and this elder man had probably known Hank Ryder most of his life.

Standing aside, Ronnie listened as the fellow routed around inside a cove-style storage area beneath the hay. Early to mid-sixties, she estimated and considered how much this fellow might tell her about the Ryder estate and subsequent plans to countermand the old man's Will. Probably, a great deal. His farm probably butted the Ryder estate at one junction or another. Five hundred-plus acres could wind between a few hills and would connect somewhere.

Hoisting a wooden box, the man emerged from his storage room, and the crate appeared light as he lowered it smoothly to the floor. "This is it here," he said and stooped, lifting, and tipping open the lid. "Now, I'm not sure he'd want the whole load, but you're welcome to pick out whatever you think he'd be of a mind to need."

Tools, she noted while stooping alongside the filthy crate. Stamped, signed tools with solid wood handles and iron, from routers to a claw hammer and Ronnie knew precisely who Jade had in mind when mentioning his interest in antique tools.

Milt Freshcorn. It was well known that Milt collected old tools, cleaned them up, and displayed them within a room he considered a den. For months, Milt had ambled around town appearing far older than his thirty-odd years, a mere skeleton of the fun-loving hen-pecked husband he'd been before this past summer. Milt hadn't bounced back nearly as fast as a few others. An entire box of tools like his great granddaddy had willed to him, just might brighten his spirits for a little while at least. God knows, Milt was a pleasant enough guy. He could use a boost, Ronnie decided while picking through the lot.

"How much for the whole box?" Ronnie asked. All business now.

"Figure on getting about two hundred for the lot," the man said simply.

Calculating, she estimated about twenty bucks a tool. "One seventy-five?" she ventured.

"There's a couple pretty fine pieces of equipment in there," the farmer commented.

"One seventy-five and twenty-five for the pumpkins?" Ronnie mused and caught the twinkle in the fellow's eye. The pumpkins were probably worth about ten bucks.

"You drive a hard bargain, ma'am," he said solemnly. "But I guess that sounds fair. You got yourself some tools . . . and pumpkins," he added sheepishly.

Obviously, she was as bad at haggling as her husband, and they'd certainly never get rich in this business. Jade would probably sell the box to Milt for twenty bucks. "Great."

Without needing to be asked, the fellow hoisted the box and rose.

As they headed toward the pumpkin patch and pickup, Ronnie wondered, "You wouldn't know if there's any land for sale out this way, would you? Zack and I have sort of been looking for someplace to call home. We've talked about relocating a few times, and I'll tell you, the longer I'm here, the better I like this scenery. I stopped by the tax office and talked to Mabel about it, but she wasn't sure if there was anything available. We wouldn't need a lot of land. Maybe around twenty acres or so . . ."

Monty, nicknamed thus through his last name, Manson Montgomery began as if a floodgate opened. "Twenty acres or so, huh . . . 'There's a lot of land just going to seed around here. Used to be, we put out enough corn and wheat in this area to feed about ninety percent of the state, and that's saying something when you're talking all the farms over in Lancaster and Carlisle . . . Not many small chunks of land and most of the bigger tracts are getting bought up by corporations."

And suddenly, Monty was mad. Leaning against the pickup's fender, the tools, and pumpkins tucked safely against the tailgate, Monty started talking. "Tell you, old Hank would roll over in his grave if he knew what his kin was up to . . . close to six hundred acres . . ."

Suffering a condition of informational overload, Ronnie drove toward Elmview, vaguely aware of the dusk shadows settling over the highway and the sky turning a platinum gray overhead. According to Monty, Kyle Ryder, one of Hank's youngest sons and a member of the town council—retired superintendent from the power plant down the road—was singlehandedly responsible for bringing the Industrialists into the bidding for the estate. If Monty was right, the trouble had begun brewing even before Hank passed away, and Monty wouldn't be a bit surprised to learn that Kyle had something to do with that untimely event. "Hank might have been up in years, but I can tell you, he was one of those old timers who could have probably lasted another hundred or so. Tough as nails, that old son of a bitch."

Despite the derogation, Ronnie had recognized the fondness in that title and the respect belying Monty's words. On a tangent, not unlike Finn, Monty had mentioned a few of the more infamous battles he'd fought with Hank Ryder. As much as two years ago, Hank could be found on his tractor at the first signs of spring, plowing, seeding, and fertilizing the land that his father had fought in the Civil War to defend.

The Rebels had never reached this far north during that incursion, Monty had professed, but a few sizeable battles had been waged due east and a few others slightly south. Monty's grandfather and uncle had both fought alongside the Ryder males, and Monty still had a few of the medals tucked away for his grandchildren to cherish. The Ryders and Montgomerys were built of solid, down-to-earth grit and determination, traits passed down through the lines. Monty's eldest son had made a career in the Marines . . . Ryder's grandson, Jason, was off stationed in the Philippines. ". . . There's going to be hell to pay when that boy gets back. He was closer to his granddaddy than that whole passel of others, and I'll tell you, I think there's something fishy with that whole Will business . . . Wasn't like Hank to up and chuck the farm to a bunch of whiners. Last he and I talked, he was planning to turn the whole place over to Jason and his brother Scott. Between the two of them, they probably would've kept the farm going. This business of him allegedly wanting the place sold off.. .? It don't make a damn lick of sense. You'd have to know Hank to understand. If he liked you, you wouldn't find a more honest friend, but if he didn't, you never had to work hard to know it. He'd just as soon tell a freeloader where to get off as to put a coin in a hard-working boy's hands. . ." And Monty was one of those boys, Ronnie soon discovered.

The land on which the Montgomery farm was built had once been an extension of the Ryder land. The War Between the States had determined the change, but the Montgomerys had run into hard times back around the Depression. Monty was barely making enough to make ends meet when Ryder offered him a loan, holding title to the land until the debt was eventually repaid. "Took me twenty years, but by God, I hold title to my land . . ." And Ryder had never once asked for a payment.

"Ryder," Ronnie had said, feigning a need for thought as she'd idled a glance over the hills and fields which spread out from either side of the highway. "Seems to me I heard that name mentioned somewhere this morning . . . Something about a funeral . . ."

Jack Trumble's name had joined the conversation, and Monty had no qualms at mentioning his opinion that Jack hadn't accidentally sailed his Buick off Conway Rd. "Jack was never any prize . . ." Monty had commented, showing only natural respect for facts and the dead, awarding the deceased the same amount of respect he might have earned in life. "After he hooked up with the Parker clan, he learned a few new tricks, but the potential was there . . . damn shame, him getting killed and mighty convenient, too. If anybody was in on that swindling, Jack was a likely candidate. I figure it this way though—Jack wasn't as brave as all that . . . somebody probably had some dirt on him and used him. He might a got a conscience, after all, his boy and Jase Ryder were close before Jase enlisted . . . Could be Jack didn't know what he was getting into. The good Christ knows Jack wasn't hurting for money . . ."

Monty had offered a whole new twist, and the first name 'Kyle' now attached to the last name Ryder, only verified her thought. The Ryders had far more to gain than the financial retribution afforded by a quick profitable sale to a conglomerate. If Hank Ryder was the patriarch of the family, and he'd fully intended to cut his immediate heirs from his Will, it wasn't much of a stretch to imagine the hostility of a few elder clansmen. What a way to spite an old man who might have outlived his usefulness in a few opinions.

The Will.

CHAPTER 18

Devinio had returned to the chaos alone, and not surprisingly, Miss Duran caught him partway and took him aside, speaking at a volume not to be overheard. Despite his speculating gaze on the wall, Dominique heard and understood her whispering her confession and enlightening Devinio about the exchange between the DA and their French visitor. Macanders had departed, taking the chief investigator with him for a private powwow, and Dominique needed neither imagination nor psychic power to know what they were discussing. Duran had further jeopardized the already faulty lines of communication between the Bureau and the police commissioner's exclusive task force. Macanders wasn't of a forgiving nature, and he carried enough clout on every political level to apply pressure.

A man with a mission was a terrible thing to waste, Dominique mused as he continued studying the map of Cleveland as if searching for the mysteries of the universe.

A few dozen paces away, Devinio spoke in a low annoyed tone, "I really wish you hadn't done that, Miss Duran."

"What was I supposed to do?" she asked with a defensive edge. "I don't know who this guy is, but judging by Mark's reaction to him, he doesn't trust him, and I can't say that I do either. There's something not . . . right about all of this. About him."

"Taking that into consideration, Miss Duran," Devinio said in a restrained voice. "Don't you think it's just slightly possible that he understands enough

English to know you sabotaged his communication with the fucking DA? We might not have a second required language in this country, but you damn sure know most foreign countries teach a mandatory English class."

"I was following orders, Agent Devinio, and I can assure you, I didn't say anything to reflect badly on either the Bureau or this investigation. If even half of what I've heard and seen in this room is any indication, I don't think we can afford to let this Frenchman become any more involved."

"You know what's contained in that transcript you handled," Devinio said calmly. "What's your take?"

"My take is, we're dealing with more than one unstable personality, and the sooner we remove Mr. Jardonet from this investigation, the better. Where's Mr. Jarvins?"

"If you hurry, you can probably catch him outside. The last I saw him, he was calling a cab."

"What?"

"As of ten minutes ago, this case was dumped in my lap," Devinio stated. "Mark's on his way back to DC. Now, let me put this to you gently, Miss Duran—either you can enlist your skills for the greater good, which does not mean tampering with the translations you're asked to offer, or I can have you shipped out of here. Regardless of your personal opinions of our mysterious guest, someone—with a helluva lot more knowledge than either of us—feels he's not only qualified but experienced enough to help break this case. And bluntly, honey, from what I've seen in the past few hours, I don't have any doubts. Now, are you staying or leaving?"

"My orders were to come here and transcribe that tape. Unless they've changed—"

"They've changed," Devinio interrupted. "Your new orders are to act as our visitor's interpreter and to translate his words literally. I don't give a damn if someone tells him to kiss their rosy ass, I want those words conveyed to him. Diplomacy, bedamned, miss. Do not edit or censor a single word. Do I make myself clear?"

"Perfectly," she said, not pleased.

"Good," Devinio stated. "Now let's go see how much damage you've done."

A great deal more than Dominique was willing to admit. Indifferently, he glanced toward the advancing agents.

Several detectives in the room sent skeptical glances toward them, but if Devinio noticed, nothing showed on his face. Apparently, the Bureau had taught him how to handle contempt and distrust. "*Comment vas-tu?*" he asked with a wiry flash.

"French?" Dominique asked with a flash of amusement. "Fine. You?"

In Italian, he answered more comfortably, "I've been better."

"A problem?"

"My partner had to return to the capital, and I just became the senior agent in this investigation."

"Your partner . . . He makes a habit of starting things he cannot finish, no?" Dominique asked and noted Devinio's flash of memory. Four months ago, Jarvins had taken a similar approach, but doubtful he would forfeit his involvement, now, any more than he had then—not when he had his nemesis again in his sights.

Whether Devinio questioned his partner's departure or the sarcasm in Dominique's words, doubt fleeted in his eyes. "Don't underestimate him," he said with a careful warning and a hint of discontent. "Officially, he's still on this investigation."

"Ah, then he chooses to remain safely behind the lines, eh?" Dominique pushed, not well concealing his greater contempt. "I'm not surprised."

"I'm not about to defend my partner here," Devinio said with his temper on hold, his gaze steady. "It takes two to tango, and I think you've gone out of your way to make him look like an asshole."

"Such credit, I do not deserve, my friend. He manages that well enough on his own," Dominique said with a spark of dark amusement in his eyes and smirk, shrugging. "He's an asshole."

Devinio hesitated. His attention distracted momentarily to notice the hushed voices and the semi-attentive audience in the nearest vicinity. His gaze returned, "I don't have time for this shit, and neither do you. I've enlisted Miss Duran as your personal translator. Do you have a problem with that?"

Dominique glanced off the visibly uncomfortable woman, mocking speculation and a warmer smile. "Such a lovely woman? How could I object?" he asked, his sarcasm concealed behind an innocent expression. "I believe she is ah . . . afraid of me. Is it just me? Or has she heard too many romantic tales of lascivious Frenchmen?"

"Probably just you," Devinio commented offhandedly, attempting to jest. "You send off too many vibes like you're perpetually on the make."

"I should resent that, yes?" he asked with a quick smirk that suggested the opposite.

"Doubtful," Devinio commented and returned to English, addressing Duran. "He's agreed to accept you as his translator. Make sure he understands anything and everything developing in this room, and if he has questions or comments, relay them." Reverting to Italian, Devinio started, "I need to step out for a little while. I'll be back—"

"I won't be here," Dominique commented.

"Excuse me?"

"I need to visit the crime scenes, friend. The pictures in this room, even the evidence has been handled too often to gain insight. I know where this killer is. I need to know where he was."

"No," Devinio said bluntly, his gaze intent. "Not yet anyway. Maybe after I talk to—"

"We work well together, Agent Devinio, but we aren't attached at the hip. Enlist an escort—Det. McAllory—to show me around."

Tense, Devinio stated, "Knowing what I know about how those scenes could affect you, I can't justify letting you go alone—"

"You are not my keeper," Dominique stated, his gaze darkening. "And you are not personally responsible for my safety any longer. I thought you understood that earlier. I may be here at the request of the Federal Bureau, but I don't answer to you. Pave the way, my friend, and trust that I have some clue as to what I'm doing."

"I don't have any doubts about your qualifications. I'm slightly more concerned with how your escorts could react to what you do and . . . the physical problems you could encounter. I think you better stay in my company a little while longer—"

"There is no option," Dominique interrupted, holding Devinio's gaze. "We are parting company. I am traveling with McAllory, your interpreter, and my own, and ah . . ." His gaze traveled off Devinio, searching absently, landing on a female detective currently engaged in a telephone conversation at the far end of the room. He hadn't heard her name, hadn't received a formal introduction, but she'd brought him a decent cup of coffee. Blond-haired, blue-eyed, she wore plain clothes—blue jeans and a yellow blouse. Not beautiful by his standards, but attractive in a careless way which appealed to him far more quickly than the blond at his side. "Her," he said and brought his gaze to Devinio. "The young woman in the corner. Will you tell them, or shall I?

The Elmview Library resided in one of the older homes, three blocks off Maine. With a slope of grass, a dozen cement-molded steps, and a small wrap-around porch contrary to the Victorian style, the house with its gables and scallops had maintained its elegance. Within the dusk shadows and shade of a single oak in the sideyard, Donna rested on a park bench, apparently intent upon her open notebook, until Ronnie pulled to the curb. She could pass for an industrious college student even in decent light, but slapping the notebook closed and collecting her purse anxiously, she increased the image a hundredfold.

Barely opening the passenger door, she huffed, "About time. I was beginning to get a little worried."

"Sorry. I hope you weren't waiting too long," Ronnie said, still too distracted to sound entirely chastened. "Find anything good?"

"I haven't decided," she said while yanking the door closed. "I did happen to remember why I chose Interior Design and the Arts over something exotic like Academic Administration. Did I mention at all—I absolutely despise research?"

With a humph, Ronnie glanced at Donna's laughing eyes and shook her head. "Guess you forgot to mention it, and you're full of it anyway," she said offhandedly and pulled onto the street. "You hungry?"

"Should we discuss this in a restaurant?"

"How about Chinese? Carry-out? We can regroup at the Inn."

"Sounds good."

"Great. I'm starving," Ronnie decided and made the right turn toward Main. Not surprisingly, the sidewalks were a little busier than in the afternoon hours. With the college campus within walking distance and frat houses scattered throughout the general population, an abundance of food chains, pizza outlets, and hot dog shops vied for dollars. Finding a parking space was easy. Far easier than wading into the flood of hungry bodies laughing, chatting, and arguing in droves. Fast-food containers, plastic drinks, and books were as intermixed and matched as blue jeans, baggy t-shirts, streaked hair, and dangling earrings. Identity crises screamed from every ensemble, a few only slightly more outrageous than the norm.

For the most part, the groups minded their own business, slightly above the age for catcalls and macho gestures. If not genuine academics and serious students, the majority appeared to pose as upcoming intellectuals, more reserved and cloistered than a gathering of head-bangers or rock-star groupies.

Every crowd had its exception, however, and Ronnie spotted the haughty group at the next corner, almost grateful to have parked in the opposite direction. Shaved heads, chain necklaces, earrings . . . macho. The males wore only t-shirts with the sleeves torn off to display their tattoos on muscled biceps and forearms. Only four, but their presence carried an impact. Several young adults crossed the street to offer these lounging, sniggering fellows a wide birth.

Noting one of them looking in her direction, Ronnie avoided the glance, glad to stride into the din of the Chinese restaurant where snatches of conversations kindled thoughts of her college days. Funny, she felt old, but listening to these anxious voices and heated debates on such eternal subjects as existentialism and the right to vote, she remembered the zeal of those early academic days. Not that long ago, she'd stood in these youngsters' shoes, determined to change the world and right the injustices of mankind.

With Donna a step behind, Ronnie waded close enough to the counter to read the menu board and needed most of the ten-minute wait to decide what she would eat. Inevitably, whatever Donna mentioned "considering" sounded better than whatever Ronnie had "decided" to order. In a last-ditch effort to satisfy their unruly appetites, they decided on two separate entrees along with several side dishes, all of which they would split down the middle.

"We are not good for each other," Donna decided as they started back to the pickup with two large brown bags of Chinese food. "At this rate, we'll both be as big as a house before Christmas."

"I'll just switch places with Jade and move into the warehouse when I can't fit through the apartment door. You're welcome to join me. I'm sure we can convince Jade to evict his fleet, and Tim's handy with wood. He could probably build us a bed the size of a battleship." Her words fading, Ronnie recognized the four bald heads lounging around the parking meter at the pickup's rear bumper.

"Damn it," Donna uttered under her breath. "I wouldn't mind having Tim's sidearm about now."

"I never leave home without one," Ronnie said as she slid her hand smoothly from the purse strap into the rat's nest of wares within her purse. With an economy of motion and no hitch in stride, she found the cold steel grip of the Saturday Night Special, silently thanking Len who'd insisted she keep the derringer after the mishap months ago. At her side, Donna stifled a step but kept pace. Within the confines of her purse, Ronnie unsnapped the holster strap and fingered the safety off. As much as she'd always detested guns, she despised becoming a victim more, and compliments of a certain farmer, she'd vowed never to find herself in a compromising situation again.

The largest, apparently the leader, stood boldly leaning against the tailgate. His muscled forearm draped over the edge; a smile twisted on his thin lips. Well over six foot, he wore a t-shirt at least two sizes too small, stretched across his muscled chest. The logo, hand-painted in red ink, carried a racial slur, suggesting death as an answer to eradicate the lesser races. With the material stretched to the limit, however, the words appeared more pink than red, and as Ronnie advanced, she wondered if he had any idea how stupid he looked. Her thoughts halted as she spotted the tiny pumpkin in his grip, no larger than a baseball in his massive fingers. Her temper flared on the instant, and she barely controlled the urge to draw, aim, and fire . . . over a pumpkin.

Damned hormones!

Cocky, the young man, no older than twenty, fingered the pumpkin, fitting it in his hand as if he might wind up a pitch at any second. Bald pate glistening under the arc light directly overhead, he sniggered at her, then glanced to his companions as if judging his supremacy. "Didn't I tell you these bitches were hot?" he chided.

Ronnie glanced at the others as she stopped a few steps from the intruder. With Donna less than a half step behind, Ronnie wouldn't venture any closer than necessary. Without a need to raise her voice, she commented, "You really don't want to do this." Reasonably, gently, she continued, "I'd appreciate it if you'd return my merchandise to the truck, unharmed, and go about your business."

"See, that's what I'm doing," the leader chided. With his bald head and likewise bald face, he appeared ridiculous, and far too young for the macho image and muscled body. Too bland to be considered attractive, only his eyes conveyed his intellect and intensity. "I'm making you dolls my business. So, what do you say? You and me can ride up front. The bitch can ride with my pals back here. We have a party to get to—“

“You can’t possibly be as dumb as you sound,” Ronnie interrupted, noting the young man’s posture firm, the offense hitting its mark. “Return that pumpkin to my truck.”

“I don’t know who the hell you think you are, bitch—“

“The bitch who will castrate you where you stand with a twenty-two bullet unless you put the goddamn pumpkin down very carefully and get the fuck away from my truck,” she spoke in a descending tone, her eyes as cold as cobalt and chilled as dry ice. “I won’t tell you again, asshole.”

“You’re bluffing, bitch,” he said, but his pals had already firmed from their languid posture losing their thin smiles. “You don’t have a fucking gun—“

“Call my bluff, asshole,” Ronnie challenged without changing her tone. “I’d like nothing better than to give your father a daughter.”

“Even if you had a fucking gun,” he chided, struggling to maintain his smile. “You wouldn’t fucking use it.”

“I won’t kill you,” she said offhandedly as if it mattered neither here nor there, would spare him only for the hell of it. “But you won’t be using your third leg for the rest of your life. The choice is yours, shit-for-brains,” she said bluntly. “I’ll tell you though—I’ve seen the damage a bullet can do, and you won’t have enough left of the family jewels to make a decent hamburger. Now, put the pumpkin back in my truck and get the fuck out of here, or you won’t need to worry about getting expelled for misconduct or going to jail for attempted rape. You’ll be too busy learning how to piss through a plastic tube.” And to confirm her words, she lifted her hand just enough for him to see she wasn’t bluffing about the gun. Her gaze held steady, she watched his attention dart, saw the bald pate pale slightly and his lips freeze in a near comic, grizzly grin.

He needed another few seconds to figure it out and lifted his flaming blue eyes to her. “You’re one crazy bitch,” he said in a lower voice.

"A girl's gotta have fun sometimes," Ronnie said with a twitch of a smile that relieved nothing of the bright shine in his eyes. He barely started to shift his hand as if to pitch the pumpkin. "Don't even think about it," she warned in a lower tone. "Put it down very carefully, 'cause I'll tell you, that little pumpkin means more to me than you do. If you even scraped its hide, I'm liable to come looking for you in the morning."

For whatever reason, he decided not to push his luck, eased his hand over the tailgate, and lowered the pumpkin without even whispering a thump. Far more slowly, carefully, he eased away from the bumper and flashed a hot glance to his companions. "Let's get out of here. They're probably fucking dikes," he said and apparently decided he had business across the street. That he nearly walked into an oncoming car enhanced his image, not at all. At the blast of the horn, he nearly jumped out of his skin and belatedly railed curses at the elder couple behind the wheel as they passed.

With a soft string of curses, Donna released her held breath and caught up as Ronnie reached the passenger door with her truck keys in hand. "I can't believe you just did that," Donna huffed, stifling a nervous, shaken laugh.

"He had Tad's pumpkin," Ronnie said and shrugged, unlocking the door with a steady hand. Very few pedestrians had stopped, most hurrying just a little to avoid calling attention to themselves. Apparently, the skinhead was the cock of the walk and a bully on campus. Belatedly amused, Ronnie strode around the front of the pickup, glimpsing the foursome striding purposefully down the opposite sidewalk. Len had insisted on the gun, but Jade had insisted on securing a permit, right after he'd agreed with Devinio on the benefits of carrying a weapon. A girl could never be too careful, and she certainly wasn't naive to the number of crazies running loose. The trend toward closing mental institutions certainly hadn't bode well for society. In fact, she might conduct a study to determine the ratio of occupants between new penitentiaries and old state hospitals over the past ten years. What the hell was the world coming to when a woman could be accosted in broad daylight in a town which should reflect the highest caliber of young adults?

Mulling over her internal kibitzing, mad again, Ronnie drove in silence, unconsciously, navigating a course toward the Inn.

"I still can't believe you did that," Donna interrupted in a soft huff. "Tell me the truth—would you really have shot him?"

"He had Tad's pumpkin," Ronnie repeated distractedly.

After a few seconds, Donna commented, "Assuming Tad's not a nickname for Jade . . . you've nicknamed the little one Tad?"

"Short for Tadpole," Ronnie said with a glance, drawing from her anger with the amusement in Donna's voice. "Has a nice ring to it, huh?"

Donna hesitated, then laughed, "You really are a little crazy, Rem."

"Well, that asshole just picked the wrong place and the wrong time, and the wrong lady to mess with. I'm tired of it, ya know? I'm sick to death of guys like that thinking that just because we have a nice ass or breasts, we're open season. You smile at the fuckers, and they automatically think you're in love. Bullshit. If he hadn't backed off, I'd have shot his balls off and dealt with the legal issues later."

Far more soberly, quietly, Donna commented, "You're thinking about Cal, huh?"

'*Two kinds of people,*' Max Hagen had said years ago. *'Victims and would-be victims . . . no in-between. Sometimes the craziest bastards I encounter were victimized a long time before they became the victimizer . . . Poor family values, abuse, psychological or physical, it doesn't matter. One way or the other, we're the compilation of where we've been and what we've endured. Large scale, small scale, we're either potential victims or victims.*'

And he was right, Ronnie considered absently.

"It's okay, ya know, hon. I mean, we never really talked about what happened . . . If you ever need to talk, I make a good listener."

"You do make a good listener," Ronnie agreed, appreciating Donna's quiet concern and empathy. "The thing is—there's not much to talk about. I wasn't really thinking about him. It's a collective consciousness, and I think . . . I think maybe I've already spent too many years viewing the dregs of society, actively involved in the madness between victims and would-be victims." Her thoughts turned, remembering.

"There was an incident in Chicago about three years ago. It was sort of a garden variety stalker case," she said absently. "This nut was following girls home from nightclubs . . . dark-haired girls," she admitted. "Three of them mentioned to friends that they felt like they were being followed in the few days preceding his attack. Nice, upstanding communities in the suburbs . . . Two of the girls opened their door to this guy, thinking he was a telephone repairman. No fucking ingenuity on his part—no serious effort. He stole the genuine uniform from a neighbor's apartment, stole a plain white van at least twice . . . Twice, he disconnected the phones with the women standing right over him the entire time. Of course, that was his version of the story . . . Four of those women were found bound, gagged, and raped before he rigged them up to a toaster and fried them on their kitchen floor . . . His mother made him do it," she said in a leaden voice and drew from the memory to realize she'd pulled into a parking space at the hotel's side entrance.

Even in the shadowy light, Donna's lovely face conveyed a haunting fear and her eyes shined with concern.

Forcing a faint smile, Ronnie shrugged. "Victims and would-be victims," she said quietly. "Max was right, that's what we all are. It's part of the ecosystem, a built-in factor created by some divine power to determine that eventually, we'll either propagate or annihilate. Given the choice, I prefer remaining a 'would-be.' I've already come too close to becoming the victim."

"I hate to break this to you, hon, but that's an extremely depressing philosophy."

"Whoever said it was a dog-eat-dog world, hit it on the money, and this dog bites," Ronnie stated. "Before I let some bald throw-back of the forties intimidate me, he's going to know it."

"Remind me never to get on your bad side," Donna decided with a soft smile. "And I promise, I'll never touch Tad's toys."

With the mocked solemnity in Donna's voice and expression, Ronnie lost the last of her anger. "I should probably mention, it could have been Guppy's pumpkin he was holding. I didn't get a good look."

"Guppy?"

"We can't both be carrying a tadpole. Yours has to be a guppy," Ronnie said bluntly. "Let's go eat. The smell in this cab's driving me nuts."

"That's what I like—a lady who can threaten to shoot the balls off a skinhead and sit down to a ten-course meal."

"God, if Tim hears you talking like that, he'll never let you get within ten feet of me again," Ronnie laughed.

"Honey, I grew up in Detroit. Granted, not a hotbed-of-gangs neighborhood, but we certainly learned the lingo of the local hoods."

As Ronnie stepped from the cab, laughing, she caught another sense of someone taking an interest, but a quick scan of the shaded semi-full parking lot offered no verification. Whatever this niggling sense of someone in the shadows, she couldn't afford to keep ignoring it. Not with the possibility of a hired gun in Elmview . . . and that was a possibility. Either one of the local boys had panicked and sent Jack Trumble off a cliff, or someone, with a serious financial interest in an industrial-sized dump, had a loose end to knot.

How many others, like Finn, had heard about a certain antique dealer marrying a certain investigative journalist? That was the question of the hour, and the answer was all too damned simple. Quite a few. The incident in Bentwood had sizzled across the news wire compliments of a few industrious reporters, and Elmview wasn't that far away from Bentwood. Anyone who knew the former Isaac 'Zack' Bently, owner of 'Olden Time Antiques and Collectibles,' could know he'd married Miss Veronica Bryson . . . 'The journalist instrumental in identifying and stopping the killing spree in Bentwood.'

Notoriety in her line of business was a two-edged sword, and she couldn't afford to overlook or ignore the possibility—not when the conspirators in the murder of Jack Trumble, and possibly, Hank Ryder, were already nervous.

In a weird moment, Ronnie found herself reaching over the tailgate, collecting the two tiny pumpkins, and depositing both in her purse. Shrugging to the peculiar, bemused look from Donna, Ronnie headed for the hotel door. "A girl can't be too careful with her pumpkins," she said lightly.

"Or her dinner," Donna laughed, holding the two sacks protectively. "Please tell me you have your hotel key handy."

"Got it covered," Ronnie said and slipped the access card from her jeans pocket. Essentials, those items relative to a hasty getaway or security, were always carried in the most convenient, easily retrievable location. Car keys, apartment or hotel keys, quarters for telephones . . . guns were secured to the inside pocket of her purse. She opened the side door and held it for Donna to pass, managing another quick scan of the parking lot. For a split second, the red-hot glow of a cigarette flared behind a shadowed windshield across the lot. Two-door, dark paint, Chevy if she knew her cars . . . and this didn't make a lick of sense. That car hadn't entered the lot behind them. If whoever rested behind the wheel had followed her or Donna's progress, he wouldn't have assumed they were . . . shit. Chinese takeout. How smart did this fellow need to be? Where else would two gals with Chinese takeout go to dine? One certainty, Ronnie wasn't about to leave things entirely to chance. Riding the elevator with Donna to the third floor, she accessed her room and started inside. "Damn. I forgot something in the truck." Producing a handful of quarters, she handed several to Donna. "If you want to catch our sodas, I'll be right back. Make mine a diet something."

"You've got to be kidding," Donna said. "Diet?"

"You're right. I'll live it up. Something with lots of sugar and not much else," Ronnie laughed and strode to the elevator. She'd need to approach the vehicle from the rear, and enough darkness had descended to assist in that enterprise. Assuming her surveillance fellow knew her room number, he'd parked on the appropriate side of the building, which should enable her to slip through the opposite side entrance without too much risk.

On the first floor, she strode the length of the hall, passing a few doors where muffled television voices verified occupancy. Apparently, she and Donna were not the only ones to decide on takeout to eat in. At the end of the hall, she found the rear exit that opened directly into the rear parking area. Garbage dumpsters camouflaged behind tall, classy fences offered enough concealment and shadows to cross diagonally toward the adjacent wooded lot that offered a rustic backdrop for the hotel. Trotting across a dozen feet of mowed lawn, Ronnie slid through the manicured bushes and ducked lower into the shadows before orienting within the shade. To her immediate amusement and relief, she found a path wide enough to accommodate a lawnmower circling the hedge.

Trotting, low to the ground, her hand tucked into her purse and gripped around the butt of the derringer, she paused only long enough to judge the distance to the car. Advancing from the rear of the lot, she gained a far better view despite the hedges through which she peered.

Not just one man behind the wheel. Two distinctive shapes occupied the front seat in silhouette against the brighter parking lot vapor lights. Cautiously, she continued her advance, conscious of every sound from the crackle of branches under a nocturnal animal in the bushes to cars passing on the highway. Only once, she stopped, held her breath, and dropped lower to the ground as a car entered the lot sweeping the hedges in headlight beams. Arriving within ten feet of the surveillance car, Ronnie stooped and waited, letting her eyes adjust to the darkness. She could barely make out the shape, much less the numbers on the license plate, and nearly uttered a curse aloud before miracle of all miracles, a car pulled into the parking lot of the family restaurant alongside the hotel. Light beams sped across the hedge around her, lancing the leaves, slicing through the peepholes—and illuminating the numbers as if shooting a laser beam for her explicit purpose.

Her heart smacked a quick, anxious beat, her attention riveted. A government plate . . . an official government plate. In her gut, the first flutters of motion distracted her with a sudden pang of alarm. Not now! Not this minute!

Tad! Be still! Just a few minutes, she pleaded silently, recording the numbers at the same time.

Hurrying, not positive what worried her more, the advance of another bout of nausea and vertigo, or the thought of government surveillance, she retraced her path through the shadows, trotting across the pavement to the exit door. Already, the dizziness threatened to cave in around her. Not here. Not in the hall. Skimming one hand on the wall, the other holding her stomach where the rocking and rolling had begun in earnest, Ronnie continued a clumsy trot up the hall. By pure luck, no one stepped from a room in her path. She slapped the elevator button, leaning heavily, nearly rolling over the edge of the door and clasping the safety bar inside to stay afoot. Not sick now. Just dizzy. Her knees felt like rubber. The lighted keypads designating floor numbers resembled an electric light show, moving and overlapping. "Damn . . . settle, Tad," she heaved softly. "Just let me get to our room . . . I saved your pumpkin, squirt . . . that should count for something."

And the irony reached her . . . she could thwart a six-foot wall of solid stupid, and one tiny tadpole was about to knock her on her tail.

CHAPTER 19

Conversations within the unmarked sedan had started and stopped a dozen times, cut short by either confusion or the distrust to flow from one body to the other. In the front passenger seat, Dominique continued to watch the passing scenery, as indifferent to the passing sights as the tension he'd created within the cramped quarters. Battle lines, he considered absently, venturing a glance to the fading daylight overhead. Within the car and without, he mused.

Behind the wheel of the sedan, Shawn McAllory had abandoned the attempt to communicate, but he was far less annoyed with his present circumstance than intrigued by the same.

Directly behind him, his associate, Det. Davis, recruited from the city homicide division, where she'd worked her way through the ranks by sheer grit and determination, wasn't as agreeable. Already, she harbored a natural rivalry for the Bureau after crossing paths with an arrogant Agent Springer who'd treated her like a secondhand citizen. She found the current Federal representative as *fake as a three-dollar bill* and *too damned lofty* for Chelsey's liking. The only benefit to this assignment, other than being dragged off the phone lines and away from her desk, was the opportunity to meet their guest. Unfortunately, the *stuffed shirt* alongside her wore all the earmarks of a *butler* with a *bulldog* attitude.

Rudemonje would have preferred escorting his *charge* to the fine hotel where their comrade had booked an appropriate suite of rooms. Finding that the Americans had booked Dominique Jardonet, son to one of the most prestigious gentlemen in all of France, in a common room—in an Inn which Rudemonje considered no more than a flophouse—was nearly more than he could tolerate. No son of Jean-Pierre Jardonet, much less this one, should be treated so negligently.

Anita Duran just wanted to go home. Belatedly, she wished she'd accepted the escape Agent Devinio had offered. This would be the last time she romanced the notion of becoming a 'field agent.' *Leave the field to the cows!* She preferred advancing her career through the educational lines of defense. Possibly, she'd request a transfer to a teaching post. With every mile, she traveled toward what she understood to be the scene of the first murder, her muscles coiled.

Unfortunately, Dominique bested her in that respect. With every passing second, he knew he followed the path of a killer, sensed the proximity of violent death even before McAllory halted at a stop sign and looked over at him.

"The hospital's about five miles north on this stretch. If, as we suspect, the Taxidermist brought Lowenstein directly to this apartment, he would have come this way," he paused, and in the backseat, both interpreters began speaking.

Over his shoulder, neither amused nor pleased with the quick response, Dominique addressed Duran. "Leave the translations to my associate if you please, miss. If he makes a mistake, feel free to intrude." Before she could protest, he addressed his comrade. "Claude?"

In concise, far more rapid native French, Rudemonje translated the words, and Dominique looked to McAllory, sensing relief and appreciation behind the intent gaze. When the translation ended, Dominique commented, "An inconvenience to have a translator, but my associate knows how to be heard and not seen. Please, continue driving. I recognize the street signs from the map."

In the backseat, Rudemonje spoke the English words with a soft accent, and McAllory nodded, accepting the situation and the order. Pulling into the flow of traffic on the busy thoroughfare, he commented, "I've never been out of this country, except to Canada a few times, but I always thought about going to Switzerland. Guess I better stick to England, huh?"

Awaiting the translation, Dominique mused, "England is overrated, my friend. Visit France—or your own motherland. Ireland and Scotland boast some of the most beautiful lands in the world. But that's my opinion, naturally."

"I don't know, I've heard the sights in Switzerland are pretty fine," McAllory mused, flashing a glance to the rearview mirror, undoubtedly, goading his comrade.

"Yea, you would pick Switzerland," Davis obliged in a muttered voice only until she realized Rudemonje had translated her words. "Hey, you didn't have to translate that, buddy."

Again, Rudemonje spoke her words, and Dominque glanced at her, catching her focus for the first time. Offering an apologetic smile that halted her protest and stifled her embarrassment, Dominique commented, "My companion is extremely well versed in his profession, miss. Please don't fault him for bridging our communication barrier'. It is ah . . . Refreshing . . . to hear uncensored words and natural voices for a change. Hearing and not understanding the words is like listening to a radio with a faulty antenna. Not pleasant."

She glanced off Rudemonje as he finished the translation; her eyes conveyed her understanding and apology. "I guess I didn't think of it that way. But I think maybe," she paused for Rudemonje's translation, then continued, still looking at him. "I guess maybe we're just afraid of offending you or sounding pretty damned stupid by comparison. You've traveled a lot, haven't you?"

"Enough to be fascinated, not offended by the cultures I encounter," he answered with a slight smile. "I have always found the company of Americans to be pleasant. Even when you're outrageous, you're basically honest."

She smiled, then laughed, "You find us outrageous."

"Oh, yes, in the extreme often, but I find that trait particularly charming since it appeals to my nature. Perhaps I am an American at heart, eh?"

She'd relaxed considerably, huffing another soft laugh, and not doubting his intended teasing. "Trust me, you hang around guys like McAllory too long, and you'll change your mind quick enough. Now, him? Even I'd consider outrageous."

"Hey, how'd I end up in this conversation?"

"Switzerland," she stated, flashing a glance toward the mirror, chiding him without an ounce of subterfuge behind her jab. "Take my word for it, you wouldn't have any more luck there than here."

"Women," McAllory huffed and flashed a glance to Dominique. "What are the women like in France? Any chance they're easier to get along with?"

"My friend, France is extremely old world, and the oldest profession is alive and well in my country," he said smoothly, and McAllory's firm jaw twitched as he flashed a side glance, undoubtedly withholding a laugh. "But as for being easier to get along with . . . doubtful."

In English, Duran stated crisply, "I really think we should find a proper subject, detectives. I'm sure Mr. Jardonet has more important things on his mind, and if I wanted this spoken in French, Mr. Rudemonje, I would speak in French. You don't have to translate it. I'm speaking to my American colleagues exclusively."

"Wie, mademoiselle," Rudemonje interjected and commenced translating her words.

"Mr. Rudemonje—" she started.

"Hey, lady," McAllory said with a fleeting glance over his shoulder, a smirk in his light brown mustache. "The rules have changed, and unless you'd like me to ah . . . mention a certain thing or two . . .?"

"Det. McAllory, I don't think it would be in your best interest—" She stopped short, realizing Rudemonje had completed several of the translations. Her own included.

Turning slightly, Dominique caught her too-bright eyes, reading the tension. "It wasn't my imagination that I received slightly censored translations, was it, Agent Duran?" he asked directly, and Rudemonje translated French to English.

"I'm sure I don't know what you mean, Mr. Jardonet. I certainly attempted to translate—"

"Miss, I'm rather adept at reading expressions and mannerisms. A talent, you might say, and please, don't mistake my ah . . . language limitations as a meter of my intelligence. If I were an idiot, I doubt I would be in this car. A fool perhaps for choosing this profession, but an idiot by no means."

The silence after Rudemonje's words lingered only a few seconds before McAllory commented, "I had a feeling you figured that out back in the office. That bit about censored conversations a few minutes ago . . . you knew?"

"As I said," Dominique said lightly, relaxing in the seat again. "I rely on more than words, and impressions sometimes speak far more honestly. If it's any consolation," he said as he glanced over the seat toward Duran. "I'm not easily offended. I'm sure you had your reasons, my dear. But uh . . . you were wrong," he said and caught Davis's eye, smiling slightly as he continued. "Discussing the subject of beautiful women is an acceptable conversation in any country. If it offends you," he glanced again toward Duran, catching her discomfort, smirking. "Accept my apologies."

"I wasn't offended," Duran stated in French. "I'd just prefer you didn't judge all Americans by . . . the crude nature of these detectives."

Rudemonje made the fateful mistake of translating her words to English, despite her quick attempt to stop him, silence him.

"Hey, bitch?" Davis said, leaning to look past Rudemonje, who belatedly realized that he sat between two rival females. "You haven't seen crude, but I'd be happy to show you how crude I can really be."

"I'm sure Mr. Jardonet's seen and heard enough, Det. Davis—"

Obviously annoyed, Rudemonje snapped the French words and held Dominique's gaze. "This could become a problem, Dominique. Perhaps, we should ask our driver to pull over and let them fight outside the car."

"My money's on the blond," he mused and caught Duran's startled eyes pivoting on him. Smiling, he shrugged. "I could not lose, yes?"

"I think this has gone far enough, Mr. Jardonet—"

"Unfortunately, you are absolutely right," he said and turned into his seat as McAllory slowed for a turn. A half block away, slouching between several run-down tenements, most of which had been turned into warehouses in serious need of repair, the apartment building where Lowenstein had breathed his last breath loomed against a platinum sky. This wasn't the type of neighborhood where children romped and played. Several teenagers lingered on the next corner. A vacant lot, enclosed by a Cyclone fence that had long since been breached by wire cutters, held a few more teens slapping a basketball about on cracked tarmac and broken glass. Uncomfortably aware of the tension slipping down his spine, Dominique remembered the timeframe, realizing someone should have seen Lowenstein's car rolling down this street. Someone should have seen . . .

"The alley," Dominique said absently as his attention riveted on the building. "Drive around the block, my friend, approach from the rear entrance," he said, and Rudemonje translated in a noticeably different tone.

Warehouses. The front of the building faced other similarly battered buildings and dilapidated houses, but the rear angle provided far more camouflage. Even before McAllory made the two right turns and pulled into the alley, Dominique sensed his accuracy. With warehouse entrances and crumbling stone walls bisecting the narrow canyons, the killer had passed unseen to his destination . . . and he'd passed through these alleys several times in preparation. Already, Dominique's temple pulsed, drawing his hand to massage the uncomfortable pressure. Footprints, as if this maniac had left his footprints in the ruined brick and cracked gravel, the feeling of trespass grew with every second.

"Like the report said," McAllory spoke in an all-business tone. "We think our guy had a getaway car parked in one of these buildings, but we never found any evidence to prove it. As you probably noticed, this isn't the kind of place a guy would leave a car parked in the street for any length of time. It's also not the kind of place anyone would admit to seeing anything or anyone like a lone walker. The nearest decent neighborhood is about two miles away and the nearest hotspot for a crowd to linger at midnight is three miles the other way. I don't think our guy took a chance on walking too far."

"He had a car," Dominique said vacantly as McAllory stopped within a large, shadowed inlet. On one side, an industrial garbage receptacle stood against a wall, out of place within the clutter of bags and cardboard boxes strewn over the alley floor. On the other, cracked railings barely marked the subterranean entrance, which might have accommodated a handyman or building super in another era. Slipping from the car, Dominique trailed his gaze skyward to the broken fire escapes, boarded windows, and gutters dangling dangerously close to electric lines to crisscross the canyon-like clotheslines. The arc lights were long since destroyed or burned out and never replaced, but the skeletal remains suggested a pleasant atmosphere a lifetime ago.

Drawing a breath, he felt it . . . the by-gone years. Voices and music . . . shouts and friendly greetings alike. Before he could sway, a gunshot blasted him from the nostalgia, and he stood, poised to duck before he realized the sound had come from the past. Releasing his held breath in a slow, calming sigh, he drew his attention to the foursome joining him in the shadowy light.

Davis and McAllory had both planned ahead; Davis snapped on her flashlight, apparently testing the batteries, as McAllory commented, "The electric's still on down there, but that's not saying much. By now, someone probably swiped the bulbs we replaced, and most of the sockets were either broken or ripped out."

"There were ah . . . empty sockets," Dominique said hesitantly, and Rudemonje translated.

"The two main ones," McAllory answered smoothly. "You didn't miss a thing in those reports, did you?"

"Suppose not," he said, in no hurry to reach the stairwell. In fact, now that he stood within this alley, he would prefer to return to the car and race as far away as possible. Unconsciously, he lifted his cigarettes from his jacket, killing a few seconds to light a butt. Snapping the silver lighter shut, he drew a hearty inhale and stood, scanning either direction. His head thudded with an increasing pulse at his temple. Squinting, nearly flinching, he reconsidered his need to enter the lair of a madman. Too late, he nearly uttered aloud, far too late yet again to back away, and why bother?

With that simple question in his mind, the tension slid from his spine, replaced by relief. A weight had lifted. *Why bother, indeed?* This was who he was. What he was.

Turning, he found the federal agent watching him, apparently anticipating something as dramatic as Dartworth had awaited hours earlier. A great performance. An elaborate show. *A hoax?* His tone chilled considerably as he decided, "I believe you should wait out here, Miss Duran. Watch the car and see that we're not left stranded. You are armed, yes?"

"I'm armed, but I think Det. Davis—"

"Det. Davis has visited this place before," he interrupted. "She may tell me things that you cannot. Mr. Rudemonje," Dominique said as he turned his gaze to the older gentleman. "Do you have an objection to accompanying me into this scene of a murder?"

"No, sir," he answered.

"Very well," Dominique said and motioned to his escorts, flashing a glance between them that needed no translation. McAllory took the lead, igniting his flashlight before reaching the stairwell. Under his heel, Dominique crushed his cigarette and lighted his hand on Davis's back as if to assist her balance on the steps. His motives were far more selfish, demanding her touch as an anchor and distracting himself by the prickle he sent down her spine. "Miss," he said politely and noted her doubt in the flash of her eyes. She kindly considered his manners reflective of foreign etiquette and forgave him before they reached the basement door. The remnants of yellow tape and the broken lock told enough of the tale to linger within. Undoubtedly, sightseers and thrill-seeking children had corrupted the crime scene.

A few steps ahead, McAllory cursed the ineffectiveness of the lock and crime scene tape, apologizing over his shoulder. "Suppose we couldn't keep people out of here forever. Whatever evidence could be found though, we collected."

Dominique withheld a comment, passing through the door into the narrow hallway that served as an entry. What remained of plasterboard and walls had become a skeleton of support beams and tattered clumps of plaster; still, the ravages were covered in spray-painted graffiti.

"Damn it," McAllory stated. "None of this shit was on the walls a couple months ago. Kids, goddamn it. You'd think they'd have something better to do—"

"Get real," Davis growled, likewise annoyed. "This has probably become the local hangout—probably the newest thing since walking on hot coals to prove these piss-ants have balls."

Somewhat inhibited, Rudemonje translated the words literally.

"Pissing ants?" Dominique asked.

"That's what she said," Rudemonje commented with a dismissive shrug. "An Americanism, my friend."

"Interesting," Dominique answered and caught the tainted amusement in Davis's eyes when she looked up at him.

"Sorry," she said simply. "I have a feeling I just confirmed Miss Priss's opinion of us."

"No apology necessary," he commented with a half-smile, a more wicked shine in his eyes. "My translators may be sensitive. I'm not. This uh . . . pissing ants. Say it in English?"

"Piss-ant," she repeated with an attempt to restrain a laugh, her bemused eyes reflecting the glow of her flashlight. Ahead, McAllory stifled a laugh.

"Pea`zaunt," Dominique repeated and muttered a curse, shaking his head. "That didn't sound just right, did it?"

"Actually, it sounded a lot more kind. Sort of like the American word 'peasant,' and I think you better stick to French, hon. You start calling some of these teens peasants, and regardless of how fitting, you're liable to run into a world of shit."

"Unpleasant analogy, that," he said with a tainted smile and halted her forward step. They were close. The pulse at his temple threatened to blind him. "Monsieur MacAllor`et?"

"Uh, Shawn, hold up a sec," Davis stated.

McAllory turned, sweeping the floor between them with his flashlight. A single dull watt bulb offered a yellow glow, only enhancing the skeletal climate. The light barely pierced the gouges in the walls to either side suggesting rooms.

Davis asked, "What's up, French?"

"Ah . . . Dominique? Or Dom, if you please?" he suggested, straining against a slight smile.

She appeared slightly embarrassed. "Open mouth, insert foot, right?"

"There is something we need to discuss. Something I need to explain to both of you before we continue," he said as McAllory came within a few paces. "This is not something I am comfortable discussing, and I'd rather it remains between the three of us."

"There are four of us here," McAllory noted, fleeting a glance to Rudemonje.

"Mr. Rudemonje already knows, my friends. Agent Devinio knows, but no others here. I have only a sense of placing my trust in the appropriate hands. What we are about to do here is ah . . . what I describe as an alternative source of investigation. Doubtful you'll find that listed in any directory, and it's not part of a course study in law enforcement. The fact remains, I don't rely merely on tangible evidence to solve cases." He paused as Rudemonje caught up to him. Both detectives studied him, waiting, neither judging, merely curious. Slightly—genuinely—uncomfortable, Dominique continued. "I don't have time, either to prove what I am about to say or explain it, even if I were so inclined. I will say, for your ears only, what I do will speak for itself. Either you will believe what your eyes perceive, or you will not. To me, it doesn't matter, but to you . . . the difference could be detrimental to this case. I will ask only that you keep what you see to yourself."

"I'm not sure I'm following you," McAllory stated, and Rudemonje started to translate.

Looking over to Rudemonje, Dominique commented. "There's no need for you to translate their English here, sir. Translate my French to their English," he said and looked to McAllory, who was swift enough to understand something of significance had just passed. "One-on-one, I understand enough English to spare us time. I asked Mr. Rudemonje not to translate your words. I'll apologize for deceiving you if it seems that way, but uh . . . my grasp of your language isn't good enough to catch every word spoken in a crowded room," he lied smoothly. "Distractions. Here, there are none. May I continue?"

McAllory again spoke for both of them. "Please do, Mr. Jardonet."

"Dominique or Dom is preferable to Mister. What were you not understanding in my words? Following?"

"Providing I understood even half of what you just said, how are we supposed to use whatever we . . . see toward solving this case if you're asking us to keep it quiet?"

"A paradox, yes," he admitted, holding McAllory's gaze. "The details of how we learn whatever there is to learn—not what we learn—I ask you not to reveal, detective. To be clear, I will tell you things about this case, about this uh . . . crime scene that you will not be able to prove. We are . . . stepping inside the mind of a maniac."

"Come again?" McAllory stated, bouncing his gaze toward Rudemonje and back.

"This is where my life becomes complicated," Dominique said with a slight smirk, sigh, and shrug. "But I don't know any easy way of explaining this. For whatever reason, I've made a connection with your killer. It's why I am here. I see him . . . or through him. The mention of the lightbulb outside . . .? It was never mentioned in the written reports. I cannot explain how, only that I can, and will see what your murderer saw the night he butchered the Lowenstein boy. Mr. Rudemonje will continue to translate whatever I say in French . . . and I'll try to communicate impressions of my own as I walk with him. Just don't shoot me if you please. You would be shooting the messenger. I uh . . . I will try to remain outside this monster's realm. But I have been known to . . . to adopt the mannerisms. Are you beginning to understand?"

McAllory was at a loss, but Davis grasped the concept. "Goddamn," she uttered, looking up at him. "You're saying you're a psychic?"

"Touché," he said with a slight twitch of a smile. "The secret of my success."

For a long moment, they just studied him, then McAllory asked, "Agent Duran, she doesn't know. That's why you made her wait outside?"

"She knows, but she doesn't believe what she knows," he shrugged. "I have no tolerance for skeptics. She uh . . . considers me a con artist," he said offhandedly. "Who am I to dispute such a learned woman?"

Davis smiled slightly.

McAllory studied him curiously, neither prepared to doubt nor believe. "How exactly does this work?" he asked.

"You are asking for the mechanics rather than the technical aspects," Dominique understood. "And I can only admit that the next few moments will test your belief in the material world . . . I have never stood on the outside, but I know I frighten people who've seen my curse in action. I'll ask again . . . please do not shoot the messenger no matter how that thought may cross your mind. I . . . I truly have no physical proof to offer you evidence of my innocence. Nor to verify that what you hear is the unaltered truth. For that, you may need to seek your own soul."

"What do you want us to do?" Davis asked, apparently reaching her own conclusions.

Curiously, Dominique looked down at her seeing, feeling her belief and acceptance. "How is that possible? You believe?"

"Let's just say. . . I've seen some pretty weird stuff that defied the norm," she said bluntly. "And I tend to trust my soul. It also makes a certain kind of screwy sense," she said offhandedly and looked to her colleague. "Tell me you don't feel it? . . Sort of like a crackle in the air down here?"

"If anything, it's a little colder than I remember from the last time I was down here, but that was July, and this is October."

"It's about to get a lot colder, my friend," Dominique said and addressed Davis commenting, "Just don't let him shoot me." He was only half joking, she realized a half second before he withdrew his hand from her back.

The pulse at his temple slammed him, swaying him, and he staggered a half step. Swinging his head, he clamped his hand over his temple, stifled a gasp, and caught his balance on his other hand against a solid beam. "My God, that hurt," he uttered, straining. Already, his muscles quivered as though a living thing crept through him, prickling his skin, tugging at the nerves in his legs. "Oh . . . fuck," he huffed. "No holding it . . . back. Damn it . . . no." *No!* He was not—would not—bow to this beast inside of him! But the battle for control brought a growl off his lips. The air had chilled, chilled considerably in the space of a few seconds.

Hell wasn't fire and brimstone. It was ice cold.

"God-damn—" a husky voice started.

"Cold, huh?" Davis spoke in a quavering, slightly nervous voice, then, "Mister. . . Dom . . . shit. Mr. Rudemonje, can you . . ."

"Not . . . taking . . ." Dominique looked up suddenly, straightening and firming, glancing between them with worried cat-glowing eyes. Uncontrollably, he flashed his feral gaze in either direction. "Uh . . . oh" His attention landed, locked on the shadowed features of the older, faintly familiar man. "I know you, sir," he said in a softer voice, his internal fear rising in his livid green eyes. "No . . . okay? Tell me this . . . a nightmare."

"Dominique?" the man asked carefully and offered his hand.

Uncontrollably, Dominique side-stepped away from the man who seemed to glow in the strange shadowed light. Livid with fear, Dominique bumped into the strange woman and recoiled from her intended grasp. His gaze locked and held. "American . . . you're an American . . ." he said and heard his words echoed in a soft low voice. Darting his gaze to the elder, confused, he shook his head. "D-don't let him d-do this to me, sir, please," he asked softly as the tears lifted in his eyes. He was speaking French . . . his six senses spiraling to recognize the phantom world. "Don't let him keep me down here . . . I d-don't w-want to be in this—this place! Please—ta-ake me out of h-here."

"What's he saying?" the woman asked softly.

"He's talking to me, miss," the man said quietly though his eyes held on Dominique. "You know where you are, Dominique . . . Look around you. You do know."

"I—I don't want to know!" he demanded and closed his eyes, dropping his head again and lifting his hands to clasp his temples. "I don't w-want to be here! M-make him s-stop this. Make hi-im stop, Mr. Rudemonje," he pleaded on the brink of a sob. "First mamma—now him. Why? Why c-can't they l-leave me a-alone?"

"My God," the elder said softly, and Dominique jolted with the hand clasping his shoulder. "How you can even ask such a thing, my boy," the low voice cajoled and drew him forward, bringing him into a partial embrace. "This is . . . it's the place you told me about, isn't it, Dominique? The place . . . where you will leave your childhood behind you."

"Evil," he said in a soft, angry oath. "Evil be-longs with evil."

"Mister, he said you'd translate," the deeper voice stated.

"I hear them . . . The Americans . . . Tell them to—to go away! I'm not here! I'm not coming here! Tell them!" he demanded and stabilized on his feet. Wiping his eyes clear, he found the elder's concentrated gray-blue eyes. Suddenly, the face was changing, fading . . . for just a second, it was the face of his father before that too, distorted. "Oh God, no," he uttered, shaking his head, backing, and flashing his gaze toward either wall. *Tattered walls. Faded light.* "Nooo—"

Distorted, he saw something, someone coming toward him out of the darkness. Backing, stumbling, he caught himself on one of the walls and began skimming backward over the jagged surface. Gouges and cracks. Clumps of plaster broke away, and his gaze drifted momentarily watching the dust spilling like a spray of water.

"Nooo . . ." *he moaned and shook his head, backing, trying to concentrate, but everything warped, moving and shaking, rippling. Only the impact of his landing woke him to the cave-in beneath him . . . His knees, not the floor, he realized and nearly started to laugh before the sense of urgency reached him. Shaking his head, he began paddling, spider-walking on hands and feet. The shadow loomed over him . . . his father . . . not his father.* "Paa-paa . . .?" Comfort nipped *at the fringe of his mind as the familiar green-clad arms reached toward him. The surgeon's mask registered. "Paaapppa," he heaved and welcomed the hand clasping his arm, tugging him afoot.*

"That's it . . . Come to pappa," *a darker, unfamiliar voice skittered in his mind, musing.* "Pappa has something to show you."

"Show me?" *he asked, needing the hand about his waist to remain afoot, moving and stumbling. Drunk . . . he barely thought to laugh when the strangeness spilled over him. Not drunk . . . not funny. If his father caught him like this . . .* "Pappa?" *he asked as the image of his father swayed beside him, the strength of the arms dragging him. His father would be furious.* "I'm sorry . . ." *Not drunk, the thought nudged his mind. Confused, he tried shaking his muddled thoughts into order, tried remembering. Not drinking . . . he had . . . was . . . the hospital. Work. He'd finished his shift . . . a date. He had a . . . drugged?* "Nooo," *he heaved and shook his head, staggering and swaying. An odd fear tugged at the corner of his mind . . . a fear of this strangeness. He'd never taken drugs . . . rarely drank . . . work.* "Work." *Coming home from work.*

"That's right . . . How bright you are. We have work to do. . . beautiful work. You want to work with your father, isn't that right?"

"Uh-huh . . . work." *Coming home from work . . . getting in . . . the car. He remembered his car . . . starting to reach for the door. A prick . . . a bug bite.* "Bite . . . an allergic reaaaction," *he heaved, feeling better with his ability to remember.* "Sssick . . . need a cortisone injection . . . severe reaaaction . . . epppinephrine . . . Having an alllergic reaaaction."

"That's right . . . We'll just lie you down here, and I'll get your medication."

Gratefully, he half fell, half laid on the table, his gaze fanning over the gleaming medical tray, relieved to be in the emergency room. His breathing felt funny. Struggling, he skimmed his hand to find his own wrist, to take his pulse. Concentrating, he closed his eyes, and he heard the movement. The shuffle of utensils, the crackle of . . . plastic?

"Whaaat?" *he heaved and dragged his lids open, seeing a shadow and green glow of surgical scrubs. Comfort and confusion waged war inside his mind; he identified the syringe and the flick of a finger against the tube. He understood the squirt of liquid like a geyser in his mind. His gaze lifted, squinting to peer past the mask, to recognize his father.*

"Just relax, Abraham." *The doctor's voice cajoled.*

"Whooo aa-re you?" *Abraham Lowenstein struggled as his slitted eyes followed the syringe toward his arm. Something wrong . . . something was wrong with this procedure.* "Wa-aait! . . . Alcohol," *he heaved, grateful to have remembered, relieved.* "Neeed tooo—" *The prick of the needle in his arm halted and stifled his relief. For endless seconds, he stared at the syringe in his arm, the gloved hands, his attention skimming upward over the cloth as his body jerked in a spasm.* "Whooo . . ."

"That's right . . ." the deep voice *coaxed*, and Abraham felt a tingle against his cheek as his visions ebbed. "Beautiful . . . You have such beautiful skin . . . Such handsome features for a Jew. Too handsome . . . It's wasted on you . . . But that's all right, Abraham . . . Such a biblical name. That's it . . . Just go to sleep, Abraham . . . You won't feel any pain . . . I don't want to hurt you, really. I promise, no pain . . . That's more than you deserve, you Jew-dog . . . I would so much rather keep you awake for this . . . I would've liked to see the knowledge in your eyes and to let you watch . . . But I can't risk you thrashing . . . You wouldn't like this . . . Or maybe you would," the deep voice mused. "Your interest in science and all . . . Yes, it's a pity you couldn't be awake for this. You and I are going to make history together, Abraham . . . We're going to rewrite history! But we have a long way to go . . . sleep. Just sleep, you lazy dog.

Leave the medicine to those who are capable of it . . . Hmm, a bug bite," the Taxidermist huffed a laugh. "You would propose to tell me how to treat you? Fool . . . such a credit to your ignorant race . . . and let this be a lesson to all of those who would believe themselves risen above their betters . . . Ahh, just as I imagined . . . you are flawless."

CHAPTER 20

"Ronnie! Wake up, honey! That's it, honey. Can you hear me?"

Through a haze, Ronnie found the anxious face above her, felt the cold cloth brushing against her forehead, and understood the panic barely restrained in the soft voice. "Uh . . . huh," she uttered, orienting slowly. A hotel room, the lamp attached to the wall gave it away, if not the firmness of the mattress beneath her. Vaguely, she recalled staggering into the room and Donna catching her, helping her to the bed. Darkness, then, like a shutter lens closing in slow motion. Tadpole had been rocking and rolling . . . He was calm now, or nearly so. Against her palm, a vibration continued . . . Not more than a quiver as if the little fella was shivering.

"How often are you doing this?" Donna asked worriedly.

"Not too," Ronnie managed and began pushing onto her side, rising. "I'm all right—"

"Just rest," Donna stated, touching her shoulder to halt her rise. Grabbing the pillows, Donna propped them against the veneer headboard, refusing to move off the side of the bed as if she knew Ronnie would rise. "I think maybe we overdid it, big time, today, Rem. Like it or not, there's something to be said for taking a break now and again. Especially, when you're moving for two."

"I'm all right. Really, Donna," Ronnie said simply, improving far more rapidly with the little worm calming more beneath her hand. "I think what we're dealing with here is simply a matter of motion sickness, and it's just a matter of me adjusting to it."

Donna eyed her suspiciously, still not budging off the side of the bed. "What's that supposed to mean, exactly?"

"The tadpole's really starting to move. Before, when he moved, it was more like a bubble in the gut . . . A little like after one too many cans of soda. Now, he's up to the size of a small fish, and I'm not entirely familiar with the alien sensation of it."

"He shouldn't be big enough to cause you that much trouble, Ronnie," Donna said lightly. "Not saying I'm an expert, but you're only a few months along. I don't think Dee even started moving until closer to three months."

"So, uh . . . maybe me and Mr. Know-It-All miscalculated by a fraction," Ronnie said with a slight smile and shrug.

Donna studied her for about a half second before the revelation hit home. "How far along are you? And don't bullshit me, okay?"

"Let's just say, if we calculate the date from our wedding day, Tad's coming premature," Ronnie said and saw the flash of genuine amusement in Donna's eyes. "Now, how about getting up? I think our dinner's getting cold."

"When are you actually due?"

"Probably closer to May than June," Ronnie admitted and started pushing off the pillows. "But that's for your information only," she added and caught Donna's laughing eyes. "I'm serious. Don't even mention it to Tim."

"Why?"

"Honey, I have one younger and two older brothers, none of whom are entirely sure whether or not they appreciate my hasty marriage. Not that I give a damn what they like or don't like . . . But they're typical Irishmen. Give them a reason, and they'll rant till hell freezes."

"I've met your brothers," Donna said with a smile. "I think Sax could handle them."

"I'd rather not have a family feud any bigger than the one we have now."

"I didn't know things were that bad," Donna said with a touch of sobriety.

"They're not that bad now, but considering how Jade and I met, and how fast we married . . .? Let's just say, I'd rather keep things on an even keel. So, you'll keep that to yourself, right?"

"Dr. Blackwell knows, right?"

"That old sawbones is the one who told me," Ronnie said with a hint of annoyance. "Right after he drew the blood tests for our marriage certificate. I've vowed him to secrecy, and I probably should admit, I didn't tell Jade until after the wedding . . . Not that I needed to. The shit. I think he knew before I did . . . Which is what happens when you marry a psychic. Do you think we could eat now and get back to business?"

"You stay sitting," Donna stated and pushed off the bed, moving around the end to the table where Chinese containers stood with lids open and chopsticks sprouting. Collecting as much as she could carry, she made two trips to deliver the entire collection to the bed, brought the sodas off the table, and settled directly across from Ronnie, folding her long legs on the bed. Her eyes bright with laughter, she shrugged. "If the Chinese can eat on the floor, we can eat on the bed."

"I think the Japanese eat on the floor. I'm not sure about the Chinese," Ronnie commented and lifted one of the nearest containers. "God, this smells good. Wonder if I could just sniff it and get filled."

"I've tried that for the past half hour. It doesn't work," Donna confided. "So, how did your afternoon go? Any success?"

"Shit," Ronnie stated and divided her attention between the telephone and the container in her hand. The offering on the chopsticks won. She took the bite before reaching for the telephone, dragging the base to the bed beside her. "Pretend like you don't hear this, Mona. Your soulmate being a cop, it probably wouldn't go over well with him," she said while punching numbers. "Even better, you might want to take that box, visit the facilities and turn the shower water on high."

Donna hesitated, "Just tell me this . . . Is what you're about to do physically dangerous to you?"

"The opposite," Ronnie admitted and hesitated to punch the last few digits until Donna pushed off the bed and strode to the bathroom. On the third ring, Max Hagen answered with his usual gruff, threatening, "Hello."

"Hiya, Max. How's every little thing?"

"Better at this moment," Max's voice relaxed. "How's my favorite little mother?"

"God," she huffed. "To think I used to be your favorite journalist . . . next to Ms. Walters."

"Honey, you're still the best," he said huskily. "Now, tell me you and papoose are healthy and happy, and you'll make my day."

"Tadpole and I are just fine," she said lightly.

"Hubby getting nervous yet? Tripping over himself? Bragging at the local pub? Strutting just a bit—"

"Max, I have a favor to ask," she interrupted his roll. "Any chance you could look into a few things for me?"

"Please, don't tell me you're involved in something," he said, sobering.

"Okay, I won't. But I have a couple license plates I need to identify. One's PA. I think it could be a rental. The other . . . it's a G-1."

"Ahh, shit," Max grumbled and hesitated, apparently rifling for paper and pen. "Ready when you are, baby doll."

Reciting the numbers, one from memory, one from her palm, she listened as he repeated them for verification. "I probably better give you the number to reach me, too."

"I was afraid you'd say something like that, too," he grumbled and took down the Inn number before asking, "Where's your other half?"

"I wish I knew," she said honestly.

"Maybe you better explain that, baby doll. What's going on?"

"Actually, I shouldn't have said it like that. He was home when I left this morning. He had some business to tend to. Hopefully, he'll join me here." *Just a hope.* His message via Elaine had suggested a few days. "I guess I've just gotten used to having his handsome mug within hitting distance."

"Knowing how he feels about you, baby doll, I bet he loves when you swing," Max said with a vibration laughter in his voice. "So, everything's all right between you?"

"Everything's fine," she said, but a prickling doubt touched the nape of her neck, distracting and annoying as hell. "If you could contact me with that info ASAP, I'd appreciate it."

"What exactly are you getting involved in, honey?"

"As much as I love being a homemaker and wife, Max, I still have a career. When I nail down a few details, I'll let you know."

"Damn it, Ronnie, you're pregnant. The last thing you should be doing is chasing down a God-blessed story. Especially, the kind of stories you fall into. When you hear from hubby, you tell him I have a bone to pick with him. Where the hell's his head? Assuming he knows what you're up to, I'm damn sure going to—"

"Max, as much as I love your paternal instincts, and I know you mean well, think about what you're saying before you jump down Jade's throat—if you presume to jump on my behalf. If he hadn't agreed to let me run with this, I'd have run without his agreement. We're married. That doesn't make him my keeper, and you damn sure better remember that."

"Ronnie, I worry about you. Always have, always will, and you damn well know it. Bottom line—you're involved in something dangerous, and I want you out of it. No ands or buts. No arguments."

"Max," Ronnie said, remembering her promise. "I promised Jade if I found anything amiss and evidence to that fact, I'd turn it over to the proper authorities. Which leads to another little favor . . . How about checking around down your way? See if you hear anything about a company called Algen Industries. It has something to do with waste management or disposal. If I'm right, one of those license plates should connect to someone in the EPA."

"Good grief," Max muttered, barely audible through the phone. "Please don't tell me you're butting heads with someone in that fraternal order."

"Honestly, I haven't decided, but if it even looks that way, I'll back off. Right now, I have about three pounds of pepper steak to inhale, and I think the tadpole's hungry."

"Couldn't come up with something cute and cuddly, huh, Ron? Teddy bear, Curly, Kitty—short for Kitten?"

"When we're dealing with legs, maybe I'll call him Iggy—short for Iguana. Tadpole's a helluva lot more realistic than Kitty, for God's sake. Later, Max," she said and disconnected with a laugh in her voice.

The smile faded almost as swiftly as the chopsticks lifted, her attention riveted to the darkness beyond the window. Where was he? Where would he be that he would leave a message rather than pick up a phone and talk to her in person? A few days . . .? Did that mean he wouldn't even bother trying to call?

Belatedly, she remembered Donna, and only then when the shadow in the corner of her eye caught her attention. Not fast enough could she hide the concern which reflected swiftly on Donna Spencer's lovely face.

"What's wrong?"

"I'm worried about him," she said bluntly. "Something's wrong. This . . . him letting me come here . . . As much as I try telling myself that I'd have come regardless, he and I both know he could have stopped me. It still . . . it still feels as if maybe this trip is the lesser of the two evils, and that's not a relief. In fact, that scares the hell out of me," she said and blinked back a sting of tears while turning her bleary gaze to the gaping box of oriental. "There's something definitely wrong," she said in a strained voice and looked again at Donna. "Something's happened to him. I can feel it."

"Honey, you're tired, and you're pregnant," Donna said gently. "I'm sure Jade's all right."

Ronnie shook her head, never more certain of anything in her life. "He's not all right, Donna. Something's wrong."

"Did you try to call him?"

"He's not at home. He left a message with Elaine for me. When I left this morning, he was planning to join me here tonight . . . but his message said he'd see me at home in a couple days. And this . . . all day. It's been so damned screwy," she said while poking in the box with the prongs, not even attempting to snag a chunk of steak or wedge of pepper. "It's like . . . almost as like he set this up in advance," she said and found Donna's eyes. "Everywhere I went today, his name came up. Even when I stopped to buy the damn pumpkins . . . I ran into a guy who just happened to have a box full of 1800s tools waiting for *Zack* to buy. It's nuts, Donna. I feel like . . . like maybe he's trying to tell me something. Or leading me. Or maybe just letting me know he's here with me. Does that make any goddamn sense at all?"

"If uh . . . if we were talking about anyone else, I'd probably say no," Donna said as she settled onto the end of the bed, her focus listing, no longer intent on the chopsticks in her hand. Faintly troubled, Donna commented, "With him, I'd have to say it sounds just about right, and I'll tell you, Rem, with everything we're hearing, I can't say I mind having his name come up or the thought of him helping out. You know, I mentioned maybe finding out something good?"

Ronnie nodded, her attention wavering, riveting.

"Something weird happened at the library . . . I mean, like you said, something off-the-wall caught my eye. Whether it makes any sense or has any bearing on this, I don't have a clue, but remember when Finn was telling us about Trumble? The lake? The younger brother nearly dying on Shocklan Lake?"

Nodding, thinking about her search for Shocklan Lake, Ronnie waited.

"I came across that name again. Just this past spring, a few kids were out fishing—apparently after a hard rain and the spring thaw. One of them wasn't as lucky as Nate Trumble. He was a little older, too. They uh . . . this is really lousy dinner conversation," Donna said uncomfortably. "But they found his body about three miles down Blackborne River a week later. It probably has no bearing on anything but—" She shrugged and dropped her attention to fidget with the chopsticks. "Struck me odd, so I took some notes. On a brighter, more productive note," she said and attempted to lighten up. "I found Hank Ryder's obituary." A half second of silence dropped as Donna's expression waned toward astound.

I considered that a brighter note?

They both lost their dumbstruck expressions and what began as smiles, swiftly became hysterical cathartic laughter.

Slowly, all too slowly, Dominique woke to the external pulse against his ear and his heaving breaths. He recognized the weariness, an age-old weariness that left him drained. In stages, he realized he wasn't alone. A hand weighted his shoulder. Another held his head in an awkward fold against what appeared to be a wad of cloth. Blinking, widening the scope of his vision, he recognized the fuzzy glow of a flashlight beam, arched toward him without touching him. He rested on his side . . . on what vaguely appeared to be a gulf of cement floor with a scattering of debris that he couldn't begin to identify. Blinking, heaving a soft breath, he considered attempting to rise, but a greater force immobilized him.

Weariness. Exhaustion. He knew these sensations. Leaden limbs, an ache in his head lingering as if a hammer had landed a few telling blows. Not alone . . . Someone held his shoulder, and at least one other person sat within this weird, worried silence. With an effort, he dragged his hand to his head, upsetting the weight on his skull and replacing it with his own. Whoever these silent spectators were, they were worried.

"He's . . . he moved?" A soft voice whispered.

"He's waking." Another, deeper, closer voice responded. "Rest, Dominique. Just rest."

The nearer voice vibrated from the man who rested, shadowed above Dominique's head, holding his shoulder, comforting and demanding in conflict. The answers and revelations drifted toward the surface of his mind on a slow tide. He knew where he rested . . . remembered entering the building where a madman had dwelt long enough to take a life.

How much time had passed, he couldn't even guess, but he couldn't afford to rest much longer. Heaving a breath, he forced himself to move. Pushing onto his elbow, he flopped on his back, still holding a hand to his head. Muttering a curse against the leaden feel in his limbs, he squinted to view the outline of a man resting almost casually on the floor above his head.

Wearing a three-piece suit and tie, the fellow rested on his hip, leaning against the tattered wall with a drawn knee supporting his arm—as out of place within this chilled, shadowy atmosphere as the flashlight beam illuminating his frosted head.

"Rudemonje?" Dominique strained, and the head tilted at a deeper angle to study him. With the cross-current of light and shadow enhancing the sculpted features, Dominique recognized the pensive curve in the thin mustache.

"I'm here, Dominique," the man from the past spoke quietly, consolingly. "Rest a few moments more. You've been through hell."

"Ahh . . . a comedian," Dominique heaved softly, his words strained but amused.

"What's he uh . . . what's he saying?" the female voice asked quietly.

Davis . . . Det. Chelsey Davis . . . and the gentleman, silent and still a few paces away, Det. Shawn McAllory.

His hand still holding his skull, his senses swaying, Dominique tipped his head enough to glean the ethereal images hovering, likewise sitting on the floor. Davis rested on her behind, her knees folded in front of her, the flashlight directed past Rudemonje. McAllory rested on his hip, his flashlight dangling downward to light the floor between them . . . deliberately angled to keep Dominique within the peripheral glow without blinding him. Dragging his foot up and raising his knee, attempting a more natural pose, Dominique glanced between them. Both watched him, studying him critically, anticipating . . . what? A performance . . . not a performance. They waited only to see if they would need to intervene . . . tackle him? Confused, Dominique lifted his attention to Rudemonje. "Was I . . . violent?"

"No, my boy, you were not violent," Rudemonje said quietly.

Straining, doubting, Dominique sensed something of the lie, but even as he considered asking aloud, the answers flowed into him. Like liquid pouring into his mind, the images becoming crystal to see himself as Rudemonje had seen him. Frozen, now, Dominique continued to study this man who hovered like a guardian angel over him . . . and he saw it all. His staggering and mad uttering, his words . . . The muttering of a madman who'd splayed a boy on a makeshift wooden bench . . . stripped the flesh from his limbs. . . and the bones from his carcass. Ah . . . and he remembered, now. That feeling of power flowing off the madman, through him, and the maniacal words, terrifying the two seasoned officers. McAllory had drawn his gun . . . had believed with his mind and soul that he viewed a madman, and he'd, indeed, nearly shot the messenger to silence the message.

Dominique huffed a disgusted sound, nearly a laugh, as he tipped his head and sought the tense face watching him. "I . . . am glad you didn't shoot the messenger," he said heavily.

Rudemonje repeated the words in English.

"You knew I'd come close, didn't you?" McAllory asked.

"I must have . . . sensed such a thing," Dominique admitted, belatedly aware of his raised knee falling over, sinking, as surely as his elbow tilted to land on the cloth pillowing his head. Denim cloth. His head rested on Davis's denim jacket rolled into a makeshift pillow. Looking toward her, he read her concern as clearly as her belief. If not for Rudemonje, Dominique knew he'd be in a hospital. The woman had feared for his life when he'd collapsed toward the end of the 'operation.' Apologizing, he wore a faint smile, "I should have warned you, my dear. I am ah . . . sorry."

Her gaze darted off Rudemonje, back. "You were dead," she said bluntly, her gaze tense. "I took your pulse . . . Did you know that would happen?"

"I am . . . sensitive to the . . . powers of suggestion," he said with a twitch of a smile which might have been more effective if he didn't feel like roadkill splattered on the chilly cement. His pulse had increased. His blood flowed more freely, but for a time. . .? "Yes, I suspected . . . I would hover between the realm of the . . . living and the dead. A risk . . . the uh . . . danger of my trade." He managed a shrug by his tone. "I survived."

She moved as Rudemonje finished, pushing onto her feet and closing the distance, stooping at Dominique's side. Keeping the flashlight from his eyes, directing the beam just past his head, she looked down into him while touching her fingers gently to the nook of his neck. Not a word. For several seconds, she continued to study him, judging the rhythm and beat of his heart. Dominique sensed her relief before she eased onto her shin and brushed the back of her fingers on his jaw. "Yea, you should've warned me, mister. You scared the hell out of me. This bastard. . . he's taken enough lives, ya know?"

Moving his hand, he clasped her fingers before she could retract them. No tingle of excitement, no warmth spreading beneath his chilly touch. He might as well be clasping the hand of a manikin for as much attraction as he felt. Only one face . . . the soft blue eyes and thick black curls. . . fire and ice, that minx who held his heart. No other . . . there would never be another no matter what name he wore or what life he lived. Tipping his head, he closed his eyes, feeling the sorrow, the pain . . . and wishing, suddenly, that he'd died within this darkness. Such a life of abandon, he wasn't sure he could continue to live.

Gladly—gladly, he would close his eyes and slip away to that other place where the world made sense. Where the blue eyes lit with fire and ice, where the light erupted to sparkle like blue diamonds, and black bubbles slid through his fingertips, thrilling and heating him. "Ahhh . . . Mon amour . . . mon amour . . . ma copine . . ." The light in his darkness. His friend. His love. His life. "Mon amour . . . ."

From hysterics to tears, Ronnie gave vent to the retching, stifling the sobs that threatened to burst. Already, she'd laughed too hard, and she couldn't even recall what had set them off. Donna wasn't much better. Splayed on her back, heaving and wiping her eyes, she lingered nearer to tears than laughter.

For a few moments, for a few wicked moments, Ronnie had felt as though the world had collapsed on top of her and become too heavy to bear.

Max's words, his implication that something could be wrong between her and Jade . . . Nothing had come between them. Nothing had been wrong when she'd left him on the sidewalk. If anything, their love had grown stronger, balanced and counterbalanced, yin and yang. They were two parts to the same whole. Nothing could happen to him that wouldn't happen to her and vice versa. That was the promise they'd made. A vow they'd promised before ever oathing their union before God. If he wasn't all right, she would know . . . and with her thought, her gaze slid to the mirror directly across from her.

Against the pillows, she rested at an elevation to view her reflection in the silver, but she remembered too clearly, the other image she'd seen. First, him splayed in a scatter of limp, bleeding limbs . . . then him standing, wearing one of his cocky smiles, his sorrow . . . to have put her through that moment of terror when she'd believed him dead?

In the mirror, she watched her hand lift and wipe tears off her cheeks. Inconsequential this reflection. She watched, willing the image to change, demanding a change. She needed to—

She heard him then, a whisper, an oath. How far away he sounded, and for just an instant, she saw him, his face tipped and pale, his dark waves scattered in contrast to the brightness haloing him. With barely a flutter, his mustached lips moved, whispering the words she strained to hear. Panic touched her mind, barely relieved by the deep, whispered words. Something wrong . . . hurt. He was hurt . . .

"Jade," she stated and leaned slightly forward as if she might draw the answers from the mirror or improve her view. Instead, the image faded, ebbing swiftly, an apparition scattering, dispersing on the glass. "Jade!"

"Ronnie?" Donna said worriedly, her head tipped and bloodshot blue eyes tense as she started onto her elbow. "Honey, what's—"

"He's . . ." God. She'd sound nuts. One does not see her husband's image in a hotel mirror. Impressions, intuitions, no problem. Full-blown visions fell into the category of hallucinations, and on top of passing out, doubtful Donna would settle for delivering dinner and a can of soda. More likely, she'd call Tim and between the two of them, Ronnie would land in some lockdown ward in the nearest hospital. According to at least a few cases Ronnie had heard in passing, it wasn't entirely unheard of for a woman to lose her mind during pregnancy.

Not this woman! She wasn't about to become a statistic!

"What about him, hon?" Donna asked carefully.

"He's . . ." *How to explain those outbursts*?

"We've covered that one, Rem."

"He's been all over this damn town," she snapped and leveled her gaze on Donna. "Did I mention the tax collector? Did I tell you that one?" she asked with an edge of anger which only confused Donna more. "Na, I didn't tell you about that visit. This flower-braggart as much as warned me not to mention that I'm married to Zack—infamous, antique-peddler from 'Olden Time.' Can you believe that shit? He was all over this stinking town, and he didn't even bother to mention that detail once. The shit. He let me head out without so much as a town map or a few shop names. He really is a shit, you know? I'm not only going to hurt him when I see him, I'm going to hurt him real bad."

Donna had lost her alarm to a growing amusement. "Since I happen to doubt you'll threaten any part of his anatomy that could seriously alter the extension of your family, I think I'll just stand aside and watch when you do."

"Well, how would you feel if you found out that Tim was probably considered the most edible thing since apple pie, and the shit didn't feel it necessary to mention it to you?"

"I'd hurt him," Donna said with a smile. "Bad."

"There you have it," Ronnie said bluntly. "Now, since I'm fairly recovered from my fit of outrage. Let's get down to some serious business."

"Don't tell me, you're hungry again," Donna mused.

"I haven't been *not* hungry in so long I forget what life was like before hunger pains. But since we have work to do, let's clean up this mess, or better yet, let's move to the table. I'm assuming you weren't just pretending to study notes when I picked you up."

"Woman, did anyone ever tell you, you're relentless?" Donna said, heaving a breath, shaking her head as she continued into a sitting position. "A virtual slave driver, so you are, Mrs. Laquette."

"Did you call Tim when we got in?" Ronnie asked.

"I left a message with his mom for him to call me when he gets in," she said offhandedly, breezing a glance off her watch as they began collecting the half-empty boxes, a few not even opened. "He might've tried reaching my room. He should've been off a few hours ago. I'll give him a call a little later."

As they were depositing the cartons on the dresser, the knock interrupted, halting them both. A prickling sensation slid down Ronnie's spine as she connected with Donna's curious gaze. Glad she hadn't mentioned the surveillance, but not entirely sure she wanted to greet a visitor, Ronnie clasped Donna's arm, stopping her from starting toward the door. Shaking her head in silent signal, Ronnie picked up her purse as she moved to the door. The knock erupted again, a quick rap of solid knuckles. Her hand poised in her purse, gripped around the revolver, Ronnie wondered if this would become a new habit even as she called, "Yes?"

CHAPTER 21

The strangeness had come to Dominique as he'd lay holding the stranger's hand, thinking, remembering, feeling the sensations of the only woman he could ever love. Once and again, something had changed inside of him. As if the mad surgeon had severed something physical inside of him, Dominique experienced the detachment from the material world around him . . . and grasped the freedom in his discovery.

A burden, that, to feel the world, to experience the sorrow and fear of others, to be touched by madness and joy. Different. He felt different, and with every moment of discovery, he knew the integrity of his revelation. And in his way, he knew the mad surgeon hadn't initiated this change. The depth of his sorrow and the pain of his loss combined had tipped the balance of the volitions toward evil to lay dormant inside him. How could the world affect him when he'd already lost the only thing that ever mattered to him? Not an immediate or spontaneous change. He collected himself slowly within the chilled atmosphere and managed to rise as far as his hip. Nothing physical or instantaneous. He'd lingered in the pits of sorrow, slowly, surely, drawing away from the material world.

Veronica . . . Ronnie . . . Veronique . . . She held the only part of him that had ever been human, the only decency to surface inside him. The only flicker of light that he'd salvaged from the ruin of his early years. In her, with her, he had been human and alive, and so wondrously free of the loneliness that had driven him for a lifetime.

Perhaps only to fool himself, he'd refused to see and believe what his talents could have revealed even as he'd walked away from his life in the early morning hours. An irony, to be his own greatest skeptic, his own enemy. Ah, but there were others out there, as well. Enemies . . . and in a moment of crystal clarity, he knew he'd never be entirely free of them.

Jade Laquette . . . child prodigy, mystery, a visionary, persecuted by the American press, hounded . . . until the hounds had driven him into the hunter's trap. With nowhere left to run or hide, he'd landed in the hands of the American government, snatched from his home, and removed from the protective fold of Nan Duncan's arms.

They had taken him . . . and driven him slightly more mad in the wake of his mother's death.

Pandora's Box . . . the resurrection of Jade Laquette had opened Pandora's Box, and he wasn't foolish enough to believe the monsters were dead. Someone in the American government had known him, someone in the government, with enough knowledge and belief . . . feared him. Feared him enough to engage a few federal agents to enlist his services . . . and in a momentary epiphany, his thoughts moving at light speed, Dominique knew exactly what a few knowledgeable monsters – hunters – had hoped to achieve . . .

The whirl of propeller blades, the distinctive chop-chop-chop of a helicopter engine . . . Somewhere in his mind, he knew he'd heard those sounds before, perhaps in the depths of sleep. The sounds, a dream . . . but he felt the wind, now. *A noticeably cooler wind touched his hair, his face. Nothing of the air could he smell, the reason apparent with the pressure weighted around his mouth and nose. An oxygen mask. Hazy, he glimpsed the faces. His numb body jostled with the motion and floating. Not a dream. Too late, he understood, this was not a dream. Outside himself, he heard the engine drone, whirling propellers, shouting deep voices barely audible beneath the raucous of mechanical sounds. Rolling his head, he identified only the white form floating beside him, a human form propelling him. A murky face turned to him, then away, toward something beyond his head. The clatter of other machinery touched his senses, the feeling of others around him, moving with him. Confused . . . drugged, he tried lifting his head, his body. A protest formed on his lips, but no more than a groan escaped, lost within the mask and the clamor.* Nooo!

The focus of attention, Dominique understood, as surely as he felt himself somehow ignored by his white-frocked companions. They wheeled him, headfirst toward a destination he was only beginning to grasp. A helicopter . . . he glimpsed the flanks and doors. The whizzing, near invisible blades, shadowed the darkness overhead, and too soon, the ceiling turned gray above him. At the outer edges of his vision, others moved, moving with him, crowding around him. His head rolled; his eyes barely opened enough to see images veiled by his own eyelashes, which wouldn't quite lift. Wrong . . . something was wrong. *Nothing moved on his own power. A disconcerting vulnerability touched him, a touch of panic in his mind that he was seen and not heard, deliberately. Ignored. Suppressed. Restrained . . . and drugged for* . . . convenience?

He understood.

Standing within the hazy light of the basement, he realized the integrity of that vision, the outcome he'd witnessed in the depths of his dreamscape. If he'd played by the rules the American agents had outlined . . . If not for Devinio and Dr. Rhoades carrying him from that autopsy room and allowing him to recover, he would have been taken to a hospital, and from there . . .? He would have returned to the institution from which his father had rescued him years ago. A trap . . . oh, yes. No doubt remained. Only the clout and influence of Robert Bryson, Veronica's father, had spared him for these four months. A trap had been planned and he could well imagine the headlines to pour out of Cleveland in a day or two. "Psychic Slain by Serial Killer" . . . And in the weeks to come . . . "Psychic's Widow Suffers Nervous Breakdown." Veronica, they would spare . . . but his child, his son. Taken, tested . . . developed as the bastards had attempted to develop him.

Why . . . and who. Those were the questions remaining, the answers he would need . . . And Jean-Pierre's powers of observation slammed him with a force to darken the shade of his eyes to a feral shine. For his wife—for his child—he would live long enough to find those answers and his enemy. Before he could extricate himself from their lives, from the threat that he would become to them, he needed to safeguard them.

"Mr. Jardonet, Dom? . . . Are you all right?" Davis asked quietly.

He nodded absently, glancing about within the shadows, collecting more of his balance, and recovering his immediate thoughts. Jardonet. He'd taken the name Jardonet, and it was something of an irony to realize he'd depended on Jean-Pierre's power and influence, accepting his father's trap to avoid yet another trap. Cat and mouse, he considered, and chanced to wonder who was the cat, who the mouse, in this game?

Another irony. That he should find himself within the birthplace of a monster . . . and draw from the superiority in this beast's madness. "Damned fool," he uttered, too quietly for Rudemonje to translate.

With a far keener insight and a strangeness washing over him, Dominique turned and landed his gaze where a wooden workbench had stood. The state forensic technicians had removed the table, had taken it, along with every scrap of paper and grain of dust within this room. Teenagers. He needed only fleeting glimpses to know the present clutter had been created by thrill-seeking teenagers, either testing their courage to brave the haunt of a maniac or to revel in fantasies.

"This place," he said indifferently, drawing a breath of sweet tobacco from the chilled air, knowing. "It wears the mark of evil now. Those who dwell here, those who come for curiosity or thrill will be touched by it. A shame, but a fact of life," he said as Rudemonje translated.

Looking at McAllory, Dominique commented, "Pissing ants or not, my friend, if I were you, I'd join a movement to condemn and demolish this building. There is evil in the world. You've felt it, touched it, and you've now seen it. Holy water couldn't cleanse the places your maniac has been. His touch, that clammy chill you feel, will remain in this place, like a footprint in cement. A pity, that so many might have already danced here with the devil.

Get larger locks or erect steel doors," he said offhandedly and motioned to the door.

They were already in the hall when Rudemonje finished his translation, and McAllory spied over his shoulder, landing his wary gaze. "You really have a knack for giving people the creeps, right? I mean, that just goes with your territory, huh?"

"Maybe he's just telling it like it is, McAllory," Davis fired back, subdued by her tone. "Tell me you don't get the heebie-jeebies when you walk into a place like this."

"Yea, well, if we buy into his theory, honey, we're not exempt," McAllory stated. "I, for one, don't think I like that concept."

"You are uh . . . Catholic. Irish Catholic, perchance?" Dominique asked as they neared the exit, stepping over cardboard boxes and crunching candy wrappers underfoot.

"Lucky guess," McAllory commented. "My name probably gave me away."

Dominique stifled a laugh, knowing McAllory believed the opposite despite his jibe. "A religious quandary, my friend. If there is a God, then what of the devil? Does one walk the earth, dishing up love and hope, while the other is merely a myth? Good and evil . . . you feel joy when you enter your church? Or do you feel obligated and inconvenienced, buckling to a doctrine just to appease your parents? Do you attend church for the hell of it?"

"Something tells me that uh . . . oxymoron wasn't a slip of the tongue."

"Ah, then you recognize the opposite ends of the same staff, my friend. Good for you," Dominique commented and followed McAllory up the cracked steps, emerging into the natural shadows. Drawing a breath of clean air, he heard the snap of the door lock disengaging and watched as Duran slipped hurriedly from the front passenger seat. Obviously, she'd learned what Dominique had sensed on the drive to the crime scene—

"What took you so long!" she snapped, addressing one or all. "And what's wrong with the radio in that car? I tried radioing your dispatcher! I couldn't get a response!"

"Uh, shit," McAllory commented. "Must be on the fritz again. That's what happens when you're working with a task force that doesn't exist, lady. You get all the secondhand shit. Guess it's lucky we didn't need backup."

"I thought all you FBI guys carried phones and gadgets," Davis said with a touch of antagonism if not outright chiding. "You weren't getting scared out here, were you?"

"I don't know who you think you're talking to, Det. Davis—"

Dominique interrupted smoothly, "Why do I have the impression this is not a discussion about the case, Rudemonje?"

"You are observant, my boy. They are squabbling again."

"Not a pleasant place for such an event," Dominique commented and started toward the car, motioning to McAllory. "You mentioned a decent neighborhood a few miles east? Show me," he said, and Rudemonje translated as the others hustled to join him in the vehicle.

Both females, with Rudemonje between them in the backseat, maintained a tense silence until Duran spoke in a carefully controlled tone, "Mr. Jardonet, under the circumstances, I'd like to apologize for the inefficiency and unorthodox behavior you've witnessed and endured here. I hope you'll understand when I insist, we either return to the station or telephone the headquarters and have a more adequate vehicle and escort meet us. For your safety, I must insist I have a few of our own people escort you beyond this point. I'm sure Agent Devinio would agree and respond immediately."

Interrupting before Rudemonje could translate more than the first few words, Dominique commented, "Ask Det. McAllory to find the first telephone booth in a more acceptable part of town, Miss Duran."

Gladly, she made her demand, and Rudemonje verified McAllory's question concerning Dominique's agreement. Moments later, the detective pulled in alongside a telephone booth at a well-lighted gas station. Duran excused herself, and stepped smoothly from the backseat, striding purposefully to the open-air booth that barely provided an arch to protect a customer from a blazing sun much less rain. Progress. The ancient-styled glass booths offered comfort and privacy, sparing one the need to cover one ear while attempting to hear with the other. In the passenger seat, Dominique watched Duran drop a few coins in the slot, then lift her hand as anticipated. Over his shoulder, he commented to Rudemonje, "Ask McAllory to pull closer to the booth." Rolling down the window, he caught her attention as the car rolled within a few feet. Through the open window. Dominique interrupted her conversation. "Miss Duran, tell them to hurry, will you? I wouldn't want you stranded here too long alone."

"What?" she asked while lifting her palm from her ear.

"Det. McAllory, drive," Dominique stated, almost managing the English version of the word before again looking over to Duran. "Tell your superior, I will be in touch, yes?"

"Mr. Jardonet—" She started with a step, nearly dropping the phone.

Waving as McAllory stomped the gas, Dominique called, "Thank you for your assistance, miss. Until we meet again."

"Au revoir—" Davis started with a laugh in her voice, half turning, waving through the back window as she continued a litany. "Chow! Cao, baby! Adios! Arrivederci! Hasta Luego! Auf Wiedersehen! See ya, sweetie."

McAllory rumbled a low chuckle, shaking his head as he rolled smoothly into traffic, glancing over to Dominique with his laugh. "I think we just got into trouble here."

"What? You think she'll have me arrested?" Dominique mused. "Doubtful, my friend. Diplomatic immunity—a terrible privilege to waste."

Glancing over his shoulder to Rudemonje, McAllory laughed again, bouncing his glance off Dominique, "Waste not, want not. That's your motto, huh?"

Sober entirely, Dominique spoke simply, "We have a job to do, and she was uh . . . excess baggage? Drive back to that thoroughfare. I'd like to see the hospital parking lot where the Lowenstein boy was taken."

Likewise sober, McAllory commiserated in silence for a few seconds, then asked, "How uh . . . how real was that—I mean, what we saw? Was that really how it came down?"

"It was ah . . . only too real, my friend. The boy . . . If memory serves, he was drugged but not uh . . . unconscious when our killer took him. I . . . I know he believed he was bitten. It is the second time . . . and yet, the coroner has not found any unusual puncture wounds. Does this mean the doctors are lax? Or does this mean the puncture was so minuscule that it was missed with the overall ruin of the body? A syringe puncture would leave a deeper mark. What is he using to knock his victims down? A question, yes?"

Davis sat forward, leaning her elbow on the back of the seat behind McAllory. "We thought maybe he used something like ether," she commented. "Or that he managed to hold them down long enough to get the needle in their arm. In Lowenstein's case, if the kid had been held at gunpoint, he could have stuck himself and gone out like a light. Except that what you just uh . . . showed us, counters that belief. He's not using a gun, is he? He's not forcing these people into their cars at gunpoint to get them."

"I think the risk would be too great," Dominique said absently, his gaze cast through the side window. "He wants them for their flesh. He wouldn't risk a struggle." Fleeting, he remembered Frances Cummings, 'Owe . . . what . . .' And Lowenstein's reaction. "A dart gun? Small but effective . . . quick acting. If he's using something like that to give him a few seconds to come out of the shadows, perhaps, we will know something more about him, yes? A study in ancient religions? A collector of Japanese art or artifacts. Such a device might lend us insight."

"You uh . . . I guess you can't just give us a description, huh?" McAllory asked. "Or is that what you already did? Six-foot, blue eyes, blond hair, 185 to 195 lbs. . . . 'You've seen this guy?"

"Where insight fails me, collected information enhances . . . I wish I could see him clearly, my friend. It's accurate to believe he's a surgeon of sorts . . . but whether he actively practices? Whether he has an overbite? Scars? Distinctive features . . .? I cannot be sure. When I see him, he's in shadows or uh . . . already wearing his surgical scrubs. Such is the way with evil, Det. McAllory. Darkness is the cloak behind which this monster can hide even from me."

Awaiting the full translation, McAllory glanced over, speaking carefully, "Don't take this wrong, but I'm almost happy to hear that. That sort of makes you a little more human. Faults, you know?" he turned his attention fully on the road ahead. "If you could just walk into that scene and tell me who this guy is, I'd be happy as all hell, but I'd have one hard time believing it."

"Can I ask you something, Dominique?" Davis asked and awaited his gaze, continuing with his slight nod. "Why did you pick me and McAllory for this? I mean, did you have a reason? Or did we just get lucky?"

She wasn't being sarcastic; her question was sincere. Dominique shrugged, "I would like to think I had a reason other than self-indulgence and arrogance, but honestly, either could apply. I might also say, both of you were being wasted by the uh . . . politics?"

Dominique looked at McAllory, catching the glance and surprise. "You're an extremely astute investigator despite your age and experience, McAllory. I'm not very tolerant. Never was. I truly don't like waste, and your uh . . . commander saw nothing more than youth to be ordered about even though you could run rings around him." His gaze turned to Davis, and he smiled. "You, I noticed, faced the same situation for another reason. Your commander is ah . . . a chauvinist? You're an attractive woman thrust into his command, and he's a man driven by old values. Not a fault, exactly, but your value to this case was limited by the desk. Does that answer your question?"

She nodded as Rudemonje finished, but she continued to study him, a slight smile on her lips. "You have interesting eyes, Dom. I noticed that in the station . . . and it's not just the color. You have a way of looking into people, through people. That's why you dumped Duran, huh? Something about her didn't wash. She didn't have anything constructive to add. Excess baggage? More waste?"

He stifled a laugh, "I don't think she'd enjoy hearing that. In fact, I believe she'd be extremely offended to learn that I considered her litter to be left on the side of the road."

"God," she huffed, withholding a laugh with an effort. "You're a snob."

"Shit, I hope we don't get caught," McAllory mused. "We have a penalty for littering in this state. Probably wouldn't look good on my record."

"I do believe I said that wrong," Dominique decided. "I didn't mean she was trash. A misunderstanding, yes?"

McAllory laughed and glanced over, his blue eyes conveying his genuine humor at the dual meaning. "Forget it, Detective. I think you had it right. She sorta reminded me of a girl I picked up a few years ago. High class from the heels to the—"

"McAllory, I feel it's my civic duty to remind you, you're talking about a federal agent," Davis said in a mock, chastising tone. "And we wouldn't want to leave too many bad impressions on our foreign friend—not that I think we have any chance of succeeding with you behind the wheel. I'm surprised the chief even let you get close to our friend."

"I'm not the one who tried going hand-to-hand over our other friend in the backseat, honey. Good impressions probably went by the wayside the moment you started that battle."

"I didn't start it," Davis stated. "She's the one who took offense to all the testosterone flying around up there, and the bitch shouldn't have called me crude—in French, no less. I shoulda fuckin decked her and been done with it."

"You better thank our pal here for pulling the plug on that one," McAllory commented soberly. "It probably would've cost you your badge." Barely missing a beat, McAllory continued, "There are three different access roads to the hospital parking lot, but the employee lot is closer to the rear entrance. I'm taking you in that way. We're pretty sure that's the way he came since it's . . . well, you'll see in a minute."

Dominique did see. The rear entrance, not much different than the main, opened onto a busy two-lane highway. Wooded, the hospital grounds offered a golf-course atmosphere with plenty of high shrubs and thick trees crowding the pavement. The parking lot wasn't much better, with bushy islands separating the lanes and trees countering the effectiveness of streetlights. Even with the headlight beams, the darkness provided ample cover for a criminal. This madman could have stalked Lowenstein for days, following him nearly to the lighted doorways without ever stepping out of his car or the cover of a bush. Daylight. A glitch, perhaps, but not an insurmountable problem in this atmosphere. Even before McAllory pointed out the parking space—one space away from a thick collection of hedges and thick-bowed maple trees—Dominique felt the residual evidence of the maniac.

"We're pretty sure that's where Lowenstein was parked that afternoon. We're not sure if anyone was parked between him and the bushes—"

"The space was empty," Dominique said as gazed through the side window. Sensations, knowledge . . . as if he were a spectator, separate, apart from the emotional input now, he rested, unaffected as the scenery began changing in his mind's eye.

Daylight . . . overcast. Gray, the sky offered an illusion of early dusk. A soft, heated breeze swept through the parking runways, picking up dust in swirls. Hot and muggy, a taste of sunbaked tar and heated glass transcended the atmosphere. *Alone, Lowenstein strode between the cars, stripping off his sweated blue tunic. In a hurry . . .*

"Somewhere to go," Dominique said absently. "Already late . . . supposed to be home . . . a date. Shit," he said in a different voice, muttering, "Shoe's going to spit sickles . . ." *A stupid expression, Abraham smiled and shook his head . . .* "Something his grandfather used to say . . . 'spit sickles' . . . He's at the car," Dominique said in a vacant voice. "Ahh, come on boy . . . tell me—"

Fumbling with his keys, Lowenstein gasped suddenly, jolted. His keys hit the pavement; his right hand flung toward his left arm. . . He barely started to rub his bicep and turn. An arm caught about his waist, lowering him into a stoop. A hand reached for his fallen keys, but it wasn't his hand—

"He never made a sound," Dominique said absently and blinked the image away, turning his gaze to McAllory, who studied him critically. "It was windy that evening. If our surgeon rustled a single leaf, it was lost in the sound of the wind. Lowenstein didn't see him—didn't hear him. Didn't know he was there until the bite . . . Our surgeon's coming in close and . . ." And in his mind, he heard it, that tiny click, a mere whisper of sound, but he knew what it was suddenly. "And I'll be damned," he uttered, his hazel eyes flickering and landing again on McAllory. "Not a dart gun, my friend. Maybe, ah, something better? Or worse. Y– you decide. A diabetic's blood kit . . . a lancet. At the touch of a trigger, a tiny needle snaps out and draws blood. Whatever he's injecting, it is very quick . . . painless. A single prick, and voila! Down they go. He is close enough to catch them. He eased Abraham down gently. Now, we have a single problem . . . I don't recall a mention in the report, but I wonder . . . was it a coincidence that Abraham was late getting off work that eve? Was it ah . . . usual for him to work overtime?"

"That's getting ahead," McAllory stated after the translation. "Are you saying our guy's a diabetic? Or does this fall into the category of easily accessible items to substantiate our doctor theory?"

"Hmm, I did say, better or worse, for you to decide, yes?"

"Shit," McAllory stated. "Then it's possible either way."

"That explains how the coroner missed it," Davis stated. "If I remember right, that gadget's no more than a pinprick. It probably barely touches the skin through the cloth."

"Doesn't tell us what's on it . . . and it doesn't tell us how the lab missed the evidence on the clothes. If this guy's using something that powerful, you'd think it'd leave a trace on the clothes."

"It was summer, my friend, and hot that day—muggy. Abraham removed his tunic while crossing the parking lot. The bite struck his upper arm. Bicep. The left arm . . . he was lefthanded, but he swung with his right and the keys . .

. nerves," Dominique said thoughtfully, his gaze misty as he replayed the scene in his mind. "The keys fell. Either an instant effect on the nerves or jolted by the bite. Quick and painless."

"I really wish you'd quit using that word," McAllory said and appeared uncomfortable. "Painless," he stated. "You kept saying that in the basement. It's his word, isn't it? He really thinks he's a fucking humanitarian because he's not letting them feel any fucking pain while he's skinning them. And that kid was alive through most of it, wasn't he? He was alive the whole time this bastard was taking his life."

For a long moment, Dominique looked into the pale blue eyes, suffering the rage of pain and horror, the helplessness McAllory felt for the victim. Those moments in the basement, the nightmare had come alive for Shawn McAllory. "I am sorry, detective."

McAllory turned his gaze away and slapped the heel of his palm against the steering wheel, his fingers closing slowly, tensely in an iron grip. "I think I'm the one who should apologize to you, detective," he said in the wake of Rudemonje's words. Shaking his head, he continued to scan the parking lot, his young features held in a rigid set, a mask of tension highlighted in the gauge lights. "We're supposed to be trained for this shit," he continued in a low, controlled tone. "We're supposed to know how to handle this, but how the fuck do you prepare yourself for this kind of madness?"

He brought his gaze about, searching Dominique as if he might hold an answer. "I've handled some pretty rough shit, ya know? Don't get me wrong. I answered a routine call when I was working patrol—about four months out of the Academy. Routine. Domestic violence. I get there and find a six-year-old kid blown away. He's all over the kitchen floor and walls, and the old man's still sitting there holding the gun. Six years old . . . and I handled that. It happens . . . we see wackos on the street every fucking day, and we get immune to the insanity and cruelty, but this one . . .? How do you handle knowing that some twenty-two-year-old kid with his whole life ahead of him ended up on a butcher's table? And the bastard who put him there thinks he's doing the world a service? Creating fucking art? And you're right. He's a fucking doctor. Someone trained to keep people alive, to treat the sick, to mend the broken . . . A guy somebody in this city probably trusts enough to visit regularly. Or worse, somebody actually *pays* this maniac to cut into them, trusting him to fix them . . .? It's not computing in my head, ya know? How can he be this crazy—this sick—and nobody knows it? Nobody sees it?"

"You know the answer to that question, Shawn," Dominique said quietly, holding the man's intent gaze. "What I allowed you to see is the maniac behind the mask. That's not what others would see when they look at him on the street or across an operating table. He will come apart. He's already coming apart. What he did to Abraham . . . that was his fantasy coming to life, my friend, but he's already changing, growing."

"What do you mean?"

"Before I came to your headquarters today, I visited the morgue," he answered honestly. "Some of what I told you when I arrived, I drew from that experience. He is growing, my friend, and changing. The problem is this . . . I think someone does know he is mad, and they are uh . . . using his madness? Fueling it? I have a sense that uh . . . he has found a buyer for his art."

As Rudemonje finished, McAllory's expression changed. "What? What the hell are you saying."

"A feeling, my friend. Something he uh . . . words he spoke," Dominique said absently and reached for his cigarettes, shaking a butt out and glancing at McAllory. "Evil is a sickness, Shawn, and contagious . . . like the plagues of old? This maniac has taken an idea, and if he is successful, his idea will appeal to others like himself. Supremacy . . . in the name of that word, over six million Jews lost their lives in the Holocaust, and to this maniac, that word means – perfection. Art. He is perfecting an art . . . and art is to be appreciated as well as sold and collected, my friend. It is a product, and I think . . . I think he has already found a buyer, or at the least, he believes he has."

Delayed by the translation, both detectives uttered breaths of surprise and disbelief. “Jesus. You’re saying he’s actually *making* something out of h-human skin and bones . . . and *selling* it?“ McAllory asked.

“Whether it is true, or whether he is fantasizing, I can’t be certain,” Dominique said indifferently and shrugged. “But he believes it. That much I know. And that much I have said on tape, which the Federal Bureau transcribed and has in its possession. Information, which you and your colleagues would not be given. Privileged information, Shawn. You, Det. Davis, myself, and my colleague are the only ones outside the Bureau who now possess that knowledge.”

“Why are you uh . . . why did you tell us?” Davis asked hesitantly.

“Because I don’t trust bureaucrats,” Dominique said with a slight smile. “And because someone, with the ability to catch this maniac, should have whatever assistance I can offer. Good or evil, my friends, what I do isn’t for public record, and the Bureau, even Agent Devinio, who I would trust with my life, wouldn’t be permitted to admit from where that information originated. Checks and balances. Evidence. I have told you because you won’t question the source. You’ve seen enough this evening to understand.”

“You uh . . . you want us to do something with it,” Shawn said, his gaze turning from Rudemonje to Dominique. “What?”

“Consider this, Shawn. Our maniac is a doctor. We’ll assume he’s successful in his profession. Wealthy. Now, consider too . . . on the chance that he is not selling this skin for medical procedures—skin grafts or whatnot—then he is truly creating something from what he’s taking. A work of art made of human skin and bones. The uh . . . market would be limited, yes? And exclusive. And if he’s already found a buyer for his trade?”

“God almighty,” Shawn said heavily. “It would be worth a fortune to some sick bastard with more bucks than humanity.”

“Yes, unfortunately. I fear that’s possible.”

"Great," Davis said as she slumped in the seat, folding her arms across her breast as if stumped. Unconsciously, she warded off a chill. "We're dealing with at least two bull goose loonies."

"A pity you have so many hospitals and research facilities in your city," Dominique said offhandedly. "In a smaller community, this would be ah . . . piece of pie, yes?"

"Cake," Davis corrected. "A piece of cake, honey."

"Would it sound in ah . . . extremely bad form if I invited both of you to dinner?"

"Gad, you can't be serious? After everything you just said?"

"Hmm, thought it might be offensive," Dominique commented indifferently. "But the fact remains, I haven't eaten much all day. Tried Italian earlier, but it didn't sit well," he admitted, recalling too swiftly how he'd paid a visit to the restroom before finishing more than a few bites. "I'm wilting—or withering—or however the hell you'd like to put it. Do you think we could find a restaurant?"

Finishing his translation, Rudemonje continued in French. "Could I suggest we dine in your suite, my friend? By now, Paul's probably considering placing a call to the Embassy."

"Probably right," Dominique commented. "Ask our friends to deliver us and join us."

CHAPTER 22

"Special delivery," the husky voice came through the thin door.

The voice, not the words, sent relief and anticipation through Ronnie's mind. She slammed the deadbolt free and yanked open the door. Looking at the arrogant pose, the bemused, deep blue eyes, and the cocky smile, Ronnie maintained a deadpan expression. "Can we refuse delivery?"

"Smart ass," Tim chuckled and lanced his gaze past her to his wife who eyed him somewhat accusingly. "Heya, funny meeting you here," he said as Ronnie stepped aside. Casually, he sauntered into the room, eyeing both of them before dropping pretenses. Smiling, he welcomed Donna's hasty steps and drew her into an embrace. On most men, blue jeans, a checked shirt, and a sports jacket complemented by name-brand tennies might look ridiculous. Tim looked fantastic, and he knew it.

After hugs and a long, slow kiss to defy eight years of marriage, they parted, and Donna lost her misty look to an almost indignant expression. "The message was to *call* if I remember correctly. How dare you barge in here like an invited, expected guest."

"What can I say," he said nonchalantly, his blue eyes sparkling with devilment. "I had a few days off. Mom offered to stay and watch the kids, and I figured, what the hell . . .? We haven't had an opportunity like this in a helluva long time. Besides, someone mentioned this was a buying trip, and I figured unless I want a few tons of music boxes delivered—" He ducked from Donna's slap, chuckling as he continued a hasty step to the dresser. Lifting one of the open boxes, Tim peeked beneath the flap, glancing between them. "Any chance these are leftovers?"

"God, typical man," Ronnie said as she met Donna's bemused eyes. "Not here two minutes, and he's looking for dinner."

"I was hoping to get here soon enough to take a couple knockouts to dinner, but hey, like Sax says, *ce qui sera, sera*. And if that doesn't work . . . when in Rome. Any chance you have a fork handy?" he asked.

"I can't believe you came all this way just to take us out to dinner—what with a two-hour drive back," Donna said as if she meant he better plan on driving back. Her eyes betrayed her, the delight as vivid as a blue balloon.

"Ah, come on, darlin," Tim mocked a pout and plea. "Have pity on a starving man."

"You'll have to use chopsticks or fingers," Donna said bluntly.

Apparently, this carried a private joke between them. Ronnie detected the darker shine in Tim's eyes and the flush in Donna's cheeks. To offset the sudden pang of loneliness and longing—a damn detestable condition considering the short duration of Jade's absence—she routed in her oversized purse. With considerable digging, Ronnie found a set of disposable utensils in the plastic wrap and tossed the package to Tim, shrugging as the Spencers eyed her. "Always be prepared for any contingency," she said bluntly. "And if you two would rather be alone, I wouldn't take offense. Another good rule of thumb," she said toward Donna, smiling slightly. "When opportunity knocks . . ."

"Opportunity can wait a little while," Donna decided, giving Tim a look to confirm a raincheck on the horizon.

Breaking out the fork, Tim made himself comfortable, perched sidesaddle on the dresser, and dug into one of the plundered boxes, glancing between them. "So, did you ladies manage to buy half the town's store of antiques today?"

"Na, just a quarter of them so far, but we still have tomorrow," Donna said. "And there's this really cool little shop down the road. It must have at least a million music boxes."

Tim offered a withering look, and the fork disappeared under his smirking mustache.

Studying him in a moment of serious thought, Ronnie realized his visit wasn't a mere question of opportunity and considering the day she'd endured, she wondered. "Did you happen to talk to Jade today?"

"About?" he asked, betraying nothing in his vivid blue eyes. Not too unlike her husband, Tim Spencer wore a rakish handsomeness with a mop of black-walnut hair, slightly long for a law officer. Between his dark blue eyes and ever-present smile, he'd always turned more than a few female heads in Bentwood. A sorry day for the girls in town when good ole Tim had returned from a convention in Chicago with a fiancée in tow. To hear the tale, Donna had fended off half the females in Bentwood with her bare hands just to reach the altar. If not friends, this fellow and alias, Isaac Bently, would have become serious rivals.

They were friends, however. As close as brothers, if not closer than some. Doubtful Jade would have departed Bentwood without touching base with this character. "Oh, I don't know. The price of tea in China? The market value of music boxes? The possibility of a certain antique dealer going out of town for a few days?"

"Well, now that you mention it," he said with a sheepish grin. "I might have run across him for a minute or two. The way I understood it, though, he was planning to be here this evening. Why? What's up?"

"Damn good question. Did he happen to mention where he was going?"

"He didn't say. I assumed maybe you knew," Tim said, and if he was lying, he was better at it than Ronnie had ever imagined. His gaze conveyed a quiet intensity. "He didn't tell you?"

"What exactly did he say, Tim?"

"Not much. I only talked to him for a couple minutes or less. He did mention he was going to try to get here, and if I uh . . . ran into you," he said with a smile. "I was to let you know he's in good hands. He also asked me to make sure you were all right. You're all right, right?"

"I'm worried," she said bluntly and meandered toward the window before thinking twice about standing too close. Undoubtedly, a government surveillance team occupied that dark sedan in the shadowed parking lot. Tim's presence offered a strange sort of comfort. Another message, perhaps? She veered to the side of the window, drawing the drapes. Was this Jade's way of telling her to dump this entire case? God knows she wouldn't trust the local officers if what she'd overheard about Logan was any indication, but she couldn't contact the FBI without a little more proof of a crime. She turned and found Tim watching her as he scooped another helping of Chow Mein into his maw. "Did he happen to mention why I'm on this shopping trip?"

Swallowing, he commented, "Nope. I'm sort of hoping you'll fill in the details."

Either Tim knew or suspected the buying trip was a ruse. Exchanging a glance with Donna, Ronnie sensed the woman, for all her courageousness, would like nothing better than to forfeit this adventure. The element of danger had risen shortly after they'd discovered the possibility of a staged accident, and Donna was damn sure bright enough to know it. Leaning on the air conditioner unit, Ronnie hesitated a moment, then thought better of putting her back to the window where her shadow might be cast upon the curtain.

Pushing off, she moved to the small table where Donna's notebook lay folded closed. Hastily purchased at a drug store on route to the library, the notebook was of a garden variety style with a spiral binder, the kind any college kid would buy before a boring lecture. Settling into one of the two chairs, Ronnie glanced between the Spencers, reading curiosity on one, hope on the other. The decision remained hers.

Looking at Tim, judging his solid, impressive build, and knowing the intelligence behind his country-boy style, Ronnie chose the path of least resistance.

"I came here to investigate a questionable circumstance," she said simply. "About the same way I arrived in Bentwood to find out how someone—two someones were killed accidentally with a pitchfork. The circumstances were slightly more innocuous on this trip. I was tempted to believe I was following a red herring, but I have reason to believe we're onto something that could be a bit more than I bargained for. Do you know anyone in this town?"

"I'm assuming you mean someone on the local force, right?"

"Anyone at all, Tim. Have you ever been here before? Maybe with Jade?"

"Can't say that I have, and honestly, if I've ever met anyone from here, I don't recall it," he said and picked at the box, scraping the sides with a fleeting glance without losing the intensity of his gaze. "What exactly are the questionable circumstances? And start at the beginning, okay? Who turned you onto this, when, where . . .?"

"I have a knack for spotting things not quite kosher, Tim," she admitted quietly. "Something caught my eye in yesterday's paper." Considering the ambiguity of that statement, she decided to skip any explanations. If Tim hadn't figured out her *modus operandi* and similar talents to Jade by now, he never would. "To be blunt . . . a fella by the name of Jack Trumble, age 46, was killed in a car accident two days ago. He was buried this morning. We have a great deal of reason to believe—no physical evidence to support it—his death wasn't an accident. In fact, I believe that another suspicious death can be attributed to the same cause." Glancing to Donna who'd settled onto the end of the bed, Ronnie commented, "We really need to cross reference what we found today. If you could pull the obit on Hank Ryder, we'll have a springboard."

Pushing off the bed, Donna reached the table, swinging into the opposite chair. "Nothing in the obit suggests he died of unnatural causes," she said while sliding her notebook in front of her, flipping it open. "If anything, it leads me to believe a lack of suspicion. He was ninety-four years old. Died in his own home . . ." She lifted a few sheets of folded copy paper from the notebook and glanced over with a slight smile. "Figured you'd want a copy of the actual print. It's pretty conventional stuff," she said lightly, glancing over the copied print. "Surviving heirs, which like Finn suggested, aren't that many. Two sons, a daughter, a few grandchildren." She looked over. "Not a lot of familial ties to account for ninety-four years unless he survived a passel of others. It only listed two of his deceased wives. Didn't Finn tell us he had three?"

"At least three," Ronnie agreed. "We'll need to check that out. Hall of Records should be able to help there." Unconsciously, she pulled her purse about and waded into the clutter, extracting her notebook, a leather-bound affair that she'd intended to put in mothballs. She flipped it open, slid a pen from the built-in slot, and began making a notation as Tim cleared his throat.

Glancing between them with a peculiar expression, a kink in his mustache, he settled on Ronnie, commenting, "I think you were about to bring me up to speed?"

Glimpsing Donna's slightly amused eyes, Ronnie shared the same wavelength. All too swiftly, they'd fallen into the discussion, forgetting Tim entirely for a few seconds. Still amused, Ronnie commented, "The drift in thirty seconds—isn't that how the prime-time news jockeys give you the world? Here it is—we think Trumble, a local, respected realtor, got caught up in a shady land deal after a few heirs tampered with a Will. The monetary value could be in the millions. The stakes involve criminal conspiracy charges, and to top it off, a company called Algen Industries might have a claim to fame via a few shady deals with the EPA. That's the long and short of it. Add in the facts that the local sheriff might have covered the murder deliberately and that one of the heirs is on the town council—an heir who might have been written out of the Will entirely before the old man's demise. Compound the entire ordeal by the fact, the property in question is probably within pissing distance of the city limits, and I think there's probably a few regulations concerning the disposal of toxic waste and possible disposal sites . . ." She shrugged somewhat innocently, holding Tim's more tense, startled eyes. "What else do you want to know?"

"Who else knows about this?"

"Donna, me, you . . . and probably half the old timers residing in Elmview, but none of them are willing to talk too loud to the wrong people—or right people, as the case may be. I don't think some of these folks have a very high opinion of law enforcement and their government as a collective, benevolent Uncle Sam. I'm guessing, they really don't think there's much they can do legally about the issue of a toxic dump in their backyard. I'm also guessing that the whole deal's extremely hush-hush. If the college faculty and powers-that-be learn about this—or the student body gets wind—this place will be a zoo. This is just a guess, Tim, but I'm betting Trumble had a few second thoughts. Maybe he threatened to enlighten the college dean, or he figured out the Will was bogus. So far . . ." She looked at Donna. "Correct me if I'm wrong, but I have a feeling, you didn't read anything in the headlines over the past few months to suggest the possibility of a toxic dump on the horizon."

"Not even an inkling," she said smoothly, consulting her notes, and flipping through pages. "I did happen to note several town meetings. One caught my eye." She skimmed her hand down a scribbled page and halted, looking over. "April 12th. One of the local reporters—maybe a municipal secretary—cited the closed session of the town council. Backtracking, I found at least two separate occasions when the council met in closed quarters to discuss 'issues' concerning the welfare of the town. Conveniently, those articles appeared almost in conjunction—I mean, like adjacent columns in each instant to something concerning infractions with the college set. I was tempted to believe that Elmview had a great deal of trouble with the student body in the past year—if not a few years. A few 'near riots,' a small protest march about parking permits . . . The college hosted a rock concert this past summer, and a few disgruntled merchants raised a stink. Letters to the editor, petitions, that sort of thing . . . I sort of went on a binge," she said, amused. "It reminded me of my own college days. You did say to follow hunches, right? And this ongoing feud, age-old to my thought, between young adults and older adults, struck me funny. The fact is, it looks as if the town council would like to put a few restrictions on the campus fraternity. Ironically, quite a few merchants are equally frantic about leaving the kids alone. Obviously, they know how much revenue they'd lose."

"If they lose the college, this town will become a ghost town," Ronnie agreed, thinking. "Unless they have a thriving, industrial replacement."

"It still amounts to economic suicide," Donna stated, intent. "If it truly is a dump site, the probability of Finn's prediction for the town's decline is right on the money."

"And the town council wouldn't give a shit," Ronnie noted. "At least one of them stands to make a fortune, and it's not much of a stretch to guess the others could be bought."

"So where does that leave us?" Donna asked. "As the saying goes, dead men tell no tales."

"We need the autopsy and police report on Trumble's murder," Ronnie said while doodling on her notebook. "If we can find evidence of foul play, we could bring in the big guns."

Again, Tim cleared his throat. His dinner, obviously forgotten, his gaze fleeting between them with a more pensive expression. "I hate to rain on your parade here, ladies, but if even half of what you just said holds a grain of truth, this isn't a case to be handled by either a journalist or an amateur sleuth, no offense intended, darlin," he said to Donna, sincerely. "As much as I find your interest and apparent savvy in this deal fascinating, and exciting as hell, I think it's slightly passed time you turn in your badge." His gaze slid to Ronnie. "Did Sax know what you intended to do here, or is that like the world's dumbest question?"

"At this point, I'm not sure what my wayward husband did or didn't know," Ronnie said with a hint of concern. "His uh . . . powers of perception can be a bit much, but not infallible. He knew when I set out, I had an interest in Trumble's early demise. Like I told Donna, I promised I'd turn this over to the proper authorities if I found justification."

"I'm gonna have a serious talk with that boy when I see him," Tim stated. "He should have held out for at least 'probable cause,' which is what I'm going to insist on, Ronnie. If the past ten minutes are any indication, you ladies have been traipsing all over town collecting the scoop on this mess. And if there is a murderer on the loose, darlins, this is no place for either one of you. What I want you to do—"

"Tim," Ronnie interrupted soberly. "I can understand if you're slightly miffed with me and Jade for involving Donna in this situation—"

"Honey, you don't know the half of what I'm feeling at the moment," he said gravely. "Do you have any idea of how serious this could be, for Chrissake? You're talking about a conspiracy theory that could crest somewhere within the government—"

"We don't have evidence to support that, Tim, and I slightly resent the implication that I'd deliberately, intentionally, endanger another—not to mention that I happen to be pretty good at my profession. I didn't exactly race around town holding out a sign or tossing a press card in people's faces."

"Look, I'm sorry—"

"No, you look, bub," she snapped, her Irish ire rising. "I told Donna what we were doing, and I gave her the option. We came here under the pretense of buying antiques, and we've stuck to that premise with slight deviation, in so far as I made a stop at the tax office to look into the possibility of relocating Olden Time or opening a branch. Donna went to the library under the pretense of starting a market analysis regarding said endeavor. I didn't come here as Ron Bryson, investigative journalist. I came here as Veronica Laquette, wife to a well-known and apparently, adored antique dealer who's made a routine of visiting this town at least once a year. Now, if you'd like to give Donna a lift home, fine. Do so. But don't you even presume to waltz in here and tell me what I can or can't do, nor allude to the fact that you think I'm an incompetent ass. By Christ, I passed that phase long before I met the first male ego in the law enforcement profession."

Stopped, his blue eyes cobalt with the intensity and strength of his surprise, Tim rested on the dresser by sheer force. "I wasn't implying—"

"Tim," Donna interrupted in a soft, compelling voice, drawing his heated gaze to her chilly blue eyes. "If you've come here to help, fine. If not, I think you finished your dinner, and Rem and I have work to do."

"What the—"

"I had a choice, darling," she said simply. "I understood the ramifications and risks before we entered this town. God knows I love being your wife, running a small business of my own—like a hobby—between raising two beautiful children, but this . . . it's something I feel compelled to do, to continue."

"Donna—"

"You never discussed what you saw, what you felt after finding Fred Engler," she continued, holding his gaze. "We never discussed any of that because I knew how badly it bothered you. It bothered me, too, darling. For weeks after Mr. Farnsworth was killed, I walked around feeling shell-shocked, as if I was back in Detroit and at any moment something, someone would burst through the door with a gun. When Fred Engler was murdered, I was afraid even to let the kids out of my sight. I'd turn on every damned light in the house, afraid that something or someone would jump out of the shadows or around a corner. And I'm still not sure what frightened me more—the fact that a killer could have been lurking in our own backyard or how the thought of it made me feel vulnerable. I don't like that feeling. I don't like being scared out of my wits as if my safe little world could crumble in an instant. You could have been killed. You put on a uniform every evening or morning, strap on a gun, and walk out into a world I believed was reasonably safe before six months ago. No place is safe, now, and I can't keep burying my head in the sand. If we've stumbled onto something here that has the potential to ruin, if not take a lot of lives, then by God, I'm staying long enough to make a difference. If you can't understand that, or accept it, I'm sorry."

For a long, silent moment, Tim gazed at her, his jaw twitching, eyes intense. In slow, careful syllables, he commented, "You do realize the thought of you possibly coming face to face with someone, who could ultimately intend to take your life, has a grown man shaking in his boots, right? You're fully aware of the fact that I'd lose my fucking mind if something ever happened to you? Hell," he said absently and flashed a glance to Ronnie. "To either one of you under the circumstances."

"Could I make a suggestion?" Donna asked quietly, her soft smile compelling.

"Please suggest you'll check out of this hotel—"

"Stay and help," she said simply. "I'm a fair clerical assistant in this investigation, but when push comes to shove, I doubt I'd be much good in the physical department."

Again, silence, then Tim looked at Ronnie. "How far do you intend to go with this?"

"I made a promise I'll keep. When I have physical evidence to warrant a full-scale investigation, I'll bring in the Calvary."

"By Calvary, are we talking Len?"

"He'd be a quick safe bet," she agreed.

"With what you've already uncovered, darlin, you could probably give him a call right now and dump this whole deal into his hands," Tim said soberly. "Do you know how to reach him?"

"I won't waste anyone's time, Tim. Not yours, not his, without something substantial to offer. I may base my preliminary investigations on supposition, but I don't expect others to follow suit. If you're coming in on this, it's by choice, and it's not in an official capacity. If you get my meaning."

"You don't want me waving my badge," he said simply, nodding absently as his gaze trailed away, apparently, weighing options. His gaze returned directly. "Make you a deal, Ron. I'll assist, unofficially, if you promise—at the first sign of trouble, with or without the evidence to go official, you and Donna are out of here."

"I'm stubborn, not stupid," she said bluntly. "You have a deal."

"Then maybe you better finish filling me in . . . and start somewhere around the place where you think the local sheriff's involved."

CHAPTER 23

Without a doubt, Paul Lejeune had been on the verge of calling the French Consulate after placing a call to the headquarters and listening to the tirade of an angry American Agent. Dominique listened to Lejeune's angry recital with quiet indifference, slightly amused when Lejeune suggested he would have Agent Leonardo Devinio strung from the flagpole in front of the UN building. Apparently, Lejeune had said as much—in French—after the agent had threatened to have a certain French dignitary arrested on sight unless said dignity phoned the agent soon. Having heard enough, Dominique waved off Lejeune's frustration and went into a tirade of his own when he found the American menu written in English as if that should be a surprise.

Tossing the gold-embossed leather book aside, he threw a few more curses into the air while moving behind the bar and locating the complimentary liquor. As he found glasses, ice, and began mixing a drink, he told Rudemonje to order something American, then changed his mind and suggested his countryman ask the Americans to order for all of them.

Regardless of how the staged performance had begun, his anger and frustration became genuine and had nothing to do with his inability to read a menu. That part of his curse had lifted.

Fuming, Dominique leaned at the bar, halfheartedly listening to the Agents arguing over what would be a better example of American cuisine—a charbroiled T-bone or prime rib. Sipping his drink, his attention riveted, watching them going head-to-head, both pairs of blue eyes flashing fire, one just as hotheaded as the other. They stood poised over the short coffee table, oblivious of the two native Frenchmen watching them with peculiar degrees of curiosity. Sparks. The heat of their bullheadedness. In ages, they were not too far apart. Shawn held the upper hand by a few years; Chelsey compensated in attitude. Sparks . . .

His gaze drifted, drawn to the darkness through the window where the black waters of Lake Erie fused with the skyline. Sparks . . . in the candlelight, her blue eyes had drilled him, heating and touching off a hundred sensations, a thousand tiny darts to ignite a passion that he'd never experienced before. Sex had never been a deciding factor . . . In a fit of rage, he'd made love to her for the first time, and he could still feel that moment when he'd realized a shame greater than any past. After all the sparks and fire, after all her arrogance and boldness, he'd meant to spin the witch on her ear with his seductive talents, and the minx had turned the tables on him instead.

A smile played at the corner of his mustache. His gaze softened as he remembered those moments when he'd braved her strike and met her eyes, prepared for the hatred he deserved. Instead, she'd worn that soft, compelling smile which drove him to fits of madness . . . and she'd forgiven him his madness before the guilt had taken a firm hold. God, he loved her. From the saucy snap of her tongue that could blast the wind from his sails to that soft shine in her eyes, telling him no other existed in her heart, in her mind . . . Sparks . . . such sparks and fits of frenzy . . . and she'd put him in his place, driving him over the abyss and drawing him back time and again. To live a life without that wondrous woman would be to live a life of hell . . . and he would walk through the fires of hell for her.

But how he missed her already. Barely a day, and he wanted nothing more than to sweep her into his arms and carry her into their room as he had only yesterday . . .

Instead, Dominique stood listening to the heat of a battle that reminded him so much of his recent past, he suddenly felt like weeping. He needed . . . he needed to see her, damn it!

And he barely finished the thought when the window across the room burst to life, and he saw her . . . Standing as if posed for his inspection, her long silken black bubbles spilled over one shoulder. Her head tipped at a coquettish angle as if spying him beneath the shade of her thick black lashes. Immaculate, that long sleek frame wherein the seed of their creation was barely a whisper at her waist. Slim and firm, those long legs wrapped in blue denim; inviting, those full saucy lips. Her hands slid over the subtle rise at her waist as if gaging her cargo's capacity . . . and in another instant, he saw her sitting back in a cheap vinyl chair, a notebook in front of her and a pen tapping a rapid cadence. By her expression, she wasn't pleased with whatever held her rapt, and in his way, Dominique knew she wasn't alone in this room.

As if to verify his words, she began to speak, but her words meant nothing. Only her voice held him rapt, the soft melody that never betrayed the strength of her spirit. The woman never needed to raise her voice to make a point. She could flash those sultry blue orbs and send a chill tapdancing through the minds of lesser men. What a wonder she was still. As courageous and fierce as any goddess of lore, as soft and lovely as a nymph—

"Mr. Jardonet?" Chelsey interrupted.

Snapping from his reflection, he found both detectives watching him. Belatedly, he realized the fight had ended, and this was the second time his name had been spoken. "Oui?"

Whatever she'd meant to ask him with the first attempted interruption slipped away with a thought of whatever she'd seen in his expression. Starting toward him, she asked, "Is everything all right?"

"Oui," he said simply, lifting his drink and taking a few swallows while pushing off the bar. Glancing between the agents, he looked to Rudemonje. "Have they decided on dinner?" he asked.

"The decision isn't final, my friend. I think they are in love . . . or already married."

Fleeting a smile, Dominique glanced between them, then to Rudemonje, sent the order in French to order several entrees, along with a few soft drinks and pots of coffee. As an afterthought, he glanced off McAllory and added, "Add a six-pack of beer and a bottle of Irish whiskey. Doubtful he will drink either, but he might. Tell them, I appreciate their intended assistance but . . ." He looked to Shawn directly, addressing him, "If we wait for you to win this battle, we will all starve."

As Rudemonje translated, Dominique downed the remainder of his drink and started across the room toward the larger of the two bedrooms branching off the main suite. "Offer my pardons and make them comfortable, Rudemonje. I'm taking a shower." A very cold shower, he decided, uncomfortably aware of the physical effects of his reflection added to the grime from the warehouse floor.

Bracing against the icy spray, his palms flat against the ceramic wall, he stood, remembering a million other nights when he'd exercised a similar technique to escape a nightmare. If only that could work now. If only he could stagger, shivering and numb from this deep, luxurious tub, and awaken within the safety of the small fortress he'd built in Bentwood. Nothing could be that simple. The nightmare would be waiting whether he sent himself into hyperthermia or stepped comfortably from a hot spray.

Sputtering a curse, he spun the dials to warm the temperature. Relieved of the physical pressure, he dried and dressed, donning a pair of black jeans and a turtleneck, a charcoal gray jacket. Slicking his hair, he stood momentarily, taking stock of his reflection. Physically, he was his father's mirror image, just a younger version, but he'd inherited more than his father's sharp, angled features and off-colored eyes. No longer could he conceal the anger to burn behind the surface of his near emerald eyes, any more than he could hide the dark talents within . . . And in an odd moment, he recognized the freedom of that revelation. Why bother to try? Why bother to deny a birthright when he could benefit from the very same?

His arrogance, another inherent trait, had always served him well in the past, and he needed only to recall Mark Jarvins' feeble attempts to best him in that game, to realize that he'd used that aspect of his nature for the sheer sport of it.

Jarvins had no idea what he was up against, and the poor fool was too governed by his sense of invincibility to read the signs and warnings that Dominique had offered. If, by chance, those warnings had only fueled the fires . . .? *C'est la vie.*

Even when he attempted to wipe the amusement from his lips, Dominique failed, and he was only more amused when he entered the living room area in the flux of a heated argument. At the door across the room, the collection of bodies clustered, Rudemonje and Lejeune standing off against Devinio, with the two Cleveland detectives attempting to cool the rising tempers. Apparently, Devinio hadn't arrived alone, and he intended to add two American agents to the entourage presently guarding a certain French dignitary. In no uncertain terms, he'd demanded to speak to the Frenchman, and Rudemonje wasn't a fellow to accept demands any more than his younger counterpart. A request might have gained Devinio quicker cooperation.

Unaccountably amused, Dominique managed to reach the bar and pour a drink, listening to the exchange of the detectives appealing to the agent to wait a few minutes. "The guy's in the shower, for chrissake, mister. You can wait a few minutes—"

"You and I have a few things to discuss in due time, detective—" Devinio snapped, his dark eyes flashing toward McAllory and halting abruptly.

Smiling, Dominique tipped his glass toward Devinio, fleeting his glance to the others who noted the stopped gaze and caught on. Abruptly, the entire ensemble turned toward him, and a plethora of French and American words assailed Dominique, to which he waved his hand, reconnecting his gaze with Devinio. "You wanted to speak to me?"

"At your earliest convenience," the agent sniped, inflecting his Italian dialect with a dry tone.

Even Rudemonje fell silent, his gray-blue eyes watching Dominique far more intently than the others, spying him from head to heel. Jean-Pierre Jardonet . . . the name was in Claude's mind, on the tip of his tongue. The likeness was far more visible and unmistakable in this sleek, dark ensemble.

Impressions and sensations, those talents had enhanced. Leaning against the bar in a far more casual pose, Dominique motioned toward Devinio. "By all means, my friend. Join me for a drink?"

Devinio barely spared a glance toward the two men who parted before him. Annoyed, he sidestepped and passed between the detectives and closed the distance, his dark eyes intent and angry. "I'd like to know what the hell's going on here, Mr. Jardonet," he stated as he halted within arm's reach. His aggressive posture and tone drew both Frenchmen to within a few paces, but Devinio paid them no heed.

Lejeune itched to draw his holstered gun from beneath his jacket, but he held his temper; both detectives apparently sensed the possibility, likewise positioning where they might gain an instant to halt a shootout.

Taking in the scene without more than a glance, Dominique smiled as he landed his gaze on Devinio and again motioned toward the complimentary drinks. "Relax. Have a drink," he said and reached into the small cabinet, choosing a small bottle of whiskey, Devinio's brand. On rare occasions, Devinio indulged—preferring a mixed drink over beer. Handing the bottle toward Rudemonje, Dominique tossed a few French words to prepare the drink, then looked at Devinio whose anger remained on high. "I understand, you are ah . . . distraught over the treatment of your lovely comrade, yes?"

"I think it's time we have that discussion I mentioned earlier, Mr. Jardonet," he said. Not entirely oblivious to his precarious position, he glanced toward the bedroom door. "Privately."

Considering, Dominique pushed from his lean, waited as Rudemonje finished the drink, and handed it across the counter. Glancing off Devinio to Rudemonje, Dominique commented, "Dinner will arrive soon. Start without me and my colleague, and refrain from interrupting, my well-meaning friend." Toward Lejeune, smirking, he added, "Leave your gun in its holster."

Carrying his drink, he gestured Devinio toward the bedroom, following and countering Lejeune's thought to join them. The instant the door closed,

Devinio turned and spoke in low, concise English. "What the fuck's going on here, mister?"

"We are ah . . . solving a murder, yes?" Dominique asked and continued deeper into the room, forcing Devinio to follow. At the immense window, Dominique paused, less interested in the panoramic view of a very dark horizon than he appeared. Turning, he settled on the window ledge, hiking one leg to rest sidesaddle and colliding with Devinio's critical gaze. "That was the purpose of this exercise, was it not?"

"English, mister. No more games," Devinio stated.

"Ahh, English," Dominique said, almost startling himself with the simplicity of his strictly American voice. "Better?" he asked simply, his delight genuine if not slightly unsettling in Devinio's abruptly startled mind. "Obviously, I've recovered the grasp for English. And you are not nearly as happy as I am about that event. Now, what games do you propose I'm playing?"

"You can even ask something like that when you sound almost as fucking American as George Washington? What's going on here, Jade?"

"Jade, I am sorry to say, is dead, mon ami," Dominique said in a dark, quiet tone, his gaze unwavering. "A shame, but a necessity. A casualty of war."

"That I know of, we aren't at odds—not with France anyway," Devinio stated, tense from head to heel. "And you are an agent of France, aren't you, paisano?"

Acknowledging the statement with a slight nod, Dominique cast his gaze through the glass, sipping his drink, and drawing his cigarettes from his jacket. "An unwilling agent, but an agent nevertheless, I suppose," he said absently. "We aren't always given choices," he said and tilted his gaze to Devinio. "But you don't understand that statement, by no fault of your own, mon ami. You have lived a natural life. Rising from the middle-class American suburbs, touched slightly by the mafia through your ancestry. Rising . . . above whatever obstacles of class or creed were thrown into your path. You attended normal schools, excelled in sports and academics, joined the Air Force at the legal age, and chose the life you are living now. A natural progression with your intelligence and volition, your talent for solving mysteries and handling crises. You, sir, are a credit to the American way. I am an anomaly to everything you comprehend, and I won't insult your intelligence by limiting that statement to the material world. You've seen and grasped what I'm capable of doing. An agent of France or free enterprise? What's the difference?"

"Veronica Bryson-Laquette," Devinio said carefully.

Unwavering, Dominique studied the dark eyes for a few seconds, then shook his head, turning his gaze through the glass.

"Don't just shake your head, pal. Tell me where she fits into this uh . . . lifestyle or life of yours. I happen to know the lady's in love with you, and I was reasonably sure you were in love with her. Where the hell does she fit into this game?"

For a long moment, Dominique continued to study the black horizon, then slowly turned his gaze to Devinio. "Where did she fit in when you came to see me this morning, Agent Devinio? Was I what . . . expected to come here and perform a few parlor tricks then return to her as if it was nothing? All in a day's work? Do not . . . not ever, mon ami, bring up this subject to me again. When you and your partner visited me this morning, you destroyed whatever life I could share with her. Jade Laquette . . . If I could have truly killed that mythical bastard a few dozen years ago, I would have. Thanks to you and your idiot comrade, he's gone now."

"I think what bothers me most is that you actually believe that," Devinio said quietly. "And let's not make any mistakes here, I do know you have a few weird quirks. Did you know we'd be having this conversation this morning when you stopped in that elevator?"

"I'd imagine . . . sooner," Dominique admitted. "Unfortunately, my powers of observation toward my own good are often cast in doubt and less often reliable."

"Is your name actually Dominique Jardonet?"

"What's in a name, Agent Devinio?" Dominique asked smoothly. "Four months ago, you met Isaac Bently—a legitimate American entrepreneur with a wonderfully private lifestyle, comfortable home, a few close friends. Ah, then Jade Laquette popped into life. An American-born man who disappeared after an early tragedy. Now, you are meeting Dominique Jardonet, son to a French diplomat and entrepreneur with whom even your government would not dare to fuck."

"I met Jean-Pierre Jardonet if I'm not mistaken," Devinio said carefully, undoubtedly remembering a wedding reception a few months past.

"Did you?" Dominique asked, his gaze unwavering.

"Yea," Devinio stated, refusing to doubt despite the echo of sarcasm in Dominique's tone and the hazy visions in his memory. "And the resemblance was a little too obvious for you to deny." Although if he had to describe the elder Jardonet now, Lenny doubted he could. The image had faded, leaving only a vague impression.

"Then why ask if I am who you believe I am?" Dominique asked. "And that's something of a paradox, yes? I was one, then I was another, and now I am another again. What's in a name, my friend?"

"What happens if the press finds out? Or when they get wind of the French representative who's helping on this case? What happens to Ronnie then? She's going to know you're alive, and she's going to know who you are."

"I will be mortified when my bastard brother's death reaches the news," Dominique said quietly. "An affinity for the Americans was uh . . . natural, under the circumstances."

For several seconds, Devinio studied him before the enlightenment and anger sped across his eyes. "Damn you," he said softly. "I won't let you do that to her, Jade."

"You don't have a choice," Dominique said in a low scathing tone which halted Devinio's anger for a few seconds. "It would be terrible press coverage if the Federal Bureau was involved in the murder of an American citizen."

"What the hell are you talking about?"

"You were seen removing Jade Laquette from his home, sir. You and your partner, who it's well known, carried a personal grudge against said victim. Do I need to continue?"

"If you're even suggesting what I think you are, you wouldn't get away with it. For one thing, you're alive and well, and I'm fairly sure that could be proven."

"Then you are a fool, Agent Devinio, and I never thought of you as such. You have . . . what? Fingerprints? Ah, yes, fingerprints taken from Jade Laquette months ago . . . fingerprints which, I will admit, do not match my own even now. Ah, and then there is the question of Dominique Jardonet's curious arrival on the same day . . .? A coincidence which can be traced to the French Embassy along with plane tickets to verify that I flew into this city early this morning after someone in the Federal Bureau requested a favor of my friend, Ambassador Leonet." Dominique shrugged. "Are you beginning to see why it would be in your best interest to mourn the death of your friend, my half-brother?"

"How the fuck long have you been setting this up?" Devinio asked in a chilly tone.

"It's a contingency plan I was fool enough to hope I'd never need," Dominique admitted. "But as you curse me and despise me, Agent Devinio, remember who came to whom and set these wicked wheels in motion. And while you're at it, consider this . . . You were not alone when you arrived at my door. Agent Jarvins should uh . . . watch his step in the future. Dominique Jardonet is not as forgiving or ah . . . as kind as his half-brother." Letting a slow grin slip into his mustache, he added, "Diplomatic immunity is a terrible thing to waste."

For a long moment, Devinio studied him as if he might like to strike, then recovered enough to decide, "I'm rescinding the request for the French assistance on this case, Mr. Jardonet. I want you and your watchdogs on the first plane out of here tonight—"

"It doesn't work that way, mon ami," Dominique said with his slight smile intact. "As I believe I mentioned sometime this morning, I'm not playing by your rules any longer. I'm officially involved in this case. Keep your agents off my ass and out of my territory, or you'll waste a great deal of time collecting them from the side of a highway. I'll work with the two detectives in the next room exclusively. As you sanctioned that event earlier today, I see no reason to step over your head and make the request personally of their superiors. It wouldn't look good for the Feds to be at odds with the Frenchman they have enlisted. If I learn something of interest to you, as I believe I may, I'll let you know. We are, despite what you currently believe, on the same team. My cooperation will remain indisputable."

"Present circumstances, withstanding, Monsieur Jardonet, I find that really hard to believe."

"Believe what you will. My objective hasn't changed here."

"I didn't really know you at all, did I?"

"Do you expect an answer?"

"No," Devinio said soberly. "I don't guess I do."

Dominique lifted his glass in a sign of salute, not awaiting Devinio to follow suit before taking a drink. The heat flowing off the agent's posture and from his eyes, was enough to singe the air between them. Indifferently, Dominique lowered his drink. "Au revoir, mon ami."

"Yea, see ya around," Devinio said and started to turn, then paused. "Just don't push me too hard, Mr. Jardonet. Whether I know you or not, I think you know me, and we're walking a fine line here. Stay in touch."

"Wouldn't have it any other way," Dominique commented.

Devinio completed his turn and started toward the door. Halting again, a few paces away, he half turned. "Just one question, paisano . . . Was she just another piece of ass to you?"

Setting the drink aside on the ledge, he rose smoothly and advanced. His emerald gaze locked on Devinio freezing him in place an instant before his fist flew. Devinio spun and propelled several paces before he slammed the floor.

Starting forward, intent on another strike, Dominique closed the distance by half as Devinio collected as far as his hip and palm, his hand already clasping his jaw, blood glistening at the corner of his mustached lip.

The door burst open, Lejeune in the lead with his gun drawn, halted with the weapon swinging, leveling on the felled agent. Stopped, Dominique waited for the black eyes to lift, reading the intensity. In Italian, his voice dripping rage, Dominique stated, "Consider yourself lucky I am unarmed, Devinio, and get your ass out of here before I remedy that detail."

His black eyes glittering, a thought to rise to the challenge unparalleled, Devinio pushed slowly afoot, and Dominique flashed a glance and nod for Rudemonje to assist him, escort him.

Shaking off Rudemonje's hand, Devinio maintained his glare. "Stay in touch, paisano . . ." *And don't propose to tell me you're not Jade or that you don't love her.*

"Fuck you, asshole," Dominique hissed after him and stood only until Devinio passed between the Frenchmen and through the door. Fleeting his glance to Lejeune, he snapped, "See that he finds his way out and takes those other two agents with him." Turning, he returned to the window, collecting his drink.

Only Rudemonje remained in the room, coming beside him, and standing quietly a moment before asking, "Should I pack our bags, my friend?"

"Not yet," Dominique commented and stood a moment more, collecting, calming the rage still flowing freely through his veins. If another man had spoken those words, if any man ever spoke those words again, a broken lip would be the last of that fellow's worries. Drawing a breath, his eyes more naturally hazel, Dominique turned and motioned Rudemonje toward the door. "Dinner . . . Then we have a little more work to do."

CHAPTER 24

Subdued, neither detective engaged in small talk while finishing the dinner they'd barely begun before Devinio's arrival. His plate nearly empty, Dominique read the concern which spiraled off the pair in near livid color. He couldn't blame them. They were traveling in the company of a madman who'd just struck a federal agent, an agent who could probably have them busted to K-9 cleanup duty. In the past few hours, they'd seen more and learned more about their present case than they cared to know, and little could be proven by natural means. No, he couldn't blame them.

Shoving his plate aside, Dominique refilled his coffee cup, then leaned and topped off both detectives' cups. Meeting McAllory's gaze, he sat back. "You have concerns. Voice them," he said simply, and Rudemonje, seated at his opposite side, repeated the words in English.

"Guess I'm wondering just where you stand with the Federal Bureau at the moment," McAllory answered honestly, likewise moving his plate aside. "And where that leaves us."

"My differences with the agent have no bearing on this case. We are exactly where we were before, but if you'd like to speak with your commander and verify that, I wouldn't be offended." He barely paused, letting Rudemonje catch up before continuing. "In fact, it might be a good idea for you to phone your headquarters. If we're right to assume our villain crossed paths with Cummings while stalking Labinski, then we might assume he found Labinski through Demarco, Demarco through Lowenstein. If we can narrow those time frames, we'll know where our villain was and likewise, where he was not. Maybe we'll get lucky, eh? Maybe we'll find a doctor who takes a certain day off each week. Find out where your comrades are in their investigations."

"You really don't have any doubts that this guy's a doctor, do you?" Davis asked.

"No. I don't," Dominique answered smoothly, looking into her tense eyes as McAllory decided to comply and pushed from his chair. "Our villain has access and knowledge, over and above the evidence of surgical incisions we've seen on our victims. He knew which drugs to use to keep his patients breathing and reduce the bleeding while maintaining a balance to keep his patients anesthetized throughout the procedure. What type of doctor he is, remains to be seen, but he is most definitely a professional . . . and probably a specialist."

"That's sort of what we've been thinking, too, almost from the start," Davis said thoughtfully. Absently, she lifted her spoon, drumming a staccato beat on the table. "We've been looking into transplant surgeons."

Resting on the edge of the couch, McAllory spoke a few words into the phone and fell silent, apparently listening. Whatever he heard bothered him. His eyes flashed toward his counterpart then Dominique and listed as he nodded absently. "How about looking into something else for me, Rand? Send somebody over to the Clinic and find out how often Lowenstein worked overtime. Find out what held him up the evening he was killed . . . What?" For several moments, McAllory held silent, his muscles stiffening across his cheek. A few uttered curses escaped before he spoke again and signed off.

"What's going on?" Davis asked as he lowered the receiver.

"The shit hit the fan about a half hour ago," McAllory said as he pushed off the couch, sidestepping around the coffee table. "Apparently, a group of reporters caught Macanders leaving the courthouse this afternoon, and one of them asked him if there were others. Macanders handled it, but the question set off a witch hunt, and apparently, at least one reporter remembered the murder of Lowenstein.

"Connecting the dots, Jew and neo-Nazi, the reporter paid a visit to the Lowensteins, who in turn phoned the mayor." Settling into his chair, looking as if he'd aged a few years in the past few hours, McAllory looked to his partner. "If somebody doesn't string up Schleger for this shit—"

"Can't blame him, Shawn," Davis interrupted. "We've been working on borrowed time. Sooner or later, something was bound to leak."

"Yea, but we might have avoided a fucking riot, and the situation is escalating way too fast at Schleger's precinct. They just moved the two Nazi-wannabes to the county lockup for further questioning. It's turning into a fucking zoo with reporters camping outside the mayor's office, the courthouse, the morgue, and just about anywhere else they shouldn't be, and we're sitting on a timebomb."

"So how much does the Press know at the moment?"

"According to Rand, they're putting two-and-two together faster than Einstein could count to ten. If all four names aren't on the eleven o'clock news, along with most of the details, we'll be lucky." Something else bothered him, his gaze listed before landing on Dominique. "How much do you know about baseball?"

"Excuse me?"

"In baseball, when a team's slacking, they bring in a heavy hitter—a big name. Whether it's just to boost morale or help win the game, it usually works," he paused a moment. "The mayor wants to meet you. You're supposed to call DA Macanders as soon as possible. Apparently, someone's kicking around the idea to drop your name to the press. And I probably shouldn't tell you this, but I think if that happens, the weight of the press will shift. Unfortunately, they'll probably be on your doorstep, and I wouldn't be too surprised if what the DA asked you—I mean about this nutcase coming from France—will get kicked around a few times."

"Hmm, then we don't have much time left, my friends," Dominique commented. "I uh . . . don't do press conferences."

"Somehow, I had a feeling you didn't," McAllory said with a tight smile. "Are you pulling out?"

"You have the address for Carl Shumaker," Dominique said as he pushed from his chair. "I'd like to meet him and see Lowenstein's apartment." Looking to Lejeune, Dominique commented, "Have the car brought around, will you?"

"Are you phoning the DA?" Davis asked as Lejeune headed for the phone.

Amused, Dominique flashed her a glance as he started toward the door. "Can't recruit me if they can't find me, can they?"

"They can sure try," she said bluntly.

"Then they'll chase a phantom, yes?" he commented and winked.

McAllory stifled a laugh. "Somehow, I don't doubt that either."

"Do you think the connection could be with Shumaker?" Davis asked as they collected at the door. "I mean like Cummings and Jordan? You think that's the connection?"

"Shumaker was questioned and dismissed as a bystander, not unlike Jordan, while your team thoroughly investigated the Lowensteins' life. As you said, you considered the possibility of a doctor, and by your own compiled data, I'm assuming your comrades exhausted that avenue. Besides which, I don't think our villain is ah . . . stupid? He might have crossed paths with the Lowensteins in such a way that they wouldn't remember, but I don't think he would have remained a close personal friend. Their name would have been a deterrent." Reaching for the door, his thoughts vacant, he commented, "Something we're missing. Something which might connect these crimes pencil-dot form . . ."

The apartment that Lowenstein had shared with Carl Shumaker, occupied the second floor of an early Victorian mansion midway down a block of comfortably crowded houses of similar design. Without a doubt, most had transformed from single-family to multi-unit dwellings. Even in darkness, Dominique glimpsed more than a few side entrances and private, narrow stairways clinging to the sides of houses that hadn't existed on the original building plans. Like the backstreets of Bentwood, cars lined either side of the street, narrowing the road by half, but a few homes enjoyed the luxury of a driveway and garage . . . a few of those converted as well to supplement landlord incomes.

With lamps illuminating several curtained windows on the second floor, Shumaker was home, and as Dominique followed the detectives to the side entrance, he sensed the dual occupancy in the apartment. Shumaker might not have found another roommate, but he was entertaining company this evening. Narrow, the outside stairs ascended from the end of a wraparound porch, and Dominique paused a half step, sensing, feeling the annoyance of the old woman who occupied the first floor.

The landlord suffered a paradox . . . feeling sorry for the young man who resided on her second floor, at the same time, hoping he would decide to move. She hadn't minded two college boys in her house . . . *Most evenings, they were too busy studying to carouse or throw wild parties. Upcoming doctors . . . the both of them. Since the Lowenstein boy's murder though, a thought which sent a shiver through her arthritic joints, Shumaker had fallen back in his studies, more often skipping classes, and staying up all hours blasting music or entertaining guests. She'd need to put a stop to that sooner or later . . . but how she ached for that young man. To have lost his best friend . . . he should go home to his parents.*

The landing, illuminated by a single coach-lantern-style light in line with the Victorian era, barely accommodated the two detectives. Hanging in the shadows a few steps lower, Dominique listened to the offensive music emanating through the door. If the landlord could hear the lyrics, she might be more offended. Shumaker had found comfort in heavy metal and, undoubtedly, a few synthetic medications.

"He's definitely home," Davis commented after McAllory's second hammer rap of knuckles.

"Give him another moment," Dominique commented, and Rudemonje barely finished the translation.

The inside door opened; a husky voice drawled, "Who the fuck are you?"

"Detectives McAllory and Davis, Cleveland PD. Mind if we come in? We'd like to ask you a few questions."

In delay, Shumaker drawled, "I ain't done nothing, and I answered enough questions—"

"Who's it, Carl?" a female voice, likewise inebriated, joined Shumaker.

"Just a couple cops," Carl said offhandedly, apparently not even considering a reason other than Lowenstein could have brought them to his door. Either he was extremely naive, new to the drug scene, or he considered himself slightly above reproach. "They were just leaving."

"Carl," Davis said, sounding tough despite her lyrical voice. "I don't think you want us to leave right this moment. I think you'd rather answer a few questions here than make us take you downtown. If we did that, we'd probably end up running a blood test, and we'd have to insist you piss in a bottle."

Amused in the shadows, Dominique sensed Carl waking to the possibilities and felt the grip of genuine discomfort through the boy's numb limbs.

"I . . . I answered all kinds of questions," Shumaker said in a deflated tone, sounding far younger than twenty-two. More like a dejected child.

"We know you did, Carl," McAllory said in a quiet, reassuring tone. "We won't take up much of your time. Why don't we come in, and we can sit down," he continued while reaching for the door, and Shumaker agreed if only by action, backing away, letting McAllory enter.

The young woman was nowhere in sight, neither as naive nor preoccupied as Shumaker. Undoubtedly, she'd gathered whatever evidence existed in the living room. A commode flushing echoed clearly from a short hallway which probably led to the bedrooms and living room. The doorway opened into a cove that might have served as a dressing or sewing room in another life. The kitchen, sparsely furnished with a small aluminum-legged table and four chairs, hadn't been remodeled since its creation. Reflective of an earlier era, the fixtures had probably originated in the main kitchen on the first floor. White enameled cabinets and a porcelain sink, with a ridged drainboard built-in, caught and reflected the fluorescent light from a single tract directly over the sink. Dirty dishes and cups stacked, overflowing from the wide basin.

Notebooks and textbooks intermixed with empty junk food wrappers, drink containers, a milk carton, and a few odds and ends had trickled onto the floor.

As if he had no idea where the rubble had come from, the young man scanned the clutter listlessly, then leaned and shoved the papers off the nearest chair, sending them under the table and looking up at McAllory. Belatedly, he seemed to see the two others in the room, and his eyes widened a degree, swaying between Dominique and Rudemonje. Dilated, the black pupils carried a thin ring of pale blue, in line with the corn-flour color of his slightly long hair. Three months ago, he'd been a clean-cut college student working diligently toward a noteworthy profession; presently, he resembled a candidate for a drug rehab facility. Pale and gaunt, his once firm features carried the tale of his recent decline. "I ha-ave more chairs in the living room," he offered, apparently remembering the proper etiquette that had dictated his life before the tragedy. "We could ahh . . . go in there if you want."

"This is fine," McAllory said, exercising his right to be decent and rejecting the idea of compounding the boy's problems with a drug bust. Decent, despite his occupation, the young Irish detective sidled and cleared another chair, setting his notebook on a clean corner of the table. Signaling Davis silently, Sean coaxed Shumaker toward the table.

Shumaker, however, inebriated, had begun to sober up, and his focus flashed toward Dominique, uncomfortably aware of the strangeness. Buckling to his curiosity, he settled on McAllory, sensing an ally. "Who are tho-ose guys?"

Ignoring the question, McAllory dove in. "We've been reviewing the investigation of Abraham Lowenstein's death, Carl. I know you've already answered a ton of questions, but there are just a couple of things we came across—"

"Happened again, huh?" Carl said heavily, his already glazed eyes emitting a glassier shine. "I heard some stuff on the news earlier . . . They were talking about Nazis and some girl getting murdered. Did those bastards kill Abe? Is that why you're here?"

"Carl, I'd like you to think back for a few moments," McAllory continued in the same quiet voice, which offered as much reassurance as authority. "In your statement three months ago, you said that you and Abe hadn't spent a lot of time together before the night Abe was killed. You were both working and attending classes. As I recall, you and he weren't taking any of the same courses last semester. Sometimes neither one of you got home before eleven. Just out of curiosity," McAllory said smoothly, veering from the hardcore tactics that they'd discussed on the drive. "Did Abe usually work a lot of overtime? I mean, was he usually late getting off his shift?"

"Sorta," Carl drawled, slumped, and resigned. He'd pulled the chair out, his ankle drawn over his knee. His fingers played with a frayed string at the end of his faded jeans. "Abe loved the hospital . . . Like his folks, I guess. Unless he had a class or we had plans, he'd stay over or work a double. He was always on time," he said reflectively, his voice drained more by emotion than whatever he'd smoked or choked down before their arrival. "That's what sucks, ya know? He was always on time . . . 'He'd be at work sometimes a half hour early, and if he didn't get finished, he'd hang around till he got done. I uh . . . that's why I called the hospital, ya know? When he didn't come home . . . He shoulda been home. He wouldn't stand up a date . . . just wasn't his style. We didn't go out that much."

"So, you thought something came up at the hospital?" Davis asked.

He nodded, looking toward her with a slightly lost gaze. "Figured I'd find out how long he'd be, maybe have the girls meet us at the restaurant."

"Carl, can you think of anywhere that you and Abe were together before that night? Did you guys meet for lunch or something? Maybe stop off at the library? Catch a couple drinks someplace?"

"I didn't mean it to sound like we never saw each other," Carl said absently. "We were friends, ya know? We hung out together and stuff. Sometimes, like I told you guys, we'd leave each other notes—" A flicker of a smile haunted his lips; his eyes drifted to the frayed string. "Meet me at Lindy's—I'm buying," he quoted absently and looked over. "Lindy's is a dingy little bar a couple blocks from here . . . sorta like a central point between our jobs and school. It's over on 87th Street."

Both detectives electrified. This was something new. Something not mentioned in any of the prior reports. At face value, Carl was questioned, and his words were recorded, but no one sought another connection. The line of questioning had focused on where Lowenstein had spent his last few days, and Carl had been oblivious. Lowenstein had been the first, and the investigators hadn't believed the killer had stalked his victim. The investigators had sought the hospital connection with equal weight on the school scene. Not one of Lowenstein's professors or classmates had been overlooked in those first weeks. Hospital staff had been questioned. Other doctors, nurses, and associates of the elder Lowensteins were questioned extensively. High profile, the case had gained a great deal of attention in those first weeks, but Carl Shumaker was the lowest on the list despite his proximity to the victim.

"When was the last time you and Abe met at Lindy's before that night?"

Listless, Carl considered before deciding. "Hell, maybe a couple weeks," he said absently.

Davis glanced toward Dominique, searching for his reaction.

No reaction. Something wrong. Felt wrong.

"Did you meet anyone else there? Anything stick in your mind about that time?"

He tried to remember, but either time or uneventfulness clouded his memory. "Not that I can think of."

"Would it have been during the day or evening?" Davis asked.

"We generally met in the early evening, and it was probably a Wednesday," Carl said reflectively, again wearing that slight smile. "We uh . . . we both like wings and Lindy's runs a special. When we're not too busy . . ." First-person, present tense. He blinked and focused on the thread wrapped around his index finger. "Yea, probably in the early evening . . . on a Wednesday. We never did much drinking . . . anyway—" He stopped short, his brow furrowing.

"What are you thinking, Carl?" McAllory asked, watching him closely.

"Just thinking," he said absently. "Think that was around the same time I sprained my wrist. It was a bitch trying to eat wings with my arm in a splint. Abe . . . he thought it was funny as all hell," he said with a natural sadness.

"You . . .? How did you sprain your wrist?"

He looked over with a humph. "Playing racquetball," he answered before the weariness fell over his glazed eyes and his attention wavered to the string. "It was between semesters. We used to go over to his folks' club in the Heights. Abe was hell on a racquetball court. Me, I liked tennis, but I let him sucker me into it. We ended up making a trip over to the Clinic. He wouldn't let up until he made his mother read my X-rays."

"Touché," Dominique uttered under his breath, and both detectives looked toward him, their eyes bright with enlightenment. With a fleeting glance toward the door, he signaled them to close the interview, and McAllory wasted no time accepting the suggestion.

On the steps, her voice carrying a ring of excitement, Davis stated, "That's it, isn't it? That's where our killer locked onto Lowenstein? When the two of them went for X-rays?"

McAllory stated, "Or at the parents' club. But that doesn't exactly tell us how this maniac latched onto Shumaker. Wouldn't it have been to our advantage to ask Shumaker about his personal lifestyle, his friends, or acquaintances?"

"Shumaker was never the target," Dominique said as they strode off the porch, continuing down the sidewalk to where Lejeune waited. "He was uh . . . the catalyst."

"What's that mean exactly?" Davis asked. "What are you seeing that we don't?"

She'd used the appropriate words with no slip of the tongue. Reaching the car, not quick to climb inside, Dominique stood, lighting a cigarette, leaning against the fender. His gaze listed down the block of Victorian houses, and he felt it—the maniac had passed this way. He'd stood or rested behind the wheel of a car, watching, waiting.

"Two handsome boys," Dominique said absently. "A German and a Jew . . . living, playing, side-by-side . . . Ah, and the Jew boy is beautiful . . . such beautiful skin . . . Flawless," he said in a voice dripping with contempt, his gaze locked on the entrance to the house which he could see just past the porch roof of the adjoining house. "An abomination . . . and a sign . . . a sign that it was time . . . past time to begin his life's work, his aspirations. Too much freedom . . . a curse upon decent men. To have these two living and breathing the same air . . . a lesson—"

"He was here," McAllory stated shortly, drawing Dominique from his idling by no accident. Tense and sober, McAllory stood a pace away studying Dominique. "You know that for a fact, huh? This maniac locked onto these two because of their names, their heritage, and he'd stood about where we're standing, gearing up for his debut."

"He was ah . . . imbalanced, detective. Eventually, he would have begun acting on his madness, was planning it, in fact." He shrugged, "We know now, what set him off, and where, my friend. I would suggest we visit the County Medical Center and determine the date of Mr. Shumaker's accident. I have a feeling—an intuition if you prefer—we may learn the identity of your villain." With his words, he pushed off the fender and reached toward the back door handle. A sense of something touched him, a strangeness to wonder if he should send them alone.

Holding the door for Davis as McAllory strode around to the opposite door, Dominique considered asking Lejeune to drop him off at the hotel. Instead, he issued orders to drive them to the County Medical Center, suggesting he ask McAllory for directions. Obviously, whatever this ill-omen, it wasn't something he could avoid.

"Maybe we should call for backup," Davis commented as they settled into the backseat. "If you're as sure as you sound about this, we shouldn't piss around."

"What would you suggest we use as evidence, my dear? Or reason?"

"He has a point," McAllory said after the translation. "How do we investigate this without tipping this guy off, that's more the question, Chels. We won't need a warrant to get the date or the name of the doctor who treated Shumaker, but as soon as we start asking questions and the information's accessed on a computer, our guy might figure out we're getting close. Any suggestions, Det. Jardonet?"

"We are past the daylight shift," Dominique commented. "Our doctor doesn't work evenings. But there is a slight problem with our theory, comrades. Shumaker didn't need to see a surgeon for a sprained wrist. We're undoubtedly searching for an accident victim in need of emergency surgery. Our doctor's a specialist . . . and he was on-call that day. Ah, what a fool, I am. The answer is so simple . . . a plastic surgeon," he said in a tone reeking of disgust at his delayed revelation. "Who would have more freedom of hours? Who would have a greater knowledge and appreciation for the skin? Dumbass," he said to himself. "The answer stares me in the face, and I look the other way. There's the mystery, eh?"

"I'll be damned," McAllory said under his breath. "If you think you feel stupid, I don't even like to think of how stupid I feel at the moment."

"Ditto," Davis growled. "A plastic-fucking-surgeon. Some of the highest paid sons-a-bitches in the business . . . and we've wasted three fucking months looking for a medical connection to bone marrow or skin graft specialist."

"You were searching for a reasonable explanation for this madness" Dominique consoled. "A conspiracy to justify such a ruthless crime. The only other option was to believe you had a maniac who chose his victims randomly when no connection could be found. Why, then, would he take skin and bone? A paradox."

"I, for one, didn't want to believe it was a doctor," McAllory grumbled, his gaze turned through the opposite window. "Everything pointed to that, but I was really hoping we'd find out we had some nutcase sailing on PCP or some shit."

"A pity that's not the case," Dominique said, his tone descending with his thoughts. "Much worse, I'm afraid, and not so easily stopped."

"What does that mean?"

"Knowing who, will not stop him," Dominique said quietly. "Even when you have a name and face in your grasp, the law remains on his side, and he's a clever lunatic. Do you think you'll find his tools laid out before you? Do you think he'll leave the evidence lying about for you to collect? A pity life is not so simple. What a wonderful world if we could simply declare him mad and have him hung or strung from a stake to be burned. There's a lot to be said for the medieval ages, or even the more recent past when little proof was needed to exact justice. A guillotine would serve us well."

McAllory huffed a sound, nearly an angry snort. "Yea, I agree. But since we're fresh out of them, I guess we better count on setting up surveillance and nailing this guy the old-fashioned-modern way. Bearing that in mind, I think we better be careful who we talk to at County Medical."

"It'd be nice if we could talk to one of the administrators," Davis considered. "Maybe we should call in and have the chief pave the way."

"Not a good idea," Dominique commented, and his voice drifted momentarily, thinking. "It would be better not to have your names or faces involved in this endeavor. With the publicity, even the sight of your badges will raise antennas with Lowenstein's affiliation to the hospital."

"You have a plan."

"Ah . . . reasonable assumption," he answered and fell silent, his gaze turned through the glass, watching the houses passing. In the front seat, Lejeune accepted another direction from McAllory and rolled onto another busy thoroughfare. At the peak of evening visiting hours, finding a parking space would be a problem, but to McAllory's suggestion to park near the emergency room, Dominique commented, "You and your partner remain with Lejeune and return here in five minutes. If we haven't returned, you're welcome to come find us." With those words, he ordered Lejeune to the curb at the entrance and stepped out as Rudemonje finished the translation and followed. Neither detective gained a moment to object before Dominique strode away from the car, Rudemonje at his side.

"May I ask, what is your plan?" Rudemonje asked.

"I would rather you don't ask, my friend. When we get inside, we'll part company. Visit the gift shop and read a few magazine titles." Dominique said and fell into stride behind a rowdy group of teenagers crowding through the glass doors. Barely inside the lobby, they parted, Rudemonje traveling toward the sign indicating the gift shop. Dominique followed the crowd, starting toward the elevators, then veered and passed through a wide hallway, following the signs for the admission department. At this hour, a full staff wouldn't be on duty; admissions undoubtedly entered through the emergency department. In fact, as he suspected, only a single woman occupied the compact cubicle, apparently catching up on clerical duties. Leaning over and routing in a desk drawer, she never saw him enter, and when she lifted, she nearly gasped with her start. His gaze locked on her wide brown eyes, and he halted her sound, his hand touching her shoulder as if they were well acquainted.

Mind-bending again—you little monster!

Shrugging away the memory, Dominique enlisted a low, silky voice, suggesting she return to her computer screen and continue her task. Locked into her psyche, he directed her fingers with voice commands to open the necessary files for the day in question. In less time than it had taken him to find the office, he read the name on the screen . . . Dr. W. J. Reddinger.

Whitman James Reddinger . . .

In vivid detail, Dominique saw him standing within the neon glow of Olden Time's fluorescent lights. Impeccably dressed in preppy style with a starched blue shirt and dark blue cardigan vest, the fellow wore a thin smile, his eyes bright with interest. 'Doctor,' the collegiate fellow corrected Isaac's use of 'sir,' then continued in a congenial tone, offering his name as well as his slender hand. 'Dr. W.J. Reddinger. And you are . . .?'

The transition flashed at lightspeed. Rather than Olden Time's showroom, a circle of lamplight illuminated a wire-bound ledger, sprawled open on the office desk.

A page flipped, barely whispering a sound within the shadowy atmosphere. It was late . . . after hours in Olden Time.

Columns of names were scribbled on the lined tablet paper; empty spaces gaped between the wanted items and descriptions of antiques. Oriental designs . . .

The Want files. Handwritten words scrolled across the pages, volleyed between neat block print and flowing script, depending on who jotted the information in the spiral-bound ledgers. Elaine Connely or Isaac Bently . . . or Jade Laquette. Differences in style existed between those two latter names. Two separate identities . . . And Dominique Jardonet's handwriting would be even more distinctive.

Evening shadows . . . after hours . . .

'Want files,' a familiar husky voice muttered in the preternatural silence, 'Who knew . . .' A search had begun. A stout finger trailed down the page in search of an unfamiliar phone exchange, pausing to read another address, mumbling again. 'Don't suppose Texas—'

'Hurry! She says to hurry!'

'How many of these damn books does he have?'

'Mebbe five.' Elaine answered anxiously.

After hours?

Distracted, as much by the memory as the premonition, Dominique impacted the insight, aware of the familiar voices of Tim Spencer and Elaine Connelly. They'd stood in his shop, and by the dull light, the absence of symphony music echoing from the showroom, they occupied the private office of Olden Time after hours. The want files . . . Reddinger would be found in those books. A stack of binder notebooks that Isaac Bently had begun compiling nearly at the onset to accommodate his out-of-town customers. Names, addresses, phone numbers, and a description of the customer's desired 'wants,' and W.J. Reddinger had wanted a few specialty items. Oriental design . . .

No more time to waste. Holding the administrator tranced too long could become dangerous. Even now, she struggled to awaken.

In a soft silky tone, he added voice to his mind-bending suggestions for her to close the screen, then sent an order for her to forget his visit.

Retracing his steps to the lobby, Dominique found the giftshop and snagged Rudemonje's gaze through the glass. Not until he stood on the sidewalk, watching cars pass and awaiting the sedan, Dominique considered the simplicity of his undertaking. A talent . . . a far too dangerous talent, and yet he suffered no regrets. The power of suggestion. His father had used that same talent, time and again, and the lessons were well learned. Perhaps, too well learned. No longer could he disillusion himself to believe in coincidences spiraling around him.

With Rudemonje joining him as the sedan pulled in front of them, Dominique slipped into the backseat, feeling both detectives straining against the unspoken demand.

A half block from the hospital entrance, Davis burst. "Well? Did you have any luck?"

Too much luck, he might have mentioned, instead, shaking his head. "I couldn't access the files. You'll need to speak with your commander, after all. Perhaps, he has a contact who'll open the doors without drawing the press."

CHAPTER 25

In French, Dominique directed Lejeune to deliver their charges to the hotel, then continued with a signal for Rudemonje to translate. "For obvious reasons, my friends, I'm not joining you. We're returning to the hotel, and you can pick up your car. Be sure to invite Agent Devinio to join you when you speak to your commander, and if you continue to view this as a possible connection rather than a given, it would be to all our advantage."

"Why do I get the impression, you don't want the credit for this?" Davis asked.

"You are bright," Dominique said and flashed her a slight smile within the shadows. "And you know what sort of criticism we'd all face. Whatever story you create to explain where we've been and how you reached your conclusions, I won't dispute it. Deductive reasoning, brainstorming, and a fresh perspective on the case would all wear well toward explaining what we've done this evening."

"You're backing out of this investigation," McAllory grasped.

"I've done what I can," Dominique verified and probably muddied the waters more than necessary. But he had his own agenda, and catching a psychopath wasn't at the top of his list. "The rest is up to you, and I have no doubts you'll compile the facts to mete justice."

"Are we going to see you again?" Davis asked.

"I may be around for a time," he answered offhandedly.

"But not hanging around the headquarters or visiting the mayor, huh?" McAllory asked with a wry smile.

"Touché," Dominique mused. "If you can't reach me at the hotel, phone the French Consulate in New York'. They'll find me."

"I can't say it's been fun working with you, Mr. Jardonet," Davis said quietly. "But it's definitely been interesting and enlightening. When we nail this bastard, I hope you're around so we can celebrate. I think we're going to owe you one helluva night on the town."

"I think what she means is, thank you," McAllory commented.

"You're welcome," Dominique said simply and fell into his silent thoughts, preoccupied before they reached the hotel's main entrance. In rapid-fire French, Dominique enlisted Lejeune to deliver the detectives to their car. "When they drive away, bring the car to the rear entrance," he added. Saying his farewells and shaking hands with both, he waved as they pulled away, then turned and strode into the hotel with Rudemonje. Together they rode to the penthouse floor, and Dominique continued into the private bedroom.

On dual planes, he saw himself dialing Lenny's private number and watched the clandestine exchange within the shadows of the rear parking lot. If he stood near enough to the window, he could physically look down upon another government-issue dark sedan, the Federal Bureau's ride of choice. Within the rear compartment, Agent Mark Jarvins rested, anticipating the coming moments with a certain odd glee—that he should be granted the opportunity to carry out this order was yet another feather in his cap. An even split remained between those who wanted Laquette abducted for further study and those who preferred him dead before any other prognostications of yesteryear could come to pass.

Fools, bloody fools to believe themselves truly capable of subverting whatever premonitions that a tortured young soul had offered them. Had they truly meant to test their wiles against that child, they might have tried harder to eliminate him when they had the chance . . . but even that, the child had denied them. As much as Dominique might like to deny it, he knew his weird talents had reached out across an ocean to bring his father to his blasted rescue.

Sighing as the phone engaged, Dominique flashed a thought of Devinio stepping away from the gathering at the press conference, taking this call.

"I do hope this means you intend to visit me sometime soon," Lenny commented in an all-business tone, not betraying his caller to anyone within earshot.

"Wish that I were, mon ami," Dominique offered in a genial tone, sighing. "But alas, fate beckons, and I might be indisposed for some time."

"Get un-indisposed, Amico. We have a few things to discuss," Lenny said carefully.

"Unfortunately, I don't have time just now as I have a date with destiny, but there are a few things I need to share with you before I go," he said in a distracted tone. Images swirled through his mind's eye, from syringes exchanging hands within shadows—one lethal, one not—to several anxious agents setting up surveillance within a fine empty mansion. Snowbirds . . . those elusive beasts to lock up their winter homes and head south to avoid the harsh winter winds off Lake Erie. The house was empty and within clear sight of a similar mansion in the upper-class neighborhood.

"Do not be too quick to act when you find a name, my friend," Dominique spoke in a quiet rhythm. "I think . . . No, mon ami, I *know* the mon`stair you seek is not the man you will find. Your killer, he is close . . . but I am afraid, he may be mine."

"What the hell does that mean?"

"I . . . I believe that he and I have crossed paths before, Len. We were uh . . . studied in the same labor`atory. He did not fare so well, my friend. He is a mon`stair with visions of grandeur, and others exist who would use him toward their own end."

"If you know who the hell he is—"

"If, mon ami, if I knew at this moment, I might be inclined to tell you as I have a sense of things not so pleasant on the hori`zon, but *c'est la vie.* To shange this moment is to shange many more, and the path I hov shosen lies before me, now. Just do not act too swiftly against our doct`air. He may not be the man you are seeking. Not much more I can tell you."

"Jade—"

"If such a one existed, mon ami, he is no more," Dominique said quietly, sorrowfully. "Take care, my friend."

Replacing the receiver, he stood a moment, gazing through the window to the black horizon, and a crease slid across his brow. Only in his mind's eye, he saw the alabaster face sinking beneath a dark tide, watched the black hair spiraling over empty eye sockets. Against a wicked pain, he drew a breath and stepped back from the window as if he might distance himself from the horrifying image. If ever there was a circumstance he needed to subvert, that was the one, and he could only hope he'd chosen the path to thwart that possible end.

At all costs, he needed to eliminate the threat against his wife and child, and the means to that end awaited him in the parking lot.

Russian roulette, he considered as a wry smile kinked his mustache. All his life, he'd been playing Russian roulette, with his visions and his life, and this wasn't the exception. Either he would or wouldn't receive a lethal dose of whatever drug the Taxidermist used, and either way, he would have learned a great deal about his nemesis—both the one in the sedan and the ones in Washington.

Passing through the bedroom door, he found Rudemonje leaning at the slight bar, not surprised when the fellow rose to his full height, anticipating their departure. "How about collecting our bags, my friend, and book reservations on the ten-thirty flight to New York. If I'm not back, call a cab to deliver you to the airport, and I'll catch up to you in New York."

"Dominique, I'm not sure that's a good idea."

"It's far too late to question my judgment, my friend," he said simply and strode from the room. Walking down the stairwell to the fourth floor, he veered his course to the rear elevator and rode within a dozen paces of the exit where the car waited. Again, the urge to back away, to walk away nearly flattened his resolve, but he continued walking, passing through the security door before he could change his mind or course.

Rather than parked at the lighted entrance, the sedan rested half concealed in the shadows of a small tree and shrubs, not unlike the hospital parking lot where Lowenstein had been taken. Striding purposefully to the passenger door, Dominique suffered no doubts of the moments to come, nor was he surprised when the man stepped from the bushes behind him. His hand on the door handle, Dominique froze as the gun barrel touched the small of his back. In the front seat, Lejeune rested as still as stone, and Dominique knew the fellow had been immobilized by synthetics.

"Don't do anything foolish, Mr. Jardonet. My friend in the backseat has a gun on your comrade," the husky American voice came at a low volume. "Put both hands on the side of the car. No one needs to get hurt here. We're just going to take a little ride and chat."

"Reassuring, sir, with a gun in my back. A telephone call would have been more appropriate," Dominique commented but placed his hands on the door. Even anticipating the quick jab at his hip, he jolted, rising in reflex before the heated flash started through his system. "Bassstard." The word hissed off his lips as his tongue swelled and the world rippled.

"Just relax," the stranger stated and clasped his arm as he staggered against the side of the car. "Let's go. Just a few steps."

No choice, his knees buckled as the liquid raced through his muscles, stumbling and collapsing him before he reached the backseat. Not total darkness or relief from consciousness. He fell over in the seat, vaguely aware of the voices droning, the engine igniting. He would reach his intended destination, alive—barely—he harbored no doubts, but the revelation relieved nothing of the hostility rising.

"Chopper," a familiar voice ordered, barely restraining his smug tone.

In his way, Dominique knew at least two others who resided in this company. An extraction team. Coordinated, the bodies shifted and shuffled in the seats, playing musical chairs without the music, to replace Lejeune in the driver's seat, landing him alongside Dominique in the shadowed rear seat.

"Check his pockets. Make sure he's not armed and find his passport," Mark Jarvins commanded.

Silently, obediently, another faintly familiar agent rifled through Dominique's pockets, searching for weapons and removing personal items.

"Chopper . . ." It was the last word Dominique heard before the whisper slipped off his lips and he slid into darkness. "Mon amour . . ."

"Mayday! Mayday!" Harry Windell shouted into the headsets. The instrument panel lit up like a Christmas tree in front of him, screaming every kind of failure from engines to landing gear. They were going down! "Buckle up!" Harry shouted to his passengers, but if either man heard, neither responded. "We're going down!"

And it was Vietnam all over again. He saw the emerald blanket stretched before him, so vivid green that he could believe himself lying down on a bed of grass in mid-summer. As a child, he'd loved to sprawl under the old oak out behind the homestead. He and Paul, his best friend, had spent hours contemplating life, planning, and dreaming of what they would do with their future.

A pilot, Harry had professed. He was going to fly jets like his Uncle Elroy, who'd gone down in a dogfight over France. His daddy called his brother a hero . . . But that's not what they called the boys coming back from Nam. On dual planes, Harry heard shouts at the airport, saw the protestors in the streets . . . He'd tried going home. A soldier, a pilot . . . he'd flown choppers. Survived the crash . . .

And on another plane, he knew the instruments screaming warnings on the control panel.

No longer afraid, or even alarmed by the screams, Harry held the yoke, merely gazing at the emerald blanket rising to greet him. No one spoke from the rear compartment. In a moment of crystal clarity, he knew he was alone inside the cabin, alone except for the body that had been strapped into the seat within the rear compartment. Mr. Smith had returned to the craft only long enough to direct his two companions to deliver the cargo into the rear seat, and in a rare moment, Mr. Smith had touched Harry's shoulder, telling him almost sadly, 'God's speed, my old friend.'

No longer even half aware of the sounds screaming in his ears, not the warning siren wails or the shouts through the headsets. On a slow tide, he saw Pauley, round, freckled face flushed from the sun, eyes livid with the excitement as he announced his plans to join the army when he finished high school . . . And later, still freckled but not so rounded, his smile beaming as they met at the malt shop, both in uniform and fresh from boot camp. So long ago, but yesterday in Harry's mind. That image remained the last time they'd come face to face . . . until now.

Oh, and to be young again! Filled with the promise of their glorious future . . . and here was Pauley, standing at ease with a beaming smile! A soft glow hovered at the edges of his immaculate green dress uniform . . . Pauley stood alongside Uncle Elroy, a young man whose face Harry had only seen in the framed photograph perched atop the TV console. Even without the photograph, Harry would have recognized him. The fellow looked like a much younger version of the man who stood with one arm draped over his shoulders, and his other arm hugging a slight woman at his side. Harold Sr. and Sally Windell . . . lovers and friends since high school . . . Both smiling and welcoming, waiting, as they'd been waiting for Harry when he'd stepped off the jet to carry him home from Vietnam. They'd hugged him then . . . as they were waiting to hug him now, but he'd been too confused to appreciate their happiness then. He understood it now as he stepped off the jet into their embrace . . .

The impact of the explosion sent a vibration through the hills and a ripple through the aether.

On the cusp of sleep, Ronnie shot awake, hearing the voice whispered in her ear. On the tip of her tongue, his name hovered, but she halted it there, waking more to the disorienting sights of a strange room. Groping, climbing, she found the lamp, startled and dismayed to realize she'd barely closed her eyes ten minutes ago. Wide awake now, she rested on her elbow, scanning the room as if she expected to find something changed. Nothing changed. In a rapid sequence of thoughts, she recalled booting the Spencers from the room. Driven as much by weariness as loneliness, which had enhanced at the sight of their silent communication. Donna and Tim had eight years of practice . . . She and Jade had shared that intimacy nearly from the instant they'd met.

Flopping back on the pillow, she stared at the corrugated ceiling, remembering. They'd met in Meg's Diner, him sitting in his usual place near the register . . . pawning his wares for a song, or so it seemed. She'd thought him nuts . . . Or a fool until he'd turned his liquid green eyes on her. *Keep my secret* . . . the eyes had said it all, halting her from mentioning the fair market price for that work of art, a price Meg would never have afforded.

Ronnie hadn't known him then, but she wondered, now, if she might have fallen in love with him at that instant. Any man who could take a five hundred percent financial loss with such innocent grace . . .? She'd fallen in love with him, but she still wondered how he'd come to love her. By what strange turn had God allowed them to meet, to fall in love, to wed . . . Or was it predestined as early as eighteen years ago? In all honesty, she had met him first then, and that memory surfaced. Filtered over the years, she remembered him resting against the bright blue A-frame of the swing set in the playground of her elementary school, a private school where some of the most prominent men and women in the country sent their children for an education. He'd been standing alone, as he'd always seemed to be alone . . . and she'd noticed him before that day. Older, wiser even then, he'd seemed untouchable, an upperclassman by two years, taller, sleek as a movie star even in his slight build. As cool and indifferent as a man, those pale green eyes had lanced her across the playground . . . and touched her then, perhaps, sealing their fate.

God, she loved him.

And what if he was hurt?

Sitting up uncontrollably, she uttered a breath of disgust and dismay. If anyone had ever told her, accused her of falling hopelessly, helplessly in love, she might have laughed herself silly . . . And would have known the truth of it on the inside. For him, she had waited . . . and in him, she trusted.

Sobering that latter thought. She did trust him. His intelligence, his love for her, his gifts, which he'd used at the onset to protect her. From what would he protect her now . . . if not from the possible murderer of Jack Trumble? What would he have found so much more threatening than a conspiracy of the magnitude that she'd uncovered?

Remembering his nightmares, his night sweats . . . the dismay in his eyes, and his attempted subterfuge when she'd broached the subject of this excursion, an uncomfortable thought fleeted in her mind. Was this venture—Jack Trumble's death—a sign of some sort? Had she unwittingly delivered an omen? Something like a messenger? Or was she again his catalyst?

He'd called her that four months ago. His catalyst. The beginning or the end . . . And they'd begun their life together in the wake of an end. An end to the murders. An end to his borrowed identity as Isaac Bently. An end to her loneliness and his own. For four beautiful months, they'd lived together, as man and wife, lover and friend. Together in nearly every moment, whether a few rooms or a town apart or wrapped together like Siamese twins beneath satin sheets. Never in her life had she known such happiness, and she sensed he shared that unnatural bliss. If she'd destroyed that . . . if she'd destroyed their happiness by following her intuition to uncover this conspiracy . . .

No. She wouldn't even romance that thought. If she'd delivered a message, a sign, she could only believe it was one he'd anticipated. One as predestined as their union. Whatever this strangeness . . . whatever had taken him away, she couldn't afford to believe that she'd somehow brought it to bear like a wind hitting a house of cards. What they had wasn't a house of cards. Like every other blasted couple alive, they'd suffer problems, but what they shared would withstand a God-blessed gale. To believe otherwise was to lose faith and trust, to weaken the very foundation on which she believed their union stood.

She was still going to hurt him. Right after she hugged the stuffing out of him and kissed the breath from his lungs. The big jerk! How dare he send her off in one direction and determine to take another?

Momma, pappa, and baby bear . . . three together, forever. Blast him.

Again, flopping backward, staring at the ceiling directly above her head, she whispered, "Be well, my love. Wherever you are—whatever you're doing—survive and succeed. I need you. Tad needs you. We love you."

CHAPTER 26

The focus of attention, Dominique understood, as surely as he felt himself somehow ignored by his white-frocked companions, who wheeled him headfirst toward a destination he had anticipated. A helicopter . . . he glimpsed the flanks and doors. The whizzing, nearly invisible blades shadowed the darkness overhead, and too soon, the ceiling turned gray above him. On the outer edges of his vision, others moved, moving with him, crowding around him. His head rolled; his eyes barely opened enough to identify images veiled by his eyelashes which wouldn't quite lift. Wrong . . . something was wrong. Nothing moved on its own power. A disturbing vulnerability touched him, rising panic in his mind that he was seen and not heard. Deliberately ignored. Suppressed and restrained . . . and drugged for . . . convenience? Or out of fear?

One of them hovered over him, looking down into him, canting his head as if spying something peculiar under glass.

If Dominique had ever seen this man before, the memory eluded him, but a sense of familiarity touched him. As if looking at a double-exposed picture, he saw another masked face, glasses reflecting the light. The Taxidermists . . . the fellow wore blue hospital scrubs, surgical scrubs. Rather than this sober, intense, young face above him, Dominique suffered the certainty of the taxidermist occupying the hospital attire, knew the twisted excitement hidden behind the mask . . .

'Alas, you are mine . . .'

"Just relax, Mr. Laquette," the low voice, at closer range, cut through the monotonous sounds. "You're in good hands . . . We're just taking a little trip. Nothing you need to worry about."

A lie, he sensed it, felt it. A great deal to worry about, but the thought slipped away as the sturdy face tipped away, addressing another.

"How's his vitals?"

"Still low, but steady," a crisp voice answered.

"Ready when you are—"

The increase in engine sound registered within the fog, more muffled now, but the noise remained overpowering. Numb, drifting, Dominique knew when the craft lifted, sensed the vibrations of motion, and the significance of the sounds changing tempo around him. Whether he dreamed of flying or flew now, he lost thought to wonder. Fading in and out, the images of strangers and the sounds fleeted through his consciousness, nothing remaining long.

Sleep . . . he knew the sleep he needed. In fluting rhythms, he heard his mother's voice whispering at the edges of his mind, telling him to sleep now, to recover. Mesmerizing, that distant voice, but even now the fear lingered at the edges of his consciousness. Dying . . . He'd always felt the dying, the numbing death in the wake of his curse. Nothing moved. Whether he struggled now against the sleep of the dead or against the drugs mainlining in his system, he had no clear grasp. Against his mother's chanting rhythm and the vibrations, he was no match. Sleep . . . he needed to sleep to recover. Still, he battled . . .

Fear. He knew the fear at his deepest levels of awareness, knew what she asked of him, demanded of him was dangerous . . . for him, for her. Other boys . . . he wanted to be like other boys. Not a monster . . . Nanna understood. She treated him like other boys . . . and he wanted her now. He wanted her to come and wake him as she had so many other times before . . . She knew how this frightened him, knew he feared that the sleep of the dead would take him one day and not let him go . . .

R'ed for me, bab'be boy . . .

*Nooo! Pleeease nooo . . . not again, mam`ma . . . Plllease not again . . .* but she made him read again. No playing ball like other boys . . . no walking to the park with Nanna now . . . Different. He was different . . . she knew it. Nanna knew it. He was a warlock . . . like his pappa. 'A warlock . . . like your pap`pa,' that's what mamma told him. Not like other boys. Things he touched . . . talked to him. The dead talked to him. He had to read . . . learn to read. *A monster* . . . and they would come for him.

". . . He's getting restless . . . due for meds . . . How soon before we land . . . make sure the unit's on standby . . ."

"How the fuck did this happen. . .? That wasn't supposed to be a goddamn lethal dose!"

. . . *A monster . . . to be feared . . . to be afraid.* And he was afraid . . . more afraid now of living . . . than of dying. What they could do to him . . . would do to him. *Had already done to him?*

'Do you want them to take you, bab`be boy? Is thot what you want. . .? If they knew whot you were . . ..'

"Blood pressure's climbing . . . Pulse is increasing . . . He's waking up, Conners!"

"Calm down," the husky voice demanded. "We'll have you down in a few minutes. Just relax."

Not relaxed. Numb. And he was waking. The voices were more real. The sounds amplified. Offensive. Struggling on the edges of consciousness, he dragged his lids open enough to spy the faces above him. He rested in a helicopter. Nothing moved, but his entire body vibrated, numb and tingling against the thin cushion on which he lay. Around him, the portable medical equipment hummed in tune with the propeller blades and engine roar. A trip . . . a little trip. A little chat . . . trip to a hospital . . . another hospital he knew at this moment.

Time had lapsed. He'd passed through another hospital—undergone emergency treatment to counteract the poison.

His head shook; his liquid gaze drifted, searching the faces. Strangers again. Those within his view were strangers. The one who'd spoken to him earlier, dark-haired, crisp blue suit . . . not a doctor. The man no longer wore the white smock in reflection of a medical technician. An agent . . . another federal agent, but a mere pawn, an expendable pawn, accepting orders blindly . . . manipulated.

Within his chest, Dominique recognized the leaden beat of his heart as he studied this stranger who watched him with equal intensity. Not right . . . a lie. He knew the lie. He knew at this moment, he'd been taken to a hospital, received the antidote to counter a near-lethal injection . . . A pity he needed to endure this ordeal to reach his destination. He might just as easily have walked into this next facility as easily as he'd walked into that admissions office.

C'est la vie. He was here, now, en route to the hospital that had threatened his life and his sanity many years ago.

He doesn't look so tough. Surely not a threat to national security, the young man considered silently, fully unaware of the interloper in his psyche.

One day, perhaps, Dominique might need to thank this young zealot for retaining enough of his humanity to accept the silent suggestions. A perfected art, that bit of mentalism, to play in another's mind and bend his conscious will. The key, Dominque had discovered long ago was to align his desire with the volition of the recipient. He could no more turn a good man evil than he could turn an evil man good although he'd certainly tried a time or two. If this young Agent Burns had buckled to his orders to transport a body, doubtful the fellow would have reacted when he identified the sign of life and recognized the possibility of an overdose. Without intervention, things might have happened differently and unfolded as a select group of Americans had apparently planned. Dominique might be, at this moment, lying on a metal table, awaiting a visit from the Taxidermist.

But then, that wasn't likely either.

Americans, the son of Jean-Pierre trusted them no more than he trusted the French, and he had no intention of forfeiting this game so easily. A game, a gamble, but a necessary evil. If he intended to subvert this threat, he must first allow himself to appear vulnerable, and allowing himself to be nearly killed should lend his enemy a sense of comfort if not superiority.

One would think these idiots would know differently; after all, Jean-Pierre had enlisted similar tactics years ago to spare his son this final odyssey—with a little help from his son.

Zealots. They truly believed themselves superior—a superior race.

Dominique shook his head slowly, his gaze held steady. Anger and amusement vied for attention within his throbbing leaden mind. Nothing moved. He found the substantial straps on his wrists, his ankles, across his chest, and thighs. Immobilized. His muscles were wasted within the effects of whatever medication flowed through his veins. Whether physical exhaustion or the drugs held him immobile, he couldn't decide. His fingertips tingled, numb from vibrations. With an effort, he formed fists, and for a moment, he believed his hands wrapped around a steering wheel, flying . . . racing.

Loved to drive . . . fast. Needed to drive fast . . . the devil raced at his heels. Forever. Chased, hounded by the devil, and the faces never mattered, these were just more of the same entity.

Aware, but paralyzed, Dominique listened and watched, understanding the activity around him as clearly as he recognized the engine tempo changing once again. They were landing, making him ready for landing, for transporting. Nothing could he move, nor would the words rise off his swollen tongue. Time and again, these ones avoided his direct gaze, feigning distraction when they caught him watching. Only the nearest, this sharp-dressed man with the close-cropped hair, ventured a few glances and reassuring words that offered nothing of comfort or relief.

Feigning to remain powerless, his body numb and swollen, Dominique jostled under the anxious hands rolling him from the bowels of the helicopter, hoisting and gliding him from beneath the blades. Overhead, the sky had darkened, nearly purple-black. Like tiny diamonds on black velvet, he glimpsed the stars . . . soft blue diamonds.

All too swiftly, the comfort of those sparks abandoned him, lost in a wash of blinding florescent light. Suffering blindness, his stomach rolled with the change in motion, a downward motion. An elevator. Hazy, the faces and bodies stayed with him, the voices subdued now, barely above a whisper without the helicopter engine intruding. Droning, he heard the verbal exchange, his vision only beginning to improve when other faces appeared around him, taking control of him . . . possession.

Black and white, gray, and darker gray, the bodies tread in the broken animation of an old film. The clatter of a movie projector remained as vivid as the faces turning away and ducking in shame and fear of the spotlight. Huddled, men and women marched, cleaving youngsters to their hips and shoulders, their tattered coats and brimmed hats suggesting the chill in the air around them. White spots and spider-webbed lines cluttered the film, blotching and spotting the broken animation. Still, the barbed wires and enclosures, the smoke of steam engines and trains, the walls of a factory . . . a barracks . . . chambers . . .

He knew this fellow. Dr. Carson . . . a face from the past. Or the present? So, it had begun, with the film reel clattering in the background—

Animated abruptly, Jade stood within a faded light. Sun streams filtered through sheer curtains, slanting between the heavy gold drapes held aside by woven gold cords. Lifting his hand to the light to catch the sunbeam in his palm, he watched the rainbow sparkle of dust particles shifting about his splayed fingers. The aroma of a rich Havana cigar mixed with the faint musty scent of old paper. He canted his head, reading the titles on the tomes lined up on a wall of shelves. Law books, journals . . . an entire collection of the Encyclopedia Britannica. These were new. He held a set in his private collection, c. 1768, 15th edition, gold inlaid leather bindings in mint condition . . .

His focus slid, landing, locking on the wide pale blue eyes staring at him.

The fellow rested behind a wide, stately old desk, his liver-splotched hands resting loosely on the leather inset mat; one held the thick cigar with the smoke petering to a mere thin vapor, already left too long without a puff. Impeccably dressed in a dark blue, double-breasted suit as if for an important meeting, as he surely was, he wore a stark blue tie in a perfect double Windsor, snug against his thin neck. Steel gray, his hair cut in precision, styled no differently now than forty years earlier. In stark contrast, his nearly translucent skin clung to his patrician features, his thin mustache punctuating his thin parted lips.

He'd aged. Lines creased his thin flesh, but he was the same man who'd stood at a conference table nearly forty years past. No differently than he'd stood twenty years earlier . . . at the head of another table. Like the captain of a ship surrounded by subordinates, he'd stood within a sub-level room, as heavily guarded as the White House war room.

Simple and direct, he commanded, *'You have your orders. . .'*

'We need to know what all she knows . . .'

'She has a son . . .'

'If we have to get rid of him, too, so be it. We've come too far to have some charlatan threaten our mission.'

'I think you're overreacting, Matt. It was just a blasted drawing—'

'What do you think's going to happen if this harlot goes to the press?' the mid-aged man had demanded, his pale blue eyes flashing over the half dozen others at the table. 'And she will—mark my words. As soon as my wife stops paying her, she'll make those calls—'

'How the hell did she find out—'

"I told her," Jade said in a quiet cadence, intruding on the old man's memory. "And she knew more," he continued as the pale eyes flickered with doubt and disbelief. "She knew about you and your band of madmen—about Herr Schreiber—about your intention to create the perfect race. I might even have mentioned my own abduction in the wake of her passing. Of that, I can't be certain."

"You—you're him. Laquette," the elder found voice, firming and flashing outrage. "How did you get in here?"

"Perhaps, I died in a plane crash. Perhaps, I'm the ghost of the late Jade Laquette," Jade said and shrugged, testing his corporeal self by taking a step forward. He found the oriental rug beneath his soles and continued forward to one of the two leather receiving chairs. Lifting a brow and offering a slight smile, he wondered, "Do you mind if I sit? It's been a rather long day." And occupying this space could be wearing him thin, he might have added.

That his image might have wavered with his motion, occurred to him as the old man blinked owlishly. Doubtful sitting would improve his fading essence. Too clearly, suddenly, he knew himself divided, one aspect of himself sprawled, near to comatose, on a gurney in the sublevel of a private hospital—the other fully animated within the office of Matthew Jarvins, head of the New Order, as he deemed to call himself. He'd groomed his grandson toward that order and intended to supplant the fellow into the hierarchy of the New Order come a day.

"I don't know how you got in here or what you hope to gain, young man."

"Your confession would be nice," Jade commented. "Although, I don't think it's necessary under the circumstances. There's really no statute of limitations on murder or conspiracy of the same, Mr. Jarvins."

"How dare you come into my home and accuse me of some nonsense—"

"You ordered my mother murdered, sir," Jade said quietly. "Others were involved, but you issued the order. Just as you lent the order more recently to have me removed."

"You're insane—"

"Careful, sir, that's not a word I'd speak aloud if I were you."

"I've heard enough of this—"

"About eighteen years ago, Mr. Jarvins, I occupied a room in the sub-level of a hospital where your Herr Schreiber continued with some of the worst atrocities known to man. I wonder, sir, did you know I was psychic? Or was I merely a sacrifice to Dr. Carson? A convenience, for me to become another test subject with the ultimate end to be mentally twisted?"

"I don't know what you think you know—"

"I know that you are plotting to launch a new order," Jade said with a bemused smile, another shrug. "I know that you've turned a madman loose in Cleveland to test your effects. A social and moral test, I think. One, you've been planning for years."

"You are mad—"

"If you mean pissed, you'd be accurate," Jade said without the whimsy, his gaze darkening. "You had my mother murdered because your wife showed you a child's drawing of a swastika and referenced Dr. Schreiber, a doctor who practiced his inhumane experiments in such fine establishments as Auschwitz and Dacha. At least in Germany, he had the excuse to believe he was conducting his madness to improve the German armed forces. You and your group of merry madmen brought him to this country to further your eugenics program at the cost of American lives. White supremacists and anarchists—nothing more, nothing less. Fanatics to the extreme.

"So, here we are, Mr. Jarvins—" Jade cocked his head, hearing engines—or merely sensing the approach. "Hm, and your time is running out. Someone has, or will, blow the lid off your scheme, and I think, even as we speak, the hounds of hell are racing toward your door." he barely paused, fleeting an image, "I wonder, sir . . . Will you face a jury of your peers? Or simply do what you should have done years ago? You have the means in the drawer beside you. I'd not mind assisting you with that decision, but I'd rather it be your choice which was more than you offered my mother—or me, for that matter."

"You are insane," the man stated, indignant and yet, worried behind his scheming eyes. Something had happened recently. Someone had contacted the acting director of the FBI and launched an investigation into Felicity Laquette's demise. The son, Jarvins knew as he stared at the wavering image across from him. If everything had gone as planned, this fellow wouldn't be sitting here, but the attempted assassination had gone awry; someone had indeed switched the doses of an injection that should have ended the threat of the young man seated across from him. Instead, there were reports of Laquette boarding a Cessna, crashing somewhere in Kentucky . . . and a Frenchman, two of them, in fact, lying in critical condition in the sublevels of a top-secret facility. And both the crashed plane and the dying men were linked to a

Frenchman, who was rumored to be as dangerous as he was connected. Once if not a dozen times over the years, Matthew had attempted to enlist Monsieur Jardonet's services to handle delicate situations overseas . . . to no avail.

No possible way was Jean-Pierre Jardonet and Jade Laquette connected . . . but a Dominique Jardonet had arrived in Cleveland and usurped Laquette.

A hoax, Mark had insisted when mentioning that name only a few days past . . . nothing more than a hoax created by Laquette. And Matthew had trusted his grandson's judgment; after all, there was no record of a Dominique Jardonet connected to the DGSE. With a few phone calls, Matthew had verified the absence of such a person—

"Do you truly believe the French government would risk exposing one of their most highly regarded field agents?" Jade asked and reverted to simple American slang to make his point, his accent gone. "Get serious, old man. They'd no more blow his cover than they'd admit he's as psychic as Jade Laquette—as if those two entities are two separate beings."

"You . . . you're Jardonet."

"Suppose there's no point in denying that. I was, wasn't, and am," he said and shrugged, flashing a faint smile before sobering completely. "I wonder, sir, are you brave enough to answer for your crimes now? The last of the Nuremberg trials have ended. You won't likely hang even if you stood on foreign soil, though I'd consider that justified as many of your predecessors of like mind met that end. Alas, it's a more civilized world. They won't even stand you before a firing squad and offer you a quick end. The most you'll get is a life sentence in Leavenworth . . . and truly, how long could it be? You must be nearing eighty. What . . . no more than twenty years max as I wouldn't think you'll live past a hundred even with decent health care and evil on your side."

"I think I've heard about enough of this nonsense, young man—"

The buzzing sound erupted from the phone base, and the elder huffed indignation before he reached, stabbing an intercom button. "Yes? What is it?"

"Sir," the static voice erupted, anxious. "The FBI's coming through the gate! I tried to stop them, but they have a warrant for your—"

The finger released the button as if shocked.

"Arrest," Jade finished simply and saw the instant when the old man grasped the reality. Insane, perhaps, but no fool this old man who'd been plotting and planning for the apocalypse for years. A new order, a pure race . . . a world order if he had his way. When democracy imploded as it surely would with the riots spanning the continent, he and his followers, of which there were many, would merely take the helm. A dictatorship. Jarvins had the vision and foresight, the social status in his own mind, to be king. He would lead the New Americas--

"Fool," Jade stated, no longer even slightly amused. With a push, a touch of mind-bending, he could put an end to this lunatic. But could he live with the consequence? Could he ever look at his wife—his son—with the love and devotion they deserved if he simply nudged this lunatic over the edge?

A knock came at the door, a frantic tapping to draw the opaque eyes even before his wife's soft call. "Matthew? Matthew? A dozen cars are coming up the lane. Are you expecting company?"

The gray eyes shifted, as blank as an iced lake, studying Jade even as his hand reached toward the drawer to his right. "They'll blame you, you know?" the old man spoke in a firm, nearly musing tone. "When they find you here, they'll know you did this."

"A pity, you are wrong, sir," Jade said quietly, merely leaning back in the leather chair, ankle crossed in leisure repose as the elder lifted the .45 from the drawer. In his mind's eye, he saw his mother splayed, arms and legs sprawled into the points of the pentagram. "If I might ask—or need I even bother to wonder why you insisted she was posed within that star? Was it for my benefit? Your thought to drive me mad? Or more basic? For your wife's?"

"I couldn't have Trisha seeking another charlatan," he said matter-of-factly while fitting the grip in his hand, sliding his finger into the trigger guard. "Suppose it was a bit theatrical, but she took heed."

"Never occurred to you that you might be unleashing a monster with that bit of symbolism, eh?"

"Matthew! Please, dear, open this door! What are you doing?"

"Mom? What's going on? Who are all those men outside?"

"Matthew! Open this door—"

"Nonsense, of course," Jarvins said loftily. "You're just as much of a charlatan as your mother was. All that nonsense about finding your mother's killer in Cleveland. I read those transcripts, you know? The ramblings of a mad child no differently than with Albert."

"I don't quite get it, Mr. Jarvins. How did you justify those transcripts if you don't believe in psychic phenomena? You know he and I were never in the same room."

"Don't be foolish, boy, or think me the fool. You, of all people, should know how Carson doctored those recordings if only to keep his funding."

"Dad! Open this door!" The voice had aged, but the rhythm was the same. Mid-aged, Carolyn Jarvins sounded just as lofty and demanding as she had when she confronted Felicity Laquette about her mother's continued client status. That drawing had affected the old woman, especially when compounded by Felicity's mention of Auschwitz and the subsequent hangings at the onset of the inquisitions in Nuremberg. Jade hadn't even known the significance of that drawing, hadn't understood such things as the Holocaust or the horrors to begin there. He'd barely heard of WWII or the impact of Pearl Harbor. At ten years old, he'd wanted to be like other boys . . . but the images had assailed him and increased tenfold after touching that silk, monogrammed handkerchief belonging to the wife of the man across from him. A monster, this pathetic old man, and Jade suffered no regrets watching him lift the muzzle to his temple.

One down, he dared to believe and hope that the madness ended here . . . hope.

That was the candle Veronica had ignited and held for him.

If only he could believe that this old man's passing would remove the threat.

He was the threat . . . and the fact that he could idly sit and watch this wicked old man pull the trigger was proof enough in his own mind.

That he let himself fade a split second before the index finger squeezed was only more confirmation. All things at once. The old man's flaming madness flashed shock and enlightenment as his visitor evaporated. The gunshot resounded, and blood exploded to spray the gold drape. The wife screamed her husband's name. The daughter shouted louder than the FBI agents, a dozen of whom plowed into the austere front parlor . . .

In the sublevel of a private facility, Jade awoke, only to wonder why.

Even if he cut off the head of the snake, two others would appear. Evil had reigned since the dawn of time if one believed in the holy bible . . . and it was a woman who had partaken of the forbidden fruit. Could that be Veronica's single flaw? To be tempted by the darkness no differently than him to the light. She was the light.

Staring at the corrugated ceiling and fluorescent light overhead, he drew the vision from the playground a million years ago in his mind. Like a miller to light, he'd been drawn to that lovely little girl, who'd stood beneath the bows of an immense oak. A rainbow of color had glowed about her ebony locks, and he'd stood in as much awe as excitement. He'd found her—his holy grail—and was it only an irony that he couldn't look into her and know her mind? Couldn't fully grasp her future or his own if he was a part of hers?

Flashing images assailed him, too quick for his child's mind to comprehend, but he understood those visions from an adult perspective. She was a part of him, now, a part of his past, a part of his future, as he was a part of her and hers. To secure their future, he needed to remove the threat. Oh, and a threat existed, but whether the danger remained without or within remained the only question.

He'd just assisted a man in dying . . . Or had he merely borne witness?

Could he be a threat to his wife and child?

Hope. She was the light; he was the darkness. And hope was the candle she need carry for both of them.

CHAPTER 27

Long before Max Hagen returned her call, Ronnie was awake, kneeling at the commode and retching with a force to rock the foundations at her feet. Obviously, Tad wasn't ready to just swim about in his own little world, determined, it seemed, to make his unyielding presence known. By the time Max returned her call, she'd returned to the bed within reach of the phone. Calmer, quieter, Ronnie had listened to Max's information, not surprised by his findings, nor affected by his suggestion.

"You need to drop this, baby doll, and let the Feds handle it. I'm certain they have it under control . . ."

By habit, Ronnie had moved to the table, and rested now, studying her notes in the wake of Max's call.

As she'd surmised, at least one of the fellows who'd visited Trumble's funeral, and likewise the Ryder estate, was a government official. If anyone other than Max Hagen had told her that this entity was acting on the request of Algen Industries, she wouldn't have believed it. Max might have been duped, but considering the federal agent was traveling with an Algen executive, Max had his facts in order. Apparently, Ronnie wasn't the only one to suspect something seriously wrong with the timing of Trumble's death. An executive of Algen Ind., Coleman Sheridan, had interacted with Trumble at the onset. After Jack's accident, Sheridan had contacted the FBI rather than the EPA with his suspicions.

Which led to the second traced license plate.

Definitely a government issue, she considered while lifting another cracker from the half-empty package. Unfortunately, whoever they were, they were not enlisted through any usual chain of command. Max's connections were good. He'd worked in Arlington for over twenty years, stacking up friends and acquaintances by the scores even before he'd risen to the higher ranks. If Max had no clue who these fellows were, what they were assigned to do, or why, it was a good bet they were working slightly outside normal parameters. So, why the hell were they camped outside her window?

And why waste time pondering when the answers were probably well within her grasp?

Dropping the pen, she pushed from the chair and strode around the bed, grateful for Tad's reprieve. Settling onto the mattress near the nightstand, she lifted the receiver, connected an outside line, and dialed the long series of numbers. The animated voice of a switchboard operator intruded on the second ring, and within seconds, the next leap of phone lines was underway. Waiting, Ronnie punched her pillow into a backboard and repositioned, keeping one foot to the floor. Upon a time, she might have requested a different name at that automated junction and only then in an emergency. That detail should have told her everything she needed to know about her relationship with Agent Mark Jarvins. As a last resort, she might have reached out to him, but that emergency had never come to pass by the grace of God.

At any hour of the day, Len's husky voice sounded wide awake, and this wasn't the exception. He was a fellow who seemed always to expect a phone call.

"Hiya, Len. How's every little thing?" Ronnie asked in her most cheery voice.

Hesitation, not entirely unnatural, descended on the line as Len apparently identified her voice and suffered a momentary surprise. "Can't complain, Ronnie. What's up with you?"

Something in Len's voice . . . A sudden tension? Dread? Something. He sounded reluctant, struggling to sound lighthearted, about as natural for Len

Devinio as a curse off the Pope's lips. "I uh . . . is everything all right?" she asked, abruptly worried about him, for him.

"You uh . . . you didn't just ring me up to ask me that, right?"

"Well, no, but you sound . . .? Don't guess you'd want to tell me where you are, would you?"

"Uh . . . no. I don't think I would. Is there something I can do for you?"

This wasn't Len Devinio's norm, not one bit, but did she have any right to probe further? They were friends, more so now than before four months ago, but his line of work tended to strain personal relationships. If he was working on something serious, he wouldn't discuss it over a phone line even with a *former* investigative journalist. Just not done.

"There is something, Len," she said hesitantly, wondering if she should even bother. Hell yes, damn it. If nothing else, talking to Len might counter whatever these fellows were up to. "Without asking for a whole lot of details, I'd like to ask a slight favor of you."

"Sounds ominous," Len said offhandedly. "What favor?"

"If I give you a government license plate, could you find out who's behind the wheel and why? Without jeopardizing yourself, of course."

"Maybe you better mention just a few details, Ron. Where are you?"

"I'm in Elmview, PA, sort of working on something, but uh . . . shit. I've picked up government surveillance, and I'd like to know why. My usual channels of information seem to be at a loss, and I'm just a wee bit curious as to why I've had these two characters outside my window for the past twelve hours. What I'm working on shouldn't be related . . ." *Not with a far more visible agent on the scene.* "Think you could be a pal and find out what's going on?"

"When did you notice the tail?"

"Last night when I returned to my hotel. I'd imagine that means someone knew where to find me and where to wait. I'd like to know why."

Hesitation again then, "How long are you going to be in Elmview?"

Why did that matter? "Probably only until this afternoon. Why?"

"Give me those plate numbers and a number where I can reach you," he said, apparently readying a pencil and pad at the other end of the phone line.

"You really do sound strange, honey," Ronnie said lightly. As if he were distracted. Reciting the requested numbers, she listened as he repeated them. "You'd tell me if something was seriously wrong, wouldn't you, Len?"

"You know me, Ronnie," he said in a low tone. "I'll see what I can find out and get back to you ASAP. If I miss you at the hotel, I'll reach you at home, and uh . . . if they're just hanging out, don't let it bother you. In fact, knowing the kind of *sort-ofs* you work on, honey, I'm almost happy to hear you have a few of our guys watching your back. Speaking of which . . . what the hell are you 'sort of' working on? Why the hell aren't you in Bentwood watching the idiot box and keeping your feet up? Isn't that what expecting mothers are expected to do?"

"You watch too much TV," she said offhandedly, distracted by this offbeat, delayed reaction to her admission. "And something's out of kilter here, Len. If you intended to launch into big brother mode, it should've happened about three minutes ago. I do know you. You're not generally a delayed-reactionary type personality. Methodical, brilliant, but by no means restrained. Are you sure you're alright?"

"You have my word, Ronnie, I'm fine," he said bluntly. "But I am in the middle of something, and I'm a little preoccupied. How about I check this out and get back to you? In the meantime, try not to worry, and goddamn it, stay out of trouble, huh? You're carrying my adopted niece or nephew, and I have enough to worry about without getting an ulcer worrying about you."

"Your confidence in my common sense is well noted and appreciated, Mr. Devinio," she said with a mocked edge. "Are you sure I shouldn't worry about this surveillance team?"

"If I find out otherwise, Ronnie, you can bet I'll take care of it," he said in a husky, confident voice.

This was the Len Devinio she knew and appreciated. "Thanks, Len. Talk to you soon."

"ASAP," he answered. "See ya."

Long after she replaced the receiver, Ronnie rested gazing at the telephone. Something seriously wrong. Even those parting words, Len's promise, offered no quick reassurance. On top of everything else, the last damn thing she needed was to add another worry.

And she hadn't heard from her wayward husband in over twenty-four hours. What the hell was he up to?

Muttering a curse, Ronnie shoved off the bed and started to collect her purse, tempted to head toward the door. The dizziness came then, startling and veering her to the bed. "Not finished yet, huh?" she uttered and rested, leaning her weight on one palm.

Joining Donna and Tim downstairs was out of the question.

Grumbling another curse, Ronnie settled against the propped pillow, checking the time as she lifted the TV remote control. On the outside chance that some third-world country had launched a nuclear missile and declared war, she might as well catch the early news edition. God knows, growing up near the capital had enlightened her to sensationalism along with the propaganda relative to world affairs via Capital Hill's press agents.

She'd probably learn more by watching Sesame Street.

Breezing through several channels, Ronnie landed on her regular station where the faces were familiar, and the anchorpersons were generally gifted with a talent to appear sincere and sympathetic. For a moment, however, she wondered if she'd zoomed in on an off-color commercial or movie preview. With a fleeting glimpse of the angry mob, she flashed a thought of her confrontation last evening. Skinheads. Leathers and chains, bald heads, faces embittered with voices raised shouting apparent obscenities, and banners waving, reflecting some rendition of the Swastika.

From the apparent safety and comfort of his studio, the anchorman offered a voice-over while a small block of print trailed at the bottom of the screen. 'Trent Heights, Ohio.' ". . . Outside of Trent Heights police station early yesterday afternoon where two well-known activist leaders were held for questioning in connection to the murder of Frances Cummings. The investigation began late Tuesday evening when Cleveland Police answered an anonymous call and found the body of Miss Cummings, age 26, in an abandoned warehouse in the waterfront district . . ."

The screen flipped to a shot of an industrial building, yellow police streamers, and emergency vehicles along with a crowd of sightseers.

"It is believed that Miss Cummings who was reported missing only hours before her death, was abducted and brought to this warehouse in the early hours of Tuesday evening." Again, the on-screen scene changed, showing a small, one-story house no larger than a cottage cramped among several other shabby structures on a desolate street. A few neighbors stood on the sidewalk, idly watching the activity as several police officers loitered on the small porch.

"Cleveland Police are not revealing any details; however, our sources indicate that evidence at the scene suggested a possible connection to the Freedom Crusaders who have publicly rallied and demonstrated in several highly controversial cases throughout the past several months in the Cleveland area."

The scene flashed again, apparently digging into the studio archives to offer a few blips of previous demonstrations.

Watching the scenes unfold, a chill skittered down Ronnie's spine. Stone-faced, the bald-headed leader faced off with another anchorman, chest puffed, eyes as cold as blue glass. The voice of James Bergen lacked emotion, as surely as his deadpan features as he glared into the camera, spouting off a sermon on the rights of every American. Alongside Bergen, an apparent companion held his leather vest aside to let the camera zoom in on his obscene t-shirt.

James Bergen and Ralph Gehring—the two men were in police custody; Ronnie knew before the anchorman verified her belief. The camera flashed toward a courthouse shot where a platoon of industrious reporters had caught up to the DA. Over the raucous of shouted questions, at least one reporter managed to be heard. "Will you indict Bergen and Gehring for the murder of Frances Cummings?"

The DA's voice carried with a flash of angry eyes, "No comment at this time . . ."

Another reporter shouted, further away, the words almost lost in the din, "Is it true this is the second body found near the warehouse district . . .?"

As reporters continued shouting and trotting at his heels, the DA strode down the steps, waving away the microphones. "No comment"," he spoke over his shoulders.

The morning anchorman and his female partner returned to the screen then the station cut to a commercial break.

Unconsciously, Ronnie began pushing the remote, searching for another news station, finding one. Her nausea forgotten, she sat forward slightly as another anchorman recapped the story with the help of an on-site reporter camped outside the local precinct where the neo-Nazis remained in police custody. According to this reporter, the Federal Bureau had joined the investigation, and there were 'rumors' suggesting the possibility of another murder attributed to the same killer or killers. Blips of another press conference from the prior evening flashed on the scene with a few quotes from the Cleveland mayor concerning the combined efforts of the local authorities and the FBI . . . and there stood Special Agent, Mark Jarvins, awaiting his turn at the microphone. Tall, blond, and tailored, his sculpted features were set in camera-friendly sobriety.

Whether her revelation came before or after listening, Ronnie stared at the screen as the story changed with some fantastic aerial shots of an immense fire ". . . burning out of control on Pittsburgh's Southside." And another blurb depicted a chaotic scene of emergency vehicles and strobe lights. Apparently, a small-engine aircraft crashed last evening in a horse pasture in northern Kentucky, with two confirmed dead. A chill skittering down her spine, she watched the flashing lights a few seconds longer before the screen switched to a commercial.

Len Devinio was in Cleveland . . . Mark Jarvins was in Cleveland. Tim Spencer was in Elmview. And Jade Laquette was nowhere to be found.

'. . . found late Tuesday evening.'

"Damn him," Ronnie uttered as her gaze trailed to the telephone, recalling Len's preoccupation. Jade was somewhere to be found. He was in Cleveland or had been, she knew at this moment, and when she caught up to Len Devinio, she might need to strangle him right after she wrung Jade's neck for sending her in the opposite direction.

'. . . You have one mystery to solve, and I, another,' Jade's words came to her and whatever doubts remained, vanished. He was in Cleveland attempting to solve this crime . . . or had already solved it if those two in custody were the guilty parties.

A niggling doubt touched the nape of her neck as she rose unconsciously, moving toward the door in automation. Barely, she reached for the nob when she realized the light rap of knuckles had drawn her. Distracted, she pulled open the door and barely glanced off Donna and Tim before turning, striding partway back toward the television.

"Ahh, good morning—" Tim started.

Snapping off the television, Ronnie turned and caught Tim's eye with a slightly angry shine. "When you talked to Jade yesterday, did he happen to mention Lenny?" she asked.

Tim ambled a few steps, appearing faintly troubled and surprised. "The name never came up," he answered somewhat evasively.

Studying Tim for the lie, she sensed his subterfuge.

"Ronnie?" Donna asked, coming forward, offering a cup of coffee. "What's wrong?"

Aside from her husband sending her toward the apparent lesser of two evils? And an uncanny sense of dread on his behalf . . .? "Not a damn thing," she said and bounced a somewhat angry glance off Tim, who undoubtedly knew more than he was sharing. Shaking her head, attempting to soften her glare, she looked at Donna. "I'm not feeling up to the chase this morning," she decided. "Tad's giving me a few normal fits, and there's no reason for you to sit around here. Why don't you take Tim on a sightseeing tour for a little while? Maybe pop into The Music Box. I'm sure I'll feel a little more human in an hour or so."

"I thought I might go have a chat with the county coroner over in Johnstown this morning," Tim commented.

"Actually, we're wasting our time," Ronnie admitted, recalling the conversation with Max. "I have it on good authority that the Federal Bureau's already actively pursuing an investigation into Trumble's untimely demise, and I'm fairly sure the coroner's report is already under the appropriate microscope." Realizing the dual startled glances, she shrugged and smiled slightly. "Bluntly, our job's done," she said to Donna and looked at Tim. "I took your advice. After my stomach settles, I plan to do a little more shopping, then head home."

"Just like that?" Tim asked somewhat skeptically.

"Just like that," she verified. "Since I don't plan to write this story, I see no point in wasting any more time. Eventually, we'll probably hear about it in the local news if it even breaks print. I'm guessing, the heirs are behind this ordeal, and it's an old story—wealthy old man attempts to smite his greedy heirs, and they attempt to get even as well as wealthy at his expense. Even if Algen brings in a waste site, they'll do it by the book, and it's apparently not as bleak as the locals seem to believe. The EPA is involved, and that agency will handle the crises along with the PR concerning environmental and health concerns. I wouldn't be surprised to learn that Algen's already formed an alliance with the college—probably offered some sort of scholarship or research grant regarding waste disposal and storage."

She shrugged and moved to the bed, unconsciously tossing the remote control on the nightstand. Both Spencers continued to eye her suspiciously. Neither appeared willing to believe she'd walk away in the middle of an investigation, but then, neither knew her all that well. Looking at Tim, settled against the pillow, Ronnie admitted. "If I fully believed my hands-on investigation could prevent another crime, or if I believed I could handle a human-interest angle to relieve one of the victim's grief, I'd stick this out regardless."

"What about uh . . . Trumble's family or uh . . . Ryder's grandson who's been swindled out of his inheritance?" Donna asked, sounding slightly miffed by Ronnie's indifference.

"If, as I believe, the FBI uncovers the bogus Will or discovers who paid to have Trumble killed and thereby link the Ryder heirs, both the Trumble family and Jason Ryder will receive justice as well as just compensation. In either event, I'd imagine any number of bright college students could catch wind of this fiasco and put the details in print." Ronnie hesitated before shrugging again. "Either way, this isn't my type of story."

"Just like that," Tim said again, studying her far more critically as if he sought an ulterior motive in her rapidly switching mood.

"Consider it a hormonal thing, Tim, and I'm sorry I jumped on you when you walked in," she said offhandedly. "Now, why don't you kids run along? I'm really not good company in the wee hours of the morning or the dawn." Convincing the twosome to depart took a few more moments, and it was an odd moment when the door closed behind them—an extremely odd moment for Ronnie to find hot tears spilling down her cheeks. Something was wrong. If not with Jade, then with her, or Tad, or this town, or . . .

"Damned hormones," she uttered and flopped onto the bed, tugging the pillow from its fold to bury her face. She only wished she'd been lying to the Spencers, but in her heart, in her head, this case was finished, her interest past. What she would do in Bentwood for a few days without Jade—or if she would even stay in Bentwood—remained the only question of the hour. Maybe she would take a drive and visit her parents . . .

Or Cleveland.

Either way, she wasn't taking Tad any closer to this investigation . . . or any other investigation, she decided abruptly. If, as she suspected, her wily husband had decided to begin actively pursuing a career in crime solving, she couldn't afford to pursue her own career and risk Tad's welfare by subjecting him to any more violence. If the past twenty-four hours had taught her anything, it was the very real possibility that Dr. Spock was right on the money about a fetus being influenced inside the womb. Far too many times over these past several hours, her tiny passenger had reacted to external stimuli, and no doubts remained, he was his father's son.

A psychic . . . and she had a funny feeling he might be slightly more gifted than either his father or mother. A tiny force to be reckoned with.

"Oh, Lord, what have we done, Jade?" she uttered while slipping her hand over the tiny bulge at her center. Just a thought of what her husband had endured as a child . . . losing his mother to a violent crime. Being hounded by the press. She'd written her college thesis about that unsolved murder and how the press had mishandled that entire event, persecuting a mere child and somehow holding him to account as if a ten-year-old could have masterminded that ordeal.

Gaps . . . there were so many gaps between then and five years earlier when Jade Laquette had returned to the US under the assumed name, Isaac Bently. His father had taken him in at some point. Jade had lived in France for several years, Ronnie knew, but there was no love lost between those two. She need only recall her wedding day and those few seconds when her husband had first spotted his father to know they hadn't parted on friendly terms. If ever Jade had appeared more dangerous—his eyes glowing near to emerald—never more than at that moment and Jean-Pierre was no less formidable.

History wasn't going to repeat itself, she decided on the instant. She wasn't putting herself in any position to jeopardize herself, her son . . . or her husband. The choice was made. This investigation into Jack Trumble was the last of its kind for a while—possibly forever.

One way or another, she would find a means to shut down her intuition or at the least, find another vent for the same.

A children's book, perhaps, one revolving around a little warlock.

EPILOGUE

Braced against the wind whipping his long black coat, Jean Pierre Jardonet stood on a bluff, too far from the wreckage to gaze upon the activity, but he needed no clear view. The ambulance and rescue vehicles were long gone. Only a few officials remained, including at least three aircraft accident investigators still poking and sorting through the rubble of what had once been a fine Cessna aircraft. The debris had scattered over a half-mile strip, stretching from the forested hillside on the north, scarring a swatch of fine Kentucky bluegrass on a southerly slope. Engine failure, or so the officials had determined at the onset. Based on communications with the pilot, little else explained the craft descending from a bright blue sky.

With a curve slipping into his thick black mustache, Jean-Pierre panned his gaze and shook his head. Engine failure would remain the cause of this deadly crash, a flaw in the maintenance, a loose bolt, or a lapse in the seasoned pilot's care. Such was fate, the master to create a perfect storm and another master to snatch that detail from the aether and fill a need. If Jean-Pierre wasn't still slightly miffed with this turn . . . well, and he was more than *slightly* miffed since the damned plane had belonged to him. Crashed and burned, a minor inconvenience to be certain, and despite the loss, Jean-Pierre idled a dark laugh that swept away on the cool breeze. After all these years, his bastard son still held a blasted grudge, and he probably considered this a fine bit of payback.

Senses keening, Jean-Pierre canted his head as if he heard a sound, while in his mind's eye, he watched a stoic-faced investigator lift yet another shred of scorched leather from a mound of charred metal. The main parts of that bag had been recovered at the onset. Enough to identify at least one of the passengers as no other than Jade David Laquette, or so the authorities believed.

Shaking his head, still bemused behind a tight grim smirk, Jardonet turned from the scene and strode across the grassy ledge.

Standing in regimental form, Claude Rudemonje waited alongside the black Continental, prepared to open the rear door as he'd been opening limousine doors for more than three decades. Never had Claude appeared more grim or distressed, every line on his sculpted face defined with the tension.

Jade Laquette or Dominique Jardonet. The names meant nothing to this man who'd stood forever at Jean-Pierre's right hand. Without a doubt, Claude would have forfeited his own life to protect the son of *le sorcier,* and the torment in his pale blue eyes was nearly more than Jean-Pierre could endure.

When they both settled into the back seat, Jardonet sent orders through the partition, needing little more than a thought to suggest they return to the airport. Within the confines of the steel-plated Limo, Claude's distress amplified to feel like a lead weight in the ether.

With a heavy sigh, Claude began in a lower tone. "That crash . . . It was near here, yes?"

"Over the next hill, my friend," Jardonet answered in his naturally low pitch.

"Was it truly here, then, he met his end?" Claude asked, tortured by the very thought.

Jean-Pierre sighed as he decided the fellow had suffered long enough. "As much as the American authorities would like us to believe such, Claude, I have it on good authority that neither Jade Laquette nor Dominique Jardonet was physically aboard that craft."

Claude's breath halted for a tick; his gaze riveted. "But Paul . . ."

"Delivered the bag to the Cessna in Cleveland as my wily son dictated, Claude, but that was yesterday morning when he was sent to deliver your luggage to the Lakefront."

"I . . . don't understand," Rudemonje said carefully, looking over into the shadowy compartment, clearly bewildered.

Sighing, Jean-Pierre feigned to appear disgusted, when in truth, he couldn't be more pleased. "Do believe Dominique saw this coming some time ago, Claude, and by no surprise, the arrangements were made in advance. Perhaps, he knew even before his subsequent marriage, as I understand, these murders in Cleveland began before that incident in Bentwood."

"He sabotaged your plane to be free of the Laquette name?"

"It's not considered sabotage when an unchangeable end is manipulated toward a beneficial circumstance and dismissing the Laquette name is no part of his intentions."

"But the pilot? Harold—"

"If not suffering the heart attack on the Cessna, my friend, have no doubts he would have died last evening at 8:12 p.m. Such was a detail my wily son apparently witnessed on a dozen planes before deciding which end might benefit him A manipulative little bastard, so he has always been though I'm certain he would lay that blame at my feet."

"Then he . . . he truly is all right?" Claude wondered.

"He's where he wants to be at the moment," Jean-Pierre knew if not much else. Only fleeting, he glimpsed his youngest son in a dozen different circumstances and nearly cursed his failings in his son's regard. If, or when, his son needed assistance, the wily devil would undoubtedly issue a distress signal, not unlike the message received eighteen years earlier.

"Do you think the Americans still mean him harm, Jean-Pierre?"

"Claude, if the Americans couldn't murder him eighteen years ago, why would you believe they would succeed, now?"

"You saw him back then and intervened—"

"I saw what he allowed me to see, my friend.," Jean-Pierre admitted for the first time, as amused as he was pleased with that memory. "An odd turn, grant, but a fact, we are connected, and though he might not have consciously sought my intervention, his gifts had other ideas. I knew he was in trouble then, but such and it goes, we cannot change all things. When the moment came, he reached out, not too different than these recent events to bring us here."

"You . . . didn't come to bury your son," Claude dared to hope as he'd apparently believed else when they had met last evening in New York. When news of the Cessna had reached the consulate, Rudemonje had apparently feared the worst, as he was one of the few men who knew that Jean-Pierre maintained a few ties in the USA. Undoubtedly, he'd believed Dominique had occupied the plane and might have thought him en route to New York.

If only that were true, Jean-Pierre considered. An unsettling image of an emerald casket flashed neon in his mind's eye. Far and too often lately, that vision had erupted, the vision of an emerald casket under a dull gray sky . . .

Masking his genuine concern behind a faint smile, Jardonet caught up to Claude's comment and admitted, "Not today." But where his unruly son was involved, nothing remained set in stone. Attempting to keep up with him could become a full-time occupation. He was an enigma, this son of his. And if half of what Jean-Pierre had seen came to pass, the future was as unsettling as the past.

Casting his gaze through the tinted glass, Jean-Pierre watched as a series of events unfolded as if played upon a silver screen. In one scene, he watched a mid-aged bureaucrat led from his Washington home, a flock of Federal agents descending on the house like black carrions after a morsel. Oh, and they would find more than they bargained for, but only the tip of the iceberg.

Dominique Jardonet, by whatever means, had blown the lid off Pandora's Box and set the wheels in motion to uncover a conspiracy dating nearly forty years.

Fools, these fanatics, to believe they were superior to the common mass, to think they could form a new world order in the wake of what were the worst acts of genocide in modern history.

On dual planes, Jean-Pierre remembered the horrors. Himself young enough to witness that madness firsthand, an officer already in his country's gendarme and still apart from it. He'd seen those bodies, shuffled from train cars to the ovens, and he wondered, now, through whose eyes he'd seen that madness. An unborn child at the time . . .? A small boy later, nearly twenty years later?

Jean-Pierre had seen him, then, the child strapped and helpless within an underground facility on another continent. Day after day, those madmen had forced that child to watch reel after reel of those wretched films that he should tell his captors what he knew of their involvement and ultimate eugenics plan for the future.

Fools. The fools had known the child's abilities, had verified their belief in those first physical tests, and discovered the truth behind Felicity's talents. A charlatan, Felicity Laquette, but the child behind those prognostications, was far too authentic.

'I will stop you,' the child had promised in one of those final sessions, admitting at that moment, he knew far more than he should. They had believed him, with good reason, and the idiots intended to silence him.

They might have been better off disbanding sixteen years ago. Fate might have been kinder to them.

In a fleeting instant, Jean-Pierre heard the gunshot and witnessed the old man lurching and collapsing with the blood splattering the gold-swag curtains.

The first, not the last coward, to take his own life rather than risk the wrath of the child who would seek justice for his mother.

Sighing, Jean-Pierre focused on his reflection on the tinted glass, a phantom image aglow in the soft ambient lighting of the plush back seat. Others were seeking the same end, preferring to meet their maker on their own terms rather than face a tribunal of their peers. Cowards to the end. Fanatics. The child need not even lift a hand, had merely planted the seed to mete justice.

The news would travel, might already have traveled to verify that Jade Laquette was dead, and an unknown entity had usurped him. These madmen who would believe they killed the prophecy by killing the prophet might soon learn differently. . . but Jean-Pierre need not enlighten them.

Dominique Jardonet had entered the devil's lair, but he had, by no means, entered as an innocent.

Still, that image, the older man—not an ancient—loomed large in Jean-Pierre's mind, and something about that image created a prickle down his spine.

Crystal clear, he watched as another weapon fired. A bright-white flash, a circle of death erupted on an alabaster forehead . . . But this wasn't the face of Felicity Laquette, not his only true love's face sinking into the murky water. Black hair scattered Medusa-style within the current. Eyes the color of blue diamonds glowed, fading far too rapidly from the surface where a single neon bulb reflected on the rippling waves. A cry of outrage echoed across the timelines, as heart-wrenching as it was terrifying, and even in Jean-Pierre's sturdy countenance, he knew an instant of terror.

Someone would or had already paid for that vision, and in a moment of instant clarity, Jean-Pierre reached a decision. Growling a low sound, he flashed his emerald gaze to their driver. In the front seat, the driver lurched as if physically slapped in the back of the head, but he received the message as clear as a spoken word.

Cleveland, USA.

If he had any blasted choice thirty years ago, Jean-Pierre might have steered clear of Felicity Laquette who'd sought the mystical modern-day Merlin as if seeking the holy grail.

Having children—any children—let alone the likes of his youngest creation, was a burden. Hah. And the child truly thought himself more clever than the father?

A wry smile curled a corner of his mustache and reflected at him on the tinted glass.

The little witch called him Tadpole, but the little warlock wouldn't remain contained within that fishbowl too much longer.

Acknowledgments

My thanks to a few of my favorite critics, Suellen Brady, Mary Trunick, Anne Graff, Andrew Grueber, and William Grueber, for keeping me honest to my craft, adding insight to my characters, and letting me know when I'm getting it right (or wrong!) Thank you!

JKGRUEBER.COM